Sweet Jane

JOANNE KUKANZA EASLEY

Red Boots Press | Texas

Copyright © 2022 by Joanne Kukanza Easley

All rights reserved.

No portion of this book may be reproduced in any form, stored in a retrieval system or transmitted in any form or by any means without written permission from the publisher or author, except by a reviewer who may quote brief passages in a review to be printed in a newspaper, magazine, or journal.

This is a work of fiction, Names, characters, businesses, places, events, and incidents are either the product of the author's imagination or used in a fictitious manner. Any resemblance to actual persons, either living or dead, is purely coincidental.

Publisher-Red Boots Press

Cover Design-Erin Cronin Pearson

Author Photo-Spunky Cloud Photography

ISBN: 979-8-9867133-2-8

Library of Congress Control Number: 2022915808

This book is dedicated to all aspiring writers out there with great stories to tell.

Contents

1. Chapter One — 1
   Grandma June Kicks the Bucket-West Texas 1957

2. Chapter Two — 18
   Reluctant Return to Odessa-Austin 1984

3. Chapter Three — 36
   Rangerland-West Texas 1962

4. Chapter Four — 59
   Home Sweet Home?-West Texas 1984

5. Chapter Five — 80
   Putting on Some Miles-West Texas to California 1967

6. Chapter Six — 106
   Goodbye, Mama-Mama's Funeral-Odessa 1984

7. Chapter Seven — 122
   Tom to the Rescue-Austin 1970

8. Chapter Eight — 142
   Detour-Monahans, Texas 1984

9. Chapter Nine　　　　　　　　　　　　　　　　　162
   Came to, Came to Believe-Austin 1976

10. Chapter Ten　　　　　　　　　　　　　　　　　182
    Ladies who Lunch, Trouble in Paradise-Austin 1984

11. Chapter Eleven　　　　　　　　　　　　　　　　203
    When Jane met Joshua-Austin 1982

12. Chapter Twelve　　　　　　　　　　　　　　　　223
    Revisiting the Past-Austin by way of Dallas and Lubbock 1984

13. Chapter Thirteen　　　　　　　　　　　　　　　244
    Gigantic Faded Pink Fuzzy Slippers-Odessa to Austin 1984

14. Chapter Fourteen　　　　　　　　　　　　　　　263
    True Love-Austin 1984

Acknowledgments　　　　　　　　　　　　　　　　270

Chapter One

GRANDMA JUNE KICKS THE BUCKET-WEST TEXAS 1957

There I was, minding my own beeswax, reading *Charlotte's Web*, my very most favorite book, when Tom walked right in my room without so much as a howdy-do.

"Grandma June has kicked the bucket, and we gotta go to the funeral tomorrow." Tom belly-flopped on my bed, rolled over and threw his arms out in a big V. "Church on a weekday. Lord, have mercy!"

"What you talkin' about? Kicked what bucket?"

"Janie, there ain't no actual bucket." Tom rolled his eyes. "It's just an expression. She's dead."

"Oh. And we got to go to church? What about school?"

Tom grinned. "No school for us tomorrow."

I hated to miss school. "Well, I guess I'll go. I ain't never seen a dead person before!"

Tom snorted. "You're goin'. You got no choice."

I heard Mama coming down the hallway. I looked out and saw her shoulders smack the wall, once on each side of the hall. There was a cigarette hanging out the side of her mouth with a real long ash. She poked her head in my room and said, "It's too bad Grandma June's your first dead person, but, like I always say, 'That's life.'" Cackling like a crazy person, she stumbled on down the hall to her room. Her door slammed.

Tom sat up and shook his head. "Wow. She sure don't seem real broke up about her mama dyin'. Guess she's got her reasons. She's been hittin' the vodka hard."

"But she told Daddy she quit."

Tom snorted. "She tells him what he wants to hear. Maybe she can sleep it off before he gets home. If she's still drunk, he'll flip his wig."

Daddy didn't wear no wig. He had a fine head of wavy black hair.

Tom looked at me and said, "You sound way too enthusiastic about seein' a dead person. It's not exactly party time when your Grandma dies—even Grandma June." He was acting uppity again. Just because he was six years older than me didn't mean he knew everything.

"That's not fair." I got fighting mad when something wasn't fair because I believed in truth, justice, and the American way, just like Superman. 'Course I'm sad Grandma June is dead." I looked out the window, up to heaven. "Well, a little bit sad." I had to be honest. Mrs. Foster told us about being truthful every week in Sunday school. Jesus and George Washington could not tell a lie. I tried my best not to lie, but I ain't perfect.

Making an effort is real important, Daddy says. I made an effort to love Grandma June, but she could be downright mean at times, like when she laughed at how short Daddy cut my bangs. I knew Daddy didn't mean it. He was just trying to even them up, and it got out of hand. And Grandma June was always saying Aunt Penny spoiled me and gave me too many presents. One time, she took a book right out of my hands and told Aunt Penny to take it back to the store. I guess she didn't think I could read or something. That hurt my feelings.

"Look, we weren't real close to Grandma June," Tom said. "When we saw her, she was always kickin' up a fuss about one thing or another. Remember how happy Daddy was when she moved in with Uncle Rafe and Aunt Penny in town? Heck, we all were. What I'm tryin' to say is, there ain't gonna be a whole lot of tears at the funeral." Tom flopped back down on the bed and said, "I ain't so sure you know how to act at a funeral. It's not like runnin' across roadkill and pokin' it with a stick like you do. I never saw a little girl play with dead animals like that." Tom made a face like he smelled a skunk.

"Well, I ain't about to play with no baby doll. I got to practice explorin' for when I grow up and go to Africa. And I ain't so little. I'm almost seven!" I gave him my death stare, and he had to look away. After a bit, I took pity on him. "Okay, smarty-pants, why don't you give me a lesson about how to act proper at a funeral?"

Tom looked at the ceiling.

I did too. The paint was peeling pretty bad.

"Where do I start? Well, they're gonna put Grandma June in a big old box called a casket and set it at the front of the church. Then we go to church just like on Sunday and listen to Preacher Henry gas on for a spell."

That was enough, right there. I jumped up and said, "There you go talkin' at me like I was about two years old. I ain't a baby and I ain't stupid, so just go on and tell me like I was a regular person."

Tom looked surprised and laughed. "No wonder Daddy calls you a little firecracker. Okay, Miss Janie. After Preacher Henry is finally satisfied he's used every word in the English language about fifty times, everybody lines up and says goodbye to Grandma June." He sat up and stopped talking.

It was like he had more to say but was having a hard time getting it out. After a little minute he said, "You ain't allowed to go to the cemetery and see her put in the ground. Daddy said you ain't old enough to see that."

"So what? I don't care. Cemeteries are full of ghosts and skeletons and such." To tell the truth, I was a little bit scared of ghosts. But I wasn't gonna let on about that to Tom.

"Daddy said you can go to Aunt Penny's house and help her get ready for the reception."

I wanted to clap my hands and cheer but didn't think Tom would take it the right way. "What in thunder is a reception or are you makin' up big words?"

"Near as I can figure, it's like a party folks have after a funeral."

It just popped out. I couldn't help it. "You just said it ain't party time when your Grandma dies."

Tom stared at me like I just grew another head. "You're one strange kid, Janie. I never know what's gonna come out of your mouth. You might be almost seven, but sometimes I think you're goin' on forty." He got up and walked away, shaking his head.

I'd have to think on what he meant by that. I once heard Mama tell Grandma June that I was older than my years. It didn't make no sense, so I let it go.

The screen door slammed. Tom would be picking up his basketball and dribbling his fool head off like he did every spare minute of every day. Daddy said if Tom wasn't eating or sleeping, you could bet he was dribbling. He expected Tom to make the team when he got to Odessa High in a couple years. Mama said you couldn't hear yourself think with that blasted basketball thudding all the time. She got especially out of sorts when she had one of her headaches.

Dribbling, what a funny word. First time I heard it, I pictured Tom with milk leaking out the corners of his mouth. I still did.

Lying in bed that night, I heard Mama and Daddy talking in the front room. I climbed out of bed and tippytoed down the hallway so I could hear better. They were talking about Grandma June dying. When she didn't come down for supper, Aunt Penny went out back to the garage apartment where Grandma June lived and found her on the floor.

Daddy said, "I'm sure Penny was concerned. Your mother never missed a free meal unless she was passed out." Then he said, "Ouch." Mama must have gave him a poke.

"Penny said her nightgown was hiked up to her hoo-ha."

Daddy said, "Lordy, there's a sight could take years off a person's life." Then he laughed and said, "Did Penny really say 'hoo-ha'?"

Mama giggled. "Yes, she most certainly did."

It started slow, but then they were laughing up a storm. Hearing my daddy's deep hoot made me smile.

As I turned around to head back to bed, I heard Mama say, "The old bitch was deader than a doornail and stiff as a board."

"Martha, that's no way to talk about your mother."

I scooted. I'd heard enough.

What did animal families think when their grandma didn't come home for supper? Did they go out looking for her?

I knew darn well dead people ain't the same as dead animals. When I did my exploring along the county road, I saw dead hogs, coyotes, squirrels, and such. Some were squished flat, and some looked like they was just taking a rest, except for the blood and other stuff leaking out. They didn't get a box or get put in the ground. They sat out in the hot sun, getting all swole up, with no church service and no reception. They sat there until they busted wide open and the stink was so bad, it was best just to leave them be. A while later, I would go back and see their bones. The buzzards did a darned good job picking them clean. I seen plenty of animal skeletons.

But Grandma June won't go through that. She'd do all her rotting down in the ground and that was just fine with me.

The next morning, I waited for my turn for the bathroom so I could get ready. Tom finally finished and strutted out all dressed up with a tie and everything. It looked like he even combed his hair. He grinned and headed down the hall.

I yanked the milk crate out from under the sink and climbed up so I could see in the mirror. I stretched my lips wide to see if I was growing any new teeth yet. Nope. The spaces were just the same. Summer was coming soon, and I hoped the ones in front would come in so I could eat me some corn on the cob. At least I could whistle real good.

I could hardly wait to get to the First Methodist Church. Daddy said funerals were a big draw in Odessa because they were free entertainment. Everybody showed up no matter who died. I hoped he was right. Grandma June didn't get to church much. She stuck pretty close to home. She hadn't been a cookie-baking grandma like the ones other kids had. Mama said she hadn't been any fun since Grandpa Joe had his arm tore off by a flying chain out in the oilfields and bled out in the dust. That was before I was even born.

I scooped up some water from the tap to wet my bangs. Daddy hadn't done so bad this time, and they'd growed back a little too. I combed them so they would lay flat. I had on my best dress, the brown plaid one Aunt Penny gave me for Christmas. Tom said black is the color of death, and folks always wore black clothes when someone died. My brown plaid dress was as close to black that I had. I figured there was a good amount of black in the plaid, and the dress had a black sash and black buttons with diamonds in the middle. To tell the truth, they might not be real diamonds, but I liked to think so. I brushed my teeth and was all set.

After hopping down from the milk crate, I made sure to push it under the sink so Mama wouldn't trip over it. I wasn't about to go through that again. Mama had yelled and swore like I never heard, and all she done was stub her toe. The way she carried on, it was like she had her whole foot cut off.

I stepped into the hallway and heard Daddy yelling at Mama in their bedroom. He never used to, but he did it a lot lately.

"For the love of Christ, can't you put down the bottle long enough to go to your own mother's funeral?"

"George, give me a break. My mother is dead."

"She died from the same crap you're pourin' down your throat. You're gettin' to be just like her!"

I covered my ears. When Daddy yelled at Mama, I got this sick feeling in my stomach, like the time Aunt Penny took me to the county fair and I ate a corn dog, two fried Twinkies, and some watermelon pickles. Even though I didn't get no breakfast this morning, I felt a pulling in my throat, like I was gonna barf. I turned and ran outside. After I took some good deep breaths, my tummy settled.

Tom's basketball thudded on the concrete slab in time to the song he was singing. Something about a man and a fuzzy tree. I never heard tell of any such thing as a fuzzy tree. Then he sang about being in love, shaking his rear end like I never seen. "Ooh, yeah, I'm all shook up."

Who did he think he was, Elvis Presley? Not likely. He wasn't a teenager yet, but he sometimes acted like he was.

The ball clanged off the rim. Tom didn't miss very often. Daddy said Tom was a cross between Bob Cousy and George Mikan. I didn't know who they were, but I didn't think they lived in Odessa.

The bright May sunlight made me scrunch my eyes shut. I called out, "Hey, Tom. Ain't it just about time to go? You're gonna get your shirt all sweaty."

He sure looked funny playing ball in his long black pants, short-sleeved white shirt, and black tie. The tie was flying every which way like the American flag on the school flagpole on a windy day. He didn't miss a beat with the ball. He didn't even bother to look up. "Yeah? So, I'm a little sweaty. It'll dry."

The screen door screeched and slammed shut. I about jumped a foot in the air. I was afraid to turn around and see what Mama looked like.

Daddy held Mama's elbow as he helped her to the car. His 1955 light blue Ford V-8 waited in front of the porch. He was right proud of that car. When the dust covered it and made it look dirty, he complained. Since the wind never seemed to stop blowing, he complained a lot. Maybe they should make a car the color of West Texas dust.

He yelled, "Come on, kids. We gotta get moving."

I never seen Daddy wearing a suit and tie before. He looked very handsome except he was frowning, and his mouth made a thin line, like he had no lips.

Mama wore a black dress that was too big on her. The buttons weren't done up right and her white slip was showing. Her black straw hat was on sideways, leastways I think the net was supposed to be over her face, not her ear. She wasn't standing up straight like she was always telling me to do.

Daddy hooked his arm around Mama's waist so she wouldn't fall and yanked the car door open.

Tom stopped his dribbling and tossed his ball to the side. He looked at me with his eyes big and shook his head. He didn't have to say a word. We climbed in the back seat quiet as mice.

Daddy was having a time getting Mama settled in the front. "Martha, pull your skirt down."

"Leave me be." She shoved Daddy's hands away. "I know how to get in a damn car."

"You're doing a great job so far." He stood up and said, "I give up."

Daddy slammed the door, stomped around the front of the car, and got in. His jaw was all bunched up, and he was breathing hard. I thought I might have heard him say a swear real quiet. Daddy didn't believe in cussing, so he was real mad.

Tom whispered in my ear, "Daddy's goin' ape. I hope he cools off before we get to church."

I was too busy picturing Daddy in a monkey suit to answer.

Daddy put the car in gear, and I almost flew out of my seat as he hit the gas like a race car driver.

Mama sat up and grabbed her hat. "George, you're gonna kill us all drivin' like a madman!" Then she fell back in the corner of the front seat, her head hanging down and her knees flopped out. She did not look her best, and Mama always said you should look your best for church. She sure had on a lot of perfume. It smelled like old dead flowers, but I still got a whiff of that other smell. Sometimes the stink came off Mama's skin like she was sweating it. Vodka. I hated it.

Tom leaned over and whispered, "Whoopee! Daddy's driving like he's Buck Baker."

Daddy held the steering wheel so tight I thought he might could crush it. He was going so fast we had a big tall trail of dust following us. The tires squealed as he turned on to the highway and headed into Odessa. He always liked to be on time for church. I hoped we got there in one piece.

When Daddy pulled into the parking lot of the First Methodist Church, all the spaces were full. He parked right on the church lawn. I hoped he wouldn't get in trouble for leaving the car on the grass at Jesus's house.

Daddy got a good grip on Mama as we headed inside. He was right about the whole town being there.

People's heads came together, and I heard a lot of whispering as we walked down the aisle to our seats up front. I felt like everybody was staring at me. It felt funny, but not laughing funny.

"Take a picture, it'll last longer," Tom said in a real low voice.

That was the longest walk I ever took in my life. Uncle Rafe looked at his watch when we got to our seats. Aunt Penny smiled a little. I was so glad to see her.

After Daddy got Mama set down, he whispered to me and Tom, "You know everybody is gonna go up to say goodbye to your Grandma when Preacher Henry gets done talkin'. Lord knows, it might be a good long while. So, sit up straight and be on your best behavior."

Tom said, "Yes, sir."

I nodded. I was glad Daddy looked more like his regular self. While Preacher Henry went on about just rewards and heavenly glory, I got kind of tired listening and looked around at the people sitting behind us. All the ladies' hats were fun to see. If I took the fruit off those hats, I could make one heck of a salad. The fruit wasn't real, just like all those flowers on the other half of the hats wasn't real either. But the flowers around the casket were real. I never seen or smelled so many flowers at one time. I couldn't help but take big deep sniffs of the sweet-smelling air.

Why give all those flowers to a dead person? They must have cost a pretty penny, as Mama would say. It was sort of sad Grandma June didn't get no flowers when she was alive. But I could understand why. Mama said she never had a kind word for anybody. Daddy said she was mean as sin.

I sneaked a look at Mama. Oh Lord, she was sleeping. Sleeping in church was frowned upon, Mrs. Foster told us in Sunday school. Mama began to snore—right in church with Jesus watching!

Daddy's face got red, and he nudged Mama awake. He wasn't too gentle about it, either. Mama stuck her elbow right back in Daddy's side. He said Mama always gave as good as she got. I could see what he meant.

Preacher Henry finally ran out of gas, and everyone stood up for a final hymn.

"Amazing Grace, so sweet the sound," I sang.

Tom looked at me funny. "It's *how* sweet, Janie," he whispered.

I heard Mama sing that song all the time at home, and she said, "so sweet." Mama always cried when she sang it and got stuck in places, just like now. She had tears running down her face as she leaned against Daddy.

Something about those words made my throat feel full and my eyes burn. Most folks must feel the same because there was plenty of handkerchiefs and tissues when I looked around the church. I heard a few sniffs and even some soft crying. It was hard to believe any of those folks cried for Grandma June, no matter how good Preacher Henry talked her up. Besides Mrs. Wilson and Mrs. Foster, no one came to visit her anymore. But the two of them were church ladies, always busy doing good, like teaching Sunday school and visiting sick people. Mama called them do-gooders, but it didn't sound like a nice thing when she said it.

We sat back down, and after a few more prayers, Preacher Henry said, "The service is ended."

At last, it was time to say goodbye. Daddy leaned down and said something to Mama. Whatever he said made her sit up straight and shake her head. She stood up real slow and held onto Daddy's elbow.

"Tom, Janie, you two go on. We're right behind you," Daddy whispered.

I wanted to run right up front. This was my only chance to see a dead person up close. But everybody was moving slow, so I did, too. I held my breath to help settle down as we headed to the casket to see Grandma June.

When I got to the casket, I stood on my tippy-toes and leaned in to get a good look. This was the last time I would see Grandma June on this earth. I felt kind of bad I wouldn't miss her very much. Her eyes were closed. That was a surprise. Every dead animal I ever seen had their eyes open. A line of yellowy stuff showed where her eyelids met. It almost looked like her eyes were glued shut. There was something else funny. Grandma June had a real pink face, but her hands were all yellow. How could that be? Her hair looked real nice, though. It had been straight as a stick in life, but now it held a curl just fine.

Tom poked me in the back. "Come on now, Janie. For God's sake, how long does it take to say goodbye? There's a whole line of people behind us."

I didn't answer. I didn't want to make a fuss. Even though I really wanted to stomp on Tom's foot, I didn't dare in church with Jesus right there. Mrs. Foster told us "Thou shalt not kill" also meant hitting people, so I figured it went for foot stomping, too.

Daddy leaned down and whispered, "Move on, girl!"

I moved to the side. Tom took all of two seconds to say his goodbye.

Then it was Mama's turn. She threw herself across the casket and sobbed, crying out in a pitiful voice. "Oh, Mama, I can't believe you're gone." Daddy grabbed her shoulders and hustled her around the front row of pews. His lips had gone missing again, and he rolled his eyes. We all went back up the aisle to the church door to shake Preacher Henry's hand.

That was the first time I ever heard Mama call Grandma June "Mama." But that was right. Grandma was Mama's mama. Usually Mama called her "the old bitch" when she didn't think I could hear.

Outside the church, all the people headed to their cars to line up for the parade to the cemetery.

Daddy loaded Mama in the front seat. Then he stood and put his hand on my shoulder and patted me. "You go on to Uncle Rafe's house and give Aunt Penny a hand with supper. She's right over there." He pointed at Uncle Rafe's new Cadillac, where Aunt Penny was talking with the other ladies. Uncle Rafe was Mama's brother. That made him belong to Grandma June, too. He didn't make a scene in church like Mama did, but he did look a little bit sad. I tried to picture Uncle Rafe and Mama as little children together, but I just couldn't see it.

Tom said, "I'm gonna ride with Uncle Rafe. I ain't never been in a Cadillac. Look at that paint job. Like a giant emerald!" He was gone before Daddy could say a word.

Daddy looked at me and smiled. "Don't blame him one bit. Go on now."

"Yes, Daddy." I ran over to Aunt Penny and hugged her tight. "Daddy said I'm gonna help you get supper ready."

Aunt Penny smiled at me and tucked my hair behind my ears. She waved to Daddy. "Thanks, George. I appreciate you letting Janie come help me."

Daddy waved back and got in the car with Mama.

I'd much rather be with Aunt Penny. She smiled a lot. Her hair was always nice, and she wore nail polish. She was pretty and always smelled like spices and flowers. Never like vodka.

Uncle Rafe ran over to give Aunt Penny a kiss before he got his Cadillac in line behind Daddy. I guess he couldn't stand to be away from her for even a little while. Daddy could be gone for days if a well blew out. I don't recall he gave Mama many goodbye kisses, leastways not exactly the same kind of kiss Uncle Rafe gave Aunt Penny.

We watched all the cars roll up in a long, long line. Even though it was bright May sunlight, they had their headlamps on.

Aunt Penny held my hand. "Let's go, honey. I'm sure glad for your help because we have a lot of work to do."

I squeezed her hand and said a thank you to Jesus for giving me Aunt Penny. We walked to their house just around the corner from the church and went right to the kitchen. Aunt Penny put on her apron and washed her hands. She picked me up and held me so I could wash up, too.

"We're going to have a buffet," Aunt Penny said. "It's easier."

"What's a buffay?"

It turned out a buffay was just supper all set out on the sideboard so everybody could get their own food their ownself. Aunt Penny hurried around her pink and white kitchen, getting plates and bowls out of the refrigerator. The sunlight coming through the window made her beautiful golden hair glow. It looked like the halo around an angel's head in my Sunday-school book.

Aunt Penny cooked a whole lot different from Mama. She didn't have a cigarette hanging out the side of her mouth and a frown on her face as she chopped and stirred. She wasn't forever stopping to take a swig from her glass. She seemed happy even if she was slaving away in the kitchen. Mama always called it slaving, but Aunt Penny looked like she was having a good time.

She stopped her work and looked at me. "Hey, I know what's missing. Music! Can you turn on the radio, sweetie? My hands are all messy."

I put on the radio and the rock 'n' roll station came on.

Aunt Penny sang along with Elvis to "Blue Suede Shoes." "You know, when Elvis played Odessa High last year, I was there with all the teenagers, doing the jitterbug. Didn't care a fig I was ten years older. Your Uncle Rafe can cut a rug, let me tell you. It was the best time!"

"Can you teach me to dance?"

"One of these days, I sure will, honey. But right now, I need you to frost this carrot cake. Folks will be arriving before we know it."

My mouth was filling with spit, I wanted to lick the knife so bad, but I didn't take even a little taste of the frosting. Then me and Aunt Penny put cream cheese in celery and dotted raisins on top. "Ants on a log," she called them. That tickled me.

Aunt Penny wiped her hands and ran to the radio, turning it up loud. "We got a little minute. Come on and do the stroll." She grabbed my hands, and we danced around the kitchen. She sure could move, just like the teenagers on the TV.

I wished I belonged to Aunt Penny and Uncle Rafe. They didn't have any children of their own, so they could use one. Seemed like most married people had kids. When I asked Mama why they didn't, Mama said it was not-to-be-discussed and that was that.

"Honey, can you help me carry some of this into the dining room? Here, you take these biscuits and I'll take this big platter of ham."

"Yes, ma'am. You know, I never knew how much fun cookin' is."

I was getting mighty hungry, but I didn't dare say nothing. It was rude to eat before all the other people came. But those biscuits were mighty tempting, and I wanted to take a great big bite out of one of them.

Aunt Penny looked at me. "Janie, did you have breakfast?"

"No, ma'am." My stomach growled. Maybe she could hear it.

"Why, you must be starving! Fix yourself a plate of food, sweetie. Would you like a coke? I have Dr Pepper and Pepsi."

"Thank you. Dr Pepper's good."

I took my plate, napkin, and fork out on the back porch and sat down on the top step. Aunt Penny brought out my Dr Pepper, put it next to me, and kissed me on the head. She hustled back in to finish up. My eyes stung, but I didn't know why.

Alice, Aunt Penny's calico cat, came out from under the porch and rubbed against me. She purred like a little machine. She was a nice cat. I wished and wished for one of my own, but when I asked, Mama always said, "No, and hell no!" At least I could visit Alice. I fed her little bits of baked ham, but I didn't think cats ate potato salad, so I didn't give her none.

I was finishing up when folks started coming in from the cemetery. I picked up my plate and ran inside to help. Nobody looked like they was scared or seen any ghosts, but I was still glad I came to Aunt Penny's. Mama didn't much like me always asking to go visit her, but she never said why.

Tom and Daddy came in and headed right to the buffet without so much as a "hey!"

Mama walked real slow and careful, like her feet couldn't find the right place to set down. At least her hat was on straight now. "I'm not hungry, y'all. I'm gonna get me a nice hot cup of coffee."

"I'll get it, Mama," I said. It was probably best if Mama didn't go pouring hot coffee in Aunt Penny's beautiful house.

"Well, if you ain't the little helper." Mama swayed like a tree in a high wind as she stood there.

Why did Mama always sound mean even when she was saying something nice?

Aunt Penny hurried in with an apple pie someone brought. "Martha, why don't you sit down in the parlor? Two sugars and a little milk, right?"

"You remembered. How awful sweet of you." Mama gave Aunt Penny the kind of smile a person didn't mean and walked over to Aunt Penny's pale blue couch and plopped down.

I made Mama's coffee and carried it real careful and set it down on the table next to her. She was talking to herself, but I couldn't make out the words. I sure hoped Mama acted right. I took a seat against the wall so I could keep an eye on her.

Daddy came into the parlor with a huge plate of food piled up high. He grunted as he sat down on the couch next to Mama. "At least we'll get one decent meal today."

"What's that supposed to mean, George?" Mama's lips pushed together, and she had that line between her eyes.

"You know darn well what it means. The kids and me practically live on beans and franks."

"Don't get ugly," Mama said. Her hands shook as she held her coffee cup.

How could Mama say that about Daddy? I heard lots of ladies say he was a fine-looking man. He was tall and strong and had nice wavy dark hair. He looked like he could be a movie star. I seen how some of the ladies at church looked at Daddy, like they was hungry or something. Mrs. Hampton, that nasty Priscilla Hampton's mama, always gave him the googly-eyes. Even Tom noticed. And if he noticed something besides food or basketballs, it was real obvious.

Grown-ups sometimes used words in a funny way. It was one of the things I tried to figure. Their words didn't always match what they meant, sort of like a secret code. I remembered when I was little and so excited hearing some ladies at the market whisper about colored people. I closed my eyes, and in my mind, I saw purple people with pink dots. And blue folks with green hair and yellow eyes. People with stripes and swirls of every color, like in the big box of Crayola crayons. It sounded like a marvel, and

I wanted to go see the colored people. I was about to ask Daddy if I could, then I realized the ladies was only talking about brown people—people like Claude and Miss Marcy who worked at the market. It was a puzzle.

I decided to get me a piece of carrot cake. Folks were going after it pretty good, and I liked it better than apple pie. I headed to the dining room, listening to the grown-up talk. Mrs. Foster and Mrs. Wilson had their heads so close together that Mrs. Foster's hat grapes touched Mrs. Wilson's daisies.

"It positively gives me the chills to know June is gone," Mrs. Wilson said. "Why, the three of us are the same age! I guess you never know when your time is up."

Mrs. Foster said, "June pushed up her own time, you ask me. She picked her own poison."

Did Grandma June die from poison? I wished I knew, but there wasn't a soul I could ask. Behind me, I heard a fuss, then some yelling and cussing and I didn't have to turn around to know Mama was right in the middle of it. Aunt Penny came running in with a towel.

Daddy wiped coffee off the couch. His face was red. He stood up and said, "Sorry about the couch, Penny. I'll pay to have it cleaned. Martha isn't feeling well. We're headin' out."

Mama threw her head back and said, "Yeah. Let's get outta here. I need a cigarette, and I can't have one inside Penny's lovely home."

Daddy's face got even redder, like the brick red Crayola crayon. "That's enough, Martha. We're leaving. Janie, get Tom."

I gave up getting that carrot cake, wasn't too hungry anymore, anyway. I ran to Aunt Penny and gave her a goodbye hug. With the way Mama was acting, it might be a while before I saw my aunt again.

Soon as she got outside, Mama lit up one of her cigarettes with her Zippo. She switched from matches to a lighter because she said the matches always burned her fingers before she could get the damn cigarettes lit. I would get my face smacked if I said "damn." And rightly so. It was wrong to cuss. Jesus didn't like it. Still, that didn't seem to stop Mama.

That night, after I had my bubble bath, brushed my teeth, and said my prayers, I lay me down to sleep in bed, thinking about how sad Wilbur was when he knew Charlotte was dying. No one was very sad Grandma June was gone.

I thought about what it must be like to be dead. Your body stayed on earth, was put in the ground even, like they put Grandma June in the ground today. If you were good, your soul flew away, straight up to heaven. Souls were invisible. I could understand a soul flying up to heaven, but for the life of me, I couldn't figure how a soul got down to the bad place. Could a soul dig? Did they have invisible shovels? No, that couldn't be.

There had to be a door somewhere that led straight down to hell. Boy, that must be one long stairway! I prayed it wasn't anywhere near Odessa.

I sure hoped Grandma June had gone to heaven, but I wasn't sure she would make it through the Pearly Gates. Saint Peter might not let her in because she hadn't gone to church very often.

Mama said her mama was mean as a snake. I wondered how she could call Grandma June mean when she wasn't any too nice her ownself. Jesus didn't like mean people.

Then there was the vodka. I figured out my ownself Mrs. Foster wasn't really talking about poison—she was talking about vodka. And everybody knew a good Methodist didn't drink. And here was Mama drinking vodka, just like Grandma June. Would she die, too?

I held tight to my stuffed cat, Polly. She was a comfort. Poor Polly was getting a little ragged. There were bare patches on her yellow fur where I used to pick at it when I was little. How wonderful it would be if Polly was a real live cat! But I could only pretend.

I turned onto my other side, trying to get comfortable. There was a dip in the mattress, and I had to get in it just so.

As I was falling asleep, I thought about what Daddy said about Mama, that she was just like *her* mother. Most little girls did favor their mothers. Like that disgusting Priscilla Hampton, looking like a princess with her frilly dresses and her nose in the air, and her mama all dolled up at church today.

Was I just like Mama?

Did girls get to pick what they want to be when they grew up? There were mamas, aunts, and grandmas. Could I pick just one? I knew which one I'd pick. No contest. *Jesus, I don't mean no disrespect, but I'm darn sure I don't want to be like Mama.*

Chapter Two

RELUCTANT RETURN TO ODESSA-AUSTIN 1984

Jane checked her Bulgari watch as she waited in the checkout line at Whole Foods. Two thirty already. She still had to get the groceries home and whip up a fabulous dinner for Joshua's partners. Cooking, not on her list of life's pleasures, felt like drudgery, and a house full of shrinks and their wives wasn't her idea of a good time. She hadn't seen his partners since she quit working for them shortly before her wedding last year, and while they were decent and well-respected men, they were far from scintillating guests. As for their wives, she had nothing in common with those dowdy grandmothers. There were only so many niceties to say about pictures of grandchildren and so many rounds of Trivial Pursuit she could play before passing out from boredom.

She had tried to cram too much in her day, perhaps in rebellion at the thought of the dinner party. After dropping off her much-revised paper on personality integration at UT, she'd gone to an AA meeting, grabbed a taco, then stopped at the pool, determined to maintain her strict regimen of thrice-weekly swims. Now she was running late. After loading the groceries into the Mustang GT, she zoomed down Fifth Street and squealed the tires as she launched the car onto Mopac. Only a couple of miles to the Bee Cave Road exit. Hoping she wouldn't get caught behind a school bus, she gritted her teeth at every red light.

As she waited for the garage door to open, she took deep breaths and heard Joshua in her mind, telling her as he often did, she tried to do too much. He wanted her to take a break from finishing her master's in psychology, skip taking a summer course, and accompany him to a conference in Atlanta. They hadn't exactly had a fight about her refusal, but her decision further strained their relationship. Why had he made things worse with the dreaded dinner party? Jane knew the gathering would be tedious, not festive. She fumed over the timing, the day after she finished that damn paper. It was the most difficult academic task ever, because, with every point she made, she had to wrestle with her internal contradictions and lack of integration. What a fraud she was!

She rushed into the kitchen, the loaded brown paper bags testing the limits of her arm strength. One bag ripped, and mushrooms rolled across the floor. Tallulah stalked into the room, meowing her protest at Jane's long absence, and nosed one of the fallen fungi.

Jane knelt and nuzzled the cat. "We'll catch up later, Lulah."

Groaning in frustration, Jane gathered the mushrooms and tossed them in the prep sink. She began to unpack the rest of the ingredients for dinner and noticed the flashing light on the answering machine. Ten missed calls, but no messages.

Shrugging, she returned to the drudgery when the phone shrilled. She dashed to the counter and picked up, wondering if it was the hang-up artist again. For a second, she entertained a fervent hope Joshua was calling to cancel tonight's dinner.

"Hello."

"Janie, it's me," said a deep voice with the unmistakable West Texas twang she had worked so diligently to eradicate from her own speech. "Your daddy."

Jane's fight-or-flight response activated, and her mouth turned into the Sahara. It had been a long time since they had spoken. *How did he get my number? Tom promised me he'd never...* Panic, mixed with sadness and anger, swept over her. She believed she had entombed those feelings years ago when she renounced her family at the age of sixteen and hitchhiked to California.

Despite the shocking, unwanted emotions, she cringed at the West Texas drawl and poor grammar. She mentally corrected him. *It's I, dammit.* Then, guilt seasoned her emotional stew as the massive cosmic band-aid ripped from the wound of her past. *Who says, "It's I?" Certainly not an oilfield worker. When did I become so absurdly pretentious?* "Daddy. It's been a while, hasn't it? And I go by Jane now." She sounded pompous to herself.

"Janie—"

"Jane." Now she just felt hateful. *I can't seem to help myself—I'm putting on armor to repulse the invasion of my past.*

"Jane." He sighed. "Don't sound right somehow." Her father stopped speaking.

She waited through his silence.

"Reason I'm calling...I'm sorry to tell you your mama passed away last night."

"Daddy. My God!" She reached behind her for a chair and fell into it. Jane had been waiting for this phone call for years and always thought her brother Tom would deliver the news.

A thousand times, I rehearsed cool detachment in my head. Yet, now it's real, I'm not indifferent. Go figure.

Clutching the receiver like a lifeline, she laid her forehead in her left hand. The jukebox in her mind played the Shangri-La's "I Can Never Go Home Anymore," her anthem when she lived in the Haight in 1967. Mary Weiss's plaintive cry, "Mama!" rang in her ears. The song title accurately described Jane's reality, but the singer had been regretful about leaving her mama, while Jane had been triumphant. Still, she thought it was a good tune.

"Yep, the booze finally caught up with her. Always knew she'd lose that battle." His voice thickened, and he took several deep breaths before he continued, "Funeral's in three days' time." He was silent for a few moments, then asked, "You comin' home?"

Home? But it wasn't.

It sure hadn't felt like home to her when she left seventeen years ago, dropping out of high school and making her way to San Francisco—after a slight detour to Monterey Pop—right on time for the Summer of Love.

Back then, she told herself she was running *to* something, but if she were honest, she was running away.

Home? She didn't know if she had ever succeeded in creating one, even in this expensive Austin home. The excitement when Joshua bought the house after their marriage a year ago had faded; her residency felt as impermanent as it had in all the other places she had lived over the years. She had bounced around through life and come far from her beginnings, and not just in miles. But she couldn't name a place she would call "home," including here with Joshua. And that was getting to be an issue. *He made me feel safe and sane at first. Now I don't know what I feel.*

Sitting in Austin, Texas, three hundred and fifty miles from Odessa, Jane swore she could smell the odor of Mama's vodka-soaked breath. Her throat thickened. Good God—was she going to vomit?

"Daddy, when I walked out that door, I swore I'd never go back." She closed her eyes, determined to keep her boundaries, yet aching for the hurt she knew she was inflicting on her daddy.

His voice hardened. "I know that." He cleared his throat. "I was hopin' you might reconsider," he added in a gentler tone.

Jane still clutched the phone, although she felt like flinging it at the wall. She believed the past was buried, yet it rose from the grave, poking her with the bony fingers of ugliness she worked so hard to forget. This conversation was torture.

She wanted to refuse but hearing her daddy's voice brought a rush of love for him from an untapped childhood reservoir. Jane didn't want to add to his grief; he had been hurt enough by what life dished out to him. As a child, she considered him the good parent, and he had been, compared to the misery that was Mama.

"You still there, Jani-Jane?"

"Yes, I'm here." She put her hand over the mouthpiece and prayed aloud, "God, what should I do?" *What will seeing that godforsaken house do to me? I still have nightmares.* She sighed and murmured, "All right, Daddy." She winced as she said, "I'll be there."

"Thank you, honey. I'm glad. It'll be so good to see you." After a moment, he asked, "Will Joshua be comin' too? I'd like to meet the man who won my Janie's heart. When Tom told me you was gettin' hitched, I was real happy for you."

"No!" She felt sick at the thought of Joshua seeing her origins. He knew she had grown up in West Texas and, as far as she was concerned, that was all he needed to know.

Jane pulled her suitcase out of the closet and began to pack. Lingerie, pants, tops, shoes, makeup, a goodly number of long, dangling earrings—her trademark—and the outfit, the one she would wear as they lowered Mama into the ground.

"I won't be wearing a simple and tasteful black dress." She spoke aloud as she carried an armload of clothing to the bed. Tallulah, the doll-faced Persian, followed her and jumped up next to the pile of garments.

The breath went out of Jane, and she dropped on the bed. "She's dead. I'll never talk to her again, and I didn't even know I might want to." She reached for her fawn-colored cat, a gift from Andy, the trust-fund-baby-drug-addict-romantic-disaster of her last serious relationship before Joshua. Stroking Tallulah's cashmere softness, Jane fell back on the designer pillows. Fourteen meticulously coordinated pillows to be exact. Trés chic. Trés expensive. Trés not West Texas.

Looking at the embarrassment of riches in her designer bedroom, Jane wondered if this was what she wanted. The décor—or the husband.

"I should call Lauren," she told the cat. Jane knew every good AA member was supposed to call their sponsor when in crisis. Did this qualify as a crisis? Maybe. "But not now, Lulah. Maybe later."

How her mind could obfuscate, a word she first learned while working as a receptionist in the psychiatrist's office where she'd met her husband. But she couldn't escape from this. Insight—another shrink word—she had feelings about Mama's death. All right, she could admit that. But she would take baby steps. No headlong rush into the land of emotion where incalculable landmines lurked. As her AA buddies loved to say, the mind is a dangerous neighborhood—don't go in there alone. Okay, first baby step: she wasn't the stoic, impassive stalwart she had imagined. But with the tumult of emotions whipsawing through her thoughts, it would take some sorting out before she could figure out what was going on in the mess between her ears.

She twisted her mouth in self-mockery and exhaled, blowing her long bangs off her forehead. Giving Tallulah a gentle kiss on her sweet head, she rose from the bed and returned to her walk-in closet.

Black, the color of mourning, was well represented in Jane's wardrobe. As she browsed through the silks, linens, and fine cotton garments that stretched down the wall of her custom closet, she admitted she was also partial to bright colors. Exotic prints and vivid solids in magenta, peacock, emerald, and vermillion caught the light from the crystal chandelier. Black acted as a foil for these vibrant colors. Perhaps this clothing was a vestige of her hippie days. She had a romantic view of herself back then as a sort of gypsy, all scarves and swirling skirts. Stevie Nicks came to mind. Lauren, too. The tall, willowy, sixtyish diva, with her long curly red hair and silk saris or dashikis, was a force to be reckoned with—opinionated, glamorous, unconventional. Lauren would have a thing or two to say about Jane leaving Joshua at home.

And I don't want to hear it.

Psychiatric terminology from Joshua's professional journals came to her mind. Flight of ideas. Emotionally labile. Tangential thinking. Was she psychoanalyzing herself? God forbid. She had made the raging debate between the disease model and behavioral model of mental illness an artificial barrier in her marriage. Jane manned the barricade of cognitive behavioral therapy and launched scathing attacks at psychoanalysis and psychoactive medications. Joshua just shook his head and refused to engage, saying, "Who are we to be the arbiters of that controversy?" Maddening. She laughed out loud at herself. *If you can't laugh at yourself, whom can you laugh at?* Sometimes it sucked to be married to a shrink.

On the other hand, she had learned plenty of therapeutic language from her own school texts, Alcoholics Anonymous, and devouring every self-help book on the planet. She sure could analyze. Joshua claimed she dissected and scrutinized everything down to a nub, but her reaction to Daddy's news made it clear she had dodged the large looming issues from her past, despite all the talking, sharing, and reading.

Halfway through her master's degree program in psychology at the University of Texas, she was having second thoughts about that as well as other things—like her marriage. Apparently, one phone call from the daddy she hadn't spoken to for umpteen years was enough of a catalyst to spark doubts about every aspect of the life she had constructed.

Jane was folding her favorite turquoise blouse when Tallulah sat up and stretched. The cat's ears pricked up, and she scampered from the room. Joshua must be home. No doubt, he would want to accompany her to the funeral. Worse, he might expect it and tell her it was one more example of how committed he was to her. Jane suspected his implication was that she didn't have the same commitment to him. Maybe she didn't.

She would have to really work it to get him to stay home. But she was mighty good at working it. She'd need every advantage, so she dashed into the bathroom and pulled her long hair into a casual twist, securing it with a tortoise-shell clip. After a quick assessment, she positioned a few tendrils around her face and over the back of her neck. Joshua often complimented her on her cheekbones when she wore her hair this way. A dab of Vaseline on her lips to make them gleam, a fast spritz of Coco, her new favorite Chanel fragrance, no need to touch up her eye makeup—it was flawless. She nodded at her reflection, quite ready to face her husband.

Jane took a deep breath and entered the kitchen. Joshua knelt on the floor, scratching Tallulah's ears. He spoke softly to her, and the cat purred in response.

Not bad for a dog person. Lulah loves him.

Joshua glanced up and said, "Hey, babe. You do remember my partners and their wives are coming over for dinner?" He stood and looked around the kitchen with a cocked eyebrow. "I thought I'd come home to the aroma of something tasty. What's up?"

Jane sighed and slinked up to him. She put her arms around his neck, stood on her tiptoes, and gave him a soft kiss. "I remember all right. I went to Whole Foods and bought everything for beef stroganoff."

"My favorite!"

"I know—but something came up. We have to cancel." She bit her lip and stepped back to look him in the eye, waiting for his response. *I feel like a vamp in a B movie.*

"What? What came up? It's very late notice." His voice was even, but the frown and his arms folded across his chest revealed his irritation.

"My daddy called today."

"Your father? The mystery man from your mystery past. And?"

"Mama died."

"Jesus, Jane. Why didn't you say so?" His voice was all concern as he took her in his arms and held her close. "I'm so sorry, babe. When did she pass? When is the funeral?" He stepped back, still holding her shoulders, trying to make eye contact. "I'll call Jeff and Lamar to cancel."

Jane kept her head turned to the side and pulled away. "Appreciate it. Be right back." She hurried from the room, knew she had to regroup. *How do I find the courage to tell him I'm traveling solo?*

Racing upstairs, she closed the bedroom door behind her, snicked the lock, and exhaled. Despite her earlier hesitation, she decided to call her AA sponsor. Lauren, always a good sounding board, would offer her sincere, yet blunt, advice. Jane dropped onto the bed and dialed from the phone on the nightstand. Fifteen rings before she gave up. Lauren did not believe in answering machines. Part of her charm, she said.

Jane knew the standard guidance: If you can't reach your sponsor, call a friend, or get to a meeting. There was no time for a meeting, and there was no one else she cared to confide in about her marital woes. She would have to deal with this without Lauren. Jane pictured the flamboyant redhead and smiled. An unlikely friend and confidant, given the thirty-year difference in their ages and dissimilar upbringing, but their relationship worked. Thinking back to her first AA meeting, she remembered how Lauren had stood out in the improbable mix of people in that room.

She lay back on her many pillows, closed her eyes, and repeated the Serenity Prayer about fifty times.

Ten minutes later, Jane returned to find Joshua seated at the breakfast room table sorting through the mail. He sought her eyes. "There you are. I was about to mount a search party. Don't worry about dinner. Jeff and Lamar send their condolences." He leaned forward and pulled out a chair. "Have a seat, babe. We need to talk about this. No more running out."

Jane's eyes widened. She sat across from him and looked down at the flowered place mat.

"Look at me, babe."

She usually liked looking at Joshua. His strong features might not be conventionally handsome, but two years ago, the minute he walked into the psychiatrists' office where she worked, she had responded with an intensity that shook her to the core. He was tall, with long black hair that reached his shoulders. She remembered the tug low in her belly when he smiled at her and announced, "I'm Joshua Renfrew, the new psychiatrist."

Jane forced her eyes to meet his. "I'm looking."

"Well, that's a start. I can only guess what you're feeling, babe. And, it's kind of disturbing all I can do is guess." He pushed the pile of mail to the side. "Are you sad? Glad? Do you care? Help me out, would you?"

"You know I'm not close with my family." Jane looked out the window for a moment.

"That's an understatement. But it doesn't answer the question." His large, immaculate hands opened and closed—an unusual display of agitation for cool and collected Joshua.

Jane avoided eye contact. "I was raised by wolves. At least by a she-wolf. I cut the umbilical cord a long, long time ago." Almost against her will, she turned back to him and reached out her hand. "I'm not sure what I feel. What am I supposed to feel?"

Joshua studied her. "I don't know how to begin to answer that. You keep your past locked away from me, and now it appears, even from yourself. No one can tell you what you feel." He ran his hands through his hair and stared at his shoes. "I'm at a loss here. I thought you did the work on this in AA. Yet, here you are—clueless?"

"That's exactly how I feel. I've regressed." She covered her face with both hands and said through her fingers. "My daddy asked me to come home."

"Of course we're going to the funeral. When is it?"

Jane withdrew her hands from her face but couldn't meet his eyes. Addressing the placemat, she mumbled, "You don't have to come with me." She shot a glance at him.

His beautiful brow furrowed. "Of course I do. I can easily reschedule my caseload." He reached out to her. "I want to be there for you."

Here goes. "I don't want you there."

Joshua reacted as if he were sucker punched. He pushed back from the table and shook his head. "What? Are you serious?"

Jane met his gaze, her face frozen in neutrality. She was Switzerland.

He looked away first. "I guess you are serious."

"This is my business. You made that clear when you told me you couldn't help me."

"When did I say that?" His voice was rising, tight professional control giving way.

I bet his patients never see him like this. "You just said you couldn't tell me what to feel. Guess I'll have to figure it out myself." Jane hung her head, feeling a twinge of guilt despite knowing she was getting what she wanted.

As Joshua leaped to his feet, his chair crashed to the floor. Jane jumped. Tallulah dashed from the room. Joshua's face flushed crimson and his mouth contorted as he yelled, "You are impossible! I reach out, and you pull away. Time and again. When an event like a death happens, couples weather it together. It builds the bond." He took a deep breath and bent to pick up the chair. In a more controlled tone, he asked, "Do we even have a bond?"

Jane froze, staggered at his reaction. Joshua had never raised his voice to her before this.

"Honey, please. Don't yell at me. My mother just died." *Oh my God! Mama said the same thing to Daddy. Have I become my mother?*

"Good Lord, woman! Are you nuts?" He paused, then sputtered with harsh laughter. "Did you hear what I just said? All my psychiatric counseling skills have flown out the door." He gestured with his arms as if to illustrate. "I'm going to need therapy myself if I stand here another ten seconds."

"I didn't think you'd react this way."

"Really?" He scowled. "How did you think I'd take being shut out again? There is a pattern here—a very troubling pattern." He paced in a tight circle, searching the ceiling for answers. Finally, he stopped and skewered her with a glance. "You know what? I give up. I'm walking out the door and going…I don't know where." His fists clenched. "You do what you have to do. Let me know you get there safely. I'll see you…whenever."

Before Jane could gather her wits and respond, Joshua grabbed his keys and stormed out, slamming the door to the garage as if to reinforce his anger. She heard him gun the engine on his Saab turbo and peel out down Cicero Lane. Had she just driven a psychiatrist crazy? He had never lost his cool like this. She put her face in her hands and sobbed.

After two hours, Joshua returned from his drive and didn't say a word to her, simply gathered his things and retreated to the neutral territory of the spare room. For the first time since their marriage, Joshua slept in the guest room.

She lay awake, missing his presence in the lonely acre of the king-sized bed, expecting him to come to her. Why hadn't he? She couldn't make herself go to him, either. Was this the end? She covered her head with the pillow, as if that could shut out her thoughts. Eventually she fell asleep, starting awake when the alarm blared at five a.m.

Dressed in new Calvin Klein jeans, ruffled blouse, and her favorite high-heeled red boots, she called a cab. She'd be damned if she would ask Joshua to give her a ride to the airport and knew he wouldn't offer, not after that fight. In her mind, she visualized a chasm. They stood on their respective sides, backs to each other. Who would be the one to bridge the gulf? She was determined to make a dignified exit when the cab arrived in a few minutes. Maybe the time apart would make things clearer.

Jane stopped in the kitchen to leave her flight and hotel information. She jotted a brief note about Tallulah's care. Joshua stood at the bay window, holding a mug of coffee. He appeared composed, relaxed—as if last night had never happened.

He took a sip from his cup and murmured, "Goodbye. Have a safe trip."

How civil. His temperate tone of voice and detached facial expression made her feel as if they were strangers. Maybe they were.

Jane hefted her suitcase. She blurted, "You were raised by June Cleaver, and I was raised by a cross between Cruella De Vil and Ma Kettle. Can't you understand I don't want you to see where I come from?"

He stepped toward her. "I'm your husband. Can't you understand I want you to share your life with me—all of it? Yet you keep putting up walls. I want to have children with you, but sometimes I feel like I don't even know you!"

She dropped her Gucci bag. "Children? I'm not even sure I want to be married!" Gasping, she covered her mouth with her hands. *I don't mean that—or do I?*

Joshua threw his mug against the wall. "I knew it! That's why you're so remote, so closed off, so fucking opaque."

Coffee dripped into the silence as they stood there contemplating what had been said.

"I've got to go. The cab is waiting." She picked up her luggage and turned away from him.

"I want you to think about something, Jane. I've been through analysis, and I recommend you do the same. You're going to graduate school to become a therapist, yet you don't have the faintest idea of who you are or what you want out of life. How can you ever help another human being if you have no insight into yourself? You've learned nothing from all your self-discovery, have you?" His voice was as cold as the South Pole.

The words struck Jane like so many darts, but she didn't answer, just walked out the door.

The scratchy guitar lead-in from "Season of the Witch" played in Jane's head as she rode in the cab to Mueller Airport, staring out the window but not seeing the cars fly past. *Jimmy Page played that eerie guitar on the track. Is that why the song haunts me? Or is it the lyrics? Donovan thought it strange there were so many people to be. He was right. Will I ever find out who I am?*

Her body hunched in pain at the recollection of their battle's harsh words. Joshua's parting shot rankled. *He had to hurl the barb about psychoanalysis.* Even though similar insight about the mess between her ears had crossed her mind, coming from Joshua, it burned like acid.

Being married to a shrink was very hard. Was that why she was going the psychology route? Or was it a subconscious urge to heal her troubled past? *Don't go there.*

She shuddered, thinking of the damage she had seen from electroconvulsive treatments and antipsychotics during her clinicals at the state hospital and in AA meetings. In Jane's opinion, behavior change therapy was a far better mode of intervention. *Just as long as it isn't my behavior.*

After only a year, Jane had come to the conclusion that marriage to anyone was a challenge, if not impossible. There was only so much sharing and self-revelation she could tolerate. For years, she avoided the leap into legal commitment, and now there were times she had to ask herself what the hell she was doing. Maybe her serial monogamy was a preferable option. Not that those relationships turned out any better.

"Eight-fifty, lady." The cab driver sounded impatient.

She glanced at the driver's eyes in the rearview mirror. "Sorry, what?"

"Mueller Airport. You owe me eight-fifty."

Jane took her seat in the plane and leaned her head against the small oval window. She hated flying but couldn't face the prospect of a full day in the car. The trip would be tedious with a stopover in Dallas. But the problem wasn't the flight—it was what was waiting for her in West Texas.

The engines revved and soon they were airborne, ascending into the cloudless sky. Jane closed her eyes. It had been half her life since she had seen Mama. Jane had never been able to erase the mental picture of her on *that* night. The night Jane realized she was a motherless child and had been born that way. Mama would have been thirty-nine. Jane's eyes snapped open. Thirty-nine? If she looked like that at thirty-nine, she would break all land speed records getting to the plastic surgeon. Of course, the type of damage Mama inflicted on her body and face from a diet of vodka, coffee, and cigarettes was the kind no scalpel could repair. How much more damage had Mama imposed on herself in the intervening years? Jane would be finding out mighty soon. She leaned back in the seat, almost drifting off as she recalled the gift that kept on giving—the last time she had seen Mama.

Mama was out in the hallway, bouncing from wall to wall, as she headed to the kitchen for another bottle, no doubt.

I lay in my narrow, lumpy bed, alert for any clue about Mama's progress, hoping she wouldn't come in here. I couldn't deal with her yellin' or maybe she'd want to have a heart-to-heart. Hard to do when she didn't even have one. Daddy was out fixin' a pump. He could be gone for days. Tom had escaped to school in Lubbock. Lucky Tom.

"Janie! Get in here and help your mama."

Damn. I got out of bed and went to the kitchen.

"Where is it? I know I got another bottle. Help me find it."

I reached up into the cabinet and got her damn bottle. "Here you go." Our eyes met.

Mama snorted. "There's that look."

"What're you talkin' about?"

"That look. Had it since you was born."

"Since I was born? This oughta be good. Let's hear it so I can get me some sleep." When she got like this, I knew she wouldn't stop until she was good and ready.

"Yep, even when you was a baby and looked at me, I could tell you didn't love me. Not like Grace. Not like Grace."

I couldn't speak, just stood there staring at her, giving her that look, I supposed. She had that line between her eyes. Her lips were contorted in a self-pitying twist, hair stringy, gray starting to appear. She wore her uniform: wrinkled and stained baby doll pajamas that revealed scrawny arms and legs, and gigantic hot-pink fuzzy slippers.

"Amazing Grace, so sweet...so sweet...so sweet..." She began to keen.

I turned and ran to my room. Grace. I never knew of my infant sister's brief existence until I was eleven. Tom told me. He believed losing her second-born child at five weeks of age was what drove Mama to drink. Until that moment, Mama had never spoken her name to me. What she said to me next, I could never forgive or forget...

"Ma'am? What would you like to drink?"

Jane started and looked around the cabin in confusion. She must have slept right through the stop in Dallas since she now had a seatmate. She gazed at the flight attendant. "Nothing, thank you."

The woman addressed the portly, gray-haired man in the aisle seat. "Sir?" She had a big smile for him.

"How 'bout a coke. You got Dr Pepper?"

"Pardon me. Do you want a Coke or a Dr Pepper?"

"You ain't from Texas, are you, dear?" He chuckled.

"Well, no." She dimpled again. "What can I get you to drink?"

"A Dr P. Thank you kindly."

The woman nodded and poured the soft drink into a plastic cup. She bent over solicitously and handed him the beverage. "Here's your 'coke.' Enjoy!"

"Thank you, ma'am."

The flight attendant sashayed on down the aisle.

Give me a break. Flirting with anything in pants, even grandfatherly types.

The man turned to Jane.

Oh, crap.

"Sure you don't want somethin' to wet your whistle, young lady?"

"No. I mean, yes, I'm sure."

"Thad Moore. Where you headed this fine day?"

"I'm going to Odessa for my mama's funeral." *Great conversation stopper.*

His beaming face fell. "I'm sorry for your loss."

He does *sound sorry.* "Thank you, Mr. Moore."

"Headed to Midland myself."

"Really?" *As if I couldn't guess. Big, bluff oil man, what Daddy would call a company man.*

"Yep, that's home."

"Oil business?" Jane deadpanned. "*Awl bidness*" was what she heard in her aural memory.

"How did ya know?"

"Lucky guess." She gave him the tiniest fake smile and turned to the window.

"Sorry if I intruded on you. If you'd rather not talk, just say so."

Jane winced and turned back to him. "Sorry. I don't mean to be rude. I've got a lot on my mind. Haven't been back to Odessa in quite a while. Can't help but wonder what I'll find."

"When was the last time you saw your mama?" His voice held a gentle curiosity.

"Seventeen years ago. I was sixteen."

"Bet there's a story there." He repositioned his big body in the narrow seat.

"Oh, yes, there's a story."

"I didn't get your name."

"Janie, my name is Janie." *Still regressing.*

"I'm a good listener," he said.

Jane studied his face. *He has kind eyes. Wedding ring. Probably married to the same woman since high school. Bet he has a wallet full of pictures of his grandkids. What the hell. I'll never see this guy again.*

"Mama drank herself to death, just like her mama did. Daddy stayed with her through it all." Jane was surprised Mr. Moore hadn't taken off running down the aisle. He merely nodded at her.

"Even though I never went back after I ran away, I kept in touch through my brother Tom. He's like my daddy—stable, solid, faithful. He left home to go to college at Texas Tech in sixty-three." She glanced at Mr. Moore again. "That was really hard on me."

"Must've been lonely."

"Yeah, Daddy was gone a lot. There was always one crisis or another out on the oilfields."

Mr. Moore chuckled. "You're preachin' to the choir there, young lady."

Jane found it surprisingly easy to confide in this grandfatherly stranger. It was easier to talk to him than to her husband. That couldn't be a good thing.

"Anyway, back to Tom—the one constant in my life as I meandered around San Francisco and then Austin. Tom played basketball at Tech. In fact, he's still there. He's a coach for the basketball team."

"Go, Red Raiders! What's his focus—offensive or defensive?"

Mama was offensive. Tom and I were defensive. "Pardon me?"

"What position did your brother play? Point guard, forward?" He turned in his seat, interested in hearing about Red Raider basketball. "He works for Gerald Myers, right?"

Jane blushed. "Oh. Not sure, all I remember is him dribbling and talking about defense. I don't know much about basketball." Her eyes focused beyond Mr. Moore as a harried mother escorted her little boy to the restroom at the rear of the plane. *He's more interested in basketball than my story.*

Mr. Moore patted her hand. "Sorry to get off track. I'm a big Tech fan. Go on with your story."

"You sure you want to hear this?" Jane asked with a slight smile.

"Sure do!" He beamed at her.

"Tom said Mama would pull herself together from time to time. Stop drinking. Clean up. But it never lasted long. I guess Daddy never lost hope."

"He sounds like an upstanding man."

Jane nodded. "He is. He never was one for a lot of hugging, not demonstrative at all. But he was loyal, hard-working and always provided for us." *Sounds like I'm trying to convince myself, but it's all true.* "He was always a church-going man." *Is that why he stayed? Had to be more, probably sex. Quick, young marriage, Tom's birth seven months later. That bond is powerful. Got me in enough trouble over the years.*

"Why'd you leave home in the first place, Janie? Sixteen is mighty young."

"I finally had it with Mama." She sighed. "Oh, there were other factors. With my brother away at college and Daddy working all the time, I had no one. My best friend killed herself in a rather spectacular way a few weeks before I left."

"My goodness!" Taken aback, he took a swig from his Dr P as if it were something a bit stronger.

"Yeah. Quite the scandal. Every tongue in Odessa was wagging." She shook her head. "It sounds so cliché. Football hero impregnates girlfriend. He dumps her."

"That story is common." His voice became stern, and he seemed to retreat. "Taking your life isn't."

Jane's eyes welled with tears. "I really can't talk about it anymore." *A few little anecdotes from my life can scar a stranger forever.*

"Understood. I'll keep you and your mama in my prayers." He looked relieved as he picked up his Dr P and drained it.

"Thank you, Mr. Moore."

Already, the jet's engines were decelerating. Good God, the plane was on final approach into Midland. Flat, depressing West Texas looked flat and depressing out the tiny window. Ready or not, she was almost "home."

Chapter Three

Rangerland-West Texas 1962

Mama was on a roll with the housekeeping, and I was the maid. But not if she couldn't catch me. I ran out of the house every chance I got. Ran like the wind. No one was gonna catch me in the house doing woman's work.

"Get back here and help me clean up this dump! At least sweep the floor, you little—"

The rest of Mama's rant was lost as I ran down the gravel drive with the satisfying sound of the old screen door slamming on her words. She told me I was turning into a wild thing, a tomboy. I took exception to that. I was an explorer, and why the heck couldn't a girl be an explorer? She told me no man would ever want to marry me, and I better learn to cook and clean if I hoped to get me a husband. I wanted to ask her why she didn't cook and clean herself, but I bit my tongue. I wanted to tell her I wasn't ever gonna get married, but there wasn't no point talking to Mama these days.

Her meanness used to make me cry when I was little, but not for a while now. The tears just didn't come anymore—no matter what my mean old mama had to say. Eleven was too big to cry anyway. After a while, I slowed down to a walk as I headed to the boundary tree in Rangerland, the nation where I was President and Ricky Mills was Emperor.

While I walked, I thought about Mama putting on airs now that she got her a new living room suite. She put those blasted plastic covers on the couch. I couldn't bear to sit on them. Folks would sweat and stick right to them. Daddy was none too fond of the crinkly plastic couch, neither. But Mama insisted.

I heard them talking one night when I was supposed to be asleep. "George, I'll be damned if the stink of the oilfields is gonna be all over my brand-new living room suite."

"Is that right?" His voice was low and rumbly.

Mama giggled. Didn't hear that very much. For a minute or two, I couldn't hear anything.

Then Daddy said, "You didn't seem to mind last time I was home."

I heard them hurry down the hallway to their bedroom. 'Course I knew what that meant. Turning on my side, I cuddled my old toy cat Polly close and pulled the covers over my head.

The long grasses tickled my legs and grasshoppers jumped away. It was getting hot early this year, and I was already sweating. The creosote bushes were putting out their yellow flowers, and the smell of tar was in the air. Some folks couldn't abide the smell, but I kind of liked it. It meant I was outside in my territory.

A jackrabbit scooted across my feet. I almost ran over the durn thing. Wondered if there was a nest nearby. I didn't stop to look because I was on a mission.

I spent as much time outside as I could. Now I understood why Tom had always stayed out in the driveway practicing his shot. He was a junior now and practically lived at the high school gym. I didn't want to be stuck all alone with Mama. Sometimes I felt kind of bad about that, but not too bad. Truth be told, Tom said, Mama was so far into the bottle, she barely crawled out anymore.

In my mind, I pictured a tiny Mama trapped inside an empty vodka bottle and busted out laughing. She smacked her little-bitty hands against the glass and screamed—but I couldn't hear it. That was a blessing.

When she did crawl out, it was no fun dealing with her cruelty and her mess. It sure wasn't a pretty sight, Mama stumbling down the hall in her baby doll pajamas, her hair a knotted mess, headed to the kitchen for a new bottle. Sometimes she'd be talking and laughing just like someone was right there with her. Other times, she'd be singing her favorite hymn, "Amazing Grace, so sweet, so sweet." She never got the words right.

Mama couldn't be bothered to wipe up her spilled liquor and cigarette ash. I would clean it up when it got so bad my feet stuck to the old floorboards. More times than I'd like to remember, I'd come in and find Mama sprawled on the couch, snoring. If she managed to get dressed that day, her dress would be hiked way up, showing her underwear. I always tried to cover her up, at least tug her dress over her panties. Once she woke up and smacked me right in the face. She stared at me but didn't say anything. I wasn't going to wait for her to say she was sorry. I'd be waiting till the Second Coming.

Picking up my pace, I finally reached the mesquite tree that marked the boundary of Rangerland. Ricky and I went around some about who was the ruler, but we worked it out. Being President, I got to pick what our mission would be on Monday, Wednesday, Friday, and Sunday. Ricky, the Emperor, got to choose the rest of the days. He seemed to think Emperor outranked President. I let him think he was right. But this was America, not Red China or the godless Soviet Union.

Out where we lived the houses were scattered around, like somebody had the idea to build a neighborhood and then got bored and just up and quit. It looked kind of like a bad game of Monopoly, mostly vacant land dotted with a lonely house here and there. Our house was the oldest one around, been there since water was wet and looked it, Mama said. It backed up to the empty grasslands, with no neighbors in sight.

Across the lane and down a ways was a big rectangle of land that was once someone's dream: Eden's Acres. Daddy got a good chuckle out of that one. He said, "Yeah, ten lots to an acre, and West Texas sure ain't my idea of Eden."

When Ricky's family moved into the model house in Eden's Acres three years ago, I was a little let down there wasn't a girl my age. Turns out, it was the best thing that ever happened to me, even though it made me sad no one ever built another house there.

I sure hoped Ricky could cut loose from his mama and his pain-in-the-butt little sister, Mavis. Just thinking about the precious Mavis could ruin my day. Nosy, blond-headed, whiny Mavis. She truly was too much to bear.

While I waited for Ricky, I sat on a rock under the tree. I thought on Daddy saying Mama was "making an effort." I figured that was code for stopping drinking. Poor Daddy might could be engaged in wishful thinking. Mama was going full bore, far as I could tell. She could pull the wool over Daddy's eyes—none are so blind as those who will not see—but she wasn't fooling me none. She had some good days, but it seemed like it was only when Daddy was home. He'd been gone four days this time, out fixing a broken oil rig, so he wasn't around to see what I saw.

Once I asked Daddy why we couldn't live in town like Aunt Penny and Uncle Rafe. He told me to keep out of grown-up business. He usually wasn't short with me like that, and it stung me.

How I wished for a real home, like in picture books I had when I was little, with sunshine coming in the windows and smiling people. Like on *Ozzie and Harriet* or *Donna Reed*.

Aunt Penny and Uncle Rafe's house was filled with the yummy sugar-cinnamon smell of cookies baking and the sounds of foot-tapping music and laughter. Just thinking about them made me feel good. Aunt Penny would never put plastic covers on her couch. It was getting to be I only ever saw them at church. Once in a while, if Daddy got home in time to wash off the oilfield smell Mama always complained about, we'd pile in the car and drive over for Sunday dinner. Those dinners were few and far between—Mama made sure of that. She never got over it that Grandma June used the money from the oil company when Grandpa died to send Rafe to college.

Mama said, "Rafe got him a college education, a snooty big-city wife, and a highfalutin' job. What did I get? Nothin'." She took a drag off her cigarette and blew the smoke out through her nose. I hated when she did that, but I couldn't look away.

"No, that ain't true," she said. "I got pregnant. Pregnant. Well, stupid is as stupid does. And pregnant is about as stupid as it gets!" Then she cackled and took another swig from her glass. She wasn't drinking the milk of human kindness, neither. I figured she missed out on going to Sunday school with Mrs. Foster, or if she did go, she didn't learn anything.

I'd been sitting for a spell and figured Ricky couldn't get loose today. Oh well, I'd just go on patrol myself. Looking around, I found a nice long stick I could use to poke around the brush, so I picked it up and got going. I was burning daylight. There wasn't a critter to be seen on my rounds. A few birds cawed and trilled, but that was about it. My shadow was getting longer, so I didn't have much time left before I had to head home. I covered a lot of ground but had one more stop to make.

About three weeks ago, Ricky and I had run across something real interesting—a leg off a fawn. Had to be, it was so small. We looked high and low but didn't find a trace of evidence of where it came from. Nothing—no pool of blood, no innards, just this pathetic little leg. I'd been thinking on what might could have happened and decided there was no way to know. I hated that—not knowing. One or the other of us went by and checked on the leg most every day. In the dry heat, it hadn't changed at all since we first found it.

Sure enough, there it sat in the gully. Untouched—far as I could tell. The little black hoof had a coating of dust. We hadn't had a drop of rain in weeks. The tan fur didn't have a sign of any insect activity and that seemed unusual. I wished Ricky was there to discuss it.

One afternoon in June, Mama was passed out again. For once, Tom was home practicing his jump shot in the driveway instead of at the gym, so I went to talk to him. I heard him before I saw him.

"Sweet dream baby, sweet dream baby."

I guess he was Roy Orbison these days. He was so dang tall. He sure did favor Daddy. Everybody said so. He had the same dark, wavy hair and the same serious look in his eyes. I stood there, scuffing my shoe, examining the cracks in the concrete, not knowing where to start.

"Dream baby—"

"Hey, Tom?" I wasn't about to listen to the whole dang song.

The ball clanked off the rim. "Shit!" He ran to get the rebound and dribbled over to me.

"What? Can't you see I'm busy? Now my concentration is gone." Tom dribbled the blasted ball the whole time he was talking to me. He didn't even appear to be embarrassed I caught him singing again. He never did.

"Sorry to bother you."

"Oh, Jeez, it's okay." He gave me the grin that was supposed to melt the high school girls' knees, at least according to the gossip. "What's going on?" He kept bouncing the ball, right hand, then left hand.

My mouth dried up, and it was hard to start talking. "I don't know what's happenin' to Mama. She's getting worse, back to how she was before the last dry spell. She's just so mean."

"Well, you're right about that. She's mean as all get-out." Tom spit off to the side.

I couldn't abide when he did that and shut my eyes to block the sight.

"So, what do you think *I* can do? What do you think *you* can do? Look, Dad can't do anything about it. The woman's a drunk, just like her mama."

My eyes teared up. There *were* tears left inside me. "Well, it ain't right. And it ain't fair! Why can't Mama be like other kids' mothers?" I rubbed my eyes furiously, mad at myself for being a stupid crybaby. I didn't even want to look at Tom.

He stopped his dribbling and sighed. "You know, I remember when she used to be—but that was a long time ago."

"I hate how she is." I crunched down so hard my teeth hurt.

Tom held the ball and looked longingly at the hoop. Then he did something that surprised me. He tapped the ball to the side and squatted on his heels. Looking me straight in the eye, he said, "It's because of Grace."

"Who's Grace?"

"I don't guess anyone's ever told you. Not sure I should be doing it, neither." He turned his head and spit again.

I didn't mind so much this time.

"Who's Grace?"

"When I was about four, Mama had a little baby girl, Grace. She died real soon after she was born."

I about swallowed my teeth. I got chills. It explained a lot. *Amazing Grace, so sweet...*

He stood back up and got his ball. The thumping sound echoed off the driveway, and it felt like my heart was keeping time. "Don't let on I told you, okay?"

"I got more sense than that! Why ain't I ever heard about this before? You'd think—"

"Yeah, kid, that's exactly what you do. Think. Way too much if you ask me." He stopped dribbling. "Well, I don't know what to tell you. Just do like I do and stay out of her way." He turned and shot the ball one-handed. It passed through the hoop without even touching the rim.

I had a lot to ponder, so I headed back to Rangerland—that's where I did my best thinking.

Another Saturday. Another trip to town to do the grocery shopping. As I climbed in the pickup with Daddy, I felt like my face was hanging down to my shoes. How I wished I was going to see a friend or to a movie instead. "The Brain That Wouldn't Die" was playing. I saw the poster outside the movie theater when the school bus drove me home yesterday. It looked great. But I didn't have any friends in town. None of the town girls gave me the time of day. I was the hick-from-the-sticks to them. So, I hated going to town. And I hated food shopping. That was a job for a mother to be doing.

Each week, when I went down the aisles looking for the cheapest macaroni and finding out which cookies were on sale, I couldn't help but hear the whisperings from "the busybodies" as Daddy called them. Things like: "I don't know how he stands for it." Meaning Daddy putting up with Mama, I figured. "I hear her girl, Janie, has gone half-wild, always outdoors, playing with that Ricky Mills." No mistaking who they were running on about there. "That Tom is living in the gymnasium—my Tyler says he's only ever home to sleep," one old gossip said. "Like mother, like daughter," said another one. "You ask me, Martha is going to beat her mother to the grave—dead by forty is my guess."

I tried not to hear, but I did have ears after all. I tried not to pay attention, but the words got through anyway. Couldn't very well go around the shopping aisles with my fingers in my ears going, "Nananana-nana." Yep, I hated going to the grocery store.

That Saturday, as Daddy drove down the lonely county road, I looked out the window, checking to see if there were any interesting dead animals on the side of the road. If I spotted something, I'd have to tell Ricky so we could check it out. There weren't any buzzards circling that I could see. Buzzards were the easiest way to spot a new specimen.

The country music station wasn't coming in today, and Daddy grumbled as he shut off the radio. The rest of the drive was silent. That was okay. I was used to him not talking much.

I knew Daddy was doing the best he could to keep the house running. He worked a lot, but he pitched in with the chores when he was home. He even got Tom roped in to scrub the floor every so often. We ate simple. The three of us took turns cooking, such as it was. A new invention—instant mashed potatoes—was the best thing that happened to me in ages, saved me hours of peeling potatoes. We ate a lot of canned vegetables. Tinned beef stew, hot dogs, and burgers were the specialties of the house, Daddy would joke—when he was in the mood to joke, that is. That seemed to be less and less often.

For once, Daddy found a spot right in front of the market. I climbed out of the pickup and said "Hey" to Claude who ran the market with his mother, Miss Marcy. Whenever I saw them, I laughed to myself when I remembered how I used to think colored people were pink, purple, blue, green, and yellow before I figured out the quiet grown-up talk about "the colored people" was referring to folks I knew my whole life.

As I grabbed a couple cans of corn off the shelf, I heard some giggling and froze. I didn't want to turn to look but couldn't help myself. There they were—the two prissiest, most hateful girls in the sixth grade—Priscilla and Agnes. They had their heads together, hands to their flapping mouths, whispering, and staring right at me. I hadn't had the pleasure of seeing them since school let out for the summer, and I could have waited a whole lot longer, thank you very much. I took another look and couldn't believe my eyes. Were they wearing lipstick? By God, they were! And nail polish, too. I felt my forehead crunch up as I turned back to the shelves, trying in vain to shut out the image of the baby Marilyn Monroes.

Daddy came down the aisle. "Hey, Janie, I got the meat and bread—you about done there?"

I was never so glad to see my daddy. "Yep, I'm ready to go."

Walking past the two little snots, I held myself tall and kept my back straight. My eyes looked forward, and I tried not to see their stupid giggly painted faces out the corner of my eye.

Priscilla said, "There goes Miss White Trash. I bet she's in a big hurry to go see her boyfriend, that *divine* Ricky Mills." I didn't twitch even though their nastiness hurt. Their laughter followed me all the way to the truck and all the way home.

The only bad thing about being friends with Ricky was dealing with Mavis, his nuisance of a sister. She was one of them Shirley Temple kind of little girls. All frilly and dainty, always wearing a dress and crossing her ankles when she sat down. I never saw her without hair ribbons. She was always sitting on her mama's lap and giving her hugs and just being sweet—it was really hard to take. Ricky said she was too precious for words and then made barfing sounds. That always got a laugh out of me. Worst of all, Mavis had blond curly hair. I would *die* to have blond curly hair. All these things made me dislike Mavis intensely. Ricky disliked her intensely, too, but that was only natural.

If we stayed indoors at Ricky's house watching our favorite TV shows, Mrs. Mills would urge us to "include Mavis." So, Ricky and me headed outdoors at every opportunity. Ricky said, "Include Mavis, my ass." I had to giggle at that one. We ran out the door and couldn't help but laugh at Mavis, trailing behind us like a lost calf bawling for its mother.

We played explorer. *Jungle Jim* was our favorite television show and we watched every chance we got.

"Ain't we seen this one?" Ricky asked.

"Yep. Wish they would make new adventures." It seemed like we had seen every episode about fifty times, and it got so we could say the lines right along with Jim. Me and Ricky took turns being Jim and Kaseem, Jim's faithful friend. Taking turns was only fair. Mavis begged and pleaded to be Skipper. I rolled my eyes. Skipper was a bother—just like Mavis. We said maybe Mavis could be Tamba, the chimp. Mavis would get all red-faced and start to cry for her mama. That made us fall out, clutching our stomachs and rolling on the floor, choking with laughter.

Sometimes we played cowboys. My proudest possession was my six-gun and holster. The holster was real leather and even had a big giant red ruby on it. The six-gun had pearl handles. It was really something. Okay, it might not be a real ruby or real pearl or even a real gun, but I liked to think so.

I was always Annie Oakley, and Ricky was Roy Rogers. No way was I gonna be Dale Evans because I would never, ever consider kissing Ricky, and kissing was something you *had* to do if you were married like Dale Evans and Roy Rogers. Besides, Annie Oakley was a great shot. Bull's-eye every time. And she had that pretty yellow hair. Of course, you couldn't see the color on the TV, but you sure could see her hair was light-colored. She always wore pigtails, but you just knew her hair was curly when she combed it out. Like a golden halo around her head, like Aunt Penny's hair. I had straight-as-a-stick brown hair, same as my mother, same as Grandma June, God rest her soul.

I had learned you couldn't say "Grandma June" anymore without saying, "God rest her soul" right along with her name.

All summer, we explored the prairie on the long, sun-filled days. I usually brought peanut butter and jelly sandwiches, and Ricky brought Kool-Aid and fruit. Mrs. Mills was big on fruit.

Ricky got the idea for the underground fort from all the air raid drills we had at school. "If the bombs ever do fall, our desks won't do a damn thing to save us," he said. He was right.

Everyone had heard the big kids talking. "When the Commies start bombing us, just bend over and kiss your ass goodbye."

Ricky explained the bombs were something called "nukuler" and they poisoned the air so everybody would die. The only safe place was underground.

"You know, Janie, we could build us a bomb shelter." He pushed his straight, white-blond hair out of his eyes and squinted in the sun.

"Oh yeah, how we gonna do that? We ain't got no money, no tools, no nothing."

"Well, we do so got somethin'. We got us. We can get tools from our daddies. Look around at all the junk folks have dumped out here. There's tons of stuff we could use."

I had to give credit where credit was due. Ricky did have him some good ideas. This was one of the times I was glad we were friends. The heck with the snooty town girls—Ricky knew how to have adventures.

The bomb shelter would be a great addition to Rangerland and a place to play away from Mavis. Ricky made me pledge on spit to meet there when the air raid came. What was it with boys and spit?

But first, we had to build it.

We each snitched a shovel from our houses. The location was important—it had to be as far from any of the houses as we could get. I wanted to build it beside a tree. Not that West Texas was known for its trees, but even a good mesquite would make it harder for anyone to see. After hours of patrolling Rangerland and lots of discussions, Ricky found the perfect spot. He stuck his shovel in the ground and said, "This is it, Janie. The perfect spot."

I turned around in a circle and nodded. I had to agree. Couldn't even see a house from here. Ricky was a good Emperor—much better than Emperor Ming on *Flash Gordon*, for sure.

We dug every day for as long as we could stand being out in the hot sun. When we got too tired and sweaty, we camouflaged our trench with brush. I pointed out how the tall grasses of the prairie hid the small pile of dirt we had dug.

"Hey, Janie, we got any of that grape Kool-Aid left?"

"Yeah, but it's probably warm by now."

"Okay, but is it wet?" Ricky could really deliver a line—always with a straight face, like Jack Benny.

I was right proud of how much we got done with two shovels and some determination. School would start again all too soon, so it was important to get on with it.

One morning, we got to the trench and saw dirt had slid down the sides. We looked closer and noticed some holes a few inches below ground on the side across from the mesquite. Had to be those ground squirrels. They were everywhere, hundreds of them, building their tunnels and hidey-holes. We would have to think on how to keep the dirt from sliding down the walls.

In just two weeks, we dug us a pit almost four feet deep, three feet long, but only about two feet across because of the mesquite roots. When we got down inside, it was like our own palace, but still a little too small for comfort. We had big plans for expansion, but for now, the most important thing was to figure out how to make a roof.

We scrounged the prairie and abandoned home sites for old wood and tin and made a pile at the side of the pit. The roof would be the last part of construction. Even if we had to overlap some of the tin pieces, we thought it would work. The plan was to dig in the edges about six inches below the surface of the ground so we could pile dirt back on top. We wanted it to stay hidden. And the dirt would keep out the poisoned air from the nukuler bombs.

I told Ricky we had to make sure no one could see the heap of dirt around the edge of the shelter.

"Good thinkin.' Can you run on out to the road there and see if you can make out anythin'?"

"Well, okay, but next time it's your turn to be the scout." I wasn't about to let Ricky run things, but we had agreed to share chores.

Ricky wiped the sweat off his forehead, raised one eyebrow at me, and said, "Sure, Janie." Then he shook his head, slumped his shoulders and grumbled, "Women—can't live with 'em, can't live without 'em."

I thought my eyes might just pop out of my skull. "Don't you go callin' me your woman, Ricky Mills. That'll happen when pigs fly!"

He looked at me with his lip curled. "You got nothin' to worry about, Janie Jennings. I told you a long time ago I wasn't never gonna get married. I'm gonna go to Africa and be a big-time explorer, gonna find lost cities made outta gold. It's dangerous work, and Africa ain't no place for a woman."

"Oh, yeah? This here woman is goin' to Africa and ain't nobody gonna tell me I can't. Or maybe I'll go to Asia, stake out my own claim. Maybe I'll see you there, and maybe I won't. But you're still bein' the scout next time. And, just so you know, I ain't ever gonna get married neither." I did like to get the last word and, being President, it was only right that I did.

The left-over dirt wasn't noticeable at all from the road. We congratulated ourselves that our project was secret and safe from prying eyes.

One afternoon Mrs. Mills had a doctor appointment in town, and she asked me and Ricky to watch Mavis. She said she'd give us each a quarter if we took care of her.

I was mighty interested in that quarter. That much money would buy a big supply of caps for my gun.

Ricky said there wasn't enough gold in King Solomon's mine to get him to babysit.

"I'm not a baby!" Mavis wailed and cried and whined like to make us go crazy.

Mrs. Mills bent down to the little whiner. I caught a whiff of Mrs. Mills' spicy perfume. She always had a cloud of sweet-spicy-smelling air following her as she walked.

"Now, Mavis, no one is calling you a baby. It's just a name for watching children. You are a young lady, and I know you will act like one while I am gone." Mrs. Mills was always sweet to Mavis.

Mavis beamed like the little ray of sunshine her mama said she was, showing her dimples, and giving Mrs. Mills a dear little hug. "I will, Mama."

I looked at Ricky, who was sticking his finger down his throat and making faces behind Mrs. Mills' back. I had to swallow my smile, but I couldn't help thinking I couldn't remember my mama being sweet to me. And I was pretty sure it wouldn't be happening any time soon.

It was a marvel how Mrs. Mills was so happy all the time. Why, she was earning herself a place in heaven—being nice to Mavis seemed like a real cross to bear.

Mrs. Mills was kind of sweet to me, too, if I was honest. She saved up her old *Reader's Digest* magazines and gave them to me. I read them through, over and over. I learned a lot. My favorite part was "Word Power." Every month, I studied and took the quiz and almost always got a hundred percent. My sixth-grade teacher said I had the best vocabulary in the whole school, including the teachers. She might be exaggerating.

I pulled Ricky aside. "Look, I could really use the money. C'mon, we can skip the dig for one afternoon."

Ricky reluctantly agreed. He bellowed over his shoulder, "But Janie and I get to pick what we watch on the TV."

I guess Mavis was so pleased that she would be included, she just smiled pretty and nodded. For a minute, I thought her fool head might fly off, it was bobbing so hard.

"Thank you, Ricky and Janie. I will be back in an hour or two. There's some fruit in the kitchen and milk in the fridge."

I couldn't help but think, "Of course there's fruit."

We settled in front of the TV and ignored Mavis the best we could. We wanted to plan how and when we would finish our secret bomb shelter. Mavis pretended to pay attention to *Leave it to Beaver*, but we suspected she spied on us and listened to every word we said. She was a nuisance, an irritation, and an annoyance.

When the commercial came on, Mavis was real busy playing with her stupid baby doll, dressing it and feeding it and cooing over it like to make us both puke. We figured it was safe to talk about the next steps for our secret project.

I kept my voice low. "I think the dig should be longer and wider. It's deep enough for sure."

Mavis put down her doll and said, "What dig is deep enough?"

We stared at each other, gulped, then turned to Mavis.

Ricky took the lead. "What're you talkin' about? We didn't say nothin' like that."

"Liar! You're a liar, Ricky Mills." She wagged her finger at him. "I'm gonna tell Mama when she gets home. Lying is bad, very bad. You're gonna be in big trouble."

I gave it a whirl. "Hey, Mavis, we're just talkin' in a code, is all. We're just makin' up words to hear what they sound like. Right, Ricky?" It sounded a little lame.

"Yeah, we're just foolin' with you, to see if you're payin' attention. Don't get your shorts in a knot."

Mavis jumped up and stuck out her lower lip. "I ain't wearing shorts! You know Mama said to include me." She stamped her foot. "I heard you say 'dig' and I'm gonna tell." She put her little hands on her hips and stared a hole in Ricky. She had a pretty good death stare for a baby.

Ricky balled his fists and gritted his teeth, then made an awful fake smile. "Now, Mavis, you know that 'dig' is like beatnik talk, like Maynard G. Krebs says on the TV. You know, 'I dig that?' That only means he likes somethin'. Janie was just sayin' how much she digs your doll."

I raised my eyebrows and gave Ricky a disgusted look, but I saw that it might be smart to play along. "Yeah, that's right." I gave her my own ghastly fake smile.

Mavis narrowed her eyes, seemed to think on it, then calmed down. She sat and picked up her doll. "My baby doll *is* beautiful. Beautiful Betsy Wetsy. What a sweet baby! She got my eyes and her daddy's hair. I'm glad you dig my baby, Janie." She gave me a real precious smile.

I looked daggers at Ricky, then turned to Mavis and said, "You're gonna make a real good mama someday." I closed my eyes and somehow found the strength to continue. "The way you take care of that baby is flat out amazin'."

Mavis batted her long black lashes—another sore point with me. Blond curly hair, big blue eyes, *and* long, black eyelashes. Really. it was too much to bear.

Me and Ricky hoped Mavis forgot about what she heard.

A week before school was fixin' to start, the bomb shelter was five feet long and almost three feet wide. It was better than four feet deep. We had run into rocks on the bottom. Some of them we took out, but others were just too big. We scraped the dirt away the best we could from around a huge rock, then used shovels to pry it loose. Soon we realized it wouldn't budge. I dropped my shovel and groaned.

Ricky gave the thing a kick. "That rock ain't going nowhere." He wiped his arm across his face leaving a smear of dirt.

"No kidding." I met his blue eyes and was surprised I had to look up. Over the summer, Ricky must have grown three inches. It felt kind of funny because I always towered over the boys in my class.

The ground squirrel holes continued to be a problem since we kept finding piles of dirt every morning. Ricky thought the best plan was to find some plywood or tin to line the walls, but we'd have to look farther away since we needed all we had for our roof.

I swiped a saw from the garage so Ricky could cut up a length of wood. He had the idea to dig these short pieces of wood into the side of the pit as a sort of ladder—it was getting to be hard to pull ourselves up out of the deep hole. We made a pile of rocks to stand on, but it wasn't enough. Kicking the toes of our shoes into the side only made more dirt fall into the shelter. We needed that ladder. We worked hard all day, getting hot and sweaty, but the wood pieces kept falling out of the holes we dug.

Ricky tossed his shovel out of the hole. "I give up! We gotta come up with another plan."

"Yeah, we can just use the rockpile for now. Let's work on the roof."

We laid the biggest pieces of tin across the hole and piled about a foot of dirt on top. To make it easy getting in and out, we left an opening at the end near the tree. Before the bombs fell, we would have to make a cover to pull shut behind us.

"I can't lift another shovel, Ricky. Besides, I'm gettin' hungry." The sky was clouding up, so it was hard to tell the time. I sat down.

Ricky dropped his shovel and collapsed to the ground, lying flat on his back. "I was wonderin' if you was gonna say anythin'. I'm beat, too."

I smacked myself on the forehead. "I just thought of somethin'. Weren't we gonna bury the edges of the roof into the side of the shelter? We still doin' that?"

Ricky groaned and sat up. "Not today, that's for sure. And we still got to find a way to keep the sides from fallin' in. And make a danged ladder. Guess we're not done, after all." He got to his feet. "Let's go to my house for a snack."

I stood and brushed the dirt off my bottom. "Good idea."

We watched *The Millionaire* at Ricky's house, drinking chocolate milk and eating yet more fruit—what I wouldn't have given for some Oreo cookies.

Mavis came in the living room and announced, "I'm gonna read my dear little baby a bedtime story." She plopped herself down in the corner. I rolled my eyes. Mavis didn't know how to read. She held the Golden Book, *Prayers for Children,* upside down. But I had to admit, she knew her prayers cold.

We agreed to meet at the shelter that night. Ricky had a flashlight, and I didn't, but being an explorer, I wasn't scared of the dark, at least not too afraid. We planned to meet up on the road after everybody was asleep and go to the shelter together. Ricky said he could bring some food and a few things from home to decorate the place. I told him I would see what I could scrounge up too. Since we might have to stay underground for a while after the bombs, we'd have to stock up on water, canned goods, candles, and blankets. It'd take time to collect all we needed, but we might as well start now that the roof was in place.

I knew I could get clean away. Mama would be drunk and most likely passed out, Tom would be out like a light, and Daddy would be working overtime. I warned Ricky to be quiet so he could get out of the house without waking anybody, especially pesky Mavis. I sort of had the chills thinking about being out in the prairie in the dead of night, but it was kind of exciting, too.

Ricky was waiting on the road, turning the flashlight off and on. It made him easy to spot. Smart thinking. As I came running up, I heard a scream and the too-awful-for-words sounds that followed—thuds, the whooshing sound of dirt falling, a few bangs and thumps. Then silence—total, final silence.

"What the hell!" Ricky shouted.

"Who screamed? That wasn't an animal." My stomach dropped to my shoes.

We looked at each other in panic and ran to our shelter. The moonlight, peeking from behind the clouds, and the flashlight beam, revealed the cave-in. Mavis's baby doll was sitting in the dirt at the side of the pit. There was only stillness.

I fell to my knees. "Oh, God! Did Mavis fall in?" This couldn't be real.

"We gotta get help. Fast!" Ricky's voice sounded shaky.

We ran faster than we had ever run before to Ricky's house and woke up his parents. Ricky flipped on the light and babbled as he yanked the covers off them. "Help! Mavis fell in our bomb shelter! The roof caved in! We gotta get her out. Hurry!"

Mr. and Mrs. Mills blinked and looked confused, but Ricky's panic got them moving fast. Mrs. Mills ran right out the door in her nightgown and bare feet. Mr. Mills pulled on trousers over his pajama bottoms and stepped into his shoes. He didn't take time to put on a shirt over his hairy chest. I was embarrassed to look at it but, somehow, I couldn't help but stare.

We flew out the door and soon passed Mrs. Mills, although I was impressed with her speed over the ground in her bare feet. I knew there would be questions later. Lots of them. But right then, we raced back to the cave-in with Ricky's folks close on our heels.

Once she realized Mavis was buried under the pile of dirt, boards, rocks, and tin, Mrs. Mills collapsed at the edge of the pit. She picked up Betsy Wetsy and stared at the stupid doll like it could give her some answers. She tossed the doll aside and screeched, "Mavis, baby, I'm coming. Mama's here." Mr. Mills tried to stop her, but she was determined to save her little girl. She pulled away and leaped right in the pit, landing hard on her knees. She dug into the dirt with her bare hands, crying and calling for Mavis over and over again.

Mr. Mills clutched Ricky's shoulders and shouted at him to go home and call the fire department and the sheriff.

I pointed the flashlight down at the cave-in. The sight of Mrs. Mills in her pink nightgown, hair hanging in her face, as she scooped armfuls of dirt and flung them up and out of the pit, seared into my brain. The wind picked up, and my arms broke out in goose bumps.

Mr. Mills jumped down in the pit and tried to get her to climb out and go home with Ricky to call for help. Mrs. Mills paid him no mind. She shook him off and cried and screamed and dug—just dug and dug. Mr. Mills stood, his chest and arms covered with dirt, bellowing at Ricky to get his ass in gear and bring some shovels. There was a flash of lightning, a huge crack of thunder like a judgment from God, and it began to rain.

I stepped back and knocked into a shovel. Grabbed it. "Got a shovel here!"

Mr. Mills reached for the tool. His eyes bored into me—his lips a thin line.

I understood then what folks meant when they said, "If looks could kill."

He plunged the shovel into the cave-in and dug as the rain turned the pile of dirt around the pit into a mudslide. It was a losing battle.

I crumpled to the ground and watched them. It only seemed like a minute or two until Ricky got back. My body wouldn't move. I wanted to grab a shovel and dig too, but I was paralyzed. Kneeling in the mud, I watched the three remaining members of the Mills family dig until the fire truck got there, then watched the firemen while they dug.

They found Mavis and brought her up. She was filthy. And limp. And blue. And dead.

The coroner ruled Mavis's death an accident. How could it be an accident when Mavis had done it to herself? The little pest had followed Ricky that horrible night. She hadn't forgotten what she heard that day we watched her.

I didn't want to go to the funeral, but Daddy said the Jennings family had to show up. Mama was in no condition to go, and Tom had a basketball game in Midland for his traveling league, so it was just the two of us.

Daddy said, "Why Mrs. Mills had an open casket is a mystery to me." He shook his head and looked about as miserable as I felt.

I couldn't speak. My words were gone. I sat next to Daddy in the pew at the First Methodist Church. Mavis's horrible death sure had the town talking and probably would for years. I felt the eyes of the entire congregation on me, like I had a big target painted on my back. I hung my head. Not a single person even said "Hey" to us when we walked into the church. Even Mrs. Wilson and Mrs. Foster wouldn't look me in the eye.

I saw Mrs. Mills and her family in the front row but didn't have the nerve to stop and say anything to her. Mr. Mills met my eyes, then turned away. Ricky looked awful, like he hadn't slept in days, dark circles under his eyes, his hair a mess. I couldn't imagine how bad things were for him at home.

My stomach felt all hollow and my throat felt full when I trudged up to the coffin. The smell of the flowers made me want to barf.

Sure, they cleaned Mavis up as best they could, washed her yellow hair until it was shiny again—it was the only part of that poor child that looked alive. But her face was dark, dusky, grayish. Her color was off, like she was bruised just under her skin. It ruined the whole effect of the blond curly hair and the frilly yellow party dress. Yellow never had been Mavis's color, and with her face that odd shade, it just looked wrong.

I guessed the funeral home people didn't put makeup on little kids, but maybe they should've made an exception in this case. Folks usually said the dead looked peaceful or like they were just sleeping so natural-like. If anyone said that to Mrs. Mills, they were a damn liar. Mavis's hands were dark, too. Her nails were clean, but she just looked dirty somehow. Betsy Wetsy, dressed in her finest white dress with pale blue ribbons, cuddled against Mavis's side. Ricky's little sister wasn't pretty anymore, and I wished my last view of her wasn't like this. I wished I could see her little pink face and her big blue eyes again.

We left the church with no one so much as nodding at us. I told Daddy there was no way I was going to the cemetery, no matter what he said. "I can't bear to watch Mavis get put underground again."

Remembering how Grandma June had looked in her coffin, I shivered. But she was kind of old and drank herself to death. I didn't think about her much anymore. The sight of Mavis, so little, so young, and dying the way she did, would haunt me forever.

Daddy didn't say anything. He just patted my shoulder and drove us home.

The first day of seventh grade was a disaster. Not a single person spoke to me, but there was plenty of whispering and talk behind my back.

Priscilla breathed "murderer" when I passed her in the hall. Agnes whispered, "Why isn't she in jail?" I almost dropped my books. Ricky Mills cut me dead—that was the worst. Now I had no one to sit with at lunch. He was my only friend. For the first time in my life, I couldn't wait for school to end.

When the school bus dropped me off, I ran all the way from the county road to the house. Racing into my room, I threw myself on the bed and sobbed. I cried me a river. I cried until I was dry, and then I cried some more. Stupid Mavis, dumb enough for twins, had ruined my life. I didn't even feel sorry for her anymore.

I screamed into my pillow. "I ain't got a single friend in this world. And no family to speak of."

After a while, I sat up, wiped my face, and found me some gumption. Why should I lie around feeling sorry for myself? That's what Mama did, and I wasn't about to act like her. I needed to get back outdoors—to Rangerland. I leaped out of bed and yelled at the top of my lungs. "Who needs Ricky Mills anyway?"

I changed into jeans and a t-shirt. There was a shuffling sound outside my door, then banging.

Oh no, I woke up Mama!

"What the hell is goin' on in there? Janie?" She kept up a resounding hammering on the door. "Shut up, shut up, shut the fuckin' hell up! A body can't sleep with all your wailin'." Her voice rose to a shriek, then faded to a croak.

I held my breath and hoped she'd go away. The shuffle receded, and then her bedroom door slammed. Inching my door open, I took a peek, saw and heard nothing, and tiptoed through the house, making sure to ease the screen door shut. I was overdue for patrol.

The sky was blue. The fresh air was just what I needed. I took a few deep breaths and headed out to Rangerland. There had been a gully-washer a couple days ago, so I decided to check on the status of the fawn leg. The ground felt a little bit springy under my shoes, but there wasn't a puddle to be seen anywhere. Typical after a West Texas rain. Ricky and I had marked the spot with a pile of stones, so I knew I was in the right place, but no sign of the leg. I looked high and low—but it was gone.

The days dragged by. I went to school every day and ate my lunch alone. Daddy was hardly ever home. Tom neither. For all my brave words I didn't need Ricky Mills, turned out I did. There was a hole in my life and an ache in my heart. Lonely didn't even begin to describe how I felt. I waited at the boundary tree every day for weeks after Mavis died, hoping he would come.

One day, as fall set in, I found Ricky's final message—a note impaled by his Swiss Army knife to the boundary tree: "Hit by a car most likely. Leg probably dragged away by a critter and dropped." Short and to the point, like he resented giving me even those few words and each syllable cost him dearly. Beneath the note lay the skeleton of a fawn with all four legs, the left rear pelvis shattered.

It was over. Rangerland was gone forever. I fell to my knees and cried my eyes out. Like Matthew said in the Bible, I was cast out in the darkness and there was weeping and gnashing of teeth. It was like part of me was dying.

With my bare hands and a jagged rock, I dug a shallow grave. The skeleton fell apart when I picked it up and placed the frail bones in the hole. When I covered the fawn and Ricky's knife with dirt, it felt like I was burying Rangerland, too. I stood up and wiped my eyes with my filthy arm. It took me a good long while to walk home.

Would Annie Oakley act like this? Would she wallow in misery? No, she surely would not, and I wasn't about to either. The time had come to pull myself up by my bootstraps and do something about my life. After three years of digging in the dirt with Ricky, I was going to change my ways.

I would be a teenager soon, going to high school. I needed to act like it—time to forget Annie Oakley and hang up my six-gun. I figured if Priscilla got herself all gussied up, I could, too. Being like Shelley Fabares and the girls on *American Bandstand* wouldn't be so bad. Maybe Aunt Penny could give me some advice—about my hair and clothes and all that girly stuff.

Chapter Four

HOME SWEET HOME?–WEST TEXAS 1984

Jane hoisted her Gucci bag into the trunk of the dark blue Toyota rental and settled behind the wheel. No use getting on the new interstate just to go a few miles. No more lollygagging. Time to head out toward the squalid dump she left more than half her lifetime ago. She wanted to run right back into the terminal and get the next flight out—wouldn't even care where it was headed as long as it wasn't Austin. She turned the key and adjusted the mirrors. Rock and a hard place—Austin and Odessa.

Maybe Joshua was right in saying that all her self-discovery and AA work had been in vain, that she had no idea who she was. Would she find answers in Odessa?

I'm fixin' to find out.

Jane was mortified at the ease with which her West Texas poked its head out of hibernation. Was listening to Mr. Moore's twang enough of a catalyst to reconnect those old neural pathways and bring back the accent and language she had struggled so hard to eliminate? Or was it in the air and absorbed through osmosis?

The oil derricks were gone. They used to tower over each section of land, like sentinels, gigantic in her remembered childhood perspective. Their absence forever altered what she had considered the permanent skyline of her youthful world. Jane turned on to the county road and passed a few slowly bobbing pump jacks set out in the fields. There were a few more trailers and a couple of fledgling neighborhoods along Kermit Highway. A rueful smile flitted across her lips as she recalled those long-ago days spent hunting for roadkill. She spent hours inspecting each carcass; the stilled feet and empty gazes fascinated her for so many years as she ran the plains, first alone, then with Ricky Mills.

Her mind turned to Rangerland and its disastrous end with the death of Mavis, and she shivered. To this day, the sight of a blond curly-haired little girl plunged an arrow of pain into her heart. If she had lived, Mavis would be college age. Jane shook her head as if she could dispel her guilt.

She executed the final turn down the bumpy, narrow track that led to ground zero. AC/DC had been down the same road—the highway to hell.

Her former home still hunkered all by its lonesome out in the mesquite-dotted grassy plain. Despite what Thomas Wolfe wrote, and what she had sworn she would never do, she had gone home again.

Three dust-covered vehicles—two cars and a truck—baked under the sun in the rutted dirt. The Ford F150 most likely belonged to her daddy, a lifelong Ford man. One car would be Tom's—but who else was here? This homecoming was difficult enough—no audience required. A prayer from AA came to mind; it was becoming her lifeline again, just as it had been when she first got sober.

God, grant me the serenity, yeah, that's the ticket, serenity, as if there was ever any in that house.

Failing at the Serenity Prayer, Jane pulled up between the truck and one car, shut down the engine, and glared at the house. *"Some things never change..."* The pitiful little bungalow was just as she remembered—faded, peeling white paint and too-small windows with rusty screens. Sunlight had never seemed to penetrate those stingy openings.

The screen door slammed, and goose bumps chilled her arms. That evocative sound brought up a jumble of feelings: dread about Daddy coming home to find Mama drunk again, joy at running outdoors to play in the prairie, desperation to escape Mama's clutches and her demands to dust and scrub and sweep.

Resolve on the night she left.

She lingered behind the wheel, stomach churning, breath catching in her throat. She reminded herself it was only this one visit for Daddy, and not for Mama.

There came Tom, running out the door as if he were in the starting line-up of the Final Four, bouncing that blasted basketball. He didn't appear to be in the throes of grief, but why should he be? He took his patented jump shot at the misshapen, netless hoop. Of course, he made it. Dribbling behind his back and between his legs, he spun and stopped as he noticed her car. He palmed the ball, then spun it on his fingertip for a few moments, grinning with pleasure at handling his favorite object. He tapped the ball to the side and sauntered up to her car.

"You plannin' on gettin' out of your vehicle, Jane?" Tom's lively eyes and kidding tone of voice made Jane smile.

Nope, not the picture of the bereft son. Far as I know, he's only been back a handful of times since he left for college.

"Since I came all this way, might as well." She opened the door an inch at a time as if afraid to make the commitment. She stood tall—the very picture of determination—hugged herself and turned to the house. "Looks the same. Exactly the same." Her frown revealed distaste at the view. She pivoted back to him and said, "So, Mama finally kicked."

"Drop the tough-girl act. It's me. I have a good idea of how you're feeling and why. I was right there with you." His voice had an edge.

"Not for those last four years!"

Tom's brow creased. "History, sis, ancient history. What could I do, take you to Tech with me?"

Jane sniffed and shot him a sideways look. "You're right. I know you felt bad leaving me. This is old territory. It's probably seeing the scene of the crime that brings it all back." She rubbed her arms as if she were chilled.

"You always found a way to deal with...the situation."

Jane glared at him. "Situation?"

He held up his hands. "Okay, Mama's drinking. You are a survivor, girl."

"Well, I survived." She attempted a smile, but it died a quick death. "Now here I am, 'home'." She tapped her heels together, but gently, so as not to mar her red high heel boots, and intoned, "There's no place like home."

Tom slapped his leg and threw back his head, laughing that rich laugh of his. "You're still a pistol, ain't you?"

"Since you like the Oz reference, how's this…the wicked witch is dead."

He grew serious at that. "Maybe a little harsh there."

She tilted her head and met his eyes. "No. I don't think so." Her lips were tight with anger.

Tom looked away. "Well, I guess it wasn't as bad for me as it was for you."

"You got that right." Realizing her resentment was misplaced, she softened her tone and placed her hand on his arm. "Well, big brother, I have learned to look on the bright side. Because of my fraught childhood, I have developed a fondness for black humor. What a gift! Laugh or cry, I always say." Her eyes filled, and a sob escaped from a place she didn't think existed anymore.

"Hey, c'mere." Tom held out his arms, and she fell against his strong chest.

Jane took a shuddering breath and, with her voice muffled against his shirt, asked, "How's Daddy?"

"He's doin' all right. Same reserved, silent kind of guy as ever. He's holdin' up."

"I guess nothing has changed in all this time." She disengaged from his embrace. "Except me. Guess we better go in." She glanced at the cars on her left. "By my count, there's an extra car. Who else is here?"

"You're in luck," he said with a healthy heap of sarcasm, "Preacher Henry and Mrs. Foster are here."

"Oh, Lord."

"Yeah, He's here, too, according to Preacher Henry."

They walked in tandem to their childhood home.

Before she stepped onto the porch, Jane asked, "Where's Jolene and the kids?"

"They're on the way. She's driving separately in case I stay an extra day. Doubt I will. Where's Joshua?"

She kept her face blank, and said, "He couldn't get away."

Her brother took a step back. "Really?"

Grimacing, she answered, "No, that's a lie. He wanted to come, and I told him I didn't want him to."

Tom's eyebrows rose. "Oka-ay. I'm not even gonna ask." He opened the door.

Turning to Tom, she whispered, "It's complicated." Jane girded herself as she crossed the threshold into the narrow entry hall. She paused and executed an awkward little shuffle to disguise her hesitancy. She squeezed her eyes shut and said a quick mental prayer.

A low rumble of conversation came from the front room. They walked in on Preacher Henry's oratory. Daddy sat on the company couch that was encased, as always, in plastic covers. He wore his beloved jeans and a plaid shirt. *"Some things never change..."* He leaned in toward Preacher Henry, who was jawing away.

The preacher was in excellent form. "Out of the depths we cry to You, O Lord. Hear our voice. We wait for You, O God. Our souls wait for You. Give us now Your word of hope. We know Your love is steadfast, always there when we need it. Let us feel Your presence now in our time of sorrow. Help us to look to tomorrow to see hope beyond grief, through Jesus Christ our Lord. Amen."

Mrs. Foster, a glass of lemonade in her hand, rocked slowly in Mama's favorite chair. "Amen."

Daddy mumbled, "Amen." He had always been rangy and lean; now he was downright skin and bones. His hair had turned iron gray. His face, set in sorrow, was etched with a network of lines from the West Texas sun—and from what life had dished out to him.

All eyes turned to Jane and Tom when the prayer ended. Tom didn't say a word and joined his father on the couch, leaving Jane alone to face the gauntlet.

"Well, well, here is our prodigal girl returned to us. Thank You, Jesus!" Preacher Henry did not disappoint. Jane swore she could hear the capitalization in the preacher's voice when he addressed Jesus.

Mrs. Foster, *sans* grape-festooned hat, looked much as Jane remembered her. She wore her traditional attire, a flowered shirtwaist dress with a high, ruffled neckline.

To Jane, Mrs. Foster had looked about a hundred years old when she was a kid and looked about a hundred and twenty now.

"Janie, so glad you came." Mrs. Foster said. She sniffed. "Didn't think you *would*, but I am so very glad, for Martha's sake."

Mrs. Foster's prim, proper, and patronizing tone of voice resonated in Jane's head and brought up the memory of making construction paper cutouts of Gospel figures at Sunday school. She recalled Mrs. Foster doling out stingy gobs of white paste on little cardboard squares from the giant jar, as if each dollop cost her dearly.

Jane wanted to say she was not here for Martha's sake, Jesus's sake, her own sake, or for anybody or anything else but her daddy. Instead, she showed her teeth in what she hoped passed for a smile, and said, "Hello, Mrs. Foster." That was all she managed to get past her clenched teeth.

It was so like Daddy to sit there in silence. His lips tugged at the corners when he saw her, but he didn't quite smile as he stood and held his arms out to her.

Jane didn't hesitate. She hugged him hard enough to make up for a few years. In her red high-heeled boots, she was nearly as tall as he. *He seemed so tall and strong when I was a kid. How thin he is—diminished somehow.*

Her daddy released her and stepped back but still clutched her upper arms. "Janie, I mean, Jane, it's so good to see you, girl." He smelled of Old Spice—the scent almost made her swoon and took her back to a time when she was little.

"Daddy, you can call me 'Janie.' I'm sorry I was so uppity about that when you called me. It's been tearing me up ever since." Her eyes welled, and her lips quivered.

"Hush now. It's all right, Janie. I never took no offense." He stroked her hair and patted her back.

Preacher Henry cleared his throat and got to his feet. It took a while, given he had to be approaching the century mark. He gave Mrs. Foster a pointed look.

Mrs. Foster said, "Well, I think the preacher and I will head back. Let you folks get reacquainted. You have a lot of catching up to do, I'm sure."

Jane detected a whiff of judgment, but that was par for the course. She recalled how Mrs. Foster refused to give her the time of day at Mavis's funeral. After that rebuff, Jane never had returned to Sunday school.

"Let me help you, Mrs. Foster." Daddy always had been real polite to women.

Jane said brief goodbyes to the two ambassadors from God and let Daddy and Tom see them out to their car. She was fixing to take a stroll down memory lane to her old bedroom and took the first, halting steps down that evocative hallway.

She stood before the closed door, shut her eyes briefly, then grabbed the knob. A musty smell wafted out, and, for a moment, she thought there was a trace of patchouli in the air. She inched her way past the door and gasped when she saw her Steve Miller Band poster ripped in half but still clinging to the wall. Did Mama do that? The mattress on the narrow bed was bare of sheets. She could discern the shallow trough where she had lain for most of her childhood. The room held nothing but dust bunnies and sadness. Home? Hardly.

Laughter and loud voices from the front of the house made her jump. She heard the thudding of rapid footsteps on the old creaky floorboards.

"Where is she?" piped the voice of a young girl.

"We finally gonna meet Aunt Jane?" An adolescent boy's voice cracked as he spoke.

I'd lain in bed as a child praying to Jesus to let me be an aunt when I grew up. Like Aunt Penny.

Hearing the children, Jane felt shame that she had done nothing to embrace the role of aunt; she had never even made the effort to visit. No wonder she couldn't wrap her head around the concept of having a baby. No doubt, she would carry on the grand family tradition of lousy mothering.

She took a deep breath, closed the door to her sad cell, and entered the kitchen from the hallway. "Hi y'all."

A girl squealed and ran to her. "Hi, Aunt Jane. I'm Summer!"

Jane felt an urge to reach out and push Summer's long, wild brown hair out of her eyes, but didn't act on it. The girl was a stranger because of Jane's self-imposed isolation. The desire to touch the child was disquieting, and Jane struggled to understand the impulse. Did she see herself in Summer, was she remembering the kindness of Aunt Penny, or was there a yearning to have a child in a place inaccessible to her? Just as Jane had been at her age, Summer was all gangly arms and legs.

Shane, who had to be about thirteen, stood next to Tom. He was as handsome as were all the Jennings men, with that lean-jawed, Clint Eastwood look. Shane would break hearts, no doubt about it.

Jane smiled. "So happy to meet you, Summer. And Shane. Why, you're the picture of your dad!" The juxtaposition of three generations of her male relatives disconcerted her and gave her pause for thought. What had she missed during the estrangement from her family?

Jolene was busy unloading groceries on the kitchen counter. As she emptied bag after bag from HEB, Jane remembered Saturday shopping trips to the old market run by Miss Marcy and Claude. The market was probably long gone, another victim of progress.

Jane had met Jolene only once before, years ago, when Tom brought his new bride to Austin to help Jane after the humiliating end to her first love affair. Jolene stopped stocking the refrigerator, grinned, and hustled around the counter. She clasped Jane in a warm energetic embrace and said, "Hey, Jane. I'm so glad to see you again. To say the least, it's been too long."

There was no sting to her words. Jane colored with embarrassment when she recalled what a mess she had been back then and how her brother and his bride had found her a new living situation. Jolene had been supportive and non-judgmental.

Jane blurted, "Jolene, I want you to know I've never forgotten how you helped me...in Austin. I'm embarrassed just thinking about it."

Jolene patted Jane on the shoulder. "Honey, there's no need for any of that. You were a kid in a jam and for sure did the right thing callin' us. You've come such a long way in life. No use dwellin' on the past."

"I feel so bad I never came to visit, never met your children. I'm a mess of regrets."

"Well, you're here now," Jolene said. "That's what counts. C'mon, sit down and visit while I rustle up some tuna sandwiches for lunch."

She reminded Jane of her late Aunt Penny—fun-loving, upbeat, quicksilver movements. Tom had chosen a good mate and a pretty one. And they sure made good-looking kids.

What would my children look like? No, can't go there. Still, Joshua and I would make real pretty babies.

"That's real nice of you, Jolene," Daddy said. "C'mon in the front room, Janie. I gotta ask you a favor."

"Sure, Daddy."

Jane sat in the rocking chair. She couldn't bear to sit on those plastic covers—as a child or now. Daddy took his usual spot on the couch and turned to her. His hands clenched in his lap, brow furrowed, he seemed to be having trouble getting started.

"What can I help you with, Daddy?"

He looked away and then met her eyes. "I would do it my ownself, but I just can't, Janie. I can't."

Jane's eyes widened as her rock of a father's shoulders shook and his eyes welled. Taken aback at the display of emotion, stunned that he still cared after all the drinking, the misery, the mess, the tirades.

She popped up from the rocker and, without a thought, sat next to him on the stiff, slippery plastic. Grasping his hand, she rested her head on his shoulder. "Oh, Daddy, I am so sorry. You loved her. You really loved her!"

Roughly wiping his eyes, he rasped, "'Course I did. It wasn't all roses and moonbeams, but I always loved her, ever since we was kids in school. Why else would I stick with her? For better or for worse—I meant every word of it."

"Well, I guess you did." She squeezed his hand.

Daddy chuckled weakly and said, "Things was against us from the start. George and Martha. All the jokes." He shook his head. "None of that mattered. Made us stronger if anything." He looked Jane in the eyes. "You can't help who you fall in love with."

"I can testify to that!" As she watched a tear roll down his weathered cheek, Jane felt her heart clutch. "What do you need, Daddy?" She had never considered that he might have trouble functioning without Mama.

He heaved up a big sigh. "Can you find her something nice to wear...for-for the funeral?"

Jane bit her lip, paused, and made herself say, "All right, Daddy."

He stood and nodded curtly. "I gotta get me some air." He hit the door hard.

As the screen door slapped shut, Jolene called out. "Time to eat!"

After lunch, Tom and his family gathered their things to leave for the hotel in Odessa. The hotel sounded good. A little later, she would be checking into a nice, bland, anonymous room, too. Thank God, there was a pool. Soon, she would tear up that water, washing off the day.

Jane received the last hug, said the last goodbye, and watched as Tom's family trooped down the porch stairs and got in their cars. The old place seemed to exhale. The house hadn't seen so much good energy in a long time—actually, maybe never had. She turned from the door and paused, staring down that hallway once more. She sighed from the soles of her boots and shivered as goose bumps popped up on her arms.

No sign of her daddy. Might as well get this over with, she thought. Jane threw her shoulders back, resolved to perform her duty, yet her first steps were hesitant, her feet heavy with the weight of the past.

The door to her parents' room at the end of the passage gaped open, and she entered the dim room. A long time ago, Mama had installed blackout roller shades on the windows. The ones currently hanging looked new. Jane glared at the double bed and remembered Mama sprawled there, weeping or laughing or screaming, depending on what demon haunted her that day.

Jane turned on the overhead light, for some reason unwilling to raise the shades. Recalling her childhood laundry duties, she knew Daddy kept his jeans and shirts folded in the dresser drawers, and Mama had the small closet to herself. Jane opened the door and Mama's scent, Fabergé "Woodhue," assaulted her nostrils. Mama used to slather on that fragrance in a futile attempt to mask the rank alcohol sweat from her pores.

A glimpse of faded pink fuzzy slippers in the back corner of the closet took away her breath. She staggered and leaned against the doorjamb as a vision of Mama on that last night flashed through her mind, that indelible image. Countless times, she had related the story of that night in drunken confessions to friends or lovers, shared it in AA groups, and yet, it still lived rent-free in her head. Would it never be exorcized? But the physical appearance of Mama wasn't the crux of the experience. No, that was the unforgiveable thing Mama said, the last words she had ever spoken to Jane.

Jane knew she would never make it through the funeral if she thought about those words. She would pull a Scarlett O'Hara and think about it later—much later—maybe never. *The denouement of our relationship is final, irrevocable, with no possibility of rapprochement.*

She moaned, then wailed to the empty room. "Will I ever stop this crap? Why do I wear my vast vocabulary like armor? Who even says they have a vast vocabulary? Slinging words around like weapons is my favorite sport. Am I trying to prove that I've transcended West Texas? It might could be I'm fixin' to do just that, dad gum it!"

She laughed, big gut-wrenching guffaws that tore at her throat and didn't feel the least bit funny. Maybe she did need psychoanalysis. Maybe her life had finally caught up with her, and there was no more running. She sank to her knees and wept.

When her tears subsided, Jane rose and found a box of tissue on the dresser. After patting her eyes, she returned to the closet. With no sense of how much time had passed, she knew she was still alone—except for the ghosts of the past. Gazing at the limp dresses hanging on the closet pole, the first line from the only poem she had written came to her mind: "Like forgotten flags from defunct nations."

Whoa! Where did that come from? The beginning and end of any literary aspirations I might have had. At least I got an "A."

She rummaged through the dozen or so garments, wondering what difference her choice would make. Scooping them all into her arms, she plodded to the bed, sat on the edge, and placed them beside her. Something nice? That would be a challenge. Everything was flowered. Flowered *and* pastel. Many polyesters had given their lives for Mama's wardrobe. The prettiest thing was a pink floral dress with ruffles down the front and a handkerchief skirt. Mama in a handkerchief skirt? The dress was so out of character for Mama that Jane wondered when she had bought it—and why.

She examined the tag—it was a size two, "couture" J. C. Penney, and had never been worn. Mama hadn't ever been a large woman, but a size two when she was as tall as Jane's own five-foot eight? She must have wasted away to nothing.

After deciding on the pink floral, Jane hung the other garments back in the closet and closed the door. Would this trip close some doors to her past? There were a few rooms she would like to wall off permanently. She thought she had done a good job of that, but chinks were appearing in the life she had constructed. Then again, an unexamined life is not worth living, as one of those Greek philosophers had famously said. Of course, one could go too far, and Jane was not certain she was prepared to deal with the unraveling of her personal myth. Like everything in her life these days, she was ambivalent: self-examination, her marriage, her plans for school, just about the whole kit and caboodle.

With her duty done, she left the room with the burial dress slung over her shoulder and trudged out to the front room. After she folded the frilly dress and stuffed it in her bag, she sprawled in the rocker and waited for her daddy to come home.

Jane drove down Grant Street, taking inventory of old landmarks. The Grove Drug Store had been replaced by a pool hall, The Golden Cue. The Grove sure had good nineteen-cent malts when she was in high school. Didn't the pool halls used to be over on 27th, near the tracks? The old Day's Drive-In—the scene of much teenage angst, drama, and flirtation—housed an advertising shop. The main drag looked very different; time had marched on. With the oil boom long over, change was inevitable.

Change. Her mind was certainly going through some changes, as Buddy Miles sang in one of her favorite dance tunes from the Seventies. She still loved to dance, although she couldn't remember the last time she had been on the dance floor. But it had to be to the oldies. Today's music was atrocious, either sound-alike hair bands or Euro-techno synthesized noise or quirky girl-women. Joshua didn't care to dance.

Joshua.

Had she thought of him at all today? Just once when she contemplated what their children would look like. She couldn't believe their fight was just this morning.

With tears pouring down her cheeks, Jane turned into the hotel parking lot. For someone who hadn't cried in years, she was crying like a professional. She put the car into park and wondered what it meant that her husband had scarcely crossed her mind.

Despite a swim where she churned through the water as if pursued by demons, Jane had a hard time falling asleep. She had craved the anonymity of a hotel room but found the reality uncomfortable. Jane missed cuddling Tallulah. She missed her many pillows. And yes, she missed Joshua.

Jane startled awake screaming "No!" just before five a.m. Wisps and remnants of a nightmare fogged her mind. She had been in an airplane, sitting behind the pilot. Even though it was a commercial airliner, there was no cockpit door and she had a clear view through the flight deck window. As the plane rolled for takeoff, the runway morphed into a ramp leading to a turquoise tropical sea. When the plane could not get airborne, a wall of water engulfed it.

Taking deep breaths, Jane disentangled herself from the sheets. Nonplussed by the dream, it took her over an hour to drop off to sleep again.

At eight a.m., the clock-radio woke her. She dressed and went down to the hotel dining room to join her family for breakfast.

"There's Aunt Jane!" Summer jumped up from the corner booth and grabbed Jane's hand. "Sit next to me. I'm gonna have pancakes, what about you? They have blueberry."

Jane smiled as she took the seat next to her niece. "Give me a little minute. I need a cup of coffee and a menu."

Everyone decided on blueberry pancakes. Soon, but not soon enough to satisfy the hungry kids, huge platters of mouth-watering pancakes covered in berries arrived at the table. They had blueberry syrup, which really impressed Shane.

"Can I get seconds?" he asked before he took his first bite.

Tom chuckled and said, "Hold on there, partner. Let's see how those go down first."

Shane couldn't reply because his mouth was full.

As they ate, the adults made plans for the post-funeral reception in between fielding questions from the kids about Austin.

Tom said, "I'm gonna take Summer and Shane with me to rent some chairs for tomorrow. Daddy's only got seating for about six people. Gotta make sure everyone in Preacher Henry's flock has a place to perch their butts."

The kids hooted.

"Dad said 'butt' about church folks!" Shane grinned from ear to ear.

Jolene shot Tom a look. "Kids, hush now! I'll buy a ham and go to Dad's and start cookin'. If what Tom says about funerals in Odessa is true, folks will be bringin' a lot of food. I'm told we should expect a large turnout."

Jane sighed. "The whole town will be there. Talk about a blast from the past. I don't know if I'll even recognize most of them." She downed more coffee. "I'm going to Hubbard-Kelly with the dress."

The mood at the table tempered from merriment to seriousness in a heartbeat. Tom patted Jane's hand. "You sure you want to go alone?"

Jane shrugged and pushed her hair behind her right ear. "Yeah. I'll be fine. I don't expect it'll take too long. Then I'll drive out to the house."

Tom said, "I'll walk you out."

Jane gave him a questioning glance. "Okay."

They walked to the door, and Jane asked, "What's up, brother?"

Tom gazed at her and took a breath before he said, "I don't want you to take this the wrong way...just want to give you a little perspective."

Jane looked up at him and folded her arms. "Okay. Out with it."

His brow furrowed as he searched for words. "I noticed you're fallin' back to your old MO. You always were Daddy's girl."

"And?" Jane's eyebrows rose.

"Well, okay, did you ever wonder why Daddy didn't do more to protect us when we were kids, when Mama's drinkin' got bad?" His voice rose, and he seemed to realize it. Leaning in close to Jane, he modulated his tone. "Why did he leave us alone with her so damned much? It was always about Mama. That woman had him in a stranglehold. She wasn't about to live in town, where there were other folks around—people who might've intervened." His face reddened.

Stunned, Jane said, "My God, I never knew you felt like that! You hid it well. We never talked about this."

He shook his head. "No, we didn't. With the age difference, I didn't know what to say."

Her eyes wide, she stared at him. "I can understand that. You had basketball, and I had the prairie. We each found a way to cope. And I had a rich fantasy life. I always imagined what it would be like if Aunt Penny was my mother."

Tom closed his eyes and grimaced as if in pain. He clasped her shoulder and said, "I guess I'll lay one last thing on you. No use holdin' back at this juncture." Keeping a firm grip on her, he maintained eye contact. "Aunt Penny and Uncle Rafe wanted to take you to live with them. Daddy hit the roof. Mama went…ballistic. You can imagine. That's the reason we hardly ever saw them."

Her jaw dropped. "No! When was this?"

Tom thought a moment. "I'm not sure when they first proposed the idea, but Aunt Penny really tried after Grandma June's funeral."

Jane's shocked face left no doubt about her reaction.

"I'm sorry, but I had to tell you." Uncertain he had done the right thing, Tom's furrowed brow showed contrition.

Placing her hand on her abdomen in a self-protective gesture, Jane shuddered. "Don't be sorry. I'm glad you told me. But I can't help wondering what other landmines will blow up in my face on this sojourn in Mordor." Straightening her shoulders, she pushed the door open. "I better get on my way."

Tom watched her leave.

Jane drove to the funeral home to drop off the pink-flowered burial dress. The blueberry pancakes sat like a lump of concrete in her belly. She had so much to think about besides the funeral. Martha's body would be transported to the First United Methodist Church for the service scheduled for tomorrow afternoon. As she entered the reception area of Hubbard-Kelly, the smell of flowers, so cloying, elicited a wave of sadness.

The chore took less than five minutes. With the unctuous sympathies of the current Hubbard or Kelly in her ears, she eased out the door. Instead of getting in her rental car, she decided to stroll around downtown Odessa. Walk off the pancakes. See what remained of her childhood memories. The eight-foot bronze jackrabbit still stood sentry on Lincoln Avenue. She recalled very well when it was erected—1962, the year she was eleven and lost so much.

Many of the buildings she remembered were gone or converted to other businesses. It had been so long, she wasn't sure of her bearings. Maybe her memory was playing tricks on her. She spun around in a dizzying circle. Rather than head out to Daddy's, she decided to get a cup of coffee. She firmly believed a little caffeine buzz never hurt anybody. Perhaps that conviction was a function of the addict in her—using substances to change the way she felt. Every AA member she had ever met said the urge never goes away.

Odessa hadn't joined the Eighties. There were no chic coffee shops like her favorite Trianon—with its exposed brick walls and shabby-chic armchairs—to be seen, but she spied a little place a couple of doors down the block that looked like it might do. Cheerful blue-checked gingham curtains covered the lower half of the windows. As she opened the door, the delicious aroma of fresh coffee confirmed her decision. The few patrons looked up and—she could think of no other word for it—gaped at her.

Guess I don't look too Odessa anymore. Her chin rose in defiance, and she strutted right in, without apology, wearing her embroidered silk tunic, short vest, and Calvin's. She took a seat in a red vinyl chair at a Formica-topped table for two. Glancing at the tables and chairs, she reflected that she hadn't seen so much chrome trim since she was a child.

"What can I getchu, ma'am?" twanged a seventyish gray-haired waitress. She pulled out her little green pad and took a pencil from behind her ear, careful not to disturb her beehive hairdo.

"Just coffee, please."

Service was quick and efficient. The waitress brought a big steaming mug along with thick cream in a white mini pitcher.

Jane added a small amount of cream and stirred. She sipped tentatively at first. The coffee was good and strong.

She felt eyes on her and studiously avoided looking at the other customers, tracing the Fifties' boomerang pattern on the Formica tabletop with a coral-tipped fingernail.

After a few minutes, she relaxed a bit and accepted a refill. She sat lost in thought about Tom's revelations and tomorrow's event—another Odessa funeral. As she breathed out, the force of her exhalation lifted the long feathery bangs from her forehead. Maybe she shouldn't have come back, but then she would not have heard Tom's disclosures. Sort of rocked her world—in a bad way. The information would take some time to digest.

There was still this day to get through, then the big day tomorrow. After that? Well, she had booked a return flight to Austin. But to what? Things had hit a new low with Joshua. He hadn't called her last night even though she had left her hotel information for him. When she checked in, she had expected a message, and there hadn't been one. She had to acknowledge her passive-aggressiveness in not phoning him to let him know she had arrived safely. *So it goes. And I never did get hold of Lauren. She won't be pleased she wasn't consulted about this life event.*

While rummaging through her purse to find her wallet, the sound of door chimes drew her gaze to the entrance.

"Hey, Rick, the usual?" The waitress sounded almost vivacious as she spoke to the newcomer. "How're thangs out at the park?"

The man said, "Well, Hattie, Monahans was doin' fine yesterday. I expect it still is, but I'll get back to you if that changes."

Hattie put her hand on her hip and chuckled. "Such a card! I'll get your order in."

Jane stared at Rick as he nodded to the waitress. The man was tall and lean. His hair was sun-streaked blond. His deep tan contrasted with blue eyes, the blue of the hot Texas sky that brought her back to 1962. Damned if it wasn't Ricky Mills. Adrenaline coursed through her body and left her limbs tingling.

He scanned the café and their eyes met. Approaching her table, he grinned and shook his head. "Of all the coffee shops in all the towns in West Texas..."

We haven't spoken since we were eleven—the night Mavis died. Now he's talking to me so easily, as if time has been erased.

In her lap, Jane's hands clenched, fingernails piercing her palms.

He was still grinning, thumb hitched in his belt, head cocked, eyebrow raised. "If I remember right, you weren't ever at a loss for words."

Before she left home, she heard things about him from time to time. People talked in Odessa, and you couldn't help but hear. He ran with the hot rod crowd in high school, was rumored to be drinking heavily. Then he took off one day, and no one had a clue what happened to him. To see his grin, to have him speak to her as if they had talked last week, stunned her. She felt frozen in her chair and simply stared, but she couldn't sit there gaping at him. "Ricky? Rick?"

"The one and only. What brings you back to Odessa, Janie? From what I hear, you ain't ever graced our town—since when was it—'bout sixty-seven?"

"When...where...damn, Rick. You really do have me at a loss for words." *He's gorgeous.*

"And, like I said, that's pretty darn unusual for you as I recall."

Jane blushed. "I never thought I'd come back." She blurted, "Mama died and her funeral's tomorrow." Biting her lip, she thought a moment, then asked, "Do you want to sit?"

Rick grabbed the chair across from Jane, turned it around, and stared into her eyes. He sat and folded his arms on the chair back. "Sorry to hear that. I know you had your differences, but losing your folks is tough. Learned that the hard way."

"Your folks are gone? When?"

"About eight years ago, both killed instantly in a head-on collision on I-10."

Jane's hands covered her mouth. "Oh, I'm so sorry."

He nodded and said, "You deal with it. You go on." He stood, placed the chair facing toward the table, and sat down across from her. "But I am surprised your mama lasted this long, after everything you told me way back when. Guess she never did stop drinkin'. I had my own troubles with liquor, but I've been sober almost eleven years." He reached into his hip pocket, brought out a ten-year medallion from AA, and slammed it on the table.

Jane chuckled and dug in her purse. She found her little makeup bag and pulled out her own medallion, placing it next to his. "Eight years. You got me beat."

"I'll be darned. Who'd have thunk it? Well, I guess you come by it honestly. Got the pedigree. Looks like we still got a lot in common."

"Do we?" Jane tilted her head and studied his face, trying to see the Emperor of Rangerland in the man. "The way I remember it, you weren't speaking to me after...you know. How could you treat me like that? It weighed on me something fierce."

Rick hung his head a moment, then reached across the table and placed his hand over hers. "You got to understand. Mavis's death shattered my life, my family. My parents stayed together, but in most ways, we fell apart. There was never any joy after that." He gulped and his eyes brightened with tears, then he regained his composure. "Rangerland was over for me. My folks barely let me out of the house for weeks—kept an eagle eye on me. You were a reminder of what I'd lost. It just hurt too much. But, know this, it weighed on me, too, not havin' you in my life."

Jane glanced at his hand on top of hers and gently pulled away. Memories threatened to overwhelm her. So much emotion in such a short time. She looked back at him, tamped down those pesky feelings, and asked, "Did I hear right—Monahans? The Sandhills State Park?" She raised one eyebrow, pointing at his khaki shirt with the sleeve patch.

Rick's shoulders relaxed. He seemed to be relieved at the change in subject. "It ain't Africa, but I like it. Keeps me outdoors." His eyes crinkled in the corners, "I thought about the President of Rangerland once or twice out there, I can tell you. Especially when I run across a critter."

Jane's lips formed a pensive smile. "We sure had us some adventures, didn't we?"

"Oh, yeah, we did. All that explorin' probably led me to my career in wildlife management, although now I deal with livin' critters, not roadkill. Got into it when I went to New Mexico. There's more wildlife at Monahans than you might think—saw a litter of bobcat this spring."

"Really?" *My tomboy days are long gone. Closest I come to wildlife anymore is Tallulah.* "I don't get out much in nature these days. Hard to keep a manicure." She flashed her impeccable nails.

He looked amused, then a little wistful. "Yeah, that was a long time ago. What about you, Janie—or is it Jane now? What's your life like?"

"I go by Jane." She shook her head. "Rick, do you really expect me to summarize half my life over a cup of coffee—"

The waitress placed a huge platter of eggs, sausage, and pancakes in front of Rick.

"—and the largest breakfast I have ever seen?"

He picked up a fork, dug in, and said, "You can make a start at least."

Jane checked her watch and glanced up to see Rick staring at her left hand. "I see it's time for me to go."

"And I see you got married. Thought you wasn't ever gonna get married." He opened his mouth to speak, hesitated, and came out with the question, "So, what's he like—besides rich." He pointed at her left hand with his pancake-laden fork. "I'm goin' by the size of that rock."

Jane sat up straight and put up her walls. She imagined frost coming off her body, and as she watched his grin fade, it appeared Rick picked up on her mood change right quick. She grabbed her bag, tossed a five on the table, and said, "I really do have to run. Tom and his wife are getting everything ready for tomorrow out at Daddy's and they'll wonder where I am."

Rick swallowed another massive bite, wiped his mouth with the paper napkin, pushed his chair back, and rose.

He's about as tall as Joshua.

Jane considered a hug, then thought about shaking hands, but neither option felt right. She settled for a crisp nod, clutched her bag to her chest, and just about sprinted to the door.

"See you tomorrow, Jane."

The words struck her in the back and propelled her out the door. She didn't acknowledge him, didn't even glance back, just fled the diner.

Jane had never considered how many people from her past she might run into on this visit. Did she expect to come into town incognito and make her getaway sight unseen? Odessa was a small town, and she needed to remember that.

Jane all but ran to her parking spot. She threw herself into the Toyota, started the car, shoved the gearshift into drive, and floored the accelerator in her hurry to get gone. Realizing she was not on a freeway, she slowed to a more sedate pace. Approaching the infamous Chevy dealership owned by the Taylor family, she saw a woman getting out of a Corvette. As she headed toward the entrance, she tottered on platform shoes, in danger of breaking an ankle. Something about the way she strutted with her chin tilted up and her butt waggling struck a chord in Jane's memory. The feathered, platinum-blond Farrah Fawcett hairdo almost made her burst out laughing. Then Jane spied the tight, pearl-blue, waist-length leather jacket with linebacker shoulder pads and chortled with glee. She did a double take—Lord have mercy—it was none other than her old nemesis, Priscilla Hampton. That clinched it, and she had to pull over before she crashed the car. It was too delicious not to watch.

A man and a young woman came out the front door next to the wide plate-glass window that became a legend in Odessa one night in 1967. Damned if it wasn't an older, wider, paunchy Travis Taylor. He had his arm around the young lady's waist, head bent to hers, nuzzling, whispering, and chuckling. He wasn't paying attention to his surroundings and didn't see Priscilla descending on him like a charging feral sow.

What happened next led Jane to the conclusion that Priscilla no longer went by the name of Hampton and was now Priscilla Taylor.

Mrs. Taylor grabbed the shoulder strap of what looked like a two-tone Christian Dior bag, wound up, and smacked Travis right across his fat, florid, surprised face. The other woman backed away, wide-eyed with fear, and then darted down the street.

Jane slid down in the seat until she could barely see the irate Priscilla winding up for another swing at Travis, who raised his hands in a defensive posture. The next blow knocked the sickly grin from his face.

Looks like Travis and Priscilla might be reaping what they sowed.

Chapter Five

PUTTING ON SOME MILES-WEST TEXAS TO CALIFORNIA 1967

We were in Lubeth's room, where the two of us spent most afternoons after school. She sat at her white French Provincial makeup table inspecting her worried face in the oval mirror.

Lying on the bed, studying the ceiling, I wondered if Mama would even notice if I didn't come home at all. Mrs. Williams was really nice about giving me a lift out to hell house most days. When she couldn't, I stuck my thumb out and hitched.

"I'm pregnant, Janie."

My eyes went wide and my stomach sank to my shoes. Maybe in my heart I knew Lubeth and Travis were doing the deed, but I was still shocked at the proof. "Dear God, are you sure?"

"Well, I missed my period twice now, so, yeah, pretty darn sure."

My usually even-tempered friend had been a little volatile lately. I figured Lubeth's hormones were already in overdrive.

I rolled over to my belly, propped up on my elbows, and asked, "What're you gonna do? Are you gonna marry him? You're only a junior."

Lubeth heaved a great sigh. "Travis doesn't even know yet. I'm going to tell him tomorrow night at the drive-in." She looked at me. Her chin started to quiver. "I suppose the honorable thing to do is to marry me, but what happens to his football scholarship to UT?"

Honorable? The Taylor boys weren't known for being honorable. Entitled, maybe.

I jumped up from the bed and began to pace around the spacious room. "Football? Who cares about football at a time like this? Lord above, girl. Who else knows?"

Lubeth shook her head. "Nobody. You're the only one I've told." She sat on her pink velvet stool, her shoulders slumped.

I felt bad for her and prepared myself for some prevarication. Kneeling on the plush rose carpet, I got eye to eye with her. "It'll be all right, Lubeth. Travis loves you."

I hoped Jesus would forgive me for lying. My opinion of Travis Taylor and the entire insufferable Taylor family was best kept to myself. Mr. Taylor owned the Chevy dealership on Eighth Street. Travis zoomed around Odessa in his shiny new red Corvette, giving rides to anything in a skirt. Lubeth seemed oblivious to his reputation. His three brothers were notorious hell-raisers, and the eldest got Sara Jenkins pregnant last year. She went away for the summer to visit her aunt in Dallas and came back six months later with a lumpy, flabby body and a real sad look to her.

I could see Lubeth's future even if she couldn't, and it was none too bright. I didn't have the heart to burst her little love bubble. She was my only friend and the way that happened was a pure-dee miracle. After Ricky dropped me like a hot skillet when Mavis died, I dreaded going to school until one day in seventh grade when Lubeth Williams and her family moved to town from Houston. We sat next to each other in English. Since we were both serious readers, we got along from the get-go. Lubeth's dad was some kind of manager in the oil business, and I thought she might join the Priscilla Hampton fan club, but I was wrong. I knew she must have heard the talk about me, but Lubeth was loyal. She was friends with me first, and she stayed friends with me. Like I said, it was a miracle. I would be steadfast and stand by her side. It was only fair.

Lubeth got up and walked over to look out the window. She twirled to face me. Her voice bright, she changed the topic from her own troubles to matchmaking. "Janie, are you going to go out with Cory again? He'd like to go on another date. Travis said Cory told him he felt a spark—that sounds promising."

I groaned. "Lubeth, we have nothing in common. He's never heard of Steppenwolf, and I mean both the band *and* the novel. He told me, 'If it ain't country, it ain't music.' Lordy!"

"So, you don't have the same taste in music. There's other things."

I rolled my eyes. "Yeah, football, football, and football. I don't know a line drive from a linebacker."

"He thinks you're cute."

"Cory thinks my *butt* is cute. He kept trying to squeeze it when we slow danced. I just about choked on the fumes of Jade East. Does he *bathe* in it?"

Lubeth laughed, and it did my heart good to hear it. "You're so picky!"

"I am not! I'm just selective. Has he read a book since *Dick and Jane*? The ability to speak in full sentences is not negotiable."

"Okay, okay. I get it. But I'm not giving up on you finding true love, just like I did!"

When I got off the school bus the next Monday, the schoolyard was chaos. Kids were milling around, and the noise level was high. The cheerleader-types ran from one group to another; there was excited chatter everywhere, and no one was making a move to go inside. Something was up, but I was sure it was the usual inane social gossip. I wondered who broke up with whom or what lucky girl got a promise ring over the weekend. Oh, the drama!

I headed to the door and was accosted by Priscilla Hampton and Agnes Jones, the popular girls, the ones who never gave me the time of day except to ridicule me, ever since the first grade. What was this new, alternate reality? A radical event of some sort had flipped the earth on its axis.

Priscilla was positively breathless. "Isn't it awful?" Her heavily mascaraed eyes were popping out of their sockets.

"I can't believe it." Agnes fluttered her eyelashes; she was almost panting. She glanced at Priscilla for approval. Her eagerness to please reminded me of a little terrier, looking with adoring eyes at her mistress.

All the excitement and spectacle were wasted on me. "What are y'all goin' on about?" I didn't even try to hide my distaste.

"Travis is devastated, just devastated." Priscilla shook her head and put her wrist to her forehead.

"Travis's daddy is *so* mad." Agnes yapped.

I looked at the two of them and made my face go blank. Not giving them anything. "Travis's daddy is mad about what?"

Priscilla gasped and raised a magenta-tipped index finger to her chin and—there was no other word for it—simpered. "You don't know?"

I really didn't want to deal with Priscilla's drama-queen routine. "Know what?"

"You live so far out of town—"

"I've heard that my whole life," I snapped.

Priscilla dropped her solicitous act and snarled, "If you'll let me finish…" She immediately reverted to her sweeter-than-sugar tone. "You didn't hear the sirens." Her concerned expression was utterly fake.

Agnes put her hand on my arm, and I recoiled. She didn't let go, just walked me to the side of the wide stairs at the school entrance.

Priscilla said, "You better sit down."

I shrugged away from Agnes's death grip and shook my head. "No. Just spit it out."

"Lubeth." Priscilla paused theatrically. "Lubeth is dead!"

Agnes breathed, "She killed herself Saturday night, drove Travis's Corvette right through that big display window at his daddy's Chevy dealership." She paused. "Flew right through the windshield. Can you imagine?"

I remained standing, but I don't know how. My mouth fell open, and my eyes stung. I felt separate from my body. It couldn't be true.

Priscilla and Agnes exchanged smug, satisfied looks. It took all my strength not to slap their self-important faces. My arm stayed at my side, but my hand twitched.

They were just so delighted to be the ones to give me the news. I'm sure they could never understand why Lubeth chose to be friends with me, Miss Poor Little White Trash. They didn't know me, but probably thought they did. Everyone knew my mother drank and, for some unknown reason, my daddy still hung his hat out in the sticks, when he wasn't in the oilfields.

I heard their whispers through the years. "I almost feel sorry for her, living out in so-called Eden's Acres. More like hell." Then there was the story about me and Ricky Mills killing his sister Mavis, by burying her alive. Since I wasn't in jail, I guess the dummies figured out it wasn't true.

I had such clarity at that moment. The sun glinted off the flagpole, the trees pulsated with green, and the sky was deep clear azure, with two puffy cartoon clouds. I could see every pore in Priscilla's face as she applied another coat of lip gloss. Agnes's yellow homeroom folder was covered with her spidery cursive script:

Mrs. John Benson Mrs. John Benson Mrs. John Benson Mrs. John Benson Mrs. John Benson.

I stood there motionless. They picked up their purses, patted their Jackie Kennedy hair, and backed away from me like I was a rabid dog.

"Well, Janie, class is about to start." Priscilla and her lieutenant turned smartly and sashayed away. Priscilla shot one final gleeful glance over her shoulder, then whispered into Agnes's ear.

I heard them giggling—*giggling*—as they went through the big doors.

There was no way I was setting foot in Odessa High. Not today and maybe not ever again. I was going to see Lubeth's mother and find out what had happened to my friend.

Lubeth's younger sister, Ellen, answered the door. Her eyes were red and swollen, and she clutched a box of tissue. Wordlessly, she waved me in. All the curtains were drawn, and the air was stale and hushed, like the house had stopped breathing when Lubeth did.

"I'll get Mom. Go on and sit in the parlor."

I couldn't settle down enough to sit.

Mrs. Williams shuffled in and said, "Janie, I can't believe she's gone."

My heart broke for her. I gave her a hug and got her settled on the couch next to me.

Mrs. Williams looked straight at me. "Why? You were her friend, why did she do this?" Tears rolled down her cheeks.

I had never noticed any gray in her hair before. Could it appear overnight? I gulped and came right out with it. "Lubeth told me she was pregnant."

She gasped and brought her hand to her mouth, biting her fist. "No! I've lost her *and* my grandchild?" She bent her head and wailed.

Mr. Williams came rushing in. "What the hell!"

I stood and faced him. "Mr. Williams, I'm so sorry for your loss. Mrs. Williams asked me why, and I told her the truth…Lubeth was pregnant. She was going to tell Travis that night. It must've gone badly."

He rushed to his wife and pulled her to her feet. She sagged in his arms. "You better go, Janie. We need our privacy."

"Yes, sir." I stood and hustled out of the room.

Mrs. Williams cried, "Turning up pregnant isn't the worst thing to happen to a girl. We could have gotten through it. Travis would have married her. I know he would have…"

Mr. Williams whispered, "Hush now, Milly, hush now."

I pulled the door closed behind me.

Two days later, as I walked into the First Methodist Church, I tried not to think about the other funerals I had attended there. As usual, it seemed the whole town was in attendance. For sure, the whole high school had shown up, like it was the social event of the year or something. Mrs. Williams sat in the front row with her husband and only daughter. It looked to me like the woman hadn't stopped crying since I saw her on Monday. She was hunched and shrunken. Looked like she'd aged twenty years overnight. Lubeth's daddy was sitting up straight and tall and rigid, still as a statue.

When I told Mrs. Williams about the pregnancy, I might have done more harm than good. She seemed to think Travis would have married Lubeth. I guess she didn't know about Sara Jenkins. Mrs. Williams believed an early marriage wasn't the worst that could happen to a girl. She was right. Being rejected by the baby's father and being so desperate that she took her own life was the worst thing, the very worst thing.

I ducked into a pew near the front and didn't bother to look to see who else was there. The service passed in a blur. I stood when everybody else did, followed along as best I could, but I was like a robot.

I dreaded going up to the casket. My palms were sweaty, and my stomach felt queasy. Sure enough, it was an open casket, just like Mavis's had been, just like Grandma June's had been. I hadn't liked what I'd seen in either of their caskets and didn't expect I would like what I'd see today any better. Would Lubeth's face be broken? How could they fix her up after a bad car wreck? I had to go look—it would haunt me forever if I didn't. My imagination might be worse than reality. I shoved my fear down and trudged to the front of the church.

Turned out, reality was much worse than my imagination. My knees felt like water, and I held back a scream. I knew Lubeth was dead, but actually seeing her was unbearable. What was it with these bereaved mothers having open caskets? Why put your dead child on display for the world to see? I closed my eyes, but you can't unsee something. I wished I could pray, but my relationship with Jesus hadn't been quite the same since Mavis died. Would it ever improve? After all this time, I doubted it.

Lubeth's poor pretty face wasn't pretty any longer. She'd been put back together like Humpty Dumpty and painted over with makeup layered on with a trowel.

"Powder and paint, powder and paint, makes you look like what you ain't." I heard Grandma June in my head, crowing her mad, alcoholic laugh when she used to criticize Aunt Penny for wearing makeup.

I cried for my friend, gotten up like a cracked porcelain doll with a heartbreakingly misshapen face. I didn't want to remember her this way.

Mrs. Williams had chosen to bury Lubeth in her choir gown, which obscured the shape of her upper torso—probably a good thing. My gaze dropped to her hands. Bless the Lord, they had been put into gloves, but I could see they had been damaged badly in the crash. The thin white material was stretched tight to the point of bursting, like an overstuffed sausage, on her right index finger and her left pinkie. Most of her other fingers were flattened, bent or both. I didn't even want to think about the rest of Lubeth's body. This was plenty of grist for the nightmare mill.

Travis Taylor and his family were conspicuously absent. I thought they should have made the effort to pay their respects. The spicy odor of carnations stung my nose, and I sneezed. Then I noticed a huge pink flower arrangement on a stand towering over the sea of floral offerings. A large, gilded ribbon announced it was from the Taylors. If I was Mrs. Williams, I'd take those flowers and shove them right up the collective butts of the Taylor family—mother, father, and all four boys.

No. I guessed if I was Mrs. Williams, I would be so numbed and so sad I'd just sit there in the first row of the church, like she was doing, crying her body dry.

I had enough. I turned and fled right back up the aisle and didn't stop until I was outside and halfway down Andrews Highway. I wanted to keep walking until I hit the ocean.

I left Odessa a few weeks later. The night Mama drove me over the edge, she woke me to find her another bottle of her beloved vodka. After handing her the bottle, after she told me I had never loved her like Grace did, she spoke the words that seared—and scarred—my soul:

"If I could strike you dead and bring Grace back, so help me God, I would."

With that, Mama laid the proverbial last straw on me. She almost broke me that night, but not quite.

Struck speechless by her cruelty, I ran to my room. I had been thinking about leaving for months and ever since Lubeth died, I was on my last nerve. Dragging my duffel bag from under the bed, I tossed in my few clothes. Found my stash of money. One hundred and twelve dollars. I pulled on a pair of jeans, a tie-dyed t-shirt, long-sleeved blouse, and slipped into my boots. Grabbed my book, *Stranger in a Strange Land*. I hadn't finished it and refused to leave it behind. No time to take my Steve Miller Band and Cream posters. I left them as the only remnants of life in that godforsaken dump. Glancing around my room, I vowed never to return. Tossing my hair over my shoulder, I picked up my bag, and closed the door to my room for the final time.

Without a word, I walked right past Mama. She stood by her plastic-covered sofa, swaying on her feet, wearing her uniform—wrinkled and stained powder-blue baby doll pajamas and her gigantic hot-pink fuzzy slippers—swilling vodka straight from the bottle. Singing "Amazing Grace."

The last sound I heard was the screen door slamming on Mama's wails for her long-dead daughter.

I never had a chance. How do you compete with a dead angel?

Did I have a plan? No, I didn't get that far. My goal was San Francisco, Haight-Ashbury to be precise. I heard that kids from all over the country were heading there. They were even sleeping in the park. That was fine with me. It sure beat my crater of a bed in this little shop of horrors. Tears stung my eyes as I half-ran down the lane. I swiped my arm across my face to sop up the tears.

When I got to the county road, I threw down the duffel bag and raised my face to the night sky. "Are You there, Jesus? Can You hear me? Did You hear *her*?" I was a little embarrassed to talk at the sky, but there was no one around to hear me—not even Jesus.

Odessa held nothing for me. Family? I was a motherless child. Daddy spent most of his time in the oilfields. I wondered if that was by choice. Tom escaped to college in Lubbock four years ago and had only come home twice. He gave me his phone number, and I had it in my pocket. When I got settled, I'd give him a call. Aunt Penny and Uncle Rafe moved to Dallas the year after Mavis died, just a few months before Tom left. That was quite a year, and it had gone downhill at home ever since.

Friends? Nope, no friends now that Lubeth was gone. I had two friends in my life, and they were both gone. Ricky Mills and I parted ways years ago. We had never spoken after Mavis's accident. It had hurt—hell, it still hurt. Ricky hung out with a rough crowd in high school, not that I had any contact with him. Rumor had it he drank liquor and smoked marijuana. He dropped out last year, and I heard he was in New Mexico doing God knows what. New Mexico wasn't exactly Africa, but at least it wasn't Odessa. It seemed like our years playing explorer in the grasslands were only a dream or something I read in a book. I sure wasn't the same girl I was back then.

Now my only friend, Lubeth, was in the ground, fixing to be worm food. Ashes to ashes, dust to dust. Time to move on.

I threw the duffel over my shoulder and stuck out my thumb. About ten minutes later, I got a ride from an old woman in an ancient pickup.

"Thank you for stopping, ma'am."

She grunted. "Where you headed?"

"California."

"Well, I ain't goin' that far. I'll let you out at the highway."

"Fine by me." I settled in the seat and looked straight ahead.

"What's in California?" She put the truck in gear and slowly headed down the road.

"Don't know, but it's gotta be better than…where I just left." I stopped before I told her too much.

The truck rattled to a stop. As I clambered down and turned to thank her, she said, "Hope you're headin' for a better situation. You take care now, young lady."

I watched her drive on to the south side of town until the taillights disappeared.

Turning to the west, I set my mind on my first stop—Monterey Pop. Like Bob Dylan once said, the times they are a-changin' and I was a-changin' right with them. I was going to wear a flower in my hair and join the gentle people.

I had loved rock 'n' roll since I heard my first Elvis song, "All Shook Up." A vision of Aunt Penny rocking around her kitchen, teaching me to dance flitted through my mind. Now Elvis had just gotten hitched to Priscilla. I hated the name "Priscilla."

The last Christmas I shared with Aunt Penny, she gave me a transistor radio. I still had it—my most prized possession. That radio was glued to my ear day and night. Night was the best—you could hear music from way far away. My lifeline to a different place, it connected me to another world, a world I wanted to experience.

I felt like a misfit in Odessa. The kids there seemed to care about such mundane things: prom, going steady, blah, blah, blah. The girls were planning their weddings and baby showers, years before the event. Boys talked about becoming war heroes in Viet Nam. Even though I was a proud and patriotic American, I wasn't sure why our soldiers were fighting Communism way over there. Guess I didn't buy the domino theory, but like most of my opinions that went against the grain in Odessa, I kept them to myself.

There was energy in the air in California. I saw it on *Where the Action is* and read about it in "16" magazine. That's where I wanted to be, where they made the music. Brian Wilson and Mike Love sang about "Good Vibrations." Scott McKenzie told me in his song that people were in motion and now I was, too. My final destination was San Francisco, but, since Steve Miller was playing at Monterey Pop, along with The Who and The Animals, I wanted to go there first.

Even though I couldn't play a musical instrument, I could carry a tune, if I did say so myself. And I knew all the words to all the songs, always had. Words were my thing, ever since I taught myself to read when I was five. I just picked them up and kept them in my head. Words, lyrics, whatever.

I would have to spend my one hundred and twelve dollars very frugally. My resolve was firm. As the sun came up, a faint breeze touched my face. I stuck my thumb out and got a ride straight off with a long-haul trucker. As he eased back on the highway, I hoped I was leaving behind the ghosts of Grace, Mavis, and Lubeth.

The first leg of my journey with the trucker was the easiest. He was all business, drove fast, not stopping much. He played country music, but I didn't complain. When he dropped me in Phoenix, he told me he had a daughter my age and to be careful. My next, and worst, ride was with a family in a station wagon headed to Disneyland. The screaming kids and bickering parents and way too frequent stops were hard to take. On the last stretch, a van filled with surfer kids on the way to Santa Cruz gave me a lift. All those Jan and Dean songs started to make sense.

I arrived at the entrance to the Monterey Pop Festival a little road-weary. It took two days to get there, so I missed the first day of music. Not getting to see The Animals bummed me out, but the vitality in the atmosphere was contagious, and I perked up fast. What a happening scene! A total assault on the senses. My nose tingled with the odor of incense and that burnt leaf smell I knew was marijuana—thanks to the surfers—although I had never smoked any, yet.

The noise level was staggering: the music, the laughter, the calling out, the chanting. The colors were dazzling, even the cars and buses were painted with psychedelic colors, patterns, and peace signs.

Toto, we're not in Texas anymore. The kids here looked nothing like the ones I left back at Odessa High School. Why, the boys' hair was just as long as the girls' and I kind of liked that. Well, if I was being honest, I really liked it.

A girl in a granny dress and a headband made from flowers skipped by and gave me a daisy and a smile. She flashed the peace sign as she danced away.

My clothes weren't exactly right. Most of the girls were wearing hip-huggers with huge bell-bottoms or flowing, flowered dresses. The jeans on these kids were patched or torn while my 501s were dark and plain, like all the kids wore at Odessa High. My loose print blouse was fine. I didn't feel self-conscious, just a bit like I had landed in a foreign land, like when Valentine Michael Smith arrived on earth from Mars. I finally finished *Stranger in a Strange Land*. What a trip! It would take me a while to grok it. I was but an egg, and this egg was jumping right into the frying pan.

The most amazing electric musical sound, nothing I'd heard before, buzzed through the air. Lines of people were winding through the crowd, some holding hands, some tapping on drums. Everything was exotic to my Texan eyes. I didn't know where to look first. The smells, sights and sounds overwhelmed my senses, and I couldn't take in everything.

Lots of people didn't have the dollar to get in, so they were letting everyone in for free. That was good, since I had to be careful with my cash.

"Hey there, sweetheart, you look a little lost," said a deep, masculine voice.

I must have looked like a deer in the headlights. The Texas twang was welcome to my ears. I gazed up at a tall, good-looking, smiling man, and my toes curled inside my boots. He had gorgeous blond sun-streaked hair almost as long as mine. It looked like corn silk, and I wanted to touch it.

He came close so I could hear him over the music. His brown eyes crinkled, and he smiled at me. "Cat got your tongue, sweetheart?"

My face and a few other body parts felt hot. I knew I was beet-red but there wasn't a darn thing I could do about it. I smiled back. "I'm just surprised to hear a voice from home, is all."

He grinned and stuck his thumb in the belt loop of his jeans.

I was so embarrassed when he saw me looking at his...thumb.

"Is that all?" He laughed soft and low. "Where you from, sugar?"

"Odessa." It came out in a whisper.

"You're pretty far from home. You just get here?"

I nodded and looked down. The eye contact was a bit too much.

He reached out and tipped up my chin.

I about died. Knowing all the words to all the love songs as I did, I knew what was happening. "Imagine me and you, I do...I never loved a man the way I love you...Come on, baby, light my fire." The Turtles, Aretha, and The Doors were competing for attention. I was undone, nonplussed, flummoxed.

"Name's Jeremy Bonner, sugar. I'm from Dallas originally. Been working for Steve Miller for about a year now out here in California."

"Steve Miller? For real?" I was mighty impressed, and not just about Steve Miller.

"Yeah." Jeremy smiled and lit a cigarette, the regular kind. He had a very sexy smile. "I gotta say, you're the purtiest thang I've seen in a while. Where you stayin,' sweetheart?"

"I guess here at the festival." I got brave enough to meet his eyes for a moment and decided not to address the "purty" comment. "Someone told me they're passing out blankets."

"You might not want to sleep on the ground with all these folks. It's been a little damp, too. You can crash with me if you like."

Oh, I like. "Well, okay." My stomach was fluttering like I just ate a passel of butterflies.

"We got to haul our gear to the stage for Steve's set. Come on, and I'll introduce you to the crew."

I got to hang out with the roadies and their girls through Steve Miller's set. Steve was a regular guy, friendly and laid back. I had to pinch myself to make sure it was real as I listened to The Byrds and Jefferson Airplane from my privileged perch. The last act of the evening came on before I knew it.

Otis Redding was great. Booker T and the MGs backed him. He came out in a green silk suit, grabbed the mic, and demanded, "Shake. Everybody say it! Shake." The crowd complied, getting on their feet and staying there for his whole set. He sang "Respect," a song that he said a girl took away from him, meaning Aretha. The beat so compelling, I couldn't help but dance with the other girls. No one danced like that in Odessa, but I picked up on the groove right quick. Otis tore up the stage himself. I had never seen a man move like that.

Then he slowed things down. He said, "This is the Love crowd, right?" and everyone went crazy. "I've Been Loving You Too Long," with the mournful horns, pierced my heart. The depth of feeling, the yearning he put into the words touched my soul. Even with the cold rain falling, the audience couldn't get enough.

Then he picked up the pace again with a hard-driving version of The Stones' "Satisfaction," but his last song was the best. I hadn't ever heard it before. "Try a Little Tenderness" closed out the night, and I think I fell in love during it. Jeremy stood behind me and held me as we swayed to the music that started out slow. It felt so good. He was so tender as he pulled my hair back and kissed the nape of my neck. Electricity zinged up and down my spine and a little farther south. Then Otis ended the song with foot-stomping tempo, so passionate and intense, and not the least bit tender. The buildup and crescendo gave me something to think about.

While most of the crowd was still cheering and whooping it up, Jeremy took my hand and we hurried back to his van in the cold drizzle. My innards were turning cartwheels. I was still a virgin and intended to stay that way, for a while at least. Worried about how he might get after me, I wondered if I could handle it. He was older than me and no doubt more experienced. But he was respectful so far. My mouth felt a little dry. Yikes!

"Darlin', if you're worried about stayin' here with me, don't be. I promise to be a gentleman."

Parts of me were already melting, and now my heart joined them. I let out a big breath and smiled like to split my face. "Thanks, Jeremy. I sure do appreciate it."

He came close and reached out his hand.

I thought he was going to touch my face and waited for a kiss that didn't come.

Then his outstretched hand opened the back door of his purple van, splitting the big peace sign in two. He took my hand and helped me inside.

When I saw the double mattress, there was a tiny stab of doubt, but I remembered his promise. After I stowed my bag, I said a little prayer and fell asleep thinking about love. I'd heard about free love, but I was holding out for *true* love. And maybe, I had found it.

We got up late and ate some peanut butter on bread, then headed to the stage area. We met up with the other roadies again. Jeremy found us a great spot backstage to watch Janis Joplin, this crazy chick from Texas. She sure drank a lot, even on stage, but she was really nice in person. She brought her dog Scout with her to the festival and that was cool.

It was a little chilly and damp for June. As far as I could remember, I hadn't ever been cold in June in Odessa. When I shivered, Jeremy brought me a blanket he said some church ladies had donated. I thought about Mrs. Foster for a little minute. She would freak out if she could see me now. So would the entire population of Odessa.

Jeremy was real interested in the different bands and knew all the equipment and instruments. He played bass guitar and hoped he'd get on with a band someday, but for now, he liked being a roadie.

For me, the whole thing was about the music, the pulsating ever-present sound that had taken up residence in my bones. The beat of the bass reverberated in my chest. I felt the music down to my fingertips.

The Who tore up the stage and their instruments. The Dead mellowed out the crowd. All the guys were talking about the next act. There were hardly any left-handed guitar players, and Jeremy said that Jimi Hendrix was the best. "He's been livin' in Europe and makin' a name for himself. Glad he's back in the U S of A."

Hendrix came on stage wearing a ruffled orange shirt, disturbingly tight red pants, a black vest, and a headband. No one in Odessa dressed like that, but here, no one looked cross-eyed at anyone's clothes or even noticed if they weren't wearing any.

I was still getting used to the scene and learning all the new slang. To tell the truth, I felt a little embarrassed at saying things like "far out" and "groovy." But I was determined to get with it, because I wasn't ever going back to Odessa, come hell or high water.

"You gotta hear this guy, Janie."

We listened to the most outrageous sounds coming from his guitar as he began his last song, "Wild Thing." He played that guitar behind his back, up in the air, one-handed, rubbing it against the amplifier, and still—it was music.

I asked Jeremy, "How can he make those sounds? It's flat-out amazing!"

He laughed and answered, but he kept his eyes on the stage. "He's a genius, is how."

Hendrix knelt down with his guitar, what Jeremy called a "Strat," between his knees. He plucked it and kissed it. I peeked at Jeremy, and he looked as surprised as I was.

"Man, it's like he's makin' love to the durn thing." Jeremy chuckled and shook his head.

Heat rose from my neck to my face, and I turned back to the stage.

Jimi Hendrix was pouring something on his guitar and then, honest to God, he set it on fire! He stood with the Strat over his head and started smashing it on the stage. He did Pete Townshend one better. His roadies looked a little upset at the destruction, but that was only natural since it was their job to protect the equipment.

Jeremy said, "I don't have the words for what we just saw, but this guy is something else. Nothing can top this. Let's get on the road before the crowds—that is, if you're comin' with me."

I looked him square in the eyes. He gazed back, and his face slowly broke into a grin. One eyebrow rose, and he waited for my answer.

"Yes, I'm coming."

On the drive to San Francisco, we got to talking about the war. I asked him if he worried about being drafted. He shook his head and told me he had joined the army when he was eighteen, in 1962. So, he was twenty-three, quite a bit older than me, but that didn't faze me one little bit.

"Yep, I joined up right after high school, just like my brothers, just like my dad. About a year in, my left lower leg and ankle got busted up real bad while loadin' heavy equipment. They operated on it. Put in some hardware."

"Oh, how awful! Does it bother you?"

He glanced over at me and smiled. "Not so much anymore, darlin'. Sure, I got me a little hitch in my giddyup, but I don't think ya even noticed, did ya?"

"Well, no." I'd been looking at his gorgeous hair and those warm brown eyes. And his...thumb.

"With the way things are goin' in Nam, it might've been the luckiest thing ever happened to me. Well, besides meetin' you, of course."

Angels sang as I took in his words and held them close. Could I fall any more in love?

"So, sugar, I'm done with the service. Got me a medical discharge."

He told me about the rent house on Ashbury Street and the people who shared it. He explained it was a fluid situation, folks coming and going. I felt a little uneasy about living with strangers like that, but I was determined to fit in. Most of the people were in the music business. Our house was just down the street from The Grateful Dead's place.

We got in very late, brought in our gear, and went to sleep holding hands.

Since he paid a good share of the rent, Jeremy and I had a room to ourselves. After a couple of days, he laid an ultimatum on me about having sex, even though, to my way of thinking, things were hot and heavy. I was a little scared of going all the way and stopped him once again.

He sat up in bed and moaned. "Sugar, maybe you're too young for me. You need to get with it, or I'm gonna have to move on."

That hurt me, and I turned away, not wanting him to see my tears. He pulled me close and soothed me, smoothing my hair. "Hush now, sugar. You know I love you, right? But it's gotta be soon." He groaned, "Real soon."

Hearing him say he loved me made my heart swell with joy. This was what I was waiting for. True love made all the difference. I nodded and whispered, "Okay."

The next morning, I asked one of the girls for advice. Vicky was with Al, a session keyboard player and Jeremy's best friend. I found her in her usual spot in front of the bay window doing her beadwork.

"Hey, Vicky, can I ask you something?"

She put down her project and said, "Sure, what's up?"

I didn't know where to start. Gulping, blushing, I looked everywhere around the floor, but not at her. "I know you and Al are…together…and Jeremy…."

Vicky smirked. "I'm picking up that you have a question about sex."

My face burned with embarrassment. "How'd you know?"

She shook her head and laughed. "I do have eyes. You're real young and new to the scene. I bet you're still a virgin, aren't you?"

I could only nod.

"You don't need to get hung up on it. Just make sure you protect yourself. You have to be married to get the pill, but I can turn you on to a clinic where they just take your word."

"Okay. Are you on the pill?"

"You bet your life I am. I don't want any ankle-biters just yet. I'm with Al right now, but you never know what the Universe will put in your path…" She picked up her beadwork, churning out more of the headbands she sold to the tourists.

My decision made, I wasted no time and headed out to the clinic. The moment of truth was near.

I wanted my first time to be special. Otis Redding was on the tape deck. Patchouli incense smoked in a dish next to the bed; I draped a red paisley scarf over the lampshade. I went to the bathroom and put on my new, white, lace-trimmed nightgown—at least it was new to me. Scored it at the Free Store while sorting through the castoffs of the rich people. Looking in the mirror, I saw a frightened girl looking back. Next time I gazed in the mirror, a woman would be staring at me. I shivered a little.

When I walked into our room, Jeremy was waiting for me in bed. He sat up and held out a pink rose. My vision blurred for a moment. I let out my breath. Didn't realize I'd been holding it. I went to him.

The streets in the Haight were busy day and night. Music was everywhere. There were concerts at the Fillmore, in Golden Gate Park, and even in our house. The guys hung out at the Jabberwock, hoping for a gig. I immersed myself in the music scene, although I was aware of the other, less savory, aspects of life in the Haight.

Vicky took me under her wing and showed me around the neighborhood. I was glad because I hadn't felt any friendship vibes from the other chicks and needed a friend besides Jeremy. She pointed out the Drugstore Café, notorious for hard drugs, and said to steer clear of that place. A little pot, a little Owsley, was one thing, but heroin and cocaine scared me.

We waded through the throngs of kids on the street. Vicky shook her head at them and sighed. "Thank you, Life Magazine. Man, where do they all think they're gonna stay?"

I squealed. "Watch your step! I think I just stepped on a rubber, a used one."

Vicky answered, "Yuck! And these idiots going barefoot. I saw a syringe in the gutter."

How lucky I was to have Jeremy, or I might be among the horde that lived on the streets, scrounging money for food.

We saw kids freaking out on bad trips. They covered their ears and screamed, stripped down right in public, or yelled nonsense while pulling on your sleeve. Obviously, they got hold of bad acid.

I couldn't imagine how folks in Odessa would react if they saw this. Well, maybe I could. Sure, I had misgivings when I witnessed the freak-outs, but I refused to even consider going back.

Vicky and I loved the record stores, especially the Juke Box, although we never bought anything. After all, we lived in a house full of musicians.

Another of our regular stops was to see the new artwork in the window of the East Totem West poster shop. Most of the time, I just browsed, but one day I saw two posters that spoke to me. Mesmerized, I dragged Vicky through the door and tried to decide between "Pipe Dreams" and "Morning Star." Each cost two dollars, so I could only afford one. After a few moments of vacillation, I settled on "Morning Star," with its blues and yellows. It was a splurge, but I had to have it.

When we got back on the street, Vicki looked at my 501s, her mouth puckered with disapproval. "Janie, we gotta get you some new threads. Let's hit the resale shops. I know a chick at Volunteers of America."

"I don't have much money. And I just spent two dollars I probably shouldn't have."

Vicky laughed. "You won't need much. Can you sew?"

"No, never did learn." I shuddered, flashing on Mama forcing me to sew buttons on Daddy's shirt. She was so drunk, I worried she would put out my eye with the needle.

"Don't worry. I'll help you. We can stop by the Free Store, too."

I nodded. "Yeah, I love that place. I found this shirt there."

Vicky tilted her head. "Nice. Love the bell sleeves. Great score."

When we got back to the house, Vicky took a pair of scissors to my Levi's, shredding them in strategic places and sewing on patches. She worked wonders with the rags we bought. I had a whole new wardrobe—long flowing tiered skirts, shawls, vests. All the jeans were too short for me, so she added bands of fabric to the hem. No high-water pants for me. Her eye for color and pattern was amazing. I helped the best I could. Maybe I went overboard, adding lace and fringe to every garment.

"I couldn't have done this without you. How can I thank you?" I gave Vicky a hug.

She smiled. "No need to thank me. Putting out good things into the Universe brings good karma."

Every time I ventured out, the sidewalks were more crowded. Tourists came to see the hippies they'd seen on the news. What a weird scene—all these squares and establishment-types from all over the country driving by, toting cameras with shocked looks on their faces, like they were at the zoo or something. The tour buses were the worst. Lots of the kids gave the lookie-loos a show—giving them the finger, flashing them, or acting stoned. But most of them didn't have to act.

The Flower Children were into street theater, painting their faces, and handing out flowers to the gawkers who descended on our neighborhood. They danced up and down the streets, twirling and flashing peace signs and intoning, "Peace!" I thought they were like children living in fairyland, blowing bubbles, their heads full of flower petals and rainbows. Disconnected from reality, a lot of them wore actual rose-colored glasses.

One thing that got me tied up in knots was the antiwar movement. I was torn, being raised to be patriotic and supportive of the military, but I didn't believe in the war. So, I stayed away from those folks. Just too heavy.

My focus was Jeremy. I spent every minute I could with him. I loved being in love. When thoughts of Lubeth's heartbreak and death crossed my mind, I whispered a prayer for her soul. I pictured her up in heaven smiling down on me, happy that I had found true love. Every night I gave thanks to Jesus for Jeremy, pushing away thoughts about what He would say about me living in sin. It didn't feel like sin to me, and I was sure we would get married one day.

I stayed friendly with Janis. When she was on the road, I watched her dog Scout. He was a good dog and real tolerant of my cat, Jubal. Well, Jubal came with the house so, technically, he belonged to everyone, but I liked to think we had a special bond. He was the spitting image of Alice, Aunt Penny's cat, down to having a solid white ear on his otherwise calico self.

Live in the present became my motto. Maybe I snitched it from The Grassroots "Let's Live for Today." That tune had some good advice: don't worry about the future. In addition, I did my best to forget the past. I think it was Isaiah who said: Forget the former things; do not dwell on the past.

I scrubbed my mind clean if I ever thought about my so-called mother. While I felt a twinge of guilt about leaving Daddy, I figured he was hardly ever home anyway. Tom was living his own life in Lubbock, but I did owe him a phone call. Short of cash, I panhandled for a little change from the citizens who came to stare. Not my usual thing, but my rebellion was rearing its head and why shouldn't the squares pay admission for the show? I found a working phone a couple of blocks away where it was quiet.

Digging in my pocket, I pulled out the paper with Tom's number I always carried with me and put the coins in the slot.

He answered after two rings, and I was surprised he sounded like he was right next to me.

"Hey! It's me, Janie!"

"Jesus! Daddy called and told me you'd gone missin'. Where the hell are you?"

"San Francisco, California, is where I am."

"What the hell are you doing there? How in the world did you get to California?"

"I hitched. And I'm doin' fine, by the way. How're you?"

"Janie, I'm fine, but what're you *doing* there? You're not a *hippie*, are you?"

He sounded stern and concerned, almost like he was my daddy. That got my back up. I was living my life the way I wanted and didn't need a lecture.

"Look, Tom, I just called to say hey and let you know where I am. There's no call to talk to me like I'm a little kid. I'll call you when I have more change, I mean time—"

"Wait! Don't hang up! I'll tell Daddy you're okay, but you should call him yourself."

"Never. What if *she* answers? I won't do it."

"Why? What happened between you two?"

"I don't want to talk about it, but it was bad."

Tom sighed. "So, she's drinkin' again?'

"Again?" I snorted. "She never stopped, despite what Daddy thinks."

"Yeah, he's blind to her many flaws. We know better. Okay, for now. But I want you to stay in touch with me. Take care of yourself and remember, you can call me anytime."

"Thanks. I mean that. But I'm happy and doing great. I'm with a real sweet guy. Jeremy. He's a ro—musician, and he's from big D."

"A Texan? Well, he better treat you right or your big brother will have something to say about it. Got some love news of my own. Her name is Jolene, and she just may be the one."

Had Tom finally discovered there was more to life than basketball? "That's exciting. I'm happy for you." I couldn't think of anything else to say. His life was so different from mine and I just couldn't relate. "Well, gotta go."

"Janie—"

The operator cut in and said to deposit forty-five cents I didn't have, so I hung up.

My starry-eyed fascination with Jeremy came to an abrupt halt not four months after we first made love. I know it was a Tuesday because that was the day we picked up free bread from the Diggers at All Saints. Everyone else was out on the streets, at least that's what I thought. A couple of the girls had straight jobs in the shops, some of the guys panhandled between gigs, and others hung out in the parks and played their guitars for tips.

Jeremy didn't get up, just grumbled and pulled the covers over his head, even though one of our routines was to go to All Saints together. I didn't think anything of it at the time—we had stayed up late, and he was probably tired.

I walked down Waller and glanced around for any skulking narcs left over from the raid at The Dead's place last week. No one was on the street; most likely folks were keeping a low profile. There wasn't even a line for the free bread, and I got my loaf and headed back to the house.

After putting the bread in the kitchen, I went into our bedroom to see if Jeremy was awake yet—and it turned out, he was. A fog of marijuana smoke cleared to reveal him, awake, and busy. And not alone. The chick in our bed had moved in a couple of days ago. She came in from some place in the Midwest and, if I remembered correctly, she was sleeping with Jeremy's friend Jon last night.

The sight was like a punch in the gut. I let out a cry that interrupted the action under the covers. Jeremy looked up and slurred, "Hey, Janie, come on and join us, babe." The odor of weed choked me. He was stoned out of his mind. The skanky little blond-headed chick sat up and smiled, beckoning to me.

Free Love, that's what I was seeing up close and personal—real personal. I knew about free love, but hadn't witnessed any, until now. Sleeping with people as easy as shaking hands, passing each other around like candy? Anything and anyone goes? Orgies? I knew some of the scene was like this, but where I came from, folks didn't carry on that way. That kind of behavior wasn't for me. Even if I was living in sin, I'd held out for true love. Or so I thought.

I ran out of the bedroom and slammed the door for good measure. Tears blinded me as I stumbled into the kitchen. Our bedroom door creaked open, then closed. I heard low voices and then the soft patter of bare feet. The front door slammed as the bitch left the house.

Sitting at the table with my head on my arms, I felt my heart shatter. I sobbed so hard I fought for air. Jeremy hurried into the kitchen. I took a peek. He stood there barefoot, wearing only his patched jeans, still unzipped. He looked as guilty as a dog that stole the meat loaf off the counter and got caught.

Jeremy knelt beside my chair, but I wouldn't acknowledge him. He brushed my hair back and spoke softly, "I'm sorry, sugar. I was stoned. We got to talkin' and she's a cool head, and well, one thing led to another. You know how it is…"

I stubbornly kept my face buried but couldn't help answering. "You weren't involved with her head if I recall. I seem to remember other, more intimate body parts were involved. And no, I do *not* know how it is."

"Okay, I get it—not your thing."

Raising my head, I glared at him. "You bet it ain't. I have more respect for myself." I sniffed and dabbed my eyes with my sleeve, couldn't bear to look at his cheating face.

He rubbed my back. Small, tender circles.

I didn't stop him and hated myself for that.

Jeremy stood, and I glanced up at him. He caught me looking, and his slow smile spread across his mouth. His brown eyes crinkled in the corners, and he said, "So, where do we stand?" He spread his arms like he expected me to jump right into them.

"Damned if I know." I couldn't take my eyes off his bare chest and started to cry all over again as I pictured that poaching little whore's head resting there.

He rubbed his stubbled jaw. "Hey, don't flip out." He reached out for me.

I jumped up and shrieked. "Oh, I'll flip out. You'll see flippin' out like you've never even imagined. You said you loved me!" I lunged at him and pounded my fists on his broad chest.

Jeremy didn't move, just let me pummel him. Then he said, over and over, his voice cracking, "Janie, I'm so sorry, so sorry, so sorry…"

Like a fool, I fell into his arms. We held on tight to each other until my sobs stopped. He grabbed my hand and led me out of the kitchen to the living room. I planted my feet because I wasn't about to go into our bedroom. Not until it was disinfected.

"Wait here, sugar. I'm gonna clean up our room. Then we gotta talk."

I wiped my eyes with my swooping sleeves and said, "Be sure to use plenty of bleach. I'll make us some peppermint tea." In the kitchen, I filled the kettle. I heard the washer start and pictured the sheets where Jeremy had lain with that tramp. I doubted mere water and detergent could cleanse them of betrayal—if it was up to me, I'd burn them. With two steaming cups of tea in my hands, I dragged myself out to the living room. Jubal hopped on the couch and snuggled in next to me. Such a sweet cat. Placing the tea on the side table, I scooped up Jubal and rubbed his soft ears.

A few minutes later, Jeremy came back and plopped down beside me on the ratty couch. He'd put on a shirt and zipped his jeans. He seemed to be having a hard time meeting my eyes.

Jubal scooted away. For some reason, he didn't like Jeremy. Could cats sense treachery?

We sat and sipped our peppermint tea. I stayed quiet, waiting on him to start.

"I want to make it up to you. If I could go back in time, I'd a gone with you to All Saints so it never would've happened." He put a hand on my knee. "You believe me, don't you, sugar?"

Cold needles pricked the back of my neck. I wanted to believe him, but I couldn't figure what was niggling at me. So, I didn't say anything.

Jeremy put his cup down and took mine, setting it on the end table. Grabbing my hands, he said, "Look, the scene here is over. The Haight's headin' downhill fast. You can't walk down the street without steppin' in puke or worse, or gettin' hassled. Then those dealer murders—Shob and Superspade gettin' iced this summer." He shook his head.

I couldn't help it. "And now you in bed with that...that...that slut." Determined not to cry again, I scooted to the corner of the couch and clapped my hands over my mouth.

His brow furrowed, but he didn't respond to that. "The Hippie Funeral got me thinkin.' Maybe we should get out of Dodge, go to Austin."

"Austin, *Texas*? Why?"

Jeremy moved closer and again put his hand on my knee. "When Roky was in town last week, he said the 13th Floor Elevators could use another roadie. Maybe I'd even get to sit in and play a little."

Surprised, I searched his face. "You never said anything to me."

"Well, sugar, I had to think on it. I believe it's the right thing to do for my career. And our relationship."

That's what got me, "Our relationship." I wanted a fresh start more than anything. I didn't even think to ask what happened to his Steve Miller gig.

"Just make sure we don't pass through Odessa on the way back."

"You got my word, sugar."

A few days later, we packed up his bass guitar and amp, our threads, and a few posters and books. We didn't have much. Vicky wouldn't let me take Jubal, but I guess that was only fair since he belonged to everybody. I kissed his sweet head goodbye. One of these days, I promised myself, I would have a cat of my own.

We loaded the purple van and headed out to Austin. I was putting on some miles fairly quick, and not just geographically. Seventeen might seem young, but I felt a whole lot wiser than most folks my age.

When we crossed the Texas state line, well south of Odessa, I thought about the chicks in my high school class who were probably out shopping for winter formal dresses with their mamas. So lame, mere children. Hard to believe how much I had matured in a few months. I was a woman, and I sure didn't need a mama anymore.

Chapter Six

GOODBYE, MAMA–MAMA'S FUNERAL–ODESSA 1984

"Amazing Grace, how sweet the sound..."
How sweet, indeed. Mama has come full circle, and so have I.

Jane sat ramrod straight between Daddy and Tom in the first row of the First United Methodist Church, a place she had sworn she would never set foot in again. But the last time she had darkened the door, it was the First Methodist Church, and so she had kept her word by a technicality.

Walking down the aisle to her seat had evoked unwanted memories. She shut her mind to the other funerals she had attended there, marveling that time hadn't touched the interior of the church. Her daddy gripped her hand tightly, and she clung to him just as hard. The place was nearly full. Jane wondered if the congregation had shown up for Daddy's sake or for the return of the basketball hero, Tom. Hard to believe it was for Mama. Apparently, Odessa Methodists still considered funeral attendance a solemn duty. Daddy had always claimed that people came for the free entertainment. Jane thought he was right. She heard the whisperings and flinched at the sidelong glances and staring eyes.

Take a good long look, everybody. Seventeen years since my last appearance and that's too soon.

Her eyes widened when she saw Rick Mills lounging with his arms spread across the back of the last pew, as relaxed as if he were in his own living room. He winked at her, and she felt the heat rise in her face. She averted her eyes, continued to the front pew, and slid in next to Tom. Her daddy took the aisle seat.

Jane leaned close to Tom and whispered, "The whole darn town is here. Hope they enjoy the show."

He replied, "There won't be a show—Mama's gone."

She gasped, but figured he was right.

Down the pew, Shane and Summer fidgeted in their seats. Jane sympathized with them, remembering her own difficulties sitting still in church. Jolene bent her head to speak to them, placed a hand on Shane's knee, and smoothed Summer's wild hair. Jane noted Jolene's kindness and contrasted it with Mama's lack of the same. *It still hurts.*

The cloying smell of carnations, the lugubrious organ music, the starched lace hankies, the outdated black dresses and ill-fitting suits called into use only for these times—all these things were, on one level, oddly comforting in their familiarity. But on another, deeper level, they made her hyperventilate and her stomach churn, even as she kept up her brave front.

The hymn ended with a discordant reverberation, and Preacher Henry lifted his arms to greet his flock. When he began to speak, there were audible sighs and a few groans as everyone settled in for a spell. He hadn't eased up the least little bit in his dotage, and the crowd knew it. His legendary verbosity would die with him.

Jane's eyes crossed with boredom. She caught herself and felt a twinge of shame for acting the fool at Mama's funeral. As a child, she had believed Jesus watched her every move in church; she didn't know what she believed about Jesus now. She glanced at her daddy to see if he had noticed her foolishness.

He clutched a handkerchief so tightly that his knuckles were white. As he stared straight ahead, his lips pressed together, and his chin quivered.

Even though Daddy was a little shaky, he was holding it together, at least for the moment. She felt relieved because she had no idea what she could do to help him. Her mind could not access the material about grief from her psychology classes. *What* were *those stages of grief*? She returned her gaze to the front of the church and let her mind wander.

Confused by Tom's revelations of yesterday, she pondered how this knowledge would affect the rekindled bond with her daddy. Today was not the time to address what she had learned, but she wondered why she never had the same insight as her brother. After thinking about Tom's analysis overnight, she had to agree that Daddy's priority had been shielding Mama from the consequences of her drinking. *Tom and I were what? Afterthoughts? Collateral damage?* For a moment, she heard Lauren remind her if she let resentment fester, her sobriety might be endangered.

Her mind turned to Aunt Penny and Uncle Rafe. The thought of her aunt never failed to pierce Jane's core with sorrow. *Where was Rafe?* She wondered if he couldn't bring himself to come to his sister's funeral. Jane hadn't laid eyes on him since he and Aunt Penny moved to Dallas, not long before John F. Kennedy was assassinated. Those two events were forever intertwined in her psyche, not that one had anything to do with the other. Funny the connections the mind makes, how it works—or doesn't work. That line of thought sent her spinning into the litany of loss she had suffered in her twelfth year: Mavis's death, losing Rick's friendship, Tom's departure for college, her aunt and uncle moving. How did she endure those four years until she finally left home? Didn't Nietzsche say, "That which doesn't kill us makes us stronger?" Maybe he was right.

To learn, after all this time, that her aunt and uncle wanted to remove her from her dysfunctional home was stunning and would take a lot of processing. Exhausted from the mental journey through her past, she tuned into Preacher Henry as his booming voice filled the church.

"Friends, we have gathered here to praise God and to witness to our faith as we celebrate the life of Martha Jennings," the pastor thundered.

The dance-party lyrics of Kool and the Gang's "Celebrate" played on Jane's inner jukebox. *How very inappropriate.*

Jane's life had it all: grief, regret, psychic pain, anger, guilt, shame, human angst, all the makings for a Hollywood movie—or a career as a psychologist. Personality integration, cognitive behavioral therapy, developmental psychology. Maybe her attraction to the field was only a quest for the tools to figure out her own life.

She decided not to take a summer course this year. *My mind is spinning—does being aware of it mean I'm* not *crazy?*

Preacher Henry roared, "Out of the depths I cry to You, Lord: Lord, hear my voice. Let Your ears be attentive to my cry for mercy. If You, Lord, kept a record of Sins, Lord, who could stand? But with You there is forgiveness, so that we can, with reverence, serve You." The minister was well into his groove.

Lord, have mercy! Sins. Forgiveness. There can be no forgiveness now.

Her whole body shuddered. Daddy patted her knee. Tom gripped her left hand and squeezed. Jane let out a breath she didn't realize she had been holding. She forced her attention back to Preacher Henry who was still gassing on. Tom was right, he was using every word in the English language, several more than once, like "everlasting," "praise," and "glory." She grasped Tom's hand and peeked at him. He met her eyes and winked. Jane bit the inside of her mouth, trying to keep a proper funeral face. How Mrs. Foster and the rest of the faithful would wag their tongues if she cracked a smile at Mama's service.

"You prepare a table before me in the presence of my enemies."

That about sums up the reception.

After a few more prayers, Preacher Henry intoned, "The peace of God which passes all understanding keep your hearts and minds in the knowledge and love of God, and of his Son Jesus Christ our Lord. And the blessing of God Almighty, the Father, Son, and Holy Spirit, be among you and remain with you always. Amen. The service is ended."

Jane knew the drill. Everyone would troop up front to bid a fond adieu to Mama. She set her jaw, threw her shoulders back, swallowed her dread, and held tight to her daddy's hand.

Daddy drew up to his full height, raised his head high, and with great dignity walked with Jane to the casket.

She stood hip to hip with him as they faced Martha Jennings for the last time. Jane's eyes welled as she gazed down at her. Mama looked like an aged child. Her body barely made a bump under the coverlet. No one could say she appeared natural or at peace—she looked tired, resigned, and shrunken. The flowered dress gaped away from her prominent collarbones. And damned if they hadn't put a curl in her gray-brown, stick-straight hair. What was it with these funeral home cosmeticians—was it a law that the dead must have curly hair?

Her daddy made an indescribable sound and reached out a trembling hand toward his wife. He stopped before touching her and clenched his fist.

Jane watched as he brought his hand back to his side in slow motion.

His voice was thick as he said, "Martha, 'til we meet again. As our song says, 'I'll be seeing you…'"

"Goodbye, Mama." Jane leaned against her daddy, and the two turned away in unison. It wasn't clear to her who was holding up whom. As they walked up the aisle toward the exit and some fresh air, her father said, "I see you picked the dress she bought to wear to your weddin'."

Jane's step faltered, and she exclaimed, "Daddy, my God!"

"Yep. Tom told us you was tyin' the knot, and well, she was hopin' you'd invite us."

Tears threatened, but Jane controlled herself. Why should she cry for Mama? "Oh, Daddy, I'm so sorry. We just had a civil ceremony. Nothing fancy. I never even thought…"

"It's okay, honey." As they walked into the sunshine, he reached for her hand.

Uncle Rafe leaned against his Cadillac. He had double-parked, confirming his late arrival, and explaining why Jane had not seen him in the church. He spotted them, took a step forward, and attempted a smile that didn't quite make it. There was a stiff and wary handshake between the two men, and then her daddy excused himself, saying he had to talk to the funeral director about the ceremony at the graveside.

Rafe's eyes were sad, his face lined with sorrow. Because he had never remarried, Jane believed he never got over losing his wife. Rafe opened his arms, and she fell into them as if all the years gone by didn't matter.

Aunt Penny had wanted a child desperately, and that desire resulted in her death. She would have made a wonderful mother. *She wanted to be my mother.* Jane's body trembled as she contemplated what might have been. *Then there's Mama, the "Mommie Dearest" of the West Texas working class. No, can't go there today. Must rise above my resentment. Let it go. Let go and let God.*

"It's so good to see you, girl." Rafe released her from his embrace and walked with her, placing his arm over her shoulder. "I heard you got married. Where you hidin' him?"

Jane had the grace to hang her head.

Everyone looks at me sideways when they find out I came alone. Will Uncle Rafe judge me?

"I asked him not to come."

Rafe looked as if he were swallowing a question, and it was not going down easy. He didn't comment, just nodded.

Jane relaxed. The childhood bond with her uncle remained strong and was a comfort. No explanations or words required. They stopped at her rental car. She decided now was not the time to discuss what she'd learned from Tom. She opened the car door, tossed in her purse, and turned back to him. "Are you going to the cemetery?"

He squinted in the bright sunshine, took a pause, then slowly nodded his head. "Yeah, it's the last thing I can do for my sister. Things were never the same between us after our mother set me up for college. Martha always made sure I knew she felt cheated."

Jane touched his arm. "I remember. She was so bitter about getting pregnant at such a young age. And she wasn't shy about saying so."

Rafe shook his head and grimaced. "That's Martha—laying her misery on her kids." His gaze shifted from the ground to Jane. "I'm glad you came for the funeral, honey. Hope you get some closure and some peace."

Jane's eyes brimmed. She whispered, "I do, too. Seeing her in the casket...it made me second-guess myself about not talking to her all these years."

He patted her shoulder. "Listen, kid...it is what it is. Go forward from here. You came for the living. Martha was a tortured soul. She's at rest now."

He kissed her gently on the cheek.

Jane hugged him and held on tight. "I'm not one for watching folks get put in the ground, so I'm heading out to Daddy's to help Jolene and Summer set up the food. Will you be coming out to the house?"

Rafe looked down and shook his head. "No, honey. I'm gonna get on the road after the interment."

"Oh."

"Maybe I'm not a big enough man, but the thing I can never forgive her for is the way she treated Penny. I almost didn't come today."

Jane touched his arm and said softly, "But you did come, Uncle Rafe. Thank you. It was wonderful to see you."

He smiled half-heartedly and said, "I better get in line. Don't want to hold up the works." He gave her another quick hug and walked to his car.

Jane ducked into the Toyota and watched the funeral procession pull away. *Dèjà vu all over again. Once more, I'm taking a pass on the cemetery. I'll head out to Hell House and help set up the buffet like I did all those years ago when Grandma June died.*

Summer dialed in the rock station so the three of them could dance while they set up the buffet in the dining room. The last few bars of "Hungry Like the Wolf" faded away, and Summer moaned, "That Simon Le Bon is dreamy!"

Jolene and Jane shared a glance. Jane said, "When I was your age, Keith Richard was my crush." She shook her head and continued, "Go figure. He's still alive and kicking and making music. I know it's only rock 'n' roll, but I like it!"

Jolene finished, "Like it, like it, yes, I do!" She waited a beat, then said, "Back to the task at hand. I baked an enormous ham, and it's ready to go. Clear the way. I don't want to drop this!" She grunted as she lifted the platter and carried it to the battered oak sideboard. Placing it on the buffet, she wiped her forehead with the back of her wrist.

Summer said, "That smells delicious. I'm so hungry."

"Like the wolf?" Jane giggled.

"Aunt Jane!" Summer rolled her eyes.

"Folks should be here any minute. Let's get moving. And no sampling!" Jolene picked up a cheese platter and held it high to emphasize the point.

The trio rushed around getting in each other's way as they arranged the large number of casseroles and desserts on the buffet. Jane inhaled the delicious aroma of a fragrant carrot cake with cream cheese frosting.

Dozens of deviled eggs, buckets of potato salad, a gallon of Mrs. Foster's famous secret recipe coleslaw, plenty of Ritz crackers, cheese balls and dips, various finger sandwiches piled high on trays—the sheer amount was dazzling. Everything was homemade and, Jane noted with regret, loaded with carbohydrates. The dishes soon filled the sideboard, with the overflow going on the old pine dining table.

Cyndi Lauper's anthem blared from the radio. "Girls just wanna have fun!" Summer trilled as she boogied from the counter to the table. She came to an abrupt halt, her cheeks reddened. "Should we be having such a good time? I mean...Grandma is dead and all."

Jolene enveloped Summer in her arms, assuring her she was allowed to have fun.

Jane watched the interaction. *Such a nurturant mother.* The sound of a slamming car door ended the moment.

"Ready or not, we're on." Jolene surveyed the spread with satisfaction. "We can feed half of Odessa."

"We're about to," Jane said.

The first one through the door was Mrs. Foster, with Preacher Henry trailing behind her. She was slightly out of breath after the short walk from where she parked, but that didn't stop her usual non-stop commentary. "Half the town is heading this way on Kermit Highway. I do hope I made enough coleslaw."

Preacher Henry held up his arms and pronounced, "May God bless those gathered here today for this bountiful feast." He craned his neck to see just how bountiful it was.

Jane's father, Tom, and Shane arrived right after the pastor and the church lady. Her father looked tired and worn. He listlessly returned her hug.

"It's done. She's at rest." He spoke as if the words were being pulled from his throat. He trudged to the plastic-covered couch and collapsed onto it, resting his head in his left hand, elbow on his knee.

Jane glanced at Tom.

He shrugged and went to speak to Jolene.

Jane's throat thickened and beads of sweat popped on her forehead. The tight hallway felt confining. She hurried outside and stood on the small covered front porch, taking several deep breaths.

A red Corvette pulled in and parked well away from the mundane vehicles driven by the common folk whose daddies didn't own Chevrolet dealerships. The Taylors! Jane hadn't seen them at the church, but being pillars of Odessa society, they must have been there. She leaned on the porch railing as she waited for them to exit the car.

The throaty sound of a motorcycle pulsated through the air. A badass blacked-out Harley burbled to a stop in front of the porch. Rick Mills set the kickstand, got off, and strode toward the steps.

Jane felt a tiny thrill in her chest. She ignored the line of cars that continued to turn in from the lane and focused on Rick as he ambled up to the porch. He wore leathers over his jeans, a denim jacket, no helmet, and a big grin.

Rick stopped at the top of the stairs. "You look mighty nice, Jane. I like the peasant top, a little medieval wench, a little hippie chick." His eyes crinkled as he frankly looked her up and down.

Jane colored. She had chosen her outfit with care, a long swirling black skirt, a bow to traditional funeral attire, but to offset it, she selected a bright, jewel-toned chiffon blouse in a mosaic print with a peplum and flowing sleeves.

Did I dress for Rick or myself?

Rick stepped forward and stood next to her. "I see your old buddy Priscilla and her football hero have arrived. I'm sure you're looking forward to catching up." He smirked.

She glanced at him but said nothing. It felt comfortable having her old friend beside her. When they were kids, he had always listened to her complaints about the snooty town girls. Jane appreciated his support back then—and his sarcasm now—as she steeled herself to greet the approaching Taylors.

Travis sucked in his gut; his formerly massive chest was settling into his abdomen. He sure wasn't in football shape any longer. He solicitously grasped Priscilla's elbow as she wobbled along on her platform shoes. Her black brocade suit's too-tight skirt prevented normal ambulation, so she toddled like a defective wind-up doll. The Dior bag that had recently smacked into her beloved's face hung from her free arm. Travis had to help her negotiate the two steps up to the porch.

Priscilla's pancake makeup cracked as she attempted a concerned look of sympathy. Her condolences sounded trite and rehearsed. "I am so sorry for your loss, Janie." She turned to Travis and gushed, "Isn't that right, sugar?"

Travis had the grace to look sheepish. He nodded to Jane and mumbled, "Sorry." The makeup under his right eye did a fairly good job of hiding the shiner Priscilla gave him yesterday.

Jane bit the inside of her cheek and managed to say, "Thank you for coming. Please go on inside."

Rick nodded and said, "Hey."

Travis ducked his head and grunted in return.

Priscilla did a phony little double take. "Why, if it isn't Ricky Mills! I heard you were back in town. My, it's been a long time."

Rick showed his teeth. "Hey, Priscilla."

She sniffed and turned to her football hero. "We better make an appearance, darling. We don't have much time before we're due at the Country Club." She showed her own teeth and waited for Travis to open the door for her.

Jane and Rick looked at each other, turned as one to look out to the front yard, and cracked up. They tried to keep it quiet, but a few chortles escaped.

Rick said, "She ain't changed a bit."

Jane answered, "And that's a crying shame."

They stayed on the porch for a while, greeting the procession of Odessa's professional funeral-goers. Several mourners brought covered dishes to supplement what had already been delivered. Jane hoped everyone was hungry, because she didn't know how her daddy could ever consume all the food she had seen today.

The parade of visitors slowed, and she turned to Rick. "This feels strangely right, having you next to me to face the gauntlet. Even though it should be Joshua." She regretted the words as they left her lips and peeked at him from under her long bangs.

"So that's his name." Rick tilted his head and searched her face. "Tell me about him. I'm real curious why he isn't here." He folded his arms and leaned against a cedar column holding up the porch roof.

His directness shocked her. She struggled to keep her voice even. "This isn't the time or the place. Anyway, it's so damn complicated, it would take hours."

He nodded. "Fair enough. Tomorrow you're coming with me out to Monahans. I'll give you the tour, and you'll give me the story."

Jane's eyebrows rose as she fought to collect herself before replying. "I see the Emperor of Rangerland still thinks he's top banana."

"And I see the President of Rangerland hasn't lost any of her sass."

After a moment, Jane shook her head and chuckled. She stepped close and touched his shoulder.

He looked down at her hand and then into her eyes.

She pulled her hand away and retreated a step. "I guess I better get back to the reception. Have to check on Daddy."

Rick's smile faded, and he averted his eyes.

As she stepped through the door, her lips trembled, and she whispered part of her favorite prayer from AA, a simple, but powerful, supplication attributed to St. Francis of Assisi. "Lord, grant that I may seek rather to comfort than to be comforted; to understand, than to be understood; to love, than to be loved. For it is by self-forgetting that one finds. It is by forgiving that one is forgiven."

Sure hope Preacher Henry never finds out I'm saying a Papist prayer. He'd drum me right out of the First United Methodist Church.

Several children jostled her as they exited the house with plates full of food. In the small dining room, adults were eagerly filling their plates and perching on any available surface to eat. Tom had rented some chairs, but there was standing room only. The house hummed with conversation. Daddy sat in the same place on the couch. Mrs. Hampton, Priscilla's mother, leaned into him, touching his hand.

Jane rolled her eyes. Mrs. Hampton still thought Daddy was a filet mignon. He looked as uninterested in her antics as ever.

As Jane scanned the gathering, she noticed Priscilla had located her minion, Agnes. They were deep in discussion, craning their necks, looking around the room. Putting their hands to their mouths and tittering, just like on the playground in fifth grade. Some things never changed. Agnes still performed like Priscilla's trained monkey.

Jane felt a tap on her shoulder. She prepared herself to face Rick, but when she turned, Cory stood there. Unlike Travis, he was still in football shape. He raised his arms as if to hug her, then lowered them when he realized that wasn't going to happen.

"Hello, Cory. Been a long time." Jane gave him a polite smile.

"Yes, it has. I'm sorry for your loss." He looked uncertain, as if he wanted to say something more.

A syrupy female voice carried over the ambient noise. "Cory, honey, come on over here," Agnes cooed.

Cory's shoulders slumped, and he sighed as he looked past Jane's shoulder. "Oops, the old ball and chain is callin' me. Good to see you, Jane. Take care."

Jane couldn't resist a quick glance. Agnes's lower lip protruded so far it was a trip hazard. Her plucked and darkly penciled eyebrows formed a single line at the bridge of her nose. Jane cleared her throat to disguise a chuckle. *Agnes, I have no designs on Cory, believe me.*

Cory trudged over to Agnes and bent down to listen to her as she yapped like a little terrier.

A match made in heaven—two matches, by golly—perpetual double dating. And don't all four of them look happy. Ha! Reveling in Schadenfreude. I should be better than this—but I'm not.

Jane came out of the hotel bathroom wearing her apricot silk kimono, wet hair wrapped in a thick white towel, feeling relaxed and pleasantly tired after her usual mile-and-a-quarter swim. She really attacked the water today, beating it into submission, each stroke releasing tension. Concentrating on her stroke had helped tune out the mental chatter that plagued her. The hot shower washed off the chlorine—and the funeral's residue.

Jane wondered how Tallulah was faring. She missed the feline's companionship.

The phone's message light blinked red. She froze for a moment, then hit the button. Joshua's voice growled a two-word message, "Call me."

The bedside clock-radio read eight-thirty. She dialed. The phone rang four times before he answered.

"Jane?"

"Good guess."

He sighed. "Why haven't you called?"

"Why haven't you?" She wasn't giving an inch.

"Oh, for God's sake—I *did*." He paused. "You're not going to make this easy, are you?"

She saw Joshua in her mind's eye. He was wearing jeans and a white dress shirt with rolled-up sleeves, a good look for him. He was running his hand through his hair, a habit when he was frustrated with her, and something she had noticed more often in the past month. Of course, this was all in her head—but that was where she lived—in her head.

"Why...whatever do you mean?" she said sarcastically in her best Scarlett O'Hara, unable to stop herself.

Silence on both ends of the line.

Joshua spoke first. "Lauren called me. You know it's got to be serious when the Grand Dame of AA calls the husband to find out what's going on with her sponsee."

She stammered, "I-I can't believe she'd do that!"

"Well, she did. Seems you missed your weekly 'session,' I think she called it. She was stunned to learn that you never called to tell her your mother had died. It hardly seemed like my place to fill her in, but there you go."

Jane bit her lip. Joshua's voice sounded so clipped, so cold. She shivered. His guard was up, and she guessed she couldn't blame him. He was hurt, and it was her fault.

"Well, in my defense, I did try to call her before I left. But you know Lauren, she doesn't believe in answering machines, so I couldn't leave a message." She pulled the towel off her head, fluffed her hair, and put her hand on her hip. Her voice rose. "Wait, I don't have to defend myself. I haven't done anything wrong. This is my life and my business. I'm handling things here just fine." The unspoken "without you," hung in the air.

"No need to shout, Jane." He spoke in a measured, low tone.

She stomped her foot. "Ooh...just ooh! You're just so calm, cool, and collected, aren't you?"

He sighed again. "Really? Why so hostile? I'm not your enemy. I wanted to be there with you, and you treat me like this?"

"Look, we didn't exactly part on the best of terms. God, was it only two days ago?"

"Three, but who's counting."

She couldn't stop. "Well, time flies when you're having a good time."

"Are you? Are you having a *good* time?" Joshua, who rarely raised his voice, shouted, "What the hell is going on with you?"

Jane's face crumpled, and she threw herself on the bed. She remained silent and looked for a tissue as her throat thickened.

"Jane? Oh, damn it. Sorry I yelled."

"I don't know," she whispered. "I don't know what's going on with me."

His voice became honey. "Babe, please come home. I confirmed your return flight tomorrow. Arrival at four-thirty. I'll pick you up."

She sat there, shaking her head. At last, she croaked, "No."

"No! What the hell!" He groaned. "Unbelievable. No?"

"I'm sorry, honey, I need a little more time."

His voice hardened to steel. "Define little."

"Oh, I don't know. Look, it's been an emotional roller coaster these last...three days. I'll call you. Please don't be mad." She knew he could hear the tears in her voice. "Got to go."

"Jane, wait—"

She hung up.

A box of tissue later, she went into the bathroom and looked at her red, puffy face. *I can't look like this in the morning!* She grabbed her key, stepped down the hall, and got a bucket of ice. She made an ice pack with a washcloth and lay on the bed for several minutes.

Feeling like a little kid about to get a scolding, Jane sat up, reached for the phone, and dialed Lauren. To her surprise, her sponsor answered on the second ring.

"It's your nickel. Oh, I'm datin' myself. I guess it's a quarter these days," trilled the bright and inimitable voice of Lauren.

Jane almost smiled, then sputtered, "Lauren. Uh...It's Jane."

"Oh, sweetie. I'm so glad you called. Maybe one of these days I'll break down and get me one of those answering machine things."

"I doubt that very much."

Lauren chuckled and said, "You're right, it ain't never gonna happen. Girl, I'm so sorry about your mama. I know how things were between you, but losing a parent is a big old life event. And it appears it's one you felt up to navigatin' without your husband or your sponsor!"

Jane winced. At least Lauren couldn't see that through the phone line. "I tried to call you…" Jane whimpered.

"Oh, hush. I'm sure you did. I was makin' a point. You needed someone to lean on and you flew the coop with no backup. You haven't found it necessary to drink or drug out there in the hinterlands, have you, honey?"

Jane huffed, "Never crossed my mind, Lauren."

"No need to get bowed up, dear. I had to ask. Back to Joshua. He sounded devastated when we talked. He's hurt. And confused."

"I just got off the phone with him."

"And?"

"I told him I'm not coming home tomorrow like I planned."

"Why ever not? The funeral's over. Are you stayin' because of your daddy?"

Jane hesitated. "Um, yeah. He's pretty broken up, much to my surprise."

"Jane." Lauren paused. "There's somethin' more going on. I can hear it in your voice. Come clean."

The silence stretched on for what seemed like minutes.

At last, Jane said, "I'm making some connections…reconnections w-with old friends."

"Details, please. I'm sensing there's one special friend, and my gut tells me it's a he. Am I right, or am I right?"

"Well, yes." Jane chewed on her cuticles, ruining her manicure. Realizing the damage she was doing, she stopped and looked at her ragged nails in horror.

Did I pack my coral nail polish? I'll be up all night redoing my nails.

Sarcasm dripped as Lauren asked, "Who is this male *reconnection*?"

"Ricky. Rick. The diminutive doesn't suit anymore."

"Your childhood friend, Ricky?" Lauren sounded puzzled, knowing Jane's history as she did.

"None other."

"And you're stayin' in *Odessa* because of him. What the hell are you thinkin'?" Lauren's voice rose with incredulity. She thought Austin was the epicenter of existence and the pinnacle of human culture. One shouldn't leave unless absolutely necessary, and one should return with all due haste.

"You don't understand—"

"No, I don't. Enlighten me." Lauren's tone cut like a blade.

Jane stood. "Look, I'm on my last nerve. Mama's service and the reception took the stuffing out of me. I'm so tired my eyelashes hurt. I can't talk anymore tonight. I really can't."

Lauren said sternly, "Jane—"

"Lauren, I mean it. The last thing I need right now is a lecture. Please. I'll call you tomorrow."

"Do I ever lecture you? Wait, don't answer that! I can tell you're not yourself at the moment. I'll be waitin' for your call. Get some rest, girl."

Relieved at wriggling off the hook with her sponsor, Jane hung up the phone. Her mind turned to thoughts of death—not of the body, but of love. Was her marriage over? What was this flirtation with Rick? Closing her eyes, she considered the demise of her first love and wondered if she was headed for heartbreak again.

Chapter Seven

Tom to the Rescue-Austin 1970

The phone startled me awake at 2:00 a.m. When I patted the bed next to me, Jeremy wasn't there. I grabbed the receiver and rasped, "Jeremy?"

"No, ma'am. This is Officer Clark with the Austin Police. Is this Jane Jennings?"

"Y-Yes."

"Ma'am, Mr. Jeremy Bonner gave us your name and number. He's been in a fight, and we're at the ER at Brackenridge."

I sat up and threw off the covers. "Oh, my God! Is he all right?"

"He's lost some blood from a knife wound. They're stitching him up now. Doctor says he'll recover. He wants you to get down here."

"I don't have my car. He took it." As if the police cared about my transportation issues. I stood and turned on the lamp while questions tumbled around in my mind. What now? Was a woman entangled in this new mess? Did it happen at the Spoke?

"Ma'am? Are you still there?" The officer's voice betrayed his impatience.

"Yes." With the phone receiver wedged under my chin, I stretched my arm to pull clothes out of the dresser and off the floor, trying to find something to wear.

"Are you coming to the hospital?"

"I'll be there as soon as I can."

SWEET JANE

I caught the last Night Owl bus, but it only went as far as Sixth and Congress. I had a nice long walk to the hospital in the middle of the flipping night, plenty of time to think. Congress was well lit, but I still hurried up the sidewalk, checking around me for muggers.

As I walked, I wondered if my path in life was set at twenty. Sometimes I thought so. I had made my bed, and for sure, I was lying in it. An intrusive memory made me stumble: Grandma June telling Mama that very thing. I couldn't have been more than six, but I could still see them on our front porch drinking from big glasses that I thought contained water but understood now was vodka. Grandma June said, "Pregnant at seventeen, what you think you gonna get? A maid to do your chores? You made your bed, so quit bellyaching, and lie in it."

Now I wanted to get up out of that damn bed I had so foolishly made. My daily routine had become a dull, repetitive grind. All those double shifts were taking a toll. Tonight's knife fight the only excitement I had in months. On some level, I knew this was no way for a woman my age to feel, but I was paralyzed. Waitressing certainly wasn't my dream job. Would I end up with varicose veins by the time I hit thirty?

Going back to school crossed my mind more and more lately, but I didn't know how to go about it and had no one to ask. Maybe Tom could have helped, but I hadn't called him for months, mostly because I was ashamed to let on about my troubles.

I realized I lost my faith in Jeremy a while back. He was no musician. Heck, he wasn't even a roadie anymore. His bass guitar gathered dust, untouched for weeks at a time. He never did tell me how he lost his gig with the Elevators. Maybe he thought working as a bouncer at a country music bar meant he was still in the music business. What a joke!

How foolish to think he would marry me! After years of planning my fantasy wedding, I could picture every detail. It would be held at Zilker Park, atop Rock Island. My fantasy bridal attire: a pink and white, hi-low, tiered skirt, a brown men's vest with a lace camisole underneath, and red cowboy boots. I would wear a crown of yellow and orange flowers. As we said our vows, Jeremy and I would hold hands, a gentle breeze blowing our long hair, the sun shining on our perfect love. Ha! Did they have Academy Awards for stupidity?

Jeremy said marriage was just a piece of paper. Maybe he was right, but he damn sure wasn't about to sign his name to that paper.

Despite the mild November night, I shivered as I cut over to Red River from Eleventh, skirting Waterloo Park. Thinking of all the times he came home late, leaving me to imagine all sorts of things, like an accident, or him with another girl, I got angry and my steps quickened.

I flashed on that time last year I took off work to surprise him at the Vulcan. I walked in before Moby Grape's set, and there he was, sitting on the stage bathed in the kaleidoscope colors of the light show. One hippie chick was licking his face like it was a lollipop while another sat on his lap facing him and moving like—like she shouldn't. I ran home and vowed to confront him about those two tramps when he got in, but I lost my nerve.

I faced the fact I had become a pathetic doormat. Why couldn't I leave? Was I that weak?

On top of all that misery, money was a constant worry. Since Jeremy always cashed his paycheck before I saw it, I had no clue how much he earned. When rent time came around, I had to raid my tips to make up the shortfall. I'd taken to keeping a little stash hidden under a floorboard in the closet. Last count, my little jar held ninety-three dollars and fifty cents—not enough to leave. I stopped short a block from the hospital, acknowledging for the first time my desire for freedom.

Since he began working at the Spoke, Jeremy rarely smoked pot, but came home reeking of bourbon. Given my childhood, Jeremy's drinking horrified me. He wasn't a happy drunk; I saw flashes of anger from him I had never seen when he smoked.

I clutched my arms around myself as if that would shield me from the hard, cold truth raining down on me.

As I walked up Red River, I spied our junker Chevy parked catty-wampus on the street. Did Jeremy drive himself? At Fifteenth Street, I saw the signs to the ER and followed them to the entrance. Pushing the button for the door, I stared at the cop cars and ambulances crowding the drive under the canopy, even at this hour. When I entered, I got a whiff of a harsh, antiseptic smell and realized this was my first time in a hospital. I went to the desk, asked for Jeremy, and the aide buzzed me through the door to the emergency department. A nurse directed me to the white-curtained partition where Jeremy lay on a stretcher. When I saw him, I stopped in my tracks.

A bottle blonde leaned over the stretcher. She wore skin-tight jeans tucked into aqua cowboy boots and a low-cut sequined tank top from which gigantic breasts threatened to escape. She brushed Jeremy's hair from his brow and *cooed* at him. "Does it hurt, honey?"

Jeremy saw me and pushed her hand away. "Thanks for following in my car, Crystal. My girl is here."

Crystal—maybe that was her stripper name—straightened up and her lips formed a pout. "Your girl?" She turned and looked me up and down.

I stood there with my hair uncombed, wearing no makeup.

She smirked.

Although I wanted to snatch her bald, I ignored the slut. My hands opened and closed as I imagined pulling out her bleached hair by its black-as-sin roots. I stalked up to Jeremy, the real culprit. Fury threatened to choke me. My back teeth hurt from clenching them so hard. Pushing the words past my constricted throat, I screamed, "No! I'm *not* your girl. I'm not your *anything*! But I *am* gone." Looking around for something to throw at him—something that would hurt—I spied the car keys on the bedside table and grabbed them. I was about to hurl them at his cheating face, when it dawned on me that I held the means of escape.

Jeremy's mouth fell open. He tried to sit up but grimaced and collapsed on the pillows. "Janie, wait!"

"Let her go, honey," Crystal fussed at him. "I'm here."

I ran out of the hospital, found our junker Chevy on the street, and leaned against the fender, gasping for air. Crushed, I drove back to the apartment on autopilot. What an idiot I'd been! I never wanted to see him again. Like Saul, the scales had fallen from my eyes.

I should have known he was a cheater from the first time I caught him with that tramp in the Haight. Obviously, Jeremy never changed. I considered myself lucky I never got the clap. He was a big believer in condoms—even though I was on the Pill—and now I knew why.

When I got back to our apartment, I picked up the phone and dialed a number I hadn't called in over a year.

A sleepy male voice answered. "Hello?"

"Tom, I'm in trouble. I need help."

I packed up everything I could cram in the Chevy. My clothes, books, posters, two houseplants I'd managed not to kill, even the rug, footstool, and lamp from the living room. Grabbed my cash from under the floorboard. Everything else in the dump could stay. If Jeremy and Crystal came back to the apartment, I didn't want to be there.

There was only one place I could go—Abby's house. Another waitress at Hill's, she was the only friend I had made in Austin. As I drove there, my breathing returned to normal. I vowed never to go back to him. I doubted Abby would be awake at 7 a.m., so I sat in the car and waited. After trying to tune in a music station, I turned the radio off in frustration, wondering why they couldn't play a song once in a while. At eight, I walked up the cracked concrete walk to Abby's rent house and rang the bell.

Abby answered the door in her pajamas, her black hair a mess. She stood back to let me in. "Kinda early, Janie. What's up?"

I gave her a blow-by-blow account of the miserable night.

"What a shit heel! You're better off without him. The only question I got is, what took you so long?" For months, she had listened to me vent about my growing unhappiness with Jeremy. Even though she admitted he was mighty cute when he came into Hill's once to "borrow" some of my tip money, she said he had negative energy and advised me to move on.

I collapsed into a chair. "That's what I've been asking myself. Better late than never, I guess. Crystal can have him."

"Well, you're welcome to stay on the couch until you find another place." Abby yawned. "I'm gonna make a cup of tea. Want some?"

"Sounds good." I followed her into the kitchen. "Thanks for the offer of the couch. I'll keep it in mind. My brother Tom is flying in from Lubbock. He'll help me sort through this mess. Can I lay low here until his flight gets in this afternoon?"

"Sure." Abby rummaged in the cabinet. "Where's that danged sugar?"

I sat at the table. "All my worldly belongings are in the car. I'm never going back to that apartment."

"Don't blame you a bit, girl." The kettle whistled, and she poured the hot water into the mugs, then poured it out.

"Why'd you do that?" I asked.

"Warms the mug. My English granny was a stickler about her cuppa." She put tea leaves into two small mesh balls, placed them in the warmed mugs, and poured hot water over them. "Let it steep for three minutes, take out the infuser, and enjoy."

"What's wrong with a good old tea bag?"

"So, I'm a bit of a tea snob. Shoot me."

She brought the cups to the tiny kitchen table, and we waited for the tea to steep.

Abby took a sip from her mug and swooned as she was transported to tea nirvana. "If you need a shoulder to cry on, I'm here for you."

I sighed. "All my tears are gone. I've cried enough in the last three years."

"Don't shut down. If you need to howl at the moon or beat on pillows, do it."

"I hear you. Do you mind if I take a nap on the couch?"

"Go right ahead. I'm going to get ready. Got a brunch date before work. Just lock up when you leave and put the key under the mat." Her brow furrowed. "I hope you'll keep in touch, Janie."

"Sure thing." *Maybe. Probably not. Jeremy might stop by Hill's looking for me. I need to cut ties.* "Thanks for the tea and advice."

"Sure."

Abby retreated to her room, and I settled on the couch. My mind was too active to allow for sleep. Where had that determined sixteen-year-old who set out to change her life disappeared to? I had been fearless and resolute then. Sure had hitched my wagon to the wrong star.

How had I allowed myself to be totally dependent on Jeremy? When did I become a meek mouse? One thing was certain, I wouldn't ever lose myself to another man. No, I wouldn't give my heart so easily next time.

Waiting at the gate for Tom's flight, I watched the flow of arriving travelers. There were several servicemen I figured were returning from Viet Nam. I got a few skeptical looks at my army surplus camo shirt and felt my cheeks warm.

My mouth went dry thinking about how I would explain the last three years of my life to Tom. He'd been kind on the phone, and I hoped he wouldn't get all judgmental on me. I spied his tall frame coming down the walkway. He had his arm around a smiling blonde wearing a turtleneck sweater and knee-length skirt, who gazed up at him in adoration.

That had to be Jolene. Why did he bring her along to witness my humiliation? Meeting his bride under these horribly embarrassing circumstances would make quite a first impression.

I pasted on a smile and waited for them to approach.

Before I could say anything, Jolene rushed up and threw her arms around me. "Oh, Janie. I'm so happy to finally meet you!" She let go for a moment and searched my eyes. "I'm sorry for your troubles, but we have a plan." Turning to Tom, she said, "I'll let you explain, honey."

Feeling a little overwhelmed by her effusive greeting, I managed to say, "Nice to meet you, too."

Tom put down his bag and opened his arms.

I threw myself at him. Strong and solid, he made me feel safe. Four years faded away as I recalled the last time I had seen him—Christmas, 1966, the year before I left Odessa.

He stood back and studied me. "Dang, girl. You did become a hippie, didn't you?" He shook his head, chuckling, and picked up their overnight bag.

"Hippie? Just because I'm wearing camo? Clothes don't make you a hippie. Those days are behind me. I don't have the cash to update the wardrobe."

"Hey, don't get your back up. Just joshin' you."

We trooped out to the parking lot and found my car.

Tom gaped at my junker and said, "A Chevrolet product? Looks like it's held together with spit and baling wire. Does it run?"

I shrugged. "Most of the time."

Tom took a paper from his jacket, checked it, and asked, "Will it get us to the west side, the Tarrytown neighborhood?" He eyed the Corvair with its faded green paint and frowned. "Don't these things have a rear engine?

Never thought I'd say these words but open the hood so I can stow our bag."

I unfastened the latch, and Tom managed to squeeze their small overnight case in between my "luggage"—the black plastic bags took up most of the space.

"I can find Tarrytown. What's there?"

"Your new home," my brother said with a grin.

I snorted. "What am I, an unwanted puppy being placed in a loving home?"

Tom smirked. Jolene's mouth formed an "O."

After giving Tom a questioning look, Jolene said, "Our minister found us this great couple—"

I couldn't help it. "A couple of what?"

Tom laughed. "And here I was worried you lost your edge."

He didn't know I had lost myself.

Jolene's puzzled look turned into a smile. "I see I'll have to learn y'all's sense of humor. Anyway, our minister knows the pastor at Tarrytown Methodist real well and put us in touch. We asked for someone in Austin who could help you, and the pastor thought of Dr. and Mrs. Harris. They've worked with other kids in the past and may have a place for you."

Kid? I'm twenty, feel like forty, been chewed up and spit out by life, well, by Jeremy.

"Okaaay..." My mind filled with questions, and I turned to Tom.

He explained, "That's why we took a later flight. Scrambling to make arrangements. Dr. Harris is a veterinarian, and Mrs. Harris runs the office. Since their last waif," he shot me a grin, "moved on, their garage apartment is empty. They may even have a job for you at the clinic."

First, I'm a kid, now a waif. Is urchin the next stop? If I was any lower, I'd have to look up at the sidewalk.

Jolene asked, "What do you think, Janie?"

"I think it sounds too good to be true, but I'm willing to meet them. No other options, unless y'all want to adopt me."

Jolene's eyes widened.

I burst out laughing. "I'm kidding."

"Oh! Ha! I'll try to keep up." Jolene shook her head and laughed.

Tom helped Jolene into the rear seat, then contorted his body into the front passenger side. "My knees are up to my ears. Hope it's not a long ride."

The ten-year-old Corvair started on the third try. As I drove cross-town, I had misgivings about moving in with strangers, especially if they were hyper-religious Methodists. A mental image of Preacher Henry exhorting Odessa's faithful made me bite my tongue, so I didn't laugh out loud. But if I wanted to stay in Austin—and I did—this might be my only shot. Fifteen minutes later, I pulled into the drive of a cottage with a wide front porch. The veterinary clinic, closed at this hour, sat on the lot next door.

Tom unfolded himself from the cramped seat, levered the seat forward, and helped Jolene out of the rear bench she shared with the drooping philodendron, spider plant, rug, and lamp. "Next time get a Ford. We're a Ford family. Remember your heritage."

I snorted mentally. Family? Heritage?

Feeling nervous and vulnerable, I followed Tom and Jolene to the front door, hanging back and hiding behind my brother.

I held my breath and let it out in a whoosh when the door opened to reveal two middle-aged people who didn't have the wild-eyed look of religious zealots. No Bibles in sight. Dr. Emil Harris was medium tall, medium weight, with wire-framed glasses over merry eyes. Mrs. Harris, "call me Constance," reminded me of a younger, jollier Mrs. Foster for some reason.

"Welcome. Please come in," said the woman. She wore a shirtwaist dress with a lace collar under an embroidered cardigan. Her warm smile seemed sincere.

Introductions were made. A black cat padded into the entryway and rubbed against my leg. He had one blazing green eye, the other missing. "Who's this?" I asked.

Constance replied, "That's Sammy, short for Samson. He's been a fixture around here since Emil found him on the street two years ago, shot in the eye by some so-and-so with a pellet gun." She gestured to an arched opening. "Let's sit in the parlor."

Sammy led the way, and we all found seats. Dr. Harris said, "That little cat is our clinic mascot. I take him to work every day—on a leash if you can believe it. He's a blood donor for surgical patients on occasion. More than earns his keep."

After a few pleasantries, Constance excused herself to get refreshments. Jolene offered to help, and the women left the room.

Tom leaned back in an armchair. "How long you been here in Austin, Dr. Harris?"

"Please call me Doc. I never seem to reply unless I'm addressed that way." He chuckled. "I moved here from College Station right after I graduated vet school, so almost twenty years. Now, Tom, before you judge me, I had no other option but to go to A&M. Tech doesn't have a program. Hard to go from being a Red Raider to an Aggie." Doc shook his head as if in regret.

Tom commiserated. "I bet. So, who do you root for in the Southwest Conference?"

"Red Raiders."

Tom slapped his leg and exclaimed, "Good man!"

Sammy had remained close to me since I walked in the door. I bent to stroke his sleek fur; his body vibrated under my hand. A muffled woof announced the presence of a dog, and a little terrier of some sort ambled into the living room.

"And who is this?" Tom asked.

Dr. Harris replied, "That's Hank. We've had him since he was a pup. He's a Border Terrier, almost fifteen now. He's lost some hearing I think, given his late entrance, but still sharp as a tack."

Hank sniffed my boots and wagged his tail. He settled on top of my feet. I patted his head, and he sighed.

Dr. Harris chuckled and said, "Hank seems to like you, Janie. Sammy, too."

I relaxed enough to look around the room. Cozy came to mind. Overstuffed chintz couches, a caramel-colored leather armchair, polished tables of warm wood, and a worn Oriental rug. Oil paintings of dogs, hunting scenes, and landscapes glowed under the soft lamplight. How awkward the situation could have been, and how easy things were turning out to be—at least so far.

Jolene brought in a tray with a coffee pot and cups, our hostess right behind her with a plate of baked goods. Constance said, "Not homemade, but Mrs. Johnson's Bakery is the next best thing."

During our getting-to-know-you session, the Harrises laid out the ground rules—no smoking, no drinking, no drugs, no overnight guests. Nothing I couldn't live with, I decided. Constance spoke at length about her ministry, and I realized why she reminded me of Mrs. Foster; they were both what Mama had sneeringly called "do-gooders." Why was I thinking about Grandma June and Mama so much? I needed to wash my mind out with soap.

Doc excused himself to take Hank for his nightly walk. Constance led me, Tom, and Jolene out the back door and up the exterior staircase to the room over the garage. As soon as I walked in the door, I fell in love with the space. Bare wood floors gleamed. The living area held a cushy couch and a small dining table with two chairs. A folding screen, with fabric panels of an oriental design, concealed a double bed and dresser. The bathroom, tiled in sparkling white, looked new. A bath tub! Although there was no kitchen, a tiny refrigerator sat next to a row of storage cabinets under the front windows.

Constance watched as I explored my new digs. "What do you think, Janie?"

I gave her a big smile. "It's wonderful, and better than I deserve. I'll never be able to repay you."

I feel like a refugee, an orphan. Will this "placement" work?

Constance's forehead wrinkled. Placing her hand on my shoulder, she looked into my eyes. "Don't talk yourself down, my dear. Paraphrasing Jeremiah, the Lord has plans for you to have a future and hope." She folded her hands at her waist. "Having a purpose will help. We'll get down to business tomorrow at the clinic." She turned to Tom and Jolene. "When you're done here, just come in the back door. I've made up the guest room—it's at the top of the stairs."

Jolene hugged her. "You're so kind."

My hostess smiled. "It's our pleasure. Breakfast is at seven. See you then."

Tom and Jolene helped me bring in my worldly possessions. I put my shoebox of toiletries in the bathroom and stuffed my plastic bags in the closet. Jolene watered the plants and placed them on top of the fridge. After I arranged my footstool, lamp, and rug, I felt the stirrings of what could be contentment. Hanging my posters could wait until tomorrow. Jeremy would probably be pissed I took them, especially "Morning Star," but he wouldn't have a clue about where I went. I doubted if he even cared. On the other hand, I didn't want to be found. Thinking of him, my happiness evaporated.

I started fading. Not surprising, given the day I had.

Jolene touched Tom's arm. "Honey, we'd better turn in. Janie is about to fall asleep on her feet."

"I see what you mean, darlin'," Tom said to his wife. He took an envelope from his jacket and held it out to me. "This is from Daddy."

My hands remained at my side, and I regarded Tom with suspicion. "I'm not sure I want it—whatever it is."

"Oh, I think you might want to take a look."

I reached for the envelope and opened it, scanning the contents. "My birth certificate. Why?" I would read the note inside when I was alone, didn't want Tom and Jolene watching my reaction, in case I had one.

"He sent that to me after I told him you ended up in San Francisco. Guess he figured we'd keep in touch. Now you can get a Social Security number and become a legit citizen. Stop living underground."

After they left, I unfolded the note. Five twenties fluttered to the floor. Daddy's neat printing read: "Take care, Janie. Hope to see you again one day."

I picked up the cash. "Not likely, Daddy." I brushed my teeth and fell in bed in my clothes. Tired as I was, I had a hard time falling asleep. Lying awake, I wondered why Daddy sent me a hundred dollars. Did he think I would use it to buy a ticket to Odessa? Fat chance.

I woke up a couple of times during the night, sensing I was in a strange place, but managed a few hours of sleep. When I entered the large yellow kitchen for breakfast, I was dragging. At Hill's, I worked the evening shift, so I would have to get used to my new early hours.

Four sets of eyes looked up at me, making me feel self-conscious.

"Morning, y'all." I yawned and took a seat.

Tom announced, "I called a cab for eight-fifteen. Plenty of time for breakfast." He rubbed his hands together. "Smells great."

He and Jolene chatted easily with the Harrises. Methodist stuff about their ministries. I ate and tuned it out.

"Such a delicious breakfast, Constance," Jolene said. "What do you put in your French Toast batter? Nutmeg?"

Recipe stuff. I tuned that out, too, and wondered what my day would bring. Could I trust these strangers? So far, no alarm bells. But the whole church thing made me a little nervous. Methodists—they were everywhere. On the positive side, I had my own space, so I wasn't literally living under their roof, and working at the vet was something I could get behind.

Hank shuffled in, sighed, and sat on my feet.

"I see Hank has found a new favorite pair of feet to call his own," Constance said.

I smiled and reached down to pat him. "I've always been a cat person, but I do like this little guy. He sighs like a human—so funny."

Doc finished his meal and stood. "Got to round up Sammy. Have some prep work before we open."

Tom rose and shook Doc's hand. "Thank you for your hospitality. If you ever need tickets for a Red Raider's game, just give me a call." They exchanged the "guns up" sign.

"I'll keep that in mind." Doc smiled. "Pleasure to meet you and the missus." He nodded at my sister-in-law. "Jolene."

Sammy appeared from the hallway, went to the door, and pawed the leash hanging from the knob. "Cat's got a clock in his belly," Doc said on his way out the door.

Constance said, "We'll go over in about twenty minutes, Janie."

Tom and Jolene said their goodbyes to Constance, and I walked them out to the street to catch their cab.

"Thanks for rescuing me, Tom. I feel pretty good about the Harrises. And the job."

True about the job, but did I mean it about my host and hostess, or was it just the right thing to say? Too soon to know.

I turned to Jolene and set my feet, so the anticipated hug didn't knock me over. "I'm a little embarrassed about meeting you with all holy hell coming down around my ears. You've been kind, and I'll never forget it."

Jolene threw her arms around me again. She was one exuberant hugger. "Honey, no need to be embarrassed. We're family. I know you'll do well here. You'll let us know how you're settlin' in?"

"Sure." *Maybe.*

With her blond ponytail and upbeat personality, Jolene reminded me of Aunt Penny, the only woman who ever made me feel loved—and she wasn't even blood. I touched Tom's arm. "I've been so self-involved, I never thought to ask after Aunt Penny and Uncle Rafe."

Tom and Jolene exchanged a furtive glance. They turned to me. Jolene came to my side, and Tom put his arm around me.

Something awful had happened, something I didn't want to know.

"Didn't think I should lay this on you with all you're goin' through." He took a deep breath. "I'm sorry to tell you that Penny passed away this past spring."

My stomach dropped. I stepped back, bent over, and clutched my waist as if I could stop the sinking feeling. "No! How? She wasn't even forty!" I fought back tears.

Jolene patted my shoulder. "So sorry, honey."

Tom's voice thickened. "She died from a bleeding disorder while she was pregnant. A miracle pregnancy they called it, after all those years of tryin'. But the miracle was deadly. Rafe is...holdin' up, mostly."

"He takes refuge in his job, works long hours. Practically lives at the office," Jolene added.

I squeezed my eyes shut, but I couldn't shut out the knowledge. Wallowing in my own misery, I had been out of touch with Tom, the only link to my so-called family, for too long. I kicked myself for being so stubborn, for refusing to give him my number.

Now I knew why Mama had hushed me up when I was little and asked why my aunt and uncle didn't have children. My heart hurt as I counted the years Aunt Penny had tried to have a child—and the catastrophic result. I felt sick at how easy Mama got pregnant.

Most of my childhood, I had imagined a fantasy life with Aunt Penny as my mother. Sure beat the reality with Mama. I pictured Aunt Penny in her pink and white kitchen, helping me make cookies to take to school for my birthday. I wanted to remember her that way, not bleeding out in a hospital room, losing her life and that of her baby.

The next two weeks were an education. I learned the clinic routine and soon was booking appointments and assisting Doc in the exam room like I was born to it. His calm manner and patience gave me confidence. After finishing an exam and vaccinations for an energetic German Shepherd puppy—huge, fluffy, and uncooperative—Doc said, "You have a knack for this work, Janie."

That pleased me. "Thanks, Doc. I thought Hero might lick me to death. I love animals, always have." My eyes stung as I recalled the many times I asked Mama if I could have a cat and her shrewish refusal as she took another swig from her tumbler of vodka. I blinked fast, so I wouldn't cry in front of Doc.

"Well, you'll get your fill of animals here."

"Good. It's so cool that Sammy comes to work with us." The bell in the lobby rang, bringing me back to the work at hand. I went out to greet the new patient and owner. Already. I preferred the animals to their people.

Constance and I had a routine of eating lunch in the break room. She was more interested in my future than I was.

"I know you left home at a young age, Janie. I'm not going to pry, but if you ever want to talk, I'm a good listener."

I wasn't ready to spill my guts about my early years. Not yet, and maybe not ever.

I'd tell you, but then I'd have to kill you.

"Thanks, but I'm good. I'm settling in. On the right path."

"That's positive. What about school?"

I looked up from my ham sandwich. "What about it?" I regretted how those words came out, but Constance didn't look offended.

"I don't guess you graduated high school. Have you thought about getting a GED? Tom told me you had very good grades."

"What's a GED?"

"It stands for General Education Diploma. You can take a test and get a certificate that's equivalent to a high school diploma."

I perked up at that news. "Amazing! I was afraid I'd have to go back to high school, and I just couldn't face that. I'd feel like an antique among the teeny-boppers."

She smiled. "An antique at twenty? Hmmm. I'll be happy to help you find a GED class for the certificate. Then we can talk about college."

I laughed. "College? You sure are ambitious for me."

"Don't sell yourself short. What do you want to do with your life?"

That was a good question. I would have to think on it.

The Harrises paid me sixty dollars a week and provided my room and meals. I thought the deal was more than fair. My life sure had improved. I was saving money and learning a lot. And I passed my GED test with a near-perfect score of 199.

The Harrises were impressed, and Constance called the University of Texas for admission information.

We sat down in the kitchen one Saturday afternoon to check out the course catalog. A plate of pastries rested on the table alongside the teapot.

Constance paged through the UT catalog. "Tuition is very reasonable, but you'll have to work your class schedule around clinic hours. That shouldn't be hard, especially with your core classes."

"I don't know what I want to be when I grow up," I joked.

Constance chuckled. "You don't have to decide right away. That's the beauty of it. Get those general courses under your belt and see where your interests lead. Emil thinks you could be a veterinarian."

I thought a moment. "You know, I've always been interested in animals. When I was a kid, I roamed the prairie and spent a lot of time studying critters. I dreamed of becoming an explorer in the jungles of Africa." An image of Mavis's limp dead body covered in mud made me blink back tears. I hadn't left her ghost in Odessa as I had hoped.

Forcing my mind back to our discussion, I said, "I loved being outside. Better than being at home—" I glanced at Constance, but she didn't jump all over the reference to my dark past, as I feared. "Anyway, I tracked live critters and tried to catch them." I laughed at my folly. "I studied roadkill, like the dead bodies could show me the secret life of the poor animals. Saw some grisly sights, so I guess I have a strong stomach. And so far, nothing I've seen at the clinic has bothered me. Haven't barfed once."

To emphasize my point, I reached for my favorite pastry, a powdered-sugar lemon-filled donut. I took a bite and wiped the sugar from my lips.

Constance poured more tea and smiled. "Well, veterinary school will give you ample opportunity to mess with dead animals. Is that a yes, or at least a maybe?"

Nodding, I said, "A definite maybe."

I enrolled in late afternoon and evening classes at UT so I could work full time at the clinic. Constance spent less time in the office, although she still came in to do the books. Taking advantage of her free time, she got even more involved at the Tarrytown Methodist Church. I didn't think anything of it until she stopped by the front desk on a Friday afternoon.

"Janie, would you like to accompany us to service this Sunday?" Constance asked.

My stomach did a flip, and my mouth fell open. The Harrises had rules, but nothing that chapped my hide. I found it easy to refrain from smoking cigarettes and pot, never had taken to drink, and had no friends to stay overnight. Was church attendance going to be a new requirement? Memories of the voluble Preacher Henry and his never-ending sermons popped into my head.

Constance tilted her head, waiting for my reply.

I thought back to the Haight and the philosophical discussions with my housemates when we were high. I had heard stories about Jewish guilt and Catholic guilt; everyone had a story about their religious upbringing. Was there such a thing as Methodist guilt? I hadn't set foot in a church since Lubeth's service.

After several seconds of silence, Constance said, "By the look on your face, I'd say the prospect doesn't appeal to you." She raised her eyebrows. "Just an idea," she said evenly.

I sputtered, "I...I haven't been to church since I left Odessa."

"I didn't mean to upset you, dear. It's entirely up to you." She patted my hand and walked back to her desk.

That night, I took a hot bubble bath. I had never had such a nice bathroom, and I reveled in it. Cleaning duties didn't bother me anymore. Mama would be so proud. Oh crap, where did that thought come from? I shook my head to dislodge the image of her sour face. I dried off and put on my pjs.

My habit was to read in bed until my eyes started to close. I wasn't fussy, reading everything from the best-sellers like *Coffee, Tea, or Me?* and *Valley of the Dolls* to Hemingway, Steinbeck, and Flannery O'Connor. I picked up books for a nickel at street sales and Goodwill.

Tonight, I couldn't concentrate on *We Have Always Lived in the Castle*, by my favorite author, Shirley Jackson. Merricat felt so shut out from the village, so isolated, and I could identify. I couldn't wait to find out how the book ended—even though I didn't want it to. Everything Shirley Jackson wrote, from her funny books on family life to her frightening and eerie work, was fabulous. *The Haunting of Hill House* was the scariest thing I ever hoped to read. She died in 1965, much too young. So sad there would be no more of her books to read.

Putting my book aside, I compared this warm, safe room to the shabby flat I had shared with Jeremy. I was over him. He didn't break my heart all at once—it came apart in small pieces, a shard with each betrayal—and Crystal was just the last.

The fiddle in Hank Snow's classic "I'm Movin' On" echoed in my mind. Grandma June's favorite tune.

Where did these memories come from—attacking me out of nowhere? Unwanted and unbidden. Then my inner jukebox self-corrected, and The Rolling Stone's live version cut in. That was more like it. Raucous, life-affirming, straight-ahead rock 'n' roll. Yes, I was moving on. But for damn sure, not into the arms of another man, not right now. I didn't miss Jeremy. I didn't—not the least little bit. But if I was honest, I was lonely. And a little horny.

On the other hand, I had prospects for the first time in my life. A great job where my duties varied; each day different, so I was never in a rut. Holding and comforting dogs and cats, helping them through their fear, made me feel good. My ministry—in Methodist-speak, that is, if I spoke Methodist. I wasn't sitting all day, and I wasn't on my feet for long, dreary hours hauling food. Although a few canine noses had nudged me, no one had pinched my butt in weeks. I didn't miss the come-ons from flirtatious men at Hill's. Wiping up pee and barf was preferable to my former duties.

Now that I was in school, maybe I'd make some friends. I needed to pinch myself. I was in college! From runaway teenager to college student in three easy lessons. My lot in life had improved in so many ways.

All this musing made me feel like an ingrate for not accepting the invitation to attend Sunday service. Going to church would please Constance and Doc. Couldn't I bend a little and go? Didn't have to be a regular thing. My estrangement from Jesus, starting with Mavis's death, through all of Mama's cruelty, and culminating with Lubeth's suicide, might never end. But maybe I could give Him another chance.

Sunday morning, I dressed in my most somber clothing, a long black skirt and an emerald green blouse. I met up with Doc and Constance on the front porch. We walked the few blocks to Tarrytown Methodist Church.

I stopped and gazed at the four tall white pillars fronting the red-brick church. The elegant spire reached toward heaven. Jesus's Austin home looked like Monticello if you took off the dome and replaced it with the spire, but then, First Methodist in Odessa resembled a castle with its square tower. Why was I pondering architecture?

Constance and Doc turned to me. Constance asked, "Are you having second thoughts, Janie? I think you'll find our congregation welcoming."

Sure am. Not sure there's anything for me in there.

I took her hand and smiled. Feeling a twinge of conscience, I lied, "Nope. Just thinking God's earthly home looks different from town to town. What matters is what's inside."

I was going after that Academy Award, for sure.

Doc patted my shoulder. "You're right about that."

I climbed the steps between my two saviors.

Chapter Eight

DETOUR-MONAHANS, TEXAS 1984

Jane panicked as the sides of the elevator disappeared. She, Mavis, and Aunt Penny struggled to keep their balance on the platform as it tilted and yawed. Mavis lost her footing and slid to the side. She clung to the edge. Aunt Penny lunged after her...

The phone rang, waking Jane.

She groaned and reached for the receiver. *Damned elevator dream again. First time anyone else starred in it.*

A robotic voice announced, "Good morning. This is your requested wake-up call. Have a pleasant day."

Remembering her plans for the day with Rick, she sat up straight and threw her legs over the edge of the bed. Jane reflected she usually was not raring to go at six a.m.

She dashed to the bathroom and peered in the mirror. "Not bad, even with too little sleep," she said, smiling at her reflection. After a shower, she dressed in the clothes she had laid out the night before, a pair of jeans and a loose white shirt. It didn't take but a minute to get dressed. Doing her hair and makeup would take most of her time. The fluttering in her stomach made her feel like a giggly schoolgirl getting ready for the sock hop.

"Down, girl," she told herself.

Jane decided to wear her hair in a topknot. Picking through her travel jewelry box, she chose her Texas Star earrings—they dang near touched her shoulders; her motto for earrings was the longer, the better. Violet eye shadow highlighted her green eyes. Peering over her shoulder, she assessed how her butt looked in her jeans and nodded approval. Turning back to the mirror, she took a final look, made sure there wasn't a smudge or imperfection, and picked up her bag.

As she waited for the elevator, she recalled her nightmare and shivered. Then thought about taking the stairs. The doors parted, and she stepped inside. During the slow ride to the lobby, she pulled out her compact and checked in the mirror one more time. When the door finally opened, she stepped into the lobby and tapped lightly in her black Tony Lama's to the hotel portico to wait for Rick.

It was 6:30 sharp. Headlights were approaching. Right on time. Rick pulled up to the hotel entrance in a doorless Jeep.

Jane climbed in the Wrangler with a slight twinge of worry. "At least the top is up and the windshield in place." She smiled at him.

"Good morning, sunshine. You look mighty pretty."

"Thank you, Ranger Rick. I'm ready for my VIP tour."

He frowned. "You too? Damn that children's magazine anyway!" Then he threw his head back and laughed. "Seriously, my name gives me instant credibility with the school groups comin' through the park. I really don't mind it a bit. It's like it was meant to be."

Jane looked puzzled. "What on earth are you talking about?"

"Oh, that's right, probably not on your radar. There's a kid's nature magazine called 'Ranger Rick.' I get teased about it a lot by the guys at work. Once, some joker taped a raccoon tail to my pants."

"What the heck?"

"Ranger Rick is a raccoon," he said.

"Well, that explains it. I had no idea what you were going on about." She settled back in the seat and said, "Too bad we'll have the sunrise at our back." Her voice shook, and she stopped speaking, hoping Rick wouldn't notice her nervousness.

"We might could catch the tail-end of it at Monahans."

Because of the road noise, they were silent during the half-hour drive.

Jane was grateful for the windshield but still a bit apprehensive about the no-door thing. She sat as far to the left as she could and hoped Rick didn't get the wrong idea. Maybe she was the one with the wrong idea, given the thrill of anticipation she had experienced getting ready this morning.

As the sky lightened, Rick pulled in the entrance to the park, drove up to the visitor's center, and braked. "We'll go in later." He put on a tour-guide voice and pointed at the dunes. "There's gold in them thar hills, so the legend goes. You ever heard about the Monahans wagon train?"

Jane turned to him with her eyebrows raised. "Why, yes I have! Don't you remember us planning how we'd spend the gold we found once we got us some prospecting gear?"

"Your memory is better than mine, but now that you mention it, yeah. We never did get to dig for that gold."

"We decided we were going to buy a small country in Africa, or at least a few million acres for our elephants, giraffes, and zebras." She smiled slightly as she recalled their childish plans.

"That's right. We weren't gonna have lions because they might eat the others." He put the jeep in gear and headed out to the dunes.

Jane pondered a few might-have-beens; they didn't get to do a lot of things.

After driving for several minutes, he pulled over. "These little shin oaks, or *Quercus havardii* for you French speakers, have roots that go down seventy feet in their quest for water."

"Tell me, do you write your own material?"

He brushed off the gibe. "Quiet in the peanut gallery. This is a serious tour." He pointed toward a few scraggly trees. "Mesquite's roots have been known to seek water more than a hundred and seventy-five feet below the surface. What d'ya think about that?"

"That's deep, Rick."

He looked at her out of the corner of his eye. "Pun intended?"

She gave him a wide-eyed look and did not reply.

"I see I'll have to dig deeper to impress you."

"Pun intended?"

He gave her that grin she remembered so well. She saw him as a young boy for a moment and felt a pang of loss for those times in Rangerland. Did he recall their adventures with the same degree of fondness as she did, given Mavis's fate?

Rick continued his spiel. "The shin oak ain't a dwarf version of other oaks, dontcha know. It rarely reaches over four feet tall but yields a bumper crop of large acorns."

"I bet the kids hang on every word." Jane chuckled. She recalled their rivalry as kids. Now it was a kinder, gentler kind of teasing.

"Tough audience. But I shall continue, nonetheless. Fresh water can occur at surprisingly shallow depths. Sometimes, transient ponds are found in low areas between the dunes."

"Do tell, Ranger Rick. What animals do you have out here?" She batted her eyelashes at him. Her shoulders relaxed and she began to lose her self-consciousness.

Rick thought a moment. "Let's go to one of the ponds. Sunrise and dusk are good times to see wildlife. If we're lucky, we could see anything from mule deer to cottontail. We've also seen gray fox, coyote, bobcat, possum, javelina, porcupine, skunk, ground squirrel, and of course, the ubiquitous jackrabbit."

Jane laughed. "I see you haven't stopped improving your vocabulary. Remember our competition with your mom's *Reader's Digest* 'Word Power?' I usually won."

He shot her a look. "Did you now? That's not how I remember it."

"And didn't you just say that my memory is better than yours?" Jane teased.

Rick shook his head and smiled. "Touché. Are you ready to take a little hike?"

"Sure thing!" Looking down at her boots, she regretted her choice of footwear.

He put on a John Deere gimme cap and jumped out of the Wrangler. "I'd open the door for ya, but there ain't one."

As they hiked up and down the sand dunes, Rick regaled her with stories about Monahans. "Our park contains over thirty-eight hundred acres of sand dunes, some over seventy feet high. Many of the dunes change shape in response to the prevailin' winds. An ever-changin' landscape." His love of nature and satisfaction with his choice of career was evident.

"Fascinating, Ranger Rick!"

"Thank you, ma'am," he said with a grin. "The first Europeans to discover the dunes were Spaniards. That was over four hundred years ago." He gestured grandly to the west. "These here sandhills extend all the way into New Mexico. Far back as twelve thousand years ago, Apache and Comanche camped in the area. They made a go of it because of the plentiful game and fresh water beneath the sands. Using stone tools, they ground acorns and mesquite beans into an edible paste."

They trekked in companionable silence for some distance. She wondered if the frisson of sexual tension she felt on the porch yesterday was a delusion, given how Rick stuck to his ranger script. This excursion had the same flavor as those from their childhood. *Am I relieved or disappointed?*

Jane stopped for a moment and rested her hands on her knees to catch her breath. "Hold up! Walking in this sand is hard work! Where is this pond anyway?"

Rick didn't appear to be breaking a sweat. He looked down at her from his position on top of a dune. "Just down the other side of this very small hill. Can't the President of Rangerland keep up? Those boots ain't made for walkin', girl." He laughed.

"You're right about that, but I'm trying. I will have you know I swim a mile-and-a-quarter three days a week. Somehow this sand-walking uses muscles I didn't know I had."

He bounded down from the dune. Pulling off his cap, he wiped his forehead with his shirtsleeve. "Sun's gettin' hot. It's past time when we might expect to see any critters. How about we head back to the Jeep, finish the VIP tour in the nice cool visitor's center? I'll take you out for enchiladas after that."

"Deal."

Driving back to the visitor's center, Jane fidgeted, crossing and uncrossing her legs. She pondered what, if anything, she should reveal to Rick about her marriage. What was his motive for this outing? And why had she agreed to join him?

Rick parked, and they walked to the entrance. Unhooking a massive ring of keys from his utility belt and locating the correct one, he unlocked the door and stood back, gesturing for Jane to enter first. "Air conditioning. Thank the Lord for AC. I'll be back in a flash with some *agua fria*."

Jane looked around at the exhibit cases, drawn to the native artifacts and arrowheads in the nearest one. She heard the glug-glug of a water cooler.

Rick returned with two conical paper cups and handed her one. He gave her a sharp look and said, "I seem to recall you were gonna fill me in on your complicated marriage today. Haven't heard a word yet."

She accepted the cup and took a sip. Gazing at the bright posters on the wall instead of him, she said, "I hardly had a chance to talk during your incredible presentation. Let me gather my thoughts."

He leaned against a glass case and appraised her. "You kiddin' me? I think you're stallin'."

Jane studied a wall map of the park, unable to meet his eyes. "No, as I said, it's complex, and I don't know where to start."

"Just tell me this, are you happy?"

"I don't know how to answer that." *Was he asking as a friend, or something else?*

Jane scanned the menu. Rick didn't bother to open his.

"You gotta order the chicken enchiladas *suiza*. My all-time favorite, and believe me, I know my Mexican food."

She nodded. "Sounds good to me." Fussing with her napkin, feeling unsettled, she forced her eyes to his.

Those pale blue eyes. Like that Velvet Underground song, the fact that I am married, and we were best friends. And, yes, it would be a sin. This lunch might be a bad idea.

Jane's head filled with images from their years of friendship when they had sworn undying loyalty to each other and shared disdain for the opposite sex—with the singular exception of each other. They were too young for anything romantic. *Did childhood soul mates ever end up together?*

Rick waved his hand and said, "Hey, there! Where'd you go? Come back and have lunch with me."

She startled and felt warmth spread over her face. "Goodness, I was lost in the past. My mind is so restless, working overtime." Gesturing dismissively, she said, "I'm back."

The waiter rushed up and placed ice water, a basket of chips, and a bowl of salsa on the table. Rick held up two fingers. "*Dos* usuals." The waiter glanced at Jane, raised an eyebrow at Rick and retreated.

She reached for the tall glass of water. "You promised to tell me your tale. Your own personal 'There and Back Again.'"

Rick grabbed a chip and dunked it in salsa. "A Tolkien reference. Interestin'." He popped the chip in his mouth, and mumbled, "Since you're still stallin', I'll go first."

"Okay, I'll go second then." Her discomfort with talking about her marriage hung in the air between them.

How well he knew me at one time—he'd finish my sentences. Sometimes we didn't need words at all. Am I crazy to think there's more than nostalgia at play here?

Rick gave her space. He swallowed the chip and took a gulp of water. The serranos in the salsa made his eyes water. A bead of sweat ran down his forehead. "Whoo-hee. Good salsa!"

Jane's lips twitched in amusement.

He narrowed his eyes and deadpanned, "Do you really expect me to summarize half my life over—"

"Ha! Tossing my words back at me." She laughed, releasing the tension in her shoulders. "Just give me the Cliff Notes version."

"Okay, buckle in and keep your hands inside the cart..." he said with a slow grin.

"Quite the buildup. Now I've got goose bumps in anticipation."

Two heaping platters of enchiladas arrived. The waiter placed them on the table with a flourish and left after refilling the ice water.

Rick smiled at his plate, wiggled his eyebrows, and picked up his fork with great enthusiasm. "Well, I was in pretty bad shape when I fled my humble home. Been drinkin' and druggin' like I was born to it. Rolled into Ruidoso and bunked with my cousin. He was in AA and dragged me to a meetin.'" He took a bite of his enchiladas. "Um, *delicioso*."

Jane said, "Let me do the math—that must have been in sixty-six and, since you have a ten-year medallion, I guess it didn't take?"

He shook his head. "Uh, no. Took about eight years of tryin,' but eventually it stuck."

Taking a dainty bite of her enchiladas, she nodded her approval. She drank more water to cool the chile burn.

He continued, "I got my GED right quick. Did odd jobs for a spell with my cousin, handyman sort of thing. But I never forgot my interest in the great outdoors." He pointed at her plate. "You haven't eaten much."

"I'm letting it cool a bit. Did you get yourself to college?"

He shook his head. "I was using off and on during those years. Tangled with a few women. Nothin' ever worked out. Have to admit, I was stuck in a pattern." He stared over her shoulder into the past.

Jane nodded. "Been there myself."

Their eyes met, and their gaze locked.

No, it's not my imagination.

The waiter took a few steps toward their table, but stopped in his tracks, and retreated.

Jane asked, "Anyone special in those relationships? Did you ever get married or come close?"

He grinned. "Didn't I tell you a long time ago, I wasn't ever gonna get married?" He gazed at her unabashedly.

Once again, Jane found the scrutiny from his pale blue eyes hard to handle. She broke eye contact, picked up her fork, played with her rice.

I should be looking into Joshua's brown eyes. This feels dangerous.

Rick's brow creased. He put down his fork and said, "There was one gal. We were pretty serious for a time. This was about five years ago." He picked up his glass and put it down, stared at the table.

"So, you *did* find someone."

Rick glanced at her, then looked away. "Thought I might have...for a while." He stopped speaking.

Jane waited through his silence.

"Sara showed up at my AA group, back in Ruidoso. Even though she was only three months sober, I thought she had her sh—stuff together. You know what they say, no relationships in your first year." His eyes scanned her face, then moved to another time and place. "I rationalized my way past that rule right quick. Told myself I was five years sober, and I'd be an example and support for her." His fingers beat a tattoo on the table.

He continued, "Thought she was stable. Anyway, we'd been together for a few months." He gulped. "She-she went out for some reason I'll never know." His fingers pinched the bridge of his nose, his eyes closed. "Heroin. First time she shot up, she said." He glanced at Jane, his mouth wry. "Somehow I doubt that."

Jane covered her mouth with her hand. "Oh, my Lord!"

"If there were signs, I missed them. She must've shot up between her toes."

"Yikes!"

"Yeah, nice image. Told her straight up I wasn't about to deal with smack. Guess I didn't handle it very well. She swore she'd go right back into the program, but I told her it was over. Her brother found her dead the next day, overdosed." He hung his head.

"Oh, Rick, I'm so sorry."

He raised his head, eyes bright with unshed tears. Taking a deep breath, he said, "Yeah, me too."

Silence descended like a fog. Rick slumped in his chair, looking miserable.

Jane looked around for a waiter. She needed a refill on her ice water.

"Conversation stopper, huh?" Rick asked.

Jane reached out and patted his hand. "You've had your fair share of tragedy."

He stared at her hand on his. "Most of us have in this vale of tears."

"Sunday school talk. Are you channeling Mrs. Foster?"

Rick laughed. "Ha! Until yesterday, I hadn't seen her in years."

Jane's hand felt too warm, radioactive. She removed her hand from his and said with great eagerness, "Tell me all about becoming a forest ranger in the wilds of New Mexico. Let me live vicariously through your real-life adventures." She leaned forward to show her interest.

"You always could raise my spirits." He sighed. "Not a whole lot to tell. I applied to the state, took my training at various state parks around New Mexico. Got a gig in Capitan—home of Smokey the Bear." He regained his enthusiasm as he continued, "Did you know there was a real Smokey? Poor little black bear cub found with burnt paws after a forest fire back in the

Fifties. Some firefighters saved him, and he lived out his life in the National Zoo in Washington, D.C. of all places. He was laid to rest in Capitan."

"Well now, Ranger Rick, that's the most succinct resume I've ever heard. But it tells me more about the bear than it does you. How did you end up at Monahans?"

"Just lucky. I ran into some bureaucracy at the New Mexico Forest Service. Can't stomach that stuff. There was an opening here, and I thought 'Why not?' and moved on back. So far, the Texas bureaucrats have stayed in their offices, and that suits me just fine."

"I'm glad you have a good situation—even if it ain't Africa."

They looked at each other and smiled. After a moment, they got back to the food.

Rick balled up his napkin and tossed it on the table. "Damn. They do make the best enchiladas." He studied her face, then asked, "While I was givin' you my journey there and back again, you made a rather intriguin' comment. I'd like you to expand on it, if you would."

"I said something intriguing?" Her eyes widened in innocence. "You'll have to remind me."

"It was somethin' along the lines you'd been there yourself when I mentioned romantic relationships that didn't stick."

"You heard that, did you?"

"Well, I am all ears, Jane. Pun intended. Tell me your story from when you left home until, well, now."

Jane patted her lips with her napkin. "That's a tall order, but here goes." Taking a deep breath, she began, "I hitch-hiked to Monterey Pop. That's where I met Jeremy. It ended badly."

"Judgin' by your facial expression, I guess so." Rick signaled to the waiter for another napkin, then dug in again. He gestured for her to continue.

"When I got to the festival, I must have looked like a lost lamb. He was kind, and I fell for him." Her mouth twisted in self-mockery. "He was my moon and stars, and I followed him back to the Haight. In my naiveté, his connection to the music business impressed me. Besides the fact he was mighty handsome." She paused a moment. "How can I keep this short and sweet? Jeremy was into free love, and I was into Jeremy for three wasted years. That about sums up the relationship."

Rick wiped his mouth with his napkin. "That *was* very short. You put Cliff Notes to shame. How'd it end? Don't leave me hangin'."

"He was a roadie with aspirations to play bass in a band. The musician part never came to pass. He kept losing gigs, so we moved to Austin and he got a job at the Broken Spoke as a bouncer."

"The Spoke, huh? That's one legendary honky-tonk."

"Oh, yes. We lived in a tiny apartment in South Austin. I worked as a waitress. We were barely making it. One night he got stabbed trying to break up a knife fight. When I got to the hospital, I learned he was cheating on me—again." She gulped air and pushed back from the table. "Excuse me, I'll be right back." She grabbed her bag and rushed down the hallway to the ladies' room. The past was closing in, and she was back in 1970.

In the restroom, Jane wet a handful of paper towels and put them on the back of her neck. In her mind, she saw that shabby apartment, and blinked it away. She said, "I haven't thought about Jeremy in years. Right now, I'm a throbbing raw nerve. Every trip down memory lane tweaks that nerve until I want to scream." Realizing she had spoken out loud, she craned her head to look under the stalls and was relieved to find she was alone.

Checking her makeup in the mirror, she again wondered what Rick's endgame was. *If this is a seduction, it's the weirdest one I've ever experienced.* Rick had finally broached the topic of romance in the most roundabout way imaginable, and she still had no clue about his intentions. A flashback of her devastating tumble into love with Joshua made her flush with remembered desire—and a hefty dose of guilt. She had never believed it was possible to love two men at once.

How could she even consider this love? Had to be lust, and she knew the cause—pheromones. She had just spent the day in close proximity to Rick. Jane believed in pheromones like she'd believed in Santa Claus when she was little.

Santa Claus? A childhood memory starring Mama engulfed Jane.

I heard Mama in the kitchen, slamming the cupboard doors. Right proud of writing my first letter to Santa, I ran to show her.

Her cigarette burned on the edge of the counter. "No, you can't have a stamp. Santa Claus!" Her lip curled up, nasty-like. "Do ya see a chimney, Janie? Ever see a mule deer up on the roof? Grow up! Ain't no such thing as Santa Claus, the Easter Bunny, or the damn Tooth Fairy. Your daddy buys your presents."

She took another swig from her cup and almost choked, spitting her vodka all over the floor. Then she threw her cup in the sink, grabbed my letter, and tore it up in front of my eyes.

I tasted salt on my lips as the tears rolled down my cheeks. While she ranted and raved, I stood there with my letter—and my belief in Santa—in tatters. I wished my daddy wasn't gone so much. I'd give up my presents to have him home.

Shuddering, Jane returned to the present, patted a tissue to her freshened lipstick, and went back to the table.

Rick stood and asked, "You all right there? I was about to mount a search." He held her chair and returned to his seat.

She forced a weak smile. "Yes, I'm fine—just overloaded on emotion the past few days. Hadn't thought about Jeremy in a long time. Anyway, as you can imagine, that was the end of our relationship."

"Damn. What did you do? Sounds like you were hurtin' for money and pretty much on your own."

"I had only one option. I called Tom for help."

"So, you kept in touch with your brother through all your adventures."

She nodded. "Yeah, I would call him from time to time. He didn't agree with all my life decisions, that's for sure." She picked up her fork and cut off a piece of enchilada, pushing it around her plate. "He flew into Austin the next day with his wife. You met her at the house. Jolene."

Pushing back a few tendrils of hair that had escaped the clasp, she continued. "He got me a job with a veterinarian through some Tech connections. Dr. Harris and his wife gave me a room over their garage. Constance became my surrogate mother, although I wasn't looking for one. It was like going from the West Texas Mommie Dearest to June Cleaver."

Rick let out a hoot. "Damn, girl. That gives me a real good mental picture."

Jane slapped at his arm. "Back to my tale. I had time to heal. I really got my act together."

"That was a soft landin', for sure."

"Don't I know it. Constance inspired me to go to college. I thought I wanted to be a veterinarian but was cured of that real fast during biology lab when I had to dissect a fetal pig."

Rick looked surprised and put down his fork. "Really? With your vast experience of roadkill inspection and forensic analysis? Who'd a thunk it?"

Jane grimaced. "I wasn't eleven years old anymore. Lost my taste for that stuff a long time ago. I like my animals of the living variety and domesticated. Anyway, that's when I turned from studying the body to the mind. And that is the abbreviated version of how I got into psychology." She met Rick's eyes and immediately wished she hadn't.

"By my calculations, that was 1970. You still gotta fill me in on the next fourteen years. We may be here a while." Rick asked if she wanted coffee and signaled to the waiter. "Two coffees, please, and a piece of your famous *tres leches*. Want one, Jane?"

"Dessert? No, thanks. Those enchiladas filled me up."

"Did you actually eat any?"

The waiter cleared their platters and returned with two mugs of steaming coffee and the milk-drenched white cake.

Rick patted his flat stomach and said, "I never pass on the *tres leches*." He took a bite of the dessert. "Jeremy didn't deserve you. I'm sure you were busy with school, but there must've been other men in your life. A woman as beautiful as you..." He trailed off and cleared his throat. Recovering, he continued, "Probably had to beat 'em off with a stick. Even if your first love ended in disaster, you've never been a quitter." He grinned.

Was Jeremy my first love? "Oh, my, you're making me blush. Beautiful? Thank you kindly." She picked up her coffee cup. "I hit the books hard and didn't date for quite a while. Then came Andy." She winced as she recalled the disastrous conclusion of their romance.

Rick regarded her. "Hmmm, I always could tell how you felt about things. You sure don't have a poker face. Stay away from Vegas."

Jane colored and made her expression neutral. "Our relationship, well, it was quite a ride. The only good thing to come out of that time was that I got to AA. Oh, and I finally got myself a cat."

He threw his head back and laughed. "Okay, now you're gonna have to tie that together for me."

Jane's lips made an "O," then she chuckled. "I guess I do. One afternoon, a Porsche raced up to the vet hospital, practically driving through the front window. A guy got out with a Persian cat in distress. Lolita wasn't able to deliver her kittens. Poor thing was in a bad way."

"I take it the guy was Andy?"

"Yes. Dr. Harris performed an emergency c-section and saved all three kittens. Andy was very grateful. My heart melted at his concern for Lolita and her babies."

"And he asked you out?"

"Not then, although he was flirting like a pro. Singing 'Sweet Jane' under his breath, like I hadn't heard *that* one before." She rolled her eyes.

"Which version?"

Jane looked confused. "Oh, 'Sweet Jane.' The original Velvet Underground. Mott the Hoople's cover is a little too pop for my taste. Anyway, Andy came back seven weeks later and made a nice donation to the hospital. He placed a tiny fluff-ball in my hands, the smallest of Lolita's kittens. I couldn't believe it." She paused a moment. "You can't imagine how happy I was. Her name is Tallulah. She's ten years old now. Had to leave her at home and I miss her like the dickens."

"Tallulah and Lolita. Have to admit, those are some interestin' cat names. I remember how much you wanted a cat when you were a kid. Glad you finally got your wish. Sounds like Andy was loaded." He sipped his coffee and took another bite of *tres leches*.

"Trust fund baby."

He stopped eating. "Jesus. Are those real? Never did meet one. What was he like?"

Jane tilted her head and thought for a moment. "Not long on substance, but long on fun. He was high energy—into fast cars and fast boats. He owned several of each." She frowned in disapproval. "Pretty ostentatious in his spending. Oh, I confess I was impressed at first. Who wouldn't be? We dated for quite a while, then he asked me to move in."

"Livin' in sin, were ya?"

"Well, the Harrrises sure thought so. They were serious church folk—they freaked when I left."

"I bet." He returned to his cake.

"Andy had the most amazing place on Lake Austin—a contemporary with huge windows, great views. I never thought I would *see* the inside of a house like that, let alone *live* in one. We had a blast for a while—until we got on a roller-coaster ride that involved...a quantity of cocaine."

Rick leaned in and said, "You're lucky you got out of that without some serious damage."

"Don't I know it. I was about to flunk out of school. One night, I stayed home and tried to salvage my semester." She added more cream to her coffee and stirred. "Andy drove the Porsche, said he was going to the 'wilds of Westlake' to the Soap Creek Saloon. Not sure whether he went for the music or the drugs. On the way home, he drag raced on Mopac. He took the ramp onto Enfield way too fast. The car flew off the road and rolled. Lucky for him, he was thrown clear. The car exploded." She went silent, eyes unfocused, her lips quivering. "If he had been wearing his seatbelt, he would've died. If I had been in the car, we both would have been wearing our seatbelts..."

"Dang, girl." Rick sat back and exhaled.

Jane put a hand to her throat. "That woke me up but good. When the police got there, Andy was unconscious, barely alive. He spent the next two days in a medically induced coma. When he came to, the doctors were amazed he hadn't sustained brain damage. Of course, he had loads of *mind* damage from the drugs." She shrugged. "I left him."

Rick let out a low whistle. "I guess so. The Bolivian marching powder. Imagine that. Never partook my ownself, but I've seen the damage done, props to Neil Young. You dodged a bullet, girl."

"Yeah." Jane continued, "I still have some residual guilt about the break-up, but if I'd stayed, I think I might've lost myself. Anyway, I went back to the Harrises with my tail between my legs. They were so gracious.

Gave me back my job and my room on the condition I go to AA. I'm one of the lucky ones who got it the first time—so far at least."

"The Harrises have earned their place in heaven. What happened to the trust fund baby?"

"He recovered—physically at any rate—after months of therapy. Last I heard, he had periods of sobriety followed by more backsliding. Just couldn't stay sober. So many relapses." Her mouth turned down in sorrow. "I know some in AA say each relapse is a learning experience, but Andy never seemed to learn. My sponsor heard at a meeting that he showed up at Betty Ford, right after it opened a couple of years ago, with his cat and his gun. That is so Andy. No word of him since."

"Didn't he try to get you back?"

"He tried, but I made it clear we were done. Although, he did send me a hefty check for tuition." She tilted her chin up and said, "Yes, I cashed it. It really helped."

Rick showed his palms. "No judgment here. After Andy, who did ya take a shine to?"

Jane thought a moment. "No one special. No more drama like with the first two. My heart needed a rest."

Rick placed both hands on his chest and said, "After hearing about Jeremy and Andy, my own heart needs a rest."

Jane laughed. "So appreciative of your empathy. Among others, I dated a lot of AA men. I know they're not a dating service, but you know how that goes."

Rick looked up sharply, then back at his plate. His cheeks reddened. "Yep."

She didn't know what to make of his reaction and filed it away for later review. "Mostly one date and done." She made a moue of distaste. "Nothing ever worked out. The rogue's gallery of dating failures got to be too time consuming and distracting. After four years of bad dates, I swore off men so I could concentrate on finishing my degree."

The waiter refilled their coffees. They sat without speaking for a long minute. Jane dreaded the next topic—her marriage.

Rick broke the silence. "How's the psychology business working out?"

Relieved at the conversational reprieve, she explained, "I'm not working yet, still in the process of getting my master's. Not many jobs for someone with only a bachelor's in psychology. After I finished my undergraduate work, I got a job as a receptionist for a group of psychiatrists. It was time to move on from my vet tech job, although I knew I would miss the animals—and the Harrises."

Rick looked at his watch, tapped it, and kidded her. "What year are we up to?"

She wrinkled her nose. "Funny. Remember, you asked for this. We are up to 1982 for your information."

"Okay, let me get this straight, you were still not datin', just workin' and hittin' the books. Hard to believe." He gave her a sidelong look full of skepticism.

She shrugged. "Well, it's true. I lived like a studious nun for twenty-one months. Then I met…Joshua when he joined the psychiatric practice two years ago."

Rick met her gaze, held it as he made air fingers quotes, and spoke with the portentousness of James Earl Jones. "The husband." He glanced at the rings on her left hand. "Tell me, how'd he convince the girl who wasn't ever gonna get married to tie the knot?"

Jane gazed at her sparkling diamonds. "He worked hard; I'll give him that."

"Big weddin'?"

"No. Justice of the Peace. The Harrises were the witnesses and only guests. Honeymoon in Jamaica. My AA friends threw us a party when we got back."

"Hmmm. Can I infer the honeymoon is over since he isn't here?"

Jane's eyes widened, and she stifled a gasp. "Direct, ain't you?" She struggled for words. "Well, we have been married a year, so technically yes, the honeymoon is over." She realized how that might come across and blurted, "But he wanted to come with me, and I told him no." *That sounds even worse.*

Rick lost interest in his cake and stared at her. "What? Why?"

She glanced away and said, "I didn't want him to see where I came from."

"Whoa! First off, you got nothin' to be ashamed of, and second, it ain't healthy to keep things from your husband. What else is goin' on?"

Jane's lips trembled. *Don't cry.* "I...I don't...can't..." She blinked and regarded him with misgiving. "I don't want to discuss it."

Rick looked abashed at her distress. He reached out to touch her hand. "Hey, Jane, I'm sorry. Shouldn't have opened my big mouth and inserted my big ol' foot. I got no right to pry. I'm an ass. Can you forgive me?" His thumb caressed the back of her hand.

Jane let his hand stay on hers. It was warm. And rough, so much rougher than Joshua's psychiatrist hands. "I better get back to the hotel. I need to call my husband."

Rick removed his hand as if scalded. "I guess you do."

While they waited for the check, Rick spoke about the plans to expand the exhibits at Monahans. Jane, thankful for the safe topic, listened and nodded.

After paying the check, Rick put his hand low on her back while guiding her to the Wrangler. She didn't remove it.

Before Jane could step into the Jeep, Rick pulled her to him. He reached out and lifted her chin, his thumb brushing her just below the lips, and kissed her deeply. She moaned and dropped her purse, placed her hand on his neck and pressed against him for several moments.

Then Jane came to her senses and pushed him away.

They were silent on the drive back to the hotel. Jane sat as close to the door opening as she dared, her face averted.

Rick sat ramrod straight, and he looked resolutely forward at the seemingly endless road. Finally, he pulled into the hotel driveway and turned to her. He opened his mouth, but no words came.

Jane clutched her bag to her chest as if to ward off what was coming.

He exhaled from the soles of his feet and rasped, "I gotta ask. Is it just me, or did you feel somethin' when we kissed?" His brow furrowed, and he fumbled for words. "You haven't really told me anythin' about your marriage. I'm probably just embarrassin' myself, but I can't let you leave if there's a chance."

Her eyes stung. "I have to go." The lack of a door was a blessing as she dashed from the Jeep and rushed into the hotel.

Do I have a sign around my neck that says, 'Just show her a little tenderness and she melts?'

Choking with bitter laughter, she rode the elevator up to her room. She washed her face and hung up her clothes, putting on her silk kimono. While the bathtub filled, she phoned the airline to make arrangements for her return flight. Then she called Lauren, who agreed to pick her up at the airport.

"I'll take you out to lunch, darlin'. We need to touch base."

Jane suppressed a sob. "I know. See you then."

Anticipating a nice long soak to soothe her sore muscles, battered feet, and guilty conscience, she added bath salts and turned off the tap.

Jane returned to the phone, approaching cautiously, as if it were a rattlesnake. It wouldn't strike her, but the conversation she was about to have might leave a mark.

Joshua picked up on the second ring. The sound of his voice made her shiver. So familiar and yet so strange after the slow drawl she'd been hearing the last few days.

"I confirmed my flight for tomorrow morning. Lauren is picking me up at Mueller. We're going to have lunch, then she'll bring me home."

His voice was clipped. "What time might I expect you?"

"You sound so cold." She sat on the bed.

"Cold? What do you expect after our last conversation?"

She looked at the ceiling. *God grant me the serenity...* "Please, Joshua, you know we need to talk. I'll be there tomorrow around five."

"My last session is at three, so I'll be home. And you're right, we do have to talk."

Jane heard the click that indicated Joshua had hung up on her. She said aloud, "No goodbye, honey?" She placed the receiver in the cradle and lay on her side as tears began. Wiping her eyes with the back of her hand, she wondered if she was crying for the state of her marriage or herself.

Seeing the plane was almost empty, Jane breathed a sigh of relief. She had no desire to spend the flight in polite, or self-revelatory, conversation with a stranger, even one as benign as Mr. Moore. Wondering what had possessed her to bare her soul to that kind gentleman, she promised not to spill her guts to anyone on the return trip. Taking a seat in the last row, she radiated stay-away vibes.

No sooner had the plane reached altitude, it began the descent into Dallas. The layover was brief. Again, no one attempted to sit next to her. As the last leg of her journey commenced, she leaned back and closed her eyes. *Wonder what sort of reception I'll get from Lauren. With her black belt in AA, I'll get her unvarnished opinion of the mess I'm in.*

Her thoughts turned to the start of her journey in AA.

Chapter Nine

CAME TO, CAME TO BELIEVE-AUSTIN 1976

For the last time, I stood at the panoramic windows of Andy's house, watching the sun glint off Lake Austin. My bags were packed. Tallulah was softly mewling in her carrier. The housekeeper would take care of Lolita, Tallulah's mother, until Andy came home from the hospital.

I handed Lupita my key, said goodbye, and placed my things in the Ford Maverick, a birthday present from Andy. When he'd offered me any car I wanted, and I picked the Ford over an expensive foreign car, he said, "Honey, you sure are low maintenance. I guess that's one of the reasons I love you."

Leaving him was necessary for my survival, but it still made me sad—and guilty. Before turning the key in the ignition, I laid my head on the steering wheel, taking deep breaths as I recalled how we started. Andy was such fun at first, made me see what I had been missing while I labored at my studies. We had a blast at the clubs, concerts, and parties. The lake was our playground, so many good times. We clicked sexually.

The cocaine changed everything. His personality disintegrated—mania alternated with deep depression.

Dr. Harris and Constance had agreed to see me to discuss my future. As I drove to Tarrytown, my sweaty palms slipped on the slick, plastic steering wheel. Consciously, I slowed my breathing. To put it mildly, I was apprehensive about my reception, especially considering what I had told them on the phone about my drug use. Parking in the drive, I left my belongings in the car, not wanting to be presumptuous. Tallulah kicked up a fuss in the despised carrier. "Hold on, Lulah. Of course, you're coming in with me."

In the kitchen, the three of us sat at the table with cups of Earl Grey and a tempting selection of pastries from Sweetish Hill.

Constance raved about her new favorite bakery. "Everything I've tried has been excellent. The Italian cream cake is to die for. Try a brownie."

I selected a cream cheese brownie but couldn't take a bite. With my mouth so dry I didn't think I could open it, there was no way I could eat.

The Harrises sipped tea and waited for me to speak. I didn't.

Constance broke the silence. "Jane, I was surprised, but happy to hear from you and very sorry to learn about Andy's accident. What can we do for you, dear?"

"I'm the one who's sorry," I blurted. "Sorry for ignoring your advice, sorry for leaving my job, sorry for screwing up school—" My voice gave out and my eyes stung.

Dr. Harris got up and brought me a box of tissue. He patted my shoulder, and said, "There, there, Jane. You're with friends and you're safe here. I do have to say I've missed the best assistant I ever had."

Constance coughed.

Dr. Harris glanced at her and chuckled. "Except for you, my dear. Did I really need to say it?"

Mrs. Harris beamed at him. "Just a gentle reminder, Emil."

I realized the Harrises were outstanding examples of what a marriage should be. Their kindness and solicitousness toward each other was inspiring. I would like to have that in my life someday, but with my two failed romances, I doubted it would ever happen. Did I have bad luck or bad judgment?

I decided to come right out with my request. "Would you consider letting me come back? I can't stay in Andy's house. Have to make a clean break." Choking back sobs, I confessed, "I've...I've lost my way."

Doc and Constance exchanged a glance, then turned to me. Mrs. Harris spoke, "By all means, we will welcome you back. But there is one condition."

"Anything. I'll do anything you say," I implored.

"Emil and I want you to go to AA. It is an organization we wholeheartedly support and think can help you."

My mouth fell open. "AA? Isn't that for people who live under bridges drinking from paper bags?"

"That's a common misconception," Doc said. "There are people from all walks of life and socio-economic levels in AA. It's egalitarian in the finest sense. This condition is non-negotiable, given what you confided about your time with Andy."

Constance added, "We're blessed to have many AA groups in Austin. I suggest you try the Westlake group. They are open to those who have problems with both drugs and alcohol. Some groups tend to exclude those with drug issues, which is a shame. We know from personal experience."

I said, "What? Personal—"

She held up her hand. "That is a story for another time. Right now, you need to concentrate on yourself. Settle in here. Go to UT to see where you stand academically and get to a meeting." She smiled and patted my shoulder.

Tallulah let out an indignant yowl and smacked the bars of her prison. "And for goodness' sake, let Miss Tallulah out of that crate!"

To demonstrate my total commitment to getting my life back on track, I jumped right in at the clinic. Working with Dr. Harris was going smoothly. I hadn't forgotten the routine or my vet tech skills. Life was returning to normalcy.

My counselor told me there was no way to catch up this term, and since it was November, I would have to wait until the spring semester to get back to school. I vowed to work hard and finish my undergraduate degree. The delay left me more time for swimming, which was a blessing—and for AA, but I wasn't quite sure how much of a blessing that would be.

My first AA meeting was the next day. I dreaded it, but knew I had to go. That afternoon, Andy's attorney called me at the vet's office, pressing me to visit Andy at Brackenridge. I cursed myself for giving this phone number to Lupita. So much for my clean break. I hesitated at first, but decided I owed it to him to make it clear, in person, we were finished.

Driving to the hospital, I rehearsed my goodbye speech. My stomach hurt, a sympathetic preview of the hurt I would inflict on Andy. Bits of prayers floated through my mind, but I couldn't concentrate enough to complete one. I parked and walked to the front entrance.

Inside, I followed the signs in the corridors to intensive care. The medicinal smell reminded me of the last time I'd been to Brackenridge, the night I left Jeremy. Funny how my only two long-term relationships ended in this place. Perhaps, if the need arose, I would recommend my future lovers use a different hospital. I braced myself for seeing the damage Andy had done to himself. Vowed to get this over with fast.

The nurse escorted me to Andy's room. "Fifteen minutes," she whispered as she left. I wouldn't need a fraction of that. Fluorescent lights cast harsh shadows over the form in the bed. A collection of machines beeped and flashed, displaying rows of colored lines with vital sign data. He was stable but looked ghastly.

Andy's face was almost unrecognizable, swollen and discolored—his eyes mere slits. "Jane," he croaked. He held out his left hand; his right arm was in a cast. IV lines snaked from his hand and neck to a bewildering array of bags hanging from poles. My eyes locked on a bag on the railing of his bed, half-filled with orange-brown liquid. A bulb full of bloody fluid peeked from under the covers.

I maintained my composure, barely, and forced a smile. Keeping my distance, I ignored his hand. "Hey, Andy. Glad you're awake."

"Glad...you came."

Those three words seemed to take a lot of effort. Clearly, he would be hospitalized for an extended time. Silence descended—what was there to say? If I had gone with him that night, I could be lying in the next room—or dead.

"I felt I needed to see you in person one last time. I'm leaving. All my things are out of your house, and I gave my key to Lupita." My rehearsed speech came out in a rush, and relief washed over me as I finished.

"No! Don't...leave," he rasped.

"Sorry. It's done. Goodbye." I turned on my heel and walked away without looking back. Tears sprang to my eyes as I rushed down the hall. I was abandoning him but had to save myself.

I entered the old Westlake AA house in disguise. My feeble attempt at camouflage—a long dress, baggy fisherman's sweater, oversized sunglasses, and a floppy wide-brimmed straw hat—could not hide my trepidation about going to my first meeting. I wrinkled my nose at the smell of stale cigarette smoke. This noon meeting was advertised as non-smoking, but most meetings were not, and the lingering odor permeated the walls. Across the vestibule, I saw an open door and rows of chairs. A table with a pot of coffee and disposable cups sat under the window. I peeked in and saw about fifteen people, some sitting on the shabby couches that lined the walls. Avoiding eye contact with anyone, I crept in and took a seat in the last row.

A mixture of all types populated the room, roughly half men, and half women. Granny dresses, cowboy hats, jeans and plaid shirts, nursing scrubs, even a business suit or three mingled in discordant style. I was the youngest person by at least ten years. Most of the people sat in silence, but there were a few quiet conversations here and there. The thing that surprised me most was no one appeared to be suffering from humiliation or embarrassment. I was the only one in disguise and slumping in my chair. People continued to fill the room until most of the seats were taken. A tall cute guy in motorcycle leathers strolled in and all the women in the room came to attention, including me.

Promptly at noon, a tall redhead in a gorgeous dashiki dress in tones of amethyst, cerise, and aquamarine glided to the front of the room. The woman was as fabulous as the dress she wore. She was of a certain age, at least in her forties. She looked great. How could she be an alcoholic?

"Okay, y'all, since no one else is steppin' up, I'll take the reins. We'll open the meetin' with the Serenity Prayer, then the readin's. Who will read the Twelve Steps?" The good-looking man I had noticed earlier raised his hand. She nodded in recognition. "Thanks, Vaughn." She looked around the room. "I need another volunteer to read 'How it Works.'" Her speaking voice brimmed with warmth. "Thanks so much, Grant." She handed plastic-sleeved sheets to the two men who so eagerly volunteered.

After the readings, she scanned the room and her eyes locked with mine. She raised one eyebrow, perhaps in response to my attempt at concealment. "I'm Lauren, and I'm an alcoholic. Since I've worked the Twelve Steps, I've been free of the compulsion to drink alcohol for fifteen years. Do we have any newcomers who'd like to introduce themselves?" Her tone was upbeat.

I slid down in my chair, hiding behind the large man in front of me. My face burned, and I stayed silent. No one spoke.

The woman then asked, "Who would like to share?"

The man I was using as cover raised his hand. "I'm Mac, and I'm an alcoholic. Through the grace of God and this program, I've been sober sixty days and a thousand nights."

Everyone in the room responded in cheerful tones, "Hi, Mac."

"Hi, y'all. I had a drinkin' dream last night. Hate those, but they're a good reminder. Wanted to check in and say it out loud to a room full of fellow drunks," he rumbled in a deep voice. "That's all I got."

"Thanks, Mac," they all intoned.

I wondered how sixty days meshed with a thousand nights, but figured it was an AA thing. Having no idea of what to expect, I just absorbed it all.

Another hand went up. The cute guy said, "I'm Vaughn, and I'm an addict. Don't ask me to list all the things I'm addicted to, or we'll be here all day."

Lauren rolled her eyes. Many of the women in the room laughed a little too loud.

"Hi, Vaughn," the women chorused with wide smiles. Most of the men remained silent and it was easy to see the dynamic at work. Still, he had caught my eye when he strutted in, tall, lean, shaved head. He wore riding boots, and I could envision him on a Harley.

Vaughn continued, "I've been pondering that line in 'How it Works,' about being unable to manage our own lives. For years, I thought I could. I failed miserably, but still I kept at it, thinking I was in control." He surveyed his audience. "My using of...various pharmaceuticals led to the loss of my marriage and getting kicked out of my PhD program."

He chuckled and shook his head ruefully. "I also had a problem with God." He gestured to the large poster at the front of the room. "God is mentioned how many times? Well, one time was too much for me. If there is anyone here with the same issue, I'd like to share something I heard at my first AA meeting." Vaughn paused for effect. "Look at Step Three, it says 'Made a decision to turn our will and our lives over to the care of God *as we understood Him.*'"

Vaughn made eye contact with several women in the room. "An old-timer said something that helped me take Step Three without reservation. He said you could pick your own conception of God, and it doesn't have to be what you heard in Sunday school. He said, 'Hell, you can make that chair, or the doorknob, or a tree, your Higher Power. Just so it ain't you!'" Vaughn bathed in the women's appreciative laughter for a few moments, then concluded, "That's my story, and I'm sticking to it."

Two women whispered behind their hands while gazing at Vaughn as if they were starving, and he was a juicy Hut's cheeseburger.

"Thanks, Vaughn," everyone chanted.

A skinny woman, her black hair pulled back in a ponytail so tight it looked painful, blurted, "I'm Bonnie, and I *really* need to share. I'm using again. Vicodin. Monday, I go to rehab for the *third* time. Ever since my neck surgery, I just haven't been able to kick that damn shit. Even though I haven't had a drink of alcohol in *six years*, that fucking pill is kicking my ass." Her eyes welled, and her lips quivered. Vaughn brought her a box of tissue. She mouthed "Thank you," and continued, "My husband says if I don't make it this time, he's going to leave and take the kids with him." She broke down and sobbed.

And sure enough, everyone in the room said, "Thanks, Bonnie." I wanted to get up and run out the door but had no desire to draw attention to myself. Where the hell had I landed? People sharing stuff like this in public. How could this communal confession possibly help?

Lauren asked, "Does anyone else want to share their experience, strength, and hope?"

An elderly woman with a kind face spoke. "I'm Helen, and I'm an alcoholic. Because I have relentlessly worked this program on a daily basis, I have remained sober for thirty years. For me, the key to maintaining my sobriety is acceptance—acceptance that I am, and will always be, an alcoholic. I truly believe that if I pick up, I'll be right back where I was that day I drove drunk and crashed my car into the rear end of a school bus. I am grateful every day I was alone in the car." Her voice thickened, and her face crumpled. "Thank God, no children were on the bus, and the driver was not seriously injured." After a few breaths, she continued, "There could have been a very different outcome, and I'll never forget that. My strength and hope are found in these rooms. Thank you for listening."

I sat through the entire meeting since I had sworn to the Harrises I would. Did I belong here? The people were not the desperados I had expected, but I couldn't identify with anyone I heard share.

As one o'clock approached, Lauren asked any members, who had been sober for at least a year and were willing to be sponsors, to raise their hands. Looking at Vaughn, she said, "A gentle reminder: men should sponsor men, and women should sponsor women. Let's end the meeting with the Lord's Prayer."

Everyone stood and jockeyed for position—I thought there might be a shoving match between a couple of the women trying to stand next to Vaughn—and held hands in a circle. I gravitated to Mac, the big guy I had tried to use for cover. After the prayer, I attempted to extricate my hand, but it was firmly in Mac's grip. "Keep comin' back, it works if you work it," he said as everyone bobbed their hands up and down in solidarity. Once released, I picked up my bag and turned toward the door when someone tapped my arm. My plans for a quick exit foiled.

"Hello there. I haven't seen you here before. I'm Lauren."

It was the woman who led the meeting. She had the most amazing turquoise eyes. Smiling, she extended her hand.

"My first time. I'm Jane." I took the proffered hand since I didn't want to be rude. My feet were itching to head for the door.

"Welcome, Jane. I hope to see you again. Before you go, I'd like to give you a copy of the Big Book. We call it our bible."

"Oh, I can't." My eyes drifted to the exit.

"Sure you can!" She laughed melodiously. "It's a great pleasure to do this for newcomers. Come on, let me get one out of the cabinet." She floated to the side of the room, calling over her shoulder, "I'll even autograph it for you—that's a joke." She took out a key, unlocked the cupboard door, and pulled out a blue book. "I'll jot down my name and phone number. Call me if you have any questions or just want to chat." She handed me the book. "I do have a disclaimer. I'm pretty busy with my business so I'm only available in the evening, or early morning, if you must. Not a morning person. Let's get a few of the other ladies to give you their numbers as well."

With the much-autographed book under my arm, I left the meeting feeling buoyed, but I couldn't put my finger on why. It turned out not to be the ordeal I feared, and I was willing to give it a shot. Although I felt as if the people in the room shared a secret and spoke a strange language, I had an inkling that, if I learned their secret, I might live a life free of shame. For damn sure, I didn't want to end up like Grandma June and Mama.

The Harrises were thrilled that I attended my first AA meeting. It sort of stung that they doubted I would keep my word, but I guess I deserved it. Constance and I went to the back room for a cup of coffee.

She passed me the cream and asked, "Well, how was it, Jane?"

I stirred my coffee while I framed my response. "It sure was interesting—all kinds of people baring their souls and not acting ashamed. Some of the stories were incredible. I guess I didn't need my disguise. It only drew more attention to me, I think."

Constance chuckled. "I told you it wasn't necessary. So, are you going to another meeting?"

"Yes, absolutely!" I peered at Constance. "That's part of the deal. I'll keep my promise. I'm off drugs and alcohol and don't even want any."

Constance patted my hand, "I'm so happy to hear you say that, but just remember pride goeth before a fall."

What could I say to that? I blurted, "When I came back, you said you had a personal story—"

She gaped at me, the color draining from her face. After a moment, she whispered, "Yes, I did."

"Sorry. I've upset you." Disconcerted by her reaction, I lurched to my feet and turned to go.

Constance grabbed my hand and said, "No. Sit down. This is as good a time as any." She picked up her coffee cup but didn't drink. "Our daughter. Susan." With a shaky hand, she put down the cup.

I got up to get a box of tissue, and Constance glanced at me, tears glistening in her eyes. I knew this would be a tragic story.

Constance exhaled and stared into her cup as she spoke. "Susan had such promise. Smart. But when she went away to college, she changed. I wish she'd gone to school here, but she couldn't pass up the scholarship to Radcliffe. She got involved with drugs and was expelled."

"Did she come home?"

She looked at the ceiling, then at me. "A *version* of Susan came home. We tried, oh how we tried, to get her into treatment. She refused inpatient treatment, but she agreed to try AA." She plucked a tissue from the box. "The group she went to was full of rock-ribbed thoroughbred alcoholics who didn't accept those with drug issues."

"That's awful."

Constance pressed the tissue to her eyes. "One night she went to Sixth Street to buy drugs. Hit and run. They never found the driver. My girl died of head injuries."

I scooted my chair closer and grasped her hands. "Oh, my God. I'm so sorry."

"It's been ten years. The pain lessens just the tiniest bit over time. A very tiny bit." She pressed her lips together.

"Yet, you have the heart to help me and accept me back in your home despite my problems. You and Doc may have saved my life. I never told you this, but my grandma and mama drank. I swore I'd never be like them but look at me. I'm exactly like them."

With surprising ferocity, Constance exclaimed, "No! Don't do that to yourself. Remember what Timothy said, 'For God gave us a spirit not of fear but of power and love and self-control.' You can have a good life, Jane. I know you can!"

I hadn't had a champion in my life since Aunt Penny. Mama, who never had a kind word for me, certainly wasn't one. *Is this what it's like to have a mother's love?* Humbled by Constance's belief in me, I said, "I'm going to try my best not to continue the tradition of the women in my family."

Constance patted my hand. "I have faith in you."

After we finished the coffee, I excused myself to get back to the office. We had a full afternoon schedule.

My mind wandered the rest of the day, trying to process the AA meeting and how what I'd heard there fit with my history of using. Honestly, I had no desire for cocaine—that was Andy's downfall. The few times I indulged, I was frightened by the rush, the pounding pulse, the hot flashes, the sensation my heart would explode from my chest. I swore I could feel the blood circulating faster and faster through my body. Visualized it blowing out a hole in my temples and gushing all over the walls. Andy told me the coke would help me concentrate and keep up with my schoolwork. It didn't. The pounding headache the last time I used clinched it—I would never repeat that experiment.

Pot? I was not a fan of smoking anything, taking only a token toke here and there, just to be sociable. In the Haight, most of the time there was enough smoke for a contact high. I had given up pot after Jeremy. The only "sin" left was alcohol. With my background, I should have run from it like the plague, but I didn't. Of course, I had an aversion to *vodka*, Mama's elixir. Four strong men would have to hold me down and pour it down my throat. I would *never* drink vodka.

Believing alcoholics only drank hard liquor, I thought beer was harmless. It seemed only natural to drink beer when we raced around Lake Austin in Andy's Cigarette boat. At first, I suffered no ill effects and enjoyed the bite of the cold liquid on a hot summer day. But beer became my gateway to alcoholism.

Then my downfall: Champagne. The real stuff, the good stuff, the stuff I would never have been exposed to if it weren't for Andy's profligate spending. Not that I blamed him for my failing. He didn't force it down my throat. I took to it like mother's milk—oh, the irony! When Andy saw how much I enjoyed this version of the grape, he had gone out of his way to make sure there was always chilled Champagne available. I consumed bottles of the stuff, from morning to night. Picturing that morning when I woke with a pounding headache and crawled around the bedroom, drinking the dregs of warm Champagne from last night's bottles, I cringed with revulsion. When I was able to stand, I shuffled into the kitchen and grabbed a fresh bottle, chugging until it gushed out of my nose, stinging, burning. One thought ran through my consciousness: I'm just as bad as Mama. Yet, I continued to gulp Champagne every day. When my grades started to slip, I tried to stop, but the thirst and need overcame me after a few hours and I was back at the refrigerator, popping the cork. Until the night of Andy's accident.

But that trouble was in the rearview now. Where did I fit in the AA program? I hadn't met any Champagne addicts yet.

Keeping my end of the bargain with my mentors, I continued to attend the Westlake AA group twice a week. When I spent time with Constance, I thought about Susan, and my heart hurt for her loss. But Constance never revisited the topic.

Still skeptical about the program, I had yet to share my experiences. I listened, soaking up what others had to offer. I soon recognized the regulars. There were some memorable characters—besides Vaughn and Lauren.

Mac and the other Viet Nam vets told amazing stories. They suffered from combat fatigue as well as alcoholism. Flashbacks, nightmares, and broken sleep were common complaints. One man spoke about going into the hills west of town every day, carrying a case of beer and his gun, planning suicide. He drank and held the loaded revolver to his head, but never pulled the trigger. He finally confessed his pain to his wife. She called AA, and some other vets visited him and convinced him to try the program. He stopped his treks and claimed he now had "an attitude of gratitude."

I heard the same phrases over and over and realized AA had its own language. After a few weeks, I became accustomed to their slogans, but still held back from embracing the program. To tell the truth, all the mottos made me a little uneasy. Their usage was a tad bit like groupthink. Had I joined a cult? Had I joined at all?

One woman, Darlene, fascinated me. She looked like a former nun. Her short, prematurely gray hair was cut in a bob. By the looks of the hairstyle, she may have done it herself. She wore no makeup and dressed her stout body in sober, dull attire. Her shoes were as sensible as she appeared to be. Because she devoted her life to the homeless, converting her house into a shelter, I considered her a saint. Perhaps she did this work for the sake of her brother, John. She brought him to the occasional AA meeting—when he wasn't in jail or committed to Austin State Hospital.

John was unkempt; his hair stood out in stiff clumps, his beard shaved in random swaths. Because he was malodorous, no one sat next to him in meetings except his sister. He slumped in a chair with his head bent, gazing into his lap. The layers of mismatched clothing he wore, even in the Austin heat, hung from his thin frame. His hands shook, and he made disturbing facial grimaces. His leg jiggled non-stop. When he shared, he had a hard time forming words. I wondered if there was something wrong with his jaw because he would stop speaking and move it. He seemed in obvious distress most of the time, and I felt bad for him. As they say in the program: "There, but for the grace of God, go I."

Then one day, Darlene dragged herself into a meeting and tearfully told us she found John dead. His heart gave out while he was sitting on the toilet. Weeping, she spoke about the side effects of the medication he took in the hospital and the aftermath of electroshock treatments. "They robbed me of my brother years ago, well before his death!"

Her story shook me. I recalled what happened to Roky Erickson in 1969, when they'd committed him to Austin State Hospital for possession of a single joint. He had escaped so many times, they transferred him to a more secure state hospital: Rusk. He remained there until 1972. They gave him Thorazine and electroshock therapy, too. After I left Jeremy, I never saw Roky again, but I wondered if he suffered the same treatment consequences as John.

Listening to Darlene, I had an epiphany—she stayed sober despite her grief and credited AA. Her dedication to those less fortunate put me to shame. For the first time, I truly believed the program could help me.

I wanted to be more selfless and get more involved, so I volunteered to help Darlene clean out John's room. He had lived in the converted garage behind her homeless shelter.

We caravanned to South Austin right after the meeting. Already regretting my impulse to help, I almost made a U-turn on Congress, but couldn't do that to Darlene. Tamping down my unease at what we would find inside John's quarters, I lagged behind Darlene and Helen, who had also volunteered, as we entered his space.

My eyes watered as a fetid, stale, and rancid miasma smacked me in the face, the odor so thick it felt particulate. Dirty clothes, spoiled milk, and something I couldn't name and didn't care to identify. I took shallow breaths, trying to keep my mouth closed, wishing for a gas mask. Propping the door open, I yanked open the two stingy windows, but that didn't dispel the stench.

Darlene had brought big black garbage bags and disposable gloves. I donned a pair and started picking up the stiff, dirty clothes strewn around the room. The sharp odor of urine, body odor, and vomit emanated from the shirts and pants. Nothing was salvageable. Used paper plates, newspapers, books, wads of aluminum foil, soggy cereal boxes, and other trash littered the space. A daunting task, but the three of us got right to work.

As I sorted through the well-thumbed books, I was surprised at the range of titles. *Silent Spring, Bury my Heart at Wounded Knee, The Uses of Enchantment, Walden, Doors to Perception, Gulliver's Travels, The Count of Monte Cristo, Brave New World, Lord of the Flies.* I tried to reconcile the sad, broken person I'd seen at AA with the owner of this library.

I flipped through a pile of large canvasses leaning against the wall. "These are amazing, Darlene! I didn't realize John was an artist." The paintings featured heavy strokes of black paint, like gashes, evocative of suffering and pain. As I studied them, John's torment permeated my soul. Several of the paintings incorporated small blocks of deep, saturated color: ocher, maroon, rust, purple. Dark and muted, even gloomy, yet somehow illuminating of his mental state.

Darlene stopped scrubbing the kitchenette counter and smiled sadly. "Yes. He was a very promising artist, but his mental illness—" She paused and collected herself. "His work changed after his first hospitalization. He was never the same."

She walked around the counter and pulled out a large work. "He found old canvasses at Goodwill, covered them with white gesso, then painted them."

"Wow! His work is like a cross between Franz Kline and Willem de Kooning."

"If you say so," said Darlene, apparently not impressed.

"Please don't think I'm being snooty. My boyfriend, my ex-boyfriend, collected art. I'd never heard of them myself until he educated me. But Kline and de Kooning are two famous Abstract Expressionists, and I think John's work is just as good."

Darlene shrugged. "What difference does it make now? He's gone."

No words of comfort could assuage the deep pain of losing her brother. The only thing I could do was give her a hug.

As I drove home, sick at heart for Darlene's loss and John's fate, I wondered if John was a casualty of his drug use or the doctor's prescriptions. Did drugs cause his mental illness or was he self-medicating? Chicken or the egg sort of question. I was reading Thomas Szasz' *The Myth of Mental Illness* for school. If John was an example of what psychiatry did to people, Dr. Szasz had a point.

Two days later, I went to John's memorial service and, for the first time in my life, to the cemetery afterward. I recognized several of the mourners from the Westlake group, but there were many others in attendance I had never met. It seemed that Austin AA funerals were just as big a draw as those I had attended in Odessa.

There was one face in the crowd I was astonished to see, someone I last laid eyes on in 1970. The past six years had not been kind to Jeremy. He looked terrible—and not sober, either. He had a long, scraggly beard and wore ragged jeans and a torn, faded 13th Floor Elevators t-shirt. A painfully thin bleach blonde with ample black roots, wearing oversized sunglasses, clung to him. Was that Crystal? If so, her massive bosom had shrunk along with the rest of her formerly lush body. Maybe it wasn't her. Perhaps bottle blondes with black roots were Jeremy's type.

Ducking behind Mac's shoulder, I hoped Jeremy wouldn't spot me. I had adopted Mac as a sort of AA big brother. He'd been a helicopter pilot in Korea and Viet Nam and hadn't lost his military bearing. He made me feel safe. "Mac," I whispered, "my ex is over there, the tall guy with the long, blond hair and 'Vators shirt. I don't want to deal with him. Please stick with me, okay?"

"Sure thing, Jane."

The service was lengthy and, while Darlene and several others spoke, my mind drifted. I thought about things I heard in AA, like "a hole in the soul," and "comparing your insides to others' outsides." Was that my problem, or was it genetics? Would I ever figure it out? Would I stay sober for thirty years like Helen, or relapse like so many others? For the first time in weeks, I pictured a chilled bottle of Champagne, beaded with sweat, and I wanted to pop the cork on that magnum. My mouth watered and phantom bubbles tickled my tongue. I could almost taste it, and that scared me, so I inched closer to Mac.

At last, the interment was over. Darlene announced that cake and coffee would be served at Westlake. The crowd responded with enthusiasm. I had noticed that many recovering alcoholics consumed coffee by the gallon and sweets by the pound.

"Heads up. Incoming," Mac said. He held his arm out to shield me and addressed Jeremy, who was strolling over with his girl. "Help you?"

Jeremy and his girl leaned into each other, none too steady on their feet. They stopped a couple of feet from us. "Just wanted to say 'hey' to an old friend." With his hands raised, Jeremy took a step back, stumbling a little.

Stuffing down my distaste, I appeared from behind Mac. "Hey, Jeremy. That's it. You got your 'hey,' now you can get." Damn, seeing him brought my West Texas out, and I had been doing so well at erasing it.

Jeremy smirked. "Okay, okay. I expected more from you, Janie. But I guess not." As he staggered away with his arm slung around whatever-her-name-was, he looked over his shoulder. "Watch out for those resentments, they'll bite ya in the ass."

I didn't take the bait. Searching my heart, I harbored no resentment toward Jeremy, just regret I hadn't left him sooner. The blame lay with me and my lack of self-respect and gumption, all those years ago.

Mac shook his head. "By the looks of him, he's the last guy should be handin' out advice."

After a few months, I knew it was time to get serious about working the program. How many times had I heard, "It works if you work it?" I needed to actively participate instead of just listening. So far, I'd only stuck my toe into the program, testing the waters. Even though I wasn't using substances to change the way I felt, I hadn't found anything like serenity.

Lauren had invited me to coffee several times, and, after a Saturday meeting, I finally capitulated. I asked her to be my sponsor. She accepted, with the provisions I get a back-up sponsor due to her scheduling issues, and we meet once a week to work the steps. My first assignment was to share in a meeting.

I spent hours agonizing over what I would say. Although I had written five versions of my "speech," I ended up discarding them all.

At my next meeting, I decided it was time to share, but I was having a tough time getting my hand in the air. The first speaker was a cowboy type who said he was passing through on his way back to Abilene.

"Boy, howdy! I didn't just fall off the wagon, I rolled under it and got crushed by the wheels. But I got my butt here. Whadda they say, if your ass falls off, pick it up and take it to a meetin'." He looked at the clock and said, "I got six hours of sobriety. Oh, my name is Jake."

"Hi, Jake."

"Hi, ever'body. Glad to find y'all. I came to town to visit my sister and her new baby, but I made a wrong turn and ended up on Sixth Street."

There were a few commiserative groans and headshakes.

"Yeah, ya know what they say, the further ya are from the last drink, the closer ya are to the next. Lost four months of sobriety last night, but I'm hoppin' back on that good ol' wagon. Thanks for lettin' me share."

"Thanks, Jake."

Lauren sat beside me for moral support. She nudged me in the side with her elbow. Despite my anxiety, my hand went up. "I'm Jane and...do I have to say I'm an alcoholic—"

"Ya just did, sweetheart," Jake said. "Oh, sorry for the crosstalk."

With my hands clenched in my lap, I continued, "Guess I did. I've been sober since last November, so that's what...five months."

"Hi, Jane."

I gulped, pressed a tissue to the sweat on my upper lip. Taking a few deep breaths, I began to speak, sharing about my drunken mama and leaving home, even though I hadn't planned on revealing too much. As I related my drug use in the Haight, I glanced around the room. No one looked shocked or disgusted, not even about the Owsley. Had they all dropped White Lightning, too? Once I started, the words kept pouring out, and I wondered for a moment if I was making sense. Open, friendly faces smiled, and heads nodded, just like when everyone else shared. Concluding with Andy's accident and my return to the Harrises, I said, "And that is how I got here. Glad I did. Thanks for listening." When I finished, a wave of relief swept over me, and my shoulders relaxed.

"Thanks, Jane," everyone chorused.

Lauren squeezed my hand and whispered, "Good on you."

My mind churned during the rest of the meeting, and I don't remember much of it. After the Lord's Prayer, I received lots of hugs and encouragement.

"Glad you shared," Mac said.

Helen smiled. "So good to hear your story, Jane."

Vaughn stopped on his way out, his arm around his latest squeeze, a petite and pretty redhead with a heart-shaped face. "Keep coming back!"

Lauren dragged me to the door. "We're going to Hut's for burgers. My treat!"

The aroma of burgers and fries welcomed us. Sharing was hard work; and I was famished. Luckily, the line wasn't out the door as usual, and we were seated right away.

After ordering, Lauren said, "I'm happy you shared. How does it feel?"

"Surprisingly good." I had to admit she was right.

Lauren nodded. "That's the way it usually works. I'd like to hear a little more about your journey."

"I thought you might. You're not letting me off easy today."

Lauren raised one eyebrow. "Sweetie, if you're gonna stay sober, you've got a lot of work ahead of you. Openin' up to your sponsor is a requirement."

"Where should I start?"

She tilted her head. "For now, tell me more about Andy. After all, your time with him is what got you to AA."

Our food arrived. My Fats Domino burger smelled heavenly. Lauren got the Buddy Holly, and we split a basket of fries.

I bit into the juicy burger. Delicious. After I wiped my mouth with the paper napkin, I said, "I met him at the vet clinic. At first, I wasn't interested, but he was persistent. Very." I helped myself to some fries. "My life was stable, dull even, working full time and going to school. I hadn't dated in a while." I glanced at her. "Probably only a matter of time until I let loose. And, boy, did I! I guess I was attracted to his energy and sense of fun. After a few dates, I was sure I was in love. Guess I wasn't seeing things clearly."

Lauren reached for more fries and said, "Hormones will do that. Go on."

"He took me to nice restaurants, concerts, gave me gifts. I'd never been treated like that, and, frankly, I was dazzled." I sipped my coke. "When I saw his mansion, I realized he was seriously rich. I'd never heard of a trust fund baby before. He didn't work, just played. After he graduated from UT with his degree in Art History, the trust turned on the money spigot. Andy took full advantage and commenced his lavish lifestyle."

Lauren said, "Yeah, trust fund babies in Austin, you trip over them. Lots of them come through the doors of AA—some even stay. So, what made you abandon everything you'd built, including the folks who saved your bacon after that Jeremy fiasco?"

"Why, love, of course." I felt my cheeks burn.

Lauren rolled her eyes. "Love," she huffed. "Color me jaded. Do you still think it was love?

I looked down at my plate. "Not really. Infatuation at best."

"With a little lust thrown in, is my guess. One of these days, I'll tell you my story. How'd the Harrises take it?"

I felt myself deflate as I remembered their shock and disappointment. "They did everything in their power to talk me out of it. And all the while, they were gentle and loving. I was surprised they weren't angry and shouting—but I guess that goes back to my childhood. They told me I always had a place with them and not to give up on school."

Lauren said, "They sound like great people, Jane. You're lucky to have them."

"I sure am. They didn't hesitate to accept me back after...Andy's accident. They've shown me what a family can be. I'm grateful for them every day."

As I related my misadventures with Andy, Lauren listened closely. I told her everything, from the first beer to the last bottle of bubbly. My voice shook when I spoke about the cocaine. When I hedged, she asked a few pointed questions to get me to divulge more details. I gave her the whole shooting match.

"Like Vaughn says, 'that's my story and I'm sticking to it.'" I leaned back in the booth, out of words.

"Well, darlin,' each of us who comes through the doors has their tale. Remember, the pain is necessary, but if you live according to the principles of the program, suffering is optional."

The check came and Lauren wouldn't even let me leave a tip. "Honey, I got this. Next week, we're gonna discuss the first three steps, so do your readin'. We'll grab lunch again."

We stood, and I hugged her. "I've been studying the Big Book and I'll be ready."

As I drove back to the clinic, I repeated the Serenity Prayer over and over. Would I ever achieve serenity?

Chapter Ten

LADIES WHO LUNCH, TROUBLE IN PARADISE-AUSTIN 1984

Jane strode out of Mueller Airport and spotted Lauren leaning against her red Mercedes convertible, which was in a no-parking zone. Her auburn curls in a messy topknot, indigo dashiki dress moving with her graceful arm movements, she appeared to be charming a cop out of giving her a ticket. Not surprisingly, she was successful. The chubby middle-aged patrolman tucked his ticket pad in his pocket and strutted away with his shoulders thrown back, gut sucked in, and a spring in his step. A brand-new member of the Lauren Eaton fan club.

Jane couldn't help but smile. Lauren had to be sixty, looked forty, and had the energy of a twenty-year-old. *I should be so blessed when I get there—and we all get there eventually—if we're lucky.*

Lauren turned, and when she saw Jane hustling toward her, waved her arms in a "come on down" motion. She opened the passenger door, levered the seat forward, and grandly gestured to the tiny shelf in back. "Drop your bag and get in. I'm so hungry! Let's go to Omelettry West. I'm in the mood for Love Veggies."

"Too much garlic for me. Think I'll get the California salad, something light." Jane placed her bag in the car and hugged Lauren. "Thanks for picking me up. I gave you the bare bones on the phone the other night, but I've got a lot more to lay on you. I really need some guidance."

"That's what sponsors are for, girlfriend. We'll work it out." Lauren sounded supremely confident as usual.

Since the lunch rush was over, they found a parking spot in front of the restaurant. The waitress seated them in a quiet alcove. Jane wanted privacy for this conversation.

After they ordered, Lauren tilted her head and focused her gaze on Jane. "Okay, doll, let's have it." She leaned forward, waved her hands in encouragement, and the bangles on her wrist danced along her forearm.

Jane blew her long bangs out of her eyes, "Where to begin, where to begin…"

"You know you've gotta spill," Lauren said a bit sharply. "Just start."

Jane glanced around and wriggled a little in her seat. "Okay, it was intense. Like I was in a time warp. Some things were exactly the same—the house, the church. Just the way I remembered." She took a sip of water. "But seeing all the people from my past—was overwhelming."

Lauren's lips twisted cynically. "I think maybe one person in particular whelmed you over."

Jane blushed and twisted a lock of hair around her finger.

"Did anything untoward happen?" Lauren stopped for a moment, then laughed. "God, I sound like a Victorian matron. What I meant is—did y'all have sex?"

Jane's eyes popped. "Hell, no!" She glanced away. "Not that I didn't feel a little…inclination."

Lauren smacked her open hand on the table and her many bangles clinked. "You *are* attracted to Rick. I knew it! I could hear it in your voice over the phone."

The food and Red Zinger iced tea arrived, and they stopped speaking until the server left. Jane studied the lettuce, chicken, fruit, and olives in the crockery bowl.

Lauren exhaled gustily, her curls flying about as she shook her head in dismay. "Eight years, that's how long I've known you. I remember when you slunk into your first AA meetin' with your tail between your legs. How many heartbreaks, romances, crushes have I nursed you through? And here I thought you had a happy landing with Dr. Joshua. Now, it seems not." She pointed at Jane with her fork. "I guess you're in a pickle."

Jane looked up and attempted a smile. "Did I have crushes? How jejune."

Her sponsor rolled her eyes. "There you go with the fifty-cent words. Stop hiding behind your vocabulary—it's time for straight talk. Tell me about Rick."

Jane made little pleats in the napkin in her lap. "There's nothing to tell—not really. We spent some time together talking about old times. We had lunch."

"And you stayed an extra day in Odessa for *that*?" Lauren said with a generous helping of skepticism. "You need to examine your motivations there, darlin.'"

Her head bent, Jane confessed, "There was definite attraction, from the minute I saw him in the diner. During our tour of Monahans, I thought I imagined it because he was so businesslike. Then the deep gazes at lunch. The teasing and flirtation made me feel like I was cheating on Joshua. I cut it short and told Rick I had to leave. When he dropped me off, he asked me if I felt something between us, and I literally ran away." She glanced at her sponsor, wondering if Lauren could tell she left out a few...details.

Lauren took a sip of her Red Zinger iced tea and said, "Which begs the question: *do* you feel somethin'? And you, a married woman who lives her life by AA principles."

"Ouch." Jane put down her fork, picked up her water glass, and put it down without drinking. *Time to change the subject.* "On the plane, I was thinking about my first AA meeting. You practically roped me as I was trying to leave."

"You were the walkin' wounded. I felt an obligation to help." Lauren's chin lifted with pride.

"Yeah, it was after Andy." Jane shivered. "When he crashed his Porsche, I was just so grateful I wasn't with him. He almost died, you know."

"So you've told me—many times. That's not what we're talkin' about right now."

"I was shattered. I thought Andy was the one. He was—"

"Hold it, right there." Lauren held up her hand like a traffic cop. "You're real good at deflection, ain't you? Let me summarize. Your lack of judgment led to a mutually destructive drug-drenched roller-coaster ride to hell. Then you smartened up and got your pretty little behind to AA."

Jane's mouth fell open. "You just condensed two-and-a-half years of my life into a couple of sentences. Nice work. I've been thinking about Andy lately. Leaving him flat the way I did has left me drowning in residual guilt."

"Maybe so. You might want to think about makin' some amends, but I don't recommend direct amends in his case." She paused to adjust her bangles. "And thank you for the compliment. I do have a very good recall of your romantic trials and tribulations. And there were many."

"Really? I thought I was quite demure. For the Seventies, I was downright chaste."

"Darlin', if I recollect correctly—and I do—not two months later, you were hangin' on the arm of that cad, that legendary thirteenth-stepper, Vaughn." Lauren rested her elbows on the table and propped her chin on her bejeweled hands as she skewered Jane with her turquoise gaze. "Vaughn, who has more notches on his bedpost than I do!"

Jane couldn't hold in her laughter. "Did I just hear that?"

"All right. All right. That slipped out. Never claimed to be a role model in that department, but this ain't about me. Back to the topic." She punctuated her last words by jabbing her finger on the table. "You. Joshua. The marriage."

Jane avoided the topic again. "What ever happened to Vaughn? He was mighty handsome."

Lauren dabbed her lips with her napkin. "Oh, I'm sure he still is. The last I heard, that 'over-educated and chronically underemployed perennial PhD candidate' as you christened him, hopped on his Harley and left town. Found himself a sugar mama in Ruidoso."

"Well, I wish him the best."

"Honey, Vaughn will always land on his feet or on a big fat pocketbook. I remember so many AA meetings where he had slept with darn near every woman in the room. I don't know how he could sit there for the full hour supposedly listening to those trying to live right—and then try to pick off the next newcomer afterward. The weasel was shameless."

"Weasel? He's way too pretty to be a weasel. Cock of the walk is more like it."

Lauren grinned. "You got that right. Then, after you saw Vaughn for what he was, you were smitten with Alan. Now despite that hideous beard, you gave him a shot. I disremember what happened there." She looked a question.

"Alan? Smitten? You surely do disremember. He was thirty-five, and he lived with his mother. One date and done. Then *you* fixed me up with Robert. You know I despise politics. Did you honestly think I could see eye to eye with a fundraiser for Jimmy Carter?"

The redhead looked a little embarrassed. "No, not really."

Jane snorted. "All he could talk about was Jimmy this, Rosalind that. So boring. And I could never consider being with a man who wore a cardigan at the age of twenty-eight, in Austin, in the summer."

Lauren held up one well-manicured hand. "Okay, okay. I get it." She made a moue. "I might could have made a miscalculation."

Their eyes met, and they began to sputter with laughter at the same time.

Lauren stopped first. "Who gives a flyin' fig about politics when the topic is marital strife? We're here to discuss your current situation, aren't we?" She picked up a forkful of Love Veggies and waited for Jane's answer.

Jane poked her fork in the salad bowl, trying to spear that elusive last olive. "Sure. But what memories! This is too fun. Sometimes I think I sampled men like chocolates. But I didn't get the Godiva, just the drugstore assortment."

"Now, that's a good metaphor, right there." Lauren chuckled and continued to eat.

"Some men I chose because they looked pretty, others I wanted to see what was inside. At times, I knew just looking at them what I'd find, and that was what I wanted at the moment." Jane stared past Lauren's shoulder.

"Dear Lord, are you done yet?"

"No, I'm not. This is therapeutic. Bear with me. Let's see…I took nibbles of some, devoured others. A few I spit out right on the floor. Some were sticky, some stuck in my craw, one I almost broke my teeth on." Jane sighed. "Okay, I think I've beaten that one to death." *Dating was like biting into what looked like a solid, chewy caramel and instead tasting the sickly-sweet liquid gush of a chocolate-covered cherry. Not one man suited me. Until Joshua—he's Godiva, at least I thought so. Now I can't get Rick out of my head.*

Lauren waved her hand in Jane's face. "Hello? Where'd ya go?"

"Sorry, I've been so distracted the last few days. What about Tucker? Is he still around?"

Her sponsor chuckled. "Oh, my God. The ultimate agin' rocker. Peter Pan with a Gibson—or was it a Fender? Haven't seen him in a while."

"I will never forget his pick-up line. 'Was that an earthquake, or did you just rock my world?'"

Lauren fanned her fingers on her chest. "Tell me that's not true."

"Sorry, that's what he led with. When I asked him where his girlfriend was—you remember her, rail-thin with dyed black hair in a Jane Fonda shag—he said, 'I've moved on, learned everything I could from that relationship.' I said to myself, 'Buddy, you ain't learned a damn thing!'"

"Insightful."

Jane ducked her head in acknowledgment of the compliment. "I was getting better at navigating men by that time. Another one and done. He didn't even own a car, just bummed rides from every woman he met."

"Yeah, he may have been a good bass player, but what a mooch!" Lauren got the waitress's attention by holding up her empty glass.

The waitress approached with her pitcher of tea and refilled their glasses.

Lauren smiled at the server. "Thanks, this is thirsty work."

Jane took a long swallow of Red Zinger and set down her glass. "Then there was Dylan. I remember you discouraged that one. He was just as you said, the dreaded AA vulture who got his counseling license and then preyed on newcomers for his clientele. And the John Lennon glasses and hippie-speak. Eewww!"

Lauren laughed and said, "Who was that guy who wanted to take you to Wimbledon? He rehabbed houses. I thought he was stable and sincere."

"Clint? I told him I couldn't imagine anything more boring than days of watching a bouncing yellow ball go back and forth over a net. I don't think he appreciated that."

Lauren raised an eyebrow. "Blunt, ain't you?"

"I prefer forthright."

"Since we seem to be countin' down to the putative subject, let's continue this delicious indulgence for a few more minutes. But we *will* discuss Joshua."

"Lauren, you got some fifty-cent words your ownself." *There it is again, my West Texas. Funny how I struggle to eradicate it, while most Austinites revel in putting on the country talk.*

"Why thank you, darlin'. Who's next?"

Jane put her finger on her chin and looked heavenward as she reviewed the members of the rogue's gallery with whom she had practiced serial monogamy.

"I do believe that would be Daniel." Jane's breath caught as she recalled the six-foot ten ex-pro-basketball player. "So good-looking and that long, lean basketball body! He was a little older, but I didn't care. The deal-breaker there was his bipolar ex-wife who refused to take her Lithium. And their six-month-old daughter. I wasn't ready to spend the next eighteen years of my life dealing with that chaos." She pushed her bowl away, leaving only a few wilted bits of lettuce.

"Don't blame you a bit. Now, how about splittin' some blackberry cobbler?"

"I might could do that. But only if we get a scoop of Blue Bell?"

"Count on it, sweetie." Lauren looked around and beckoned the waitress who cleared the lunch dishes. "Blackberry cobbler with ice cream and two spoons, please. And coffee. Jane, any coffee?"

"Just more tea, please."

The waitress nodded and left them alone.

Lauren folded her hands on the table and said, "Where were we?"

"Griff. I thought his job was the coolest ever. Digging up Mayan ruins all over Central America. It spoke to me of adventure and reminded me of my childhood dreams. But did he talk about that on our date? Hell, no." Jane wrinkled her nose in disapproval. "He brought along some pop psychology book about male sensitivity—how to be more in touch with your feelings so you get all the girls—ridiculous. He drew me a timeline of his marriage on a napkin—from first date through break-up—and went over each entry in excruciating detail. Why, it was just like girl talk. I was expecting Indiana Jones, and I got Sally Jesse Raphael. Have to admit, I got up and left before the entrée."

The waitress returned with the blackberry cobbler topped with a mound of vanilla ice cream just beginning to melt on the warm crust. They each took a bite.

Lauren rolled her eyes in ecstasy.

Jane swooned with pleasure as the sweet and cold mixture reached her taste buds. "Best dessert ever!"

Lauren ate a few more ladylike bites, then patted her mouth with her napkin. She made a show of looking at her watch. "Have we arrived at Joshua yet?"

Jane blushed. "Maybe I am avoiding getting to it." She shrugged. "But I can't resist mentioning my most serious AA beau—Harlan. He was so cute!"

Her mentor chuckled. "The Austin version of a surfer dude. He *knew* he was cute. I found that off-puttin'."

"Oh, eventually I saw that, but I was crazy about him for a few months—until he had his teeth and hair bleached and tried to break into acting. When he got a walk-on in *Outlaw Blues*, he talked like Peter Fonda was his best buddy and Susan St. James his paramour. He was certain there was an Oscar in his future." Jane giggled. "I was focused on getting my degree and thought that was a bit frivolous, shallow. And I was worried he'd get prettier than me."

Lauren sipped coffee and set down her mug with a thump. "We have now arrived at our destination—Joshua."

Jane shredded the napkin in her lap into tiny little pieces. She kept her face as blank as a supermodel and gulped. "When he walked into the psychiatrists' office that day, I fell hard for him right then and there."

"So you said at the time. I remember when you told me about him. In the six years I'd known you, I hadn't *ever* heard you go on like that about any man. Didn't I tell you to take a cold shower? And listenin' to you, I needed one myself." Lauren fanned herself to emphasize the point. "At this juncture, I have to ask, was it love or lust?" She raised a perfect eyebrow, one of her many talents.

"Are those my choices? Is it one or the other?" Jane's face showed her confusion. "I finally take the big leap of faith and get married because of my hormones and not my soul? I hate to think that's true."

Lauren reached across the table and patted Jane's hand. "Honey, I can't answer that for you. What's really goin' on? Not to sound judgmental, but here I go—judgin'—you were so sure that it was 'happily ever after' with Joshua. I just can't understand your ambivalence now. Or your flirtation with Rick." She leaned back in her chair and picked up her coffee cup, her eyes never leaving Jane.

Jane's mouth turned downward. A tear threatened to spill from her eye. She lifted her head to look at the ceiling, willing that tear not to ruin her makeup. "I don't understand my ambivalence, either. And here I am studying human behavior when I don't comprehend my own. I'm just one raw nerve these days." She shook her head and blinked.

"Do you love him? I mean Joshua, your husband." Lauren said tartly.

Jane gasped. "Yes, of course I do! If you had asked me a week ago, I would have said I couldn't even imagine myself with another man. What does it mean that now I can?" She bit her lip. "I'm afraid to go home and see him."

"Afraid? Why?"

"Well, we had that fight as I was leaving. Then he was upset I was staying an extra day. When I called him last night, he was so cold I almost got frostbite. He hung up without saying goodbye. I think when he sees my face, he'll know what happened with Rick."

Lauren raised both eyebrows. "Yet nothing happened with Rick. So, that doesn't wash."

Jane sat without speaking. *Rigorous honesty?*

Lauren waited, and when Jane remained silent, said, "Jane, my dear, you have a lot of thinkin' to do. But first, you have to go home and see Joshua. You need to look him in the eye. Be honest and open—and calm. Tell him about your doubts. Then listen, I mean really listen to what he has to say. And call me afterwards. I should be home by then. Now, let's settle up, and I'll drop you off."

Jane stood in her driveway watching Lauren zoom away down Cicero Lane. She wanted to run after her car and beg for a ride away from her problems but knew that was cowardly.

Instead, she picked up her bag and approached the front door. It didn't feel right to ring the bell at her own home. While she looked for her keys in her voluminous purse, the door opened. Joshua spread his arms to her, but she held back, frozen.

Why can't I go to him?

He gave her a piercing look. Each waited for the other to speak.

Joshua sighed, stepped outside, and grabbed her suitcase in silence. He held the door for her.

Feeling like a guest, Jane entered the house. Tallulah padded up to her and meowed a welcome. "Lulah, my pretty girl. I missed you so!" She picked up the cat.

The door slammed behind her. "This is ridiculous—you greet the cat and not me. Hello, darling. How was your flight? Glad to be home?" Joshua's words were clipped and bitter.

Jane flinched. Soothing Tallulah, she took a moment to make certain her face was neutral before she turned to him.

"Hello, Joshua. You seem angry." *How lame and damsel-in-distress. This isn't a soap opera—it's my damned life.*

"Angry? Maybe a little. Don't I have good reason? I'll admit to frustration and confusion as well. What's going on with you?" He folded his arms across his chest and regarded Jane.

She put Tallulah on the floor. "I'm here now and ready to have a civil discussion."

He frowned. "Is the implication that I'm uncivil? Well, I will have to be on my best behavior then. No door slamming, no yelling." Jane thought he realized how harsh he sounded because he forced a smile and relaxed his shoulders. "All right?"

"Okay." She met his eyes and tried to smile, but her face did not cooperate. "I'll make some tea. But remember, I'm tired and still trying to process my trip down the rabbit-hole."

He followed Jane into the kitchen. She busied herself making hot mint tea. When it was ready, they sat at the kitchen table.

Jane glanced at the wall where he had smashed his coffee cup before she left for Odessa. There was no physical trace of the incident, but she imagined that the anger and frustration from their confrontation loomed in the air.

Joshua said, "Since you're so tired, I'll start—"

"Was that a slam?" she interrupted. "I *am* tired."

He snorted. "No slam intended. Try not to be so damned touchy. Have we lost the ability to communicate?"

Silence.

Joshua spoke first. "I have no idea what's going on in your mind. I haven't been able to stop thinking about what you said before you left. Did you mean it—you don't want to be married?" He held out his hands as if in supplication.

Jane lifted her chin, ignoring his outstretched hands, and answered, "I don't know. Did you mean to imply that I need a shrink—oh, excuse me, a psychiatrist?"

Am I trying to sabotage our rapprochement? By the look on his face, I'm doing a good job of it. And apparently, I think I speak French. If I sound like a pretentious ass to myself, how do I sound to him?

He put his face in his hands.

She heard him muttering but couldn't make out his words. They were not complimentary, she was certain. Picking up her teacup, she took a sip. Mint was supposed to be soothing.

Joshua looked up and groaned. "Let's start over. What was it like seeing your father after all those years?"

Jane recalled Lauren's advice. "Yes, a fresh start would be good." *I poured my heart out to Rick when I should've been talking to Joshua.* "In some ways it was like those seventeen years away didn't happen. I fell into being his little girl without missing a beat. But that might be a problem." She glanced at Joshua, who regarded her closely.

"Care to explain? I'm confused."

She shook her head. "So am I. I have a lot to sort out."

"Okay, I can understand that. How did your father handle the funeral?"

"He was his usual stoic self—he got through it." Jane shrugged. "My daddy really loved her, much to my amazement."

His forehead furrowed. "Why amazement? Was she so hard to love?"

Jane gave him a withering look. "If you only knew…"

"Babe, that's what I've been saying for months, 'if I only knew'—but you won't tell me. Maybe if I knew, I could help." He reached out, took her unresisting hand, and squeezed it.

His words were like a glass of cold water in her face. *Is he right?* Her throat felt thick as she continued, "Daddy was fairly broken up."

"I would imagine so. They were married a long time."

"He held it together at the service and the reception afterward, but I had glimpses of his pain and loneliness. It hurt my heart." Jane's eyes glittered with tears.

Joshua got up and brought her a box of tissue.

"I don't know what he's going to do now. He hasn't made any plans yet." She dabbed her eyes, trying to preserve her eye makeup. "There's still so much left unsaid between us. Tom shocked me by pointing out that Daddy's top priority was protecting Mama from the consequences of her drinking." When she realized she had let slip a bit of the trauma from her childhood, she drew in a breath and froze.

He placed his hand over hers and gave her a moment.

She accepted his touch. Since Jane had never shared her past with him, this conversation was difficult—no, impossible. If she started, there would be threads unraveling in every direction, leading to places she did not want to revisit. *The absurdity is, I did this to myself.*

"At last, you reveal that your mother drank." Joshua squeezed her hand. "You never told me, but I had a hunch."

She gazed into her empty teacup. "You did? Well, now you know."

He scooted his chair closer and took both her hands in his. "Babe, I appreciate that you confided this to me. It's obvious how hard this is for you."

Jane whispered, "Thanks, honey."

"Okay, change of subject. How are Tom and his family?"

"They're fine. It was good to see him and Jolene. Their children are beautiful..." *Uh-oh, touchy subject.*

After a moment, Jane stood and went to the refrigerator for ice water. Dawdling over the task, she turned to face him but remained standing at the kitchen counter. She struggled to find a neutral topic, hoping to dodge more self-revelation. "Odessa has changed a lot, but the house was exactly the same, down to the old concert posters in my room and the plastic covers on the couch."

He laughed. "Plastic covers? Wow!"

Smiling, she replied. "Yes, indeed." She gazed into the backyard, not seeing the crepe myrtles blooming fuchsia and scarlet, instead focused on a scene from the past.

Joshua rose and joined her at the counter. He embraced her and kissed her neck in the way he had that curled her toes. "How did *you* handle the funeral, babe?"

Jane's body went rigid, and she pulled away. She straightened up to her full height, shaking her head. "Oh, honey. Odessa and funerals. Story of my life—"

"The story of your life?" Running his hands through his hair, he stared at her.

Jane's green eyes blazed. Perceiving his frustration, but unable to reveal her secrets, she managed to choke out a few oblique words. "There have been other funerals, some of which have left an indelible psychic scar."

His eyes widened, and he took a step back. "That's intense. One day I hope you'll tell me about it."

Which of his shrink techniques is he using on me? His voice is so soothing. He didn't answer when I asked if I need a psychiatrist. Funny thing, I do have a psychiatrist, and I'm shoving him away.

Jane sniffed and studied the pattern on the Talavera tile countertop, tracing it with her finger. "Not tonight."

Joshua cleared his throat. "Well, I'm here when you're ready. I'm a good listener. Remember, I do this for a living." The corners of his mouth turned up.

She regarded him from under her long bangs, then took his hand. "I hadn't seen Mama in so many years, in some ways it was like viewing a stranger in that casket." She shivered. "But I did have some feelings. Not sure that I wouldn't feel the same pity for...anyone. The wreckage of her body made me sad. Self-inflicted, but still. She looked like a wizened child. Maybe a touch of regret—but there's no going back now."

He didn't say a thing, just pulled her close and held her.

She relaxed into him. It felt good, familiar. She mumbled into his shirt, "This is what I need. Touch, not talk."

"All right, babe." After a few moments, he patted her back and released her from the embrace but took hold of her hands. "You should unwind. How about a nice hot bath?

She smiled and whispered, "Yes, that is just what I need."

"Good. I'll feed Tallulah and bring up your suitcase. Enjoy."

Jane entered the bedroom two hours later, still rosy from the lavender-infused soak. Wanting to look her best when she faced him, she spent time drying and styling her long hair, and applying body lotion. She wore her most diaphanous lingerie.

The lights were low. Perfumed candles filled the air with jasmine. Joshua turned off his reading light, put down the journal he was reviewing, and lifted an eyebrow. A slow grin spread across his face.

Jane found herself wanting him, the connection intact. She went to him and forgot the past—and future—for a while.

When Jane woke the next morning, she heard the shower running. She stretched like a languorous cat, smiling. Her stomach rumbled. No dinner last night. She was starving and thought Joshua would be as well. With a burst of energy, she pulled the covers back, grabbed her robe, and dashed downstairs to make them breakfast.

Soon, the scent of coffee, frying eggs, and bacon filled the kitchen. Jane rushed around, turning the bacon, feeding Tallulah, setting the table, pouring orange juice.

Feeling sanguine after their reunion, she was eager to impress Joshua. She darted to the first-floor bath to freshen up. She gazed in the mirror, her face flushed as she recalled last night. The sex had been tender at first, then more urgent as the heat rose and she let herself go. She trembled, recalling her abandon and his passion. With a final pat of her hair and wearing a look of satisfaction, she returned to her cooking.

Jane was plating the breakfast when Tallulah raced into the kitchen. Joshua would be right behind the cat. The phone rang. Joshua, dressed for work, answered it. "Hello? Who's calling?"

She turned from the stove and saw the question on Joshua's face. He held the receiver out to her. "It's for you. Said his name is Rick."

Mouth agape, she dropped the spatula on the floor. Joshua wordlessly handed her the phone and left the kitchen. She heard him thunder up the stairs and slam their bedroom door.

Curbing the urge to hiss at Rick, she asked calmly, "What's up, Rick?" All she heard was the dial tone.

Jane banged the receiver back in the cradle and groaned, "I'm an idiot." Her reaction to the call obviously led Joshua to think she had something to hide. But she didn't, not really. If only she had coolly accepted the call and explained later. But no, her lack of a poker face betrayed her.

Breakfast forgotten, she hurried upstairs and into their bedroom. Joshua sat on the side of the bed, head hanging, his hands between his knees. He didn't look up when she entered.

"Honey?" Jane said tentatively.

"Who's Rick?" His words felt like icicles.

"An old friend."

He turned to face her, his brow furrowed. "What does that mean? The look on your face…"

"I can ex-explain," she stuttered.

He jumped to his feet and stepped toward her. "By all means, explain."

Jane's voice quavered. "You've got to understand—"

"Do I?"

"Honey, please. In Odessa, I saw everyone from all those years ago. From the preacher, to my old high school nemesis, Priscilla, and Rick…" She trailed off and stared at the floor.

"One. More. Time. Who's Rick? And more to the point, what did he want?"

"Rick's a childhood friend. He was my *only* friend from when I was eight years old until...well, until, one of those Odessa funerals I'd prefer not to talk about."

"Christ on a crutch! My head is hurting from all your obfuscation and vague references to your mysterious past. Why can't you open up to me? I'm your husband!"

Jane bit her lip. "I...I don't know. I just can't."

He groaned. "Okay, I said I'd be patient and wait for you to talk to me. But I'm not going to wait forever. We have major problems. You have to decide if you want to stay married and if you want a family—"

"Stop! Just stop!" She covered her ears and shouted, "Not now. I can't talk about the future when I still can't handle my past." She threw her arms open in frustration. "And Rick? He hung up, so I don't know what he wanted."

He raised his hands in a placating gesture. "All right. Let's take some deep breaths and deescalate. What a crap start to the day." He narrowed his eyes and shook his head. "And after last night. I'm already exhausted. I've got to get to work—back-to-back appointments today."

She exhaled. A reprieve. "Okay. We can talk tonight."

Jane cleaned up the uneaten breakfast, checked the refrigerator, and made a shopping list. In her bedroom, she unpacked and changed the linens. Then she went for a swim, to an AA meeting, hit the grocery store, and came home feeling more centered. As she put the groceries away, the phone rang, and she froze. Was it Rick again? What could he possibly want? She knew things were left hanging between them, then wondered if there was, or should be, a "them."

She answered the call, and hearing her daddy's voice, breathed a sigh of relief.

"Daddy! How are you?"

"I'm doin' all right. A little bit lonely, just rattlin' around in this old place. Maybe I'll sell it. What d'ya think?"

Jane thought about Tom's disclosure of his resentment toward Daddy and wondered again if it would affect her future relationship with him. At some point, she knew she had to confront him. The funeral hadn't been the venue for this venture into the darkness, but she believed they should talk sooner rather than later.

"Janie, you there?" His voice brought her back to the kitchen.

"Yes, Daddy. I don't know what to tell you. It's your decision." That felt a little frosty, so maybe Tom's perception *was* influencing her.

"Well, okay then, sorry to bother you." He sounded hurt.

"Don't hang up! I didn't mean to sound uncaring. Where would you move?"

"There's apartments in town. I might could live there. Haven't looked yet. Just thought I'd run it by you."

"I see. Well, if you're feeling the house is too large for one person, I can understand a smaller place might suit you better." She bit her lip and twirled the phone cord, not wanting to continue the conversation but thinking it rude to end it. More ambivalence about Daddy.

"Yep, that's what I'm thinkin'. I...I was wonderin' if you could come out and help me. I need you to pack up Martha's things." After a pause, he continued, "She made me promise I'd have you take care of it."

Jane gulped. *Was Mama reaching out for her from the grave?* She shuddered. She hadn't planned on ever setting foot in Odessa again, considering that chapter closed with her mama's funeral. But maybe Odessa wasn't done with her. Before she moved forward with her life, she had better resolve her past, as she'd shrieked at Joshua just this morning. That meant going back to see her childhood home one more time—and seeing Rick.

"Okay, Daddy. I'll talk to Joshua and call you later." She hung up the receiver and collapsed into a chair at the kitchen table. Tallulah padded in and meowed for attention. Jane picked her up and cuddled her. The cat purred in response. "Ever had a desire to see West Texas, girl?" After a few moments of stroking the cat's soft fur, she placed the feline on the floor. Jane returned to the phone to call her sponsor.

"Lauren here!"

Jane blurted, "I've got to go back to Odessa."

"Why? Did Rick call?" Lauren asked archly.

"Damn, that smarts. As a matter of fact, he did. This morning. Joshua answered, but Rick hung up before I could talk to him. So, I don't know what he wanted."

"Really? I could make a guess." Lauren's sarcasm left no doubt about her implication.

"Lauren!" Jane was glad to have the long phone cord that allowed her to pace during the conversation.

"Well, I bet I'm right. Anyway, how did your homecomin' go? You didn't call me, so I figure it went well."

"We had an excellent night. We reconnected. And yes, that means really good sex."

"That's positive. What did he say about Rick's call?"

"He asked me who Rick was, for starters—"

Lauren cut in, "What did you tell him?"

Jane sighed and untangled the kinks in the phone cord. "I told him Rick was my best friend when we were kids…and then I sort of deflected…"

"What d'ya mean, deflected?" Lauren sounded exasperated.

"I told him I couldn't talk about it because of a funeral—Mavis's—although I didn't tell him her name."

Her sponsor gasped. "Have you told him *nothing* about your childhood?"

"No. I just told him I had scars and left it at that."

"And he, a psychiatrist, let you get away with it? Hmmm. He *must've* been head over heels."

Silence on both ends of the line.

Then Jane whispered, "I hope he still is."

"Wait! I got so sidetracked about Rick that I still don't know why you're goin' back to Odessa."

Jane heard the disdain for Odessa in Lauren's voice; she pronounced the town's name with the same inflection she would use describing nasty body fluids. "Oh, my gosh, you're right! Daddy just called and asked me to come help him sell the house and move."

"Are you gonna share *this* with Joshua?"

Jane rolled her eyes, happy Lauren couldn't see her. "Yes! We'll talk this evening. So, I guess I'll leave tomorrow morning. I'm driving this time and taking Tallulah for company."

"Sounds like you're chompin' at the bit to get back. And plan on bein' gone a while," Lauren said. "Be sure to take in a meetin' while you're there. They do have AA in the hinterlands?"

Jane scoffed, "Of course they do. By the way, I went to a meeting this morning."

"Good on you, darlin'. Give me a ring if you want to talk."

Jane fussed over beef stroganoff for dinner, hoping to soften up Joshua before she dropped the news about her imminent departure. While the stroganoff was simmering, she packed two suitcases. Tallulah's carrier and her food and toys were ready to go.

Lulah ran through the kitchen to the front door. She was always the first to know when Joshua arrived home. Jane checked on the vegetable side dish, turned off the oven, and followed the cat.

"Hi, babe. Do I smell beef stroganoff?" Joshua smiled and took her in his arms.

Jane yielded to his hug. Joshua calling her "babe" was a good sign. Wanting to please him, she had embraced domesticity for once and put effort into the preparations. Candles burned on the table in the rarely used formal dining room. She had unboxed and washed the delicate porcelain dinnerware his parents had given them for their wedding and set the table with care. During the meal, she kept the talk inconsequential, minutiae from her day: she shaved a few seconds off her swim time, found the AA meeting helpful, and was amazed at how crowded the grocery store was. Telling herself she didn't want to spoil the meal, she delayed mentioning her return to Odessa.

Joshua appeared tired after his full day and seemed content to eat and listen.

Neither of them mentioned Rick's phone call.

After dinner, Joshua insisted on doing all the cleanup. Jane accepted the goodwill gesture and went upstairs to pack her makeup and jewelry and lay out her traveling outfit. Apprehensive about his reaction to her leaving again, she propped herself in bed and read a few pages in her daily reflections book, hoping to calm her nerves. She heard his tread on the stairs and closed the paperback.

When he entered their room, she announced, "My daddy called me this afternoon. He wants me to come back to Odessa and help get the house ready for sale." Jane cringed inside as she waited for his response.

He sat down on the bed and put his hand on her thigh. "Okay, but why didn't you tell me at dinner?"

"I was afraid you'd be upset." She turned to put her book on the bedside table.

"Guess that explains the stroganoff. It sounds like he needs your help. When are you leaving?" His voice was even, conveying nothing of his feelings.

"Tomorrow." She looked into his warm brown eyes.

"So soon? Huh. You just got back." He averted his eyes. "Tell me, did Rick call you again?" His gaze returned to her, checking her reaction.

Her sharp intake of breath was audible. She scooted back, letting his hand fall from her leg. "No! I would have told you."

"I sure hope so." He sighed. "Will you see him while you're there?"

"Maybe." Jane shrugged. "I don't know. Honey, he was my childhood friend, not a lover."

Joshua frowned. "I keep seeing your face when I handed you the phone." He shook his head as if to dislodge the image. "Do I have anything to worry about?"

"No! We just had lunch, that's it." She stopped speaking, realizing she had said too much.

He jumped to his feet. "What? Was *that* why you stayed another day? To spend the day with Rick?" He thrust his hands through his hair.

Jane gulped. "Maybe." She couldn't lie. She couldn't tell the truth, either.

Joshua struggled to keep his composure. His clenched fists were the only outward sign of his agitation. He didn't quite bellow. "Well, Jane. I won't offer to accompany you this time. Actually, I can't. That conference in Atlanta, the one I asked you to attend with me, starts the day after tomorrow. With all this Rick business, I'm sure that slipped your mind."

"I told you weeks ago I'd be taking a summer course and couldn't go." Her voice rose. She felt defensive, angry, and guilty all at once.

"But you're not taking a summer class after all, are you? Your summer is all freed up—to help your daddy—and whatever!"

"That's...that's not fair! Jane sputtered.

"Too fucking bad! And, you'll have to make arrangements for Tallulah. I'm not available to pet sit."

Jane kept her voice steady as she enunciated slowly. "She's...already...packed."

Joshua turned and stalked out of their bedroom. She heard the guest room door slam.

Chapter Eleven

When Jane met Joshua-Austin 1982

I looked up from the office schedule and watched as a tall, athletic man strode up to the front desk.

He smiled. "I'm Joshua Renfrew, the new doctor."

He was not what I expected—so much younger than the two other psychiatrists in the practice. And so much cuter. Instant attraction. Tummy flips. His black hair, glossy as polished ebony, almost touched his shoulders. He had to be about six-foot five—the perfect height for me. Casual charcoal trousers and a white shirt open at the collar. He carried an attaché case. No ring.

Remembering I was supposed to work there, I stood. "Welcome. Let me show you to your office. Dr. Ellis and Dr. Tate are with patients. When they're free, I'll let them know you've arrived." Worried that he would detect my delight, I led him to the room adjacent to the lobby and opened the door to his space. "I stocked the desk with office supplies, but if you find yourself in need of…anything, please ask." Did I sound professional or overcome?

"I didn't get your name," he said as he checked out his office.

No, you didn't. I was so stupefied by your fine self, I forgot it for a minute. "Um…Jane. Jane Jennings."

He held out his hand, and I stared at it for a moment. He must have thought I was an idiot.

Shaking his hand, I looked up into warm brown eyes and just about died. Impaled through the heart. I knew what was happening, had felt it twice before, both affairs—unmitigated disasters.

How long had it been since I had a romance? Way too long, almost two years. Concentrating on graduate school, I steered clear of entanglements. I grabbed a rare cup of coffee with the occasional man, but no one I had a desire to see again. Avoiding eye contact at Whole Foods and the YMCA, I kept myself to myself, even when I got horny.

Was my reaction to Dr. Renfrew real or mere hormones? Was I squirming? Compose yourself, I ordered.

"Happy to meet you, Miss Jennings." He raised his eyebrows. "Jane."

Hmmm. First-name basis already? All right.

"How long have you been with the practice?" he asked.

Making sure I trailed my fingers down his palm, I gently removed my hand from his. I replied, "Two years. But this is just temporary. I'm getting my master's in psychology at UT. If I ever finish, that is." Ha, I was trying to impress him. And it sounded so damned obvious.

Dr. Renfrew smiled, and I felt the tug in my belly that boded infatuation. I shivered as angel fingers tickled the back of my neck—that was a new one. I didn't need this. But apparently, I wanted it...him.

He said, "I hear that. Finished my residency in Oklahoma City a few weeks ago. Sometimes I didn't think I'd ever actually get to practice."

"So, you're from Oklahoma." *Brilliant conversationalist.*

"All my life. How about you?"

"Native Texan. Been in Austin for twelve years. But don't worry, I won't hold being a Sooner against you."

He chuckled. "And I won't hold being a Longhorn against you."

I felt warm—all over. Backed up toward the door, one reluctant step at a time, not wanting to leave. "I'd better get back to work."

He opened his mouth to say something but must have reconsidered. Nodding, he put his briefcase on the desk and started opening drawers.

Don't spend the day imagining what he might have said, I instructed myself. The rest of the afternoon, I made a conscious effort not to look toward Joshua's—Dr. Renfrew's—office. But it was too tempting, and I peeked now and then. Several times, I caught him looking at me. Each time our eyes met, another tummy flip. I bit the inside of my mouth, so I didn't belt out "At Last" à la Etta James. Or, alternatively, the underrated "Forever Came Today," although I was no soprano like Diana Ross. Tingling with excitement, I hid my smile. The minute I got home, I had to call Lauren.

The office closed at 5:00 p.m. but the three doctors retreated to the conference room. Frosted windows denied me a view of the yummy new doctor. Joshua. I stuck my head in to tell them I was leaving and had notified the answering service.

Drs. Ellis and Tate nodded and thanked me. Dr. Renfrew stood. "Have a good evening, Miss Jennings."

"Jane." I smiled. The rest of my words abandoned me.

After I locked the office door behind me, I dashed to my car. I raced home to Barton Hills like I was on the final lap of the Indy 500. Not easy to pass vehicles on Lamar Boulevard, but I succeeded a few times. Two years ago, after graduating from the Harris waif program at the tender age of twenty-eight, I had taken a lease on a little jewel of a studio near Zilker Park, only a few miles from work. The drive seemed endless this evening.

I opened the car door before I finished parking. Fumbling with my key, I finally got the apartment door open. Shrugging off my jacket, kicking off my heels, I ran to the phone to call my sponsor. "Please answer, Lauren." I was vibrating with excitement.

"It's your lucky day. You've reached Lauren!"

"Oh, thank you, Jesus!"

"No. It's *Lauren*. Jane?"

"Yes. I'm *so* glad you answered." I might have been panting.

"What on earth is goin' on, *chica*? Somethin's got you all fired up."

"My dream man walked into the office today."

"Whoa, girl," Lauren drawled. "A psychiatric patient? Go slow with that, honey."

"No. No! A psychiatrist. Dr. Joshua Renfrew."

"I take it he's not an antique like the two you work for?" Lauren had stopped by the office to take me to lunch and had met the good doctors.

I hooted. "Didn't you go to UT with Dr. Ellis's wife?"

Lauren said tartly, "I'm gonna pretend I didn't hear that. Go on, tell me about this dream man."

"He's the polar opposite of Tate and Ellis. Thirty yea—quite a bit younger. He's tall, very trim. The perfect height. Black hair down to his shoulders. He's got high cheekbones, a strong nose that looks like it might have been broken at some point. I wonder if he might have some Cherokee blood. He's down-home, yet exotic somehow. His eyes! They're the warmest chocolate brown. And his lips. I want to kiss them, maybe bite them gently, just a little. His smile...amazing. He's from Oklahoma City. Just starting his practice—"

"Jane!"

"I showed him his office, and I caught him looking at me, but I was looking at him too and when I left for the day, he stood up—"

"Jane!" Lauren's voice finally broke through my monologue.

"Sorry. You're right. I am fired up. I'm on fire for *him*! He's gorgeous. No ring. But some men don't wear one. Oh, no! But he wouldn't be giving me the eye the way he did if he was married, I don't think—"

"Great God in heaven, can't you shut up for a little minute? You're babblin' like a high school girl with her first crush."

I subsided, but my smile wouldn't quit; my cheeks felt stretched. "I can't help it," I moaned. "You can't imagine how hard it was to sit at my desk until five."

Lauren chuckled. "Darlin', you need to take a cold shower. Maybe I do too after listening to all that. Does this dreamboat like...women of a certain age?"

"You'll have to kill me first. He's going to be mine!"

"Pretty sure of yourself, ain't you?"

"Well, if his eyes were saying what I think they were...yeah, I am."

"Have you thought about the fact you're gonna be workin' with him?" Lauren asked.

"Yes, I have! If I quit my job, I won't see him, so I'm going to work tomorrow and every day after that."

"What're you gonna do if he asks you out?"

"Why, say 'no,' of course."

Lauren's rich laugh came through the line. "Well then, how you gonna make him yours?"

"Oh, I know how to play it, to make him ask me again." I laughed. "I'll be gentle."

"That's a dirty little laugh there, darlin.' That man doesn't stand a chance."

At work, I maintained a cool exterior, hoping no one suspected the volcano within. I doubted Drs. Tate and Ellis would notice my tight skirt and stilettos, but I hoped someone else would. I had been gearing up for this all week. This was the day I would execute. I wasn't dressed for comfort, but for conquest.

While I was making coffee in the break room, Joshua strolled in, and I pretended not to notice. The way he moved entranced me. So lithe. Did he swim? Play tennis? No football bulk.

"Good morning, Miss Jennings."

I turned from my task. "Jane." Demure smile, eyes downcast. "Good morning, Dr. Renfrew."

"Joshua."

Cool as a November breeze. "But I call Jeff, 'Dr. Ellis' and Lamar, 'Dr. Tate.'" My script called for a sexy little pout, but I restrained myself, thinking it was too much.

"Oh, I see." He grinned. "Maybe you'll make an exception and call me Joshua, anyway."

I waited a beat. "Joshua Anyway? Hmmm. I don't think so." I looked him right in the eye and smiled like I'd been practicing in the mirror for three days.

He didn't disappoint me. He cracked up, and I joined him. Sense of humor, check.

"So, you said you've been in Austin twelve years, is that right?"

He remembered.

"Yes, Joshua Anyway."

Brushing his hair back with his hand. Chuckling. "What do you do for fun?"

Oh, I could show you, if you like. I'm a little rusty, but...

"I'm a music lover." Quick, yet intense glance when I said 'lover.' "Rock and blues. We have some great clubs in town."

"Would you like to have dinner with me Saturday, then catch some music?"

You betcha.

Stricken look. "Oh, so sorry. I have plans. Maybe another time?" My eyes left no doubt I'd say yes next time.

"How about next Saturday? Or this Friday if you're free."

I made minute, unnecessary adjustments to the cuffs of my sheer sleeves while pretending to mentally review my calendar. Touched his arm—light as a butterfly—and said, "Friday would be lovely. The Fabulous Thunderbirds are at Antone's." No way was I waiting a week. Strutting out, I could feel his eyes on me. I gave my steps a little extra pizzazz.

Trying not to explode with delight, I returned to my desk and planned what to wear on Friday.

Our first date was flawless. Joshua took me to Chez Nous, a new French restaurant. I kept the conversation focused on him and Austin, not me. No way was I going to share my life history with a psychiatrist, especially this one. The food was sensuous. We fed each other bites of *truite meunière* and *noix de St. Jacques aux pleurottes*—otherwise known as trout and scallops—between heated gazes and conversational gambits. We lingered over *Ile Flottante*, a confection of meringue, crème anglaise, and caramel sauce. Calories be damned.

On the drive to Antone's, he reached for my hand between gear changes. I thought I might levitate from joy. My mind was cotton wool, thoughts couldn't form. We found a spot on Guadalupe a few doors down from the club—a miracle. The smoke and pulsating music overcame us as we entered the former Shakey's Pizza. Standing room only. No problem. That meant there were more points of body contact. I wanted to climb inside his clothes. Standing dangerously close to Joshua, the thump of Keith Ferguson's bass kept time with my heart.

During the second set, Lou Ann Barton surprised the room and hopped on the stage to join the band on "No Use Knocking."

Joshua leaned in close and raised his voice over the music. "Damn, that woman can sing."

A frisson of excitement jittered down my spine at the feel of his breath on my neck. Our eyes met, and we moved as one toward the door. As we drove back to my apartment, I firmly resolved not to invite him in; I knew what would happen if I did. My resolve nearly crumbled when he kissed me, but I locked my knees and my mental chastity belt.

The man knew how to kiss. Breathless, I put my hand on his chest and broke contact, resisting the urge to drag him inside and lash him to my bed. "I had a lovely evening, Joshua."

He cupped my face with both hands and gazed at me. "Good night, Jane. Rematch next week?"

All the words to all the love songs flowed through my consciousness. Joshua was the one I had been waiting for. Two years of studious celibacy detonated with a force I had never experienced.

We lay in the deployed Murphy bed, turned on our sides facing each other, propped up on pillows. Tallulah, apparently scandalized, had taken cover under the couch.

He ran his hand down my bare arm. Shivers.

I understood the term "afterglow" for the first time.

"Jane Jennings."

"Joshua Anyway."

He laughed and covered me with kisses.

Joshua romanced me. Flowers, dinners out. We were compatible on many levels, especially my favorite level. His only flaw was a dislike of dancing. Not a deal-breaker.

A month later, back at my place after catching Omar and the Howlers at Liberty Lunch, another spectacular rematch.

When our breathing returned to normal, he traced my lips, gazing into my eyes with an intentness that made me tremble. "You're an alcoholic? Hard to believe."

"Believe. I've been a coin-carrying member since 1976."

"I want you to meet my parents."

You won't be meeting mine.

"Joshua, we've only known each other for a few weeks." Protesting gently while my heart soared.

"I know, but I really want you to meet them—next weekend." He smothered me in kisses, grasping each finger on both hands and kissing them one at a time, then my palm, then my mouth. Then...bliss.

Lauren was elbow-deep in paperwork at her desk in the back room of the co-op. Since she was in the midst of preparing the quarterly report, she could only spare me a few minutes.

Raising her head from the huge pile of receipts, she greeted me brightly. "Darlin,' look at you! I can see Joshua has turned on your lovelight."

"Van Morrison."

"No, I was thinkin' of the original Bobby 'Blue' Bland."

Nodding, I said, "I defer to your superior knowledge of the blues."

Lauren rose and came around the desk. "You didn't ask to see me about music."

"He wants me to meet his parents."

"How gallant! Old-fashioned. Quite charmin' if you ask me." She folded her arms and leaned on the edge of her desk.

I must have looked uncharmed.

"Uh-oh. You look all stove up, like you got hold of some bad potato salad."

"Lauren, what do I do?"

"Well, you told me he was 'The One,' so I suppose you meet his parents."

Sighing, I replied, "Yes, of course. We're flying out this weekend, staying one night only, at my insistence." I looked at the floor. "What if he wants to meet my...par—family of origin?"

"Can't even bring yourself to call them 'parents.' Lots of pain there. Someday, you're gonna have to deal with it."

I protested, "I've made it fifteen years without dealing with it, thank you very much."

"And yet, you're sober, even with all that seethin' resentment."

"That hurts! I don't think I'm resentful. At least, I can honestly say I'm not *seething*. I barely spare them a thought. There's a lot of distance between us. Time and miles. Right now, I'm focused on my man." I held out my hands as if she could take my burden. "What should I do when he asks? I just know it will come up this weekend. So far, I've put him off with vague references to an unhappy childhood, but he's a flipping shrink, and he'll want to know details."

Lauren returned to the business side of her desk. "I'm surprised he hasn't pushed you more. But, from what you told me about your 'family of origin,' having him meet them might not be a good idea."

I shook my head. "No, it isn't. The last time I spoke with Tom, he said Mama had another relapse. I'll have to make it crystal-clear I'm a *de facto* orphan. Maybe I can convince him I was hatched. Or arrived on this earth via spacecraft."

"Now you're just reachin'," the redhead drawled. "Speaking of King Alcohol, when's the last time you went to a meetin'?" She cocked her head, waiting for my response.

Realizing I couldn't recall an AA meeting in the past week, I replied, "I'm going now. With the way my emotions have whip-sawed the past few weeks, I could use a dose of serenity."

On the flight, Joshua chatted about his seemingly perfect and idyllic childhood. Summer camp in the Colorado mountains, sailing vacations in the

Caribbean, skiing in Gstaad. The antithesis of poking roadkill with a stick in the prairie—and dealing with a crazed vodka-swilling mother.

Then he described his apparently flawless family: Dad, a well-known attorney—whose firm was known for its *pro bono* work—played a lot of golf; Mom, president and chairwoman of this and that charity, had earned her place in the hearts of Oklahoma City's disadvantaged; his older brother practiced law with their dad and was heavily involved in the Big Brother program; and his younger sister, a perpetual student with a bewildering clutch of letters after her name, currently studied modern languages at Oxford.

The picture he painted left me feeling "less than," a common malady of alcoholics I had observed—and lived—during the six years of meetings I had attended. I felt myself withdrawing and wondering what his parental paragons would think of me, a little West Texas refugee.

I hoped he hadn't noticed my lack of reciprocation while he spoke. Forcing a smile and nodding, I listened to his recitation. No doubt, he intended to put me at ease. However, with each piece of information he imparted, I felt my anxiety level climb. To calm myself, I leaned against him and breathed in his scent, hints of leather and cedar. How I hoped this visit wouldn't doom us.

"Listen to me, running on without giving you a chance to talk." Leaning in, he kissed my cheek. "Sorry, babe."

"Nothing to be sorry for, honey. I love listening to you. Your voice soothes my soul. And I appreciate you telling me what I'm walking into."

"You'll get a warm welcome." He squeezed my hand. "They're so excited I'm bringing someone home."

"Someone?" I teased.

He cupped my face. "Correction, the extraordinary Jane Jennings." After a moment, he said, "When am I going to meet your family?"

Never.

I sat up, leaving the comfort of his shoulder. "I've told you, we're not close."

"But I'm showing you mine, don't you think you should show me yours?" he asked with a wicked little grin.

"Are we still talking about parents?" I deflected. Nuzzling his neck, I fantasized about joining the Mile-High Club. Too bad there wasn't time.

The impeccably coifed and well-dressed couple who greeted us at the gate were exactly as Joshua described. Mrs. Renfrew, Elaine, wore a St. John knit and, as I predicted, pearls. Junior League personified. I should have taken that bet with Lauren; she had decreed there would be no pearls. Mr. Renfrew, Robert, looked the part of a successful lawyer in his three-piece suit with matching silk tie and pocket square. Nearly as tall as his son, he exuded confidence.

Thank God, they appeared happy to see us. Or were they smiling at their son? Joshua had said they were excited about meeting me. They were the most reserved and subdued excited people I had ever seen.

My navy-blue Dillard's suit, bought on sale, was prim and proper. Far from my usual attire, I hoped it passed muster with this elegant couple. I had busted my budget on a frantic shopping trip to find demure clothing I would probably never wear again. But, if my camouflage gained me acceptance, I would consider the money an excellent investment.

Elaine approached me and grasped my hands. "Jane. I'm so pleased to meet the woman who captured our Joshua's heart." She released me, smile intact. Placing her hand on Joshua's arm, she said, "You look well, dear."

Robert nodded in my direction. "Very happy to meet you, Jane." He and Joshua shook hands.

I matched their restraint and decorum, smiling with closed lips, maintaining good posture, walking at a slower pace. Because of my nervousness, it wasn't hard.

We picked up our luggage and located their car in the parking lot. The Lincoln Continental gleamed pearl white, and the seafoam green leather seats were sumptuous. No chauffeur, although I wouldn't have been that surprised if they employed one.

I had never been to Oklahoma, and my impression was one of neatly laid-out cleanliness. Joshua had told me his parents' home was in the

Country Club neighborhood, so I was expecting a three-story red-brick mansion, maybe with stately white columns or a turret.

As we approached the house and its immaculate grounds, Harry Chapin's "Taxi" played on my internal jukebox. My story was different from Harry's, but the gut-wrenching sense of not-belonging—the same.

I whispered, "Wow," at the unexpected sight of a sprawling modern stone ranch with a cantilevered roof. I glimpsed a tennis court and swimming pool as we sailed up the drive in the land yacht. A separate guest cottage and a six-bay garage completed the picture.

Joshua hopped out and ran around the back of the car to open my door. He took my hand and helped me out of the cushy seat.

Their home was not the traditional estate I'd pictured; the only red brick in sight paved the footpath. I clutched Joshua's hand as we approached the entrance, his parents leading the way past a flowing fountain and immense planters with lush vegetation.

A uniformed housekeeper opened the door to a grand foyer and a huge soaring living area. This was so far out of my experience; I didn't have the words for the architecture or the materials. Andy's house on Lake Austin, the most luxurious I had seen until now, was a shack compared to this place.

I tried not to gape. *I'll never let him see where I come from.*

Joshua greeted the housekeeper. "Nice to see you, Carolyn. This is Jane." We received nods from her as she left the foyer.

The Renfrews were staid and formal, but genial. I wouldn't call them friendly, but their smiles seemed genuine as they excused themselves to "see to dinner." Was this the "warm welcome" Joshua expected?

Joshua led me on a tour of the rambling home, each room more stunning than the last. I felt as if I were wandering through a life-sized game of "Clue"—the library, the lounge, the study, the billiard room—the house lacked only a conservatory. Immense abstract paintings, a collection of bronze sculptures on pedestals, deep upholstered leather couches, walls of ornate, leather-bound books. Andy, my only point of reference on the ways of the wealthy, had been a collector of modern art, but the pieces in this palace made his art look like crayon scribbles. Could that orange and black square be a genuine Rothko? Not my taste, and before I saw this place,

I'd have guessed the Renfrews would collect traditional art. With growing trepidation, I girded myself for more surprises.

After viewing the kitchen with its acres of soapstone counters and gleaming wood cabinets where Carolyn, head bent, went about her preparations, we headed into a laundry room the size of my apartment. Three miniature greyhounds jumped up from their fleece beds and padded to Joshua. He knelt on the floor, and the dogs sat politely with raised paws and wagging tails. "Merlin, Magic, and Wren. Good dogs!"

"They're beautiful, so sleek. I've never seen a miniature greyhound."

He looked up and shook his head as the animals broke ranks and swarmed him. Laughing, he said, "Whippets. I guess they missed me."

"Obviously."

The three brindle and white dogs led the way outside and stayed close as we roamed the grounds, our hands linked.

"I love the pool," I said. "It must've been wonderful to have one at home. Sometimes I dread the trek to the Y."

"Yet, you never miss your swim. Three times a week is impressive. I need to get back to it."

"Do you play tennis?" The breeze blew my hair in my face, and I brushed it back. My other hand grasped his like a lifeline. Tennis had not figured in my upbringing.

He rolled his eyes. "I did. Oh, boy, I did. Tennis is my parents' religion, and I suffered through intense sermons during my childhood. If forced, I'll pick up a racket on these visits home." Joshua checked his watch. "Mom said dinner is at six. Let's settle in and dress for dinner. I'll show you your room."

"My room?"

His face, full of regret, told me he wasn't joking. "House rule. It's only one night, babe."

Of course, I was disappointed, but I would tread lightly with these intimidating strangers and comply with the house rules. They *had* produced Joshua, I reminded myself. At least they had that going for them.

I showered and dressed in a slim black sheath that hit mid-calf. Another budget buster. Modest heels, loose hair. Practiced a gracious smile, not too much teeth or gums. Wondered what they'd think of my chandelier earrings and dismissed the thought. "I gotta be me. At least a little."

Elegant china, fine silver, and crystal huddled at one end of a table that could easily seat twenty. I sat next to Joshua, to the right of Robert and across from Elaine. Scooted my chair just a touch closer to my lover.

It would have been impossible to talk without shouting if we had spread out. We managed to keep a conversation flowing while we waited for the meal to be served, small talk about Austin and Joshua's new job. No awkward pauses.

I wondered if Joshua had prepared them in advance and asked them to avoid the topic of my history. He knew that a discussion of my early life was taboo. Far from relaxed, I crossed and uncrossed my legs under the table and strangled my napkin.

Carolyn entered, pushing a cart loaded with dishes. She placed a bowl of pink soup on the large plate in front of me.

Robert said, "Thanks so much, Carolyn. Looks like you've outdone yourself." The woman smiled and nodded before removing her cart to the kitchen.

"I hope you like strawberry soup, Jane," Elaine said.

"It looks delicious."

Overwhelmed by the silverware to the left, right, and above my soup, I followed Joshua's lead during the meal. I had been to some swanky restaurants in Austin, but this presentation seemed unnecessarily complex. My anxiety didn't help. I felt sweat on my upper lip and waited for a chance to dab it away with my napkin while no one was looking.

No wine was served at dinner, although the well-stocked wine rack at the far end of the dining room made it obvious they weren't teetotalers. They struck me as connoisseurs of fine wine. They certainly appeared to be connoisseurs of just about every other highfalutin' thing from what I could see. The table settings, the furniture, the museum-quality art, clearly expensive. Everything looked expensive. Had Joshua told them I didn't drink?

No surprise that Elaine was an adept conversationalist, flitting from topic to topic like an erudite butterfly. "Rebecca is loving Oxford. She's spending the summer traveling in Italy. She was so enamored with the Uffizi in Florence, I think she might study the Italian Renaissance next."

Robert chuckled. "Our girl gets enamored quite easily. She'll settle on a field one of these days and may even become gainfully employed."

"That'll be great," Joshua said. "You can only be a student for so long, in my opinion. Maybe she'll bite the bullet and teach something. Somewhere. Someday."

Elaine's eyes widened. "Now, now, dear. Sibling rivalry at your age?"

"Hardly." Joshua snorted. "Just hoping she finds her purpose."

Carolyn appeared again with her cart and exchanged our soup bowls for dinner plates. She left as unobtrusively as she had entered.

I concentrated on the asparagus, keeping my face blank as I pondered the dynamic of the last exchange.

"Joshua tells us you are pursuing your master's in psychology," Elaine's cultured voice prompted.

Uh-oh, my turn. I looked up from my plate and swallowed a chunk of Beef Wellington. "Yes, I'm working as well, so it's slow going. I've only just started the program."

Mr. Renfrew placed his fork on the edge of his plate and clasped his hands together. Glancing at his son, then at me, he said, "You're the first girl...um...woman our son has brought home since medical school."

I expected Joshua to be embarrassed, but, to the contrary, he grinned. "Yes, she is!"

Mrs. Renfrew turned to me. "We look forward to getting acquainted with you, Jane. I already see you are special to my son. As a mother, my greatest desire is to know that my son is loved."

I'm insane about him. "He is." I gave her my gracious smile.

After dessert—chocolate mousse worth the calories—we had coffee in the library. Elaine and Robert regaled me with charming stories of Joshua's childhood. I sat close to my lover and gripped his hand, nodding and smiling at what I hoped were the right places. After one particularly lengthy anecdote about a pony ride, I felt my eyes closing.

"Mom and Dad, I think Jane has reached critical mass from delightful reminiscences. We're going to turn in."

I stood and made eye contact with both parents. "Thank you for a lovely meal. And the stories. It's been a long day." Stopping myself just in time from curtsying, I smiled with closed lips. "Good night."

Joshua and I retired to our separate rooms. Although he had prepared me for this harsh reality, I lay in the luxurious sheets, draped with a silk coverlet, and missed him.

Surprisingly, I slept well, a dreamless sleep. In the morning, I dressed in cuffed trousers, a tailored blouse, and low-heeled shoes. With this protective coloration, I would blend into the environment, but I never thought I would dress this way until I was eighty.

Breakfast, set out on a sideboard from some European king's reign, was minimal: pastries, juices, and coffee. I saw why. Elaine and Robert were dressed in tennis clothes. I gulped. I didn't own any, and I didn't play. Fish out of water. Then I noticed Joshua wore khaki pants with his white shirt, not tennis whites as I feared, and I breathed a sigh of relief that he wasn't taking part in his parent's religious ritual.

Elaine genteelly sipped coffee from a fine porcelain cup and gently placed it back in the saucer. She stretched her lips and greeted me. "Good morning, Jane. We're going to play a few sets. Would you care to join us? Rebecca's closet has some whites that should fit you. Size six?"

At least she got that right. Fetching a smile from somewhere, I replied, "Oh, no thank you. I've never played, but maybe Joshua will teach me someday." I beseeched Joshua with my eyes to let me off the hook.

To my relief, he seemed to read my distress. "Jane and I are taking a little tour this morning. I promised to show her my old stomping grounds. What time is lunch at the club?"

"We've made a reservation for two," Elaine said.

"Take the Jag." Robert stood and handed Joshua a set of keys. "Enjoy your tour, and we'll see you at two."

A little fresh air would be welcome. One more fancy meal and we would be on our way to the airport.

Bearing gifts—a box of Sweetish Hill pastries—I stopped by the co-op to check in with Lauren the day after our return. She brewed green tea, her latest kick, and I choked down the swampy, grassy drink. Lauren was off coffee these days, but I knew she'd be back, especially since she refused to use sugar.

I did my best to describe the elegance of the Renfrews and their home.

"Sounds like quite the abode. What sort of vibe did you get from his parents?"

"A distinctly moneyed vibe."

"Well, yeah, sure." She rolled her eyes. "Besides that?"

I sighed. "All I can say is, high society. Very proper. Very formal."

"All right." She sampled the green tea, not appearing to enjoy it any more than I did. "Any sign of emotional life? D'ya think they liked you?"

"Hard to tell. They smiled. They asked nonintrusive questions, said the right things, but I don't know."

"What'd Joshua say?"

"He waxed enthusiastic, said they liked me very well."

"Did he say how he got that impression, since they're so uptight?"

"I didn't say they're uptight." Frowning a little, I tried more tea, then frowned more. I'd bring my own coffee next time.

"You didn't have to." Lauren laughed. "I got the picture."

"I don't mean to make them sound unpleasant."

She shook her curls. "Oh, I'm sure they're *pleasant*. Pleasant is a life skill for folks like that. Just wondering how your lover reached the conclusion he did."

Now that I thought about it, I had the same question, but didn't want to reveal this to Lauren. "I'm not sure. He just knows."

She smirked. "When are all y'all gettin' together again?"

I frowned and swatted the suggestion away. "Never. Or as long as I can put it off. Just being with those *stellar* people made me feel like a…a…an imposter, hanger-on, fraud." I glanced at her. "Like an orphan. Meeting them just reinforced my decision that I'll never let him meet my parents."

Our courtship blazed white-hot. At work, we managed to keep it professional—except in the coffee room. At play, delirious happiness.

Tallulah was a holdout, playing coy. When Joshua came over, she would scrutinize him and stalk away with her tail held vertically. There weren't many places to hide in my studio, so she usually scooted under the couch. She must have sensed that Joshua was a dog person. Our interaction with the whippets was weeks ago, but I wondered if the cat had smelled the enemy on us and remembered. Then one night, my Persian deigned to accept him, which was a relief to me. She started to look for him when I prepared for an evening out, and I knew she was as committed as I. Like me, Tallulah did not give her heart easily.

Joshua surprised me with tickets to see The Talking Heads at Fiesta Gardens. September 7th, 1982, a date etched in my memory. They weren't my favorite band by any means—I favored straight-ahead rock and Texas blues—but with the state of music these days, they were a cut above the hair bands that dominated the scene. Smart, clever, quirky, they had a good beat and were easy to dance to, as the saying goes.

I didn't really care where Joshua took me; I only wanted to be with him.

We went to Los Comales for dinner first. After chicken mole and sopapillas, we left his car in the lot and walked to Fiesta Gardens because parking was non-existent near the venue.

Joshua explained the show was originally planned for the City Coliseum, but the band decided an open-air location would be healthier than a smoke-filled indoor setting for Tina Weymouth, the pregnant bassist.

I fanned myself with my hand. "It has to be a hundred."

"Yeah, it's toasty, all right." He pulled his loose shirt away from his body. "I've always thought you look good a little sweaty."

"Don't make me blush, not in this heat." We grinned at each other. Despite the soaring temperature, I shivered in anticipation of making love when we got back to my place.

Austinites were used to triple digits, and the heat did not stop the crowd from reveling in the dance tunes. The beat was irresistible; the band, energetic. Tina laid down her bass line. What a trouper!

Even though he disdained dancing, I teased Joshua into trying a few dance moves. I grabbed his hips and told him, "Loosen up, honey. I know you know how to work those hips."

"Thank you, babe." He grinned. "Watch this."

I bit my lip, not wanting to laugh at his efforts. Very few men I knew could really let go and let the music take them. That made me think of Andy, who could, and I pushed the thought out of my mind.

The scene got a little out of control, the perimeter fencing torn down in places by those crashing the gate by land. Other ticketless people crashed the concert by boat from the river that ran behind the stage. We learned the next day that concert-goers' cars parked in the neighborhood were vandalized. The residents hadn't been notified by the city about the concert. Maybe the heat drove them mad. We congratulated ourselves on our foresight in leaving Joshua's Saab out of the danger zone.

Back at my apartment, singing "take me to the shower, drench me with the water, washing me down," we sudsed off the concert sweat. After dressing in silk pajamas, I went to the kitchenette, scooped out a generous serving of lemon sorbet, and danced the bowl and two spoons to Joshua. Dressed only in pj bottoms, he lounged on the couch. I hit the button on my tape player and Bob Seger's "Her Strut" played.

As I put on a dance revue for his viewing pleasure, Joshua whistled, egging me on. I ended my routine with a crescendo of shoulder shimmying which he appeared to enjoy. He put the bowl on the end table and waved me over to sit beside him. I sat, a little breathless.

"Once in a lifetime, Jane. Will you marry me?"

Lucky I was sitting down. He knelt on the floor and reached under the couch cushion, bringing out a small box. If there had been a photo taken of my face at that moment, I'm sure I would have had it destroyed, along with the negative. Thankful that my dropped jaw and bulging eyes were not captured for posterity, I tried to compose my face and my emotions.

Joshua's smile faltered. "Did you say something, or has my hearing failed me?"

My shock evaporated. "Yes! Yes! Yes!" I reached for his face and cradled his strong jaw with both hands and kissed him, bowling him over and landing on top. I stayed that way for a while. This was heaven. This was real.

Chapter Twelve

Revisiting the Past-Austin by way of Dallas and Lubbock 1984

Jane woke the next morning alone in bed. The reality of last night's confrontation with Joshua rocked her like a yacht struck by a rogue wave. As she grappled with the emotions stirred by Mama's funeral, the fantastic sex she and Joshua had thirty-six hours earlier, and the fragments of the recurring dream that shocked her awake, she clasped her head as if that could stop the tumble of images hurtling through her mind.

Her astral body had been out flying again. Recalling the swooping changes in elevation—soaring to the treetops then plummeting to within inches of the earth—and the somersaults she had turned in the air, queasiness overtook her. Was the residue of the Owsley tabs from all those years ago still lurking in the synapses of her brain? If so, maybe the collision of those random molecules with a receptor caused the dreams—no, nightmares—that recently plagued her.

She rubbed her eyes to purge the vision of the faceless people on the ground pointing at her aerial acrobatics as she struggled to maintain altitude and avoid crashing into them. Glancing at the bedside clock, she was astounded to see it was after ten a.m. She would be getting a late start.

The disconcerting dream-hangover stayed with her as she rose, showered and dressed, and hauled her bags downstairs. The guest room door was open, the bed made. Joshua had already left, without even trying to make up. While it was true she hadn't tried either, she had her pride. In her worldview, the man pursued the woman. She sniffed and quoted Billy Pilgrim: "So it goes." Like Billy, she felt unstuck in time as she prepared for her journey to Odessa.

She stopped in the kitchen to get the cooler of the new Diet Coke—quite a bit tastier than Tab, that high-school chemistry-lab-experiment in a pink can—and Tallulah's belongings. Spying some papers on the counter, she snatched at them, fearing a Dear Jane letter. But it was Joshua's travel itinerary topped with a Post-It note. His handwriting was legible, unlike his usual doctor scrawl.

The simple note read: *Will you be here when I get back?*

She didn't know—deciding what path her life should take, including if she was cut out for marriage—was the purpose of the trip. She shoved the papers in her purse.

Joshua's wedding gift to her, a 1983 Ford Mustang GT 5.0, sat in the garage. She had chosen bright red, with the wide black racing stripe on the hood. She loved the spoiler but had thought the rear window louvers a bit much and declined them. Joshua expressed surprise she had turned down a BMW for one hot piece of American steel, but this racy little muscle car was what she craved. Her collection of cassette tapes was already in the car, neatly arranged in a Bruno Magli shoe box. ZZ Top's *Eliminator*, Stevie Ray Vaughan's new release *Texas Flood*, and assorted Led Zeppelin, Joan Jett, Bob Seger, and Steve Miller, whose music transcended the disastrous relationship with his roadie.

Jane managed to capture Tallulah and place her in the carrier using gentle persuasion and the allure of a catnip toy. The fawn-colored Persian resisted, perhaps connecting the crate to trips to Dr. Harris. A twinge of conscience reminded her she needed to see the Harrises soon; it had been months since she had.

Once she lugged everything into the garage, she began to load the car. As she closed the trunk, she had a brainstorm: because this trip was to resolve her past—all of it—every dark corner had to be exposed, the nasty dregs dragged out, poked and prodded, and exposed to the sunlight. Nothing less would get her mind straight. For too long, she had run from her problems, lying to herself—and her husband. That couldn't continue. How had she remained sober for eight years with the overhang of her secrets?

Getting in the car, Jane bit her lip as she contemplated how to start the excavation of her history. She pulled out the road atlas, studied the map of Texas, and decided her first stop would be to visit Uncle Rafe in Dallas. Running back into the house, she called him.

"I'm coming to see you. Should be there by late afternoon. Can you give me directions from I-35?"

"Hold on there. Who's this?" her uncle rumbled.

"Oh, sorry. It's Jane. I need to talk. Mama's funeral, seeing that old house…stirred up a toxic psychic stew. I'm driving out to Odessa to help Daddy move, but I want to talk to you first. Okay?" Her words came out in a rush.

"Honey, it's more than okay. My dance card is empty, so you're welcome to come. When I saw you at the funeral, I thought maybe something was gnawing at you. Got a pencil?"

Jane wrote down his address and the directions, then dialed her daddy.

"Jennings."

"It's Janie." *Damn, still regressing.* "I'm coming, but I have to make a couple of stops on the way, so it'll be two, three days before I get there."

"That's fine, honey. Take care of your bidness, and I'll see you soon. Drive safe!" His deep drawl and slow speech sparked memories from her childhood. Good memories that brought misgivings about her mission to confront him about what she had learned. It wouldn't be easy, but it was necessary. She hurried back to the car.

"Road trip, Lulah!" She buckled up, tapped the remote to open the garage door, and backed out of the driveway. Listening to the rumble as the door closed, she wondered if she would return with more insight than she currently possessed. She drove down Cicero Lane, turned north on Loop 360, and began the two-hundred-mile drive.

Clicking on the radio, she dialed in a rock station. An Air Supply tune came on and she yelled "No!" Immediately swerving to the wide shoulder of 360, she turned off the overly sentimental soft rock song. She shuffled through her tapes, chose *Night Moves*, and inserted the cassette into the player. She leaned back in the leather seat and breathed a sigh of relief as

"Rock and Roll Never Forgets" poured out of the speakers. "That's more like it! Right, Tallulah?" The cat didn't deign to answer.

Jane took the opportunity to pop open a can of Diet Coke. To the sound of Bob Seger rasping the lyrics and the Silver Bullet Band providing a strong backbeat, she pulled back on the highway.

Approaching Dallas, traffic snarled because of the never-ending road construction. She inched along the miles of orange and white barrels, glad to have the musical accompaniment on this boring slog. More than four hours had elapsed by the time she got to Uncle Rafe's place. She pulled in the drive, rested her head on the steering wheel, and sighed in relief at her safe arrival. Carrying Tallulah's travel case, she gave her uncle a one-armed hug and returned to the car for cat supplies.

When Jane brought in the make-shift litter box and food, Rafe had already let Tallulah out of the carrier and was snuggling her. "Beautiful cat! What's her name?"

"Tallulah."

"That's a mouthful. I made some King Ranch chicken. Hope you're hungry."

Jane smiled. "I sure am. Didn't have time to eat this morning. I woke up late."

"Well, everything's ready. I'll just get it on the table."

"Thanks, Uncle Rafe. It smells great. I'll be there as soon as I feed my girl and get her settled."

"Set up in the laundry room, through the kitchen, on the right. No rush, honey. And now you're all grown up, you can drop the uncle. Call me Rafe."

While they ate, Jane concentrated on the layered casserole of chicken, cheese, and corn tortillas in the creamy sauce, and was silent.

"For someone who wanted to talk, you're sure quiet," Rafe said.

Jane looked up. "Just gathering my thoughts. There's so much swirling through my mind after going back...not home...to Odessa."

"First time you returned hom—to Odessa, wasn't it? What made you leave back then?"

"My drunk mama, of course."

"Well, honey, she was drunk a lot. Something must've happened." Rafe's voice was neutral as he spoke about his dead sister.

She sighed and said, "Oh, yeah. It did."

"You want to talk about it?" He patted her hand.

Jane met his eyes. "Grace."

Her uncle sat back as if to distance himself from that painful topic. "That's what destroyed your mama, I do believe."

"Yeah, I think you're right. Tom spilled the beans to me when I was eleven. It's amazing I'd never heard about the poor child's brief existence until then."

"Martha, and your daddy, for that matter, made it clear the subject was off-limits."

Jane glanced at him. "I'm not faulting you…Rafe." She shook her head. "Oh no, the fault lies with my mama and daddy."

He nudged her back to the topic. "Still don't understand how Grace led to you leaving."

She said matter-of-factly, "Mama said if she could strike me dead and bring Grace back, she would." The pain from this atrocity had lessened with the years—and Mama's death. Still, as she repeated those words, her heart pounded, and her hands clenched in her lap.

"Dear God!"

Not wanting Rafe to see the depth of her heartache, Jane shrugged. "Yeah, I couldn't remain under their roof after that. If you and Aunt Penny had still lived in Odessa, I might've shown up at your door that night."

Rafe's face crumbled. "Penny. God, how she loved you." He looked at the ceiling, then down at the table. "I still miss her."

Jane squeezed his hand. "I'm sure you do. You know, I loved her, too. Tom told me about—"

Rafe gaped at her. "Told you about *what*, Janie?"

"That you and Aunt Penny wanted to adopt me, or at least take me away from them." Jane's eyes glistened with tears as she croaked, "Oh, how I wish you had."

Her uncle's shoulders began to shake. He sobbed, "I do, too." Pushing his chair back from the table, he made an effort to control his emotions. "Maybe if we had, Penny wouldn't have tried so hard to have a child and die in the trying."

Dinner lost its appeal. They abandoned the dining table and moved to the living room, sitting together on the couch, talking for a while. Jane knew Rafe had bought this place after his wife's death, so she didn't expect to see her aunt's touch on the décor. The only traces of Aunt Penny were photographic—a large portrait over the fireplace, and several pictures in tabletop frames.

Jane rose and brought back a few pictures to the couch, savoring the sight of Aunt Penny's sweet face.

"I have to know—what did my mama and daddy say when y'all wanted to take me in?"

Rafe looked past her as if seeing another time and place. "Honey, you'd better talk to your daddy about that."

She gave him a sharp look. Then she sighed, relaxing into the soft leather of the couch. "You're right. And I will."

Jane reminisced about all the ways Aunt Penny had made her childhood better with her love of life and music. Most importantly, she was the one who noticed Jane could read before she even started school. Her aunt had encouraged her reading, building her a library starting with Golden Books like *The Little Red Hen*. In grade school, Jane's favorites were the adventure tales of Jules Verne. Those memories cheered Rafe; his mood lightened and the lines in his face eased.

"You were both so good to me," Jane said. "I still have the transistor radio y'all bought me before you moved. That radio was my prized possession for years. It opened the world of music to me."

Tallulah jumped up on the couch and butted her head against Rafe's hand.

"Maybe I'll get me one of these critters." He stroked the cat's ears. "Remember Alice?"

Jane brightened. "Sure do. She was a nice cat."

"She was. Alice lived a good long life. Passed away while napping in the sun at the age of fifteen. Not long after Penny." He excused himself, got up to retrieve a box of tissue, and yanked out several sheets to dab his eyes. "Damn, girl. Never thought I'd take such an emotional journey tonight."

Jane stood and hugged him. "Speaking of journeys, I'd better get on the road."

"Sure you don't want to stay the night?"

"No, thanks. I'm going to start on the next leg of my trail of tears. When I get tired, I'll find a motel."

"Okay, honey. I hope you'll keep in touch."

"I will." Jane hesitated, then said, "There's one last thing I need to address. It's weighed on me for years." She took a deep breath and continued, "The reason I didn't get in touch with you when Aunt Penny died was because I didn't *know*. Not until Tom told me, months later. I was a mess back then, and well, when I found out, I thought it was too late to get in touch." She gripped his hand. "Can you forgive me? I promise to make amends."

"Hmm, amends. AA?" He didn't look surprised.

"Yes, eight years. I want to break the cycle of drunken women in my family."

Rafe patted her back. "Proud of you, honey. Let me help with Tallulah's things. I'll walk you out."

"Thanks, Rafe."

Jane took I-20 out of the Dallas-Fort Worth metroplex to the Texas boogie of ZZ Top. After an hour, her concentration began to flag despite the spirited efforts of Billy, Dusty, and Frank. The rest of *Eliminator* would have to wait for tomorrow.

"Well, Miss Lulah. We didn't get very far, but I'm starting to fade."

A highway sign for Weatherford loomed. "Jeremy grew up in Weatherford. All that bluster about being from big D. Ha!" She pulled off the interstate and got a room at a vintage mom and pop motel. Parking right in front of the door to her unit, she unloaded her cat, a small bag, and fell into bed. Sleep took her.

She and Rick had been arrested for murder. The body they had buried so long ago was exhumed by coyotes. Shreds of black plastic bags and clothing scraps had attracted the attention of a passing motorist on a stretch of featureless road. Peering through clumps of switchgrass, feral yellow eyes glinted with malice, delighting in their capture.

They stood on the shoulder of the highway, bathed in the red and blue lights of the sheriff's cruiser with their hands shackled behind them, hanging their heads in shame.

The travel alarm shocked her awake. The remnants of the new nightmare lingered and left her gasping. "I don't need to be a psychologist to figure out that one," she muttered to herself.

She fed the cat, showered, and dressed quickly. Taking the time to make a cup of motel coffee, she gulped it down. Vile, but she needed the caffeine. She crated Tallulah, packed the cat's things, and loaded the car for the next leg of the journey.

Consulting the road atlas, she figured she would get to Lubbock in the early afternoon. When she stopped for gas and lunch, she would give Jolene a call to let her know to expect company.

With Weatherford in the rearview, she settled in for the drive with ZZ Top's tune "Got me Under Pressure" filling her ears. "I hear you, Dusty. Feel the same way."

Half an hour later, she changed the cassette, and the speakers blasted out Stevie Ray Vaughan's flavor of good old Texas blues.

"Man, he can make that guitar do things no one but Jimi Hendrix could do," Jane told Tallulah, who yawned in response. Despite the cat's lack of interest, Jane regaled her with tales of seeing SRV with the Nightcrawlers and the Cobras back in the day. "Driving up to the Soap Creek Saloon at night was such a rush. I felt a little like an outlaw." That brought up thoughts of Andy, which she swept from her mind.

When she got hungry, she stopped at Whataburger in Abilene—skipping the fries. After eating her fast food, she called her sister-in-law from a pay phone.

Jolene picked up on the first ring. "Hello?"

"Hi, Jolene. It's Jane. Um, I'm on my way to Odessa and wondered if I could stop by to see y'all this afternoon." She feared her sister-in-law might not appreciate the late notice.

"This afternoon? Didn't you just get back to Austin?" Jolene's voice rose in surprise. "Lubbock isn't exactly on the way to Odessa. What's up?"

"I've been thinking...way too much. It's what I do." Jane stopped, realizing she sounded incoherent. "Let me start over. Mama's death ripped open old wounds, then the cosmos sprinkled salt on them. I didn't deal with things while I was there, so I'm going back."

"Cosmos? Okay. What things? Wait—I really shouldn't pry. Forget I asked. And, oh, I don't mean to seem less than gracious. We'd love to see you."

Jane breathed out in relief. "Thanks, Jolene. And you're not prying. Daddy called and asked me to come back hom—to Odessa. He's thinking of selling the house and wants my help. Also, Tom confided some things when we talked, and I'd like to... discuss them further."

"Sure. I'll call him and let him know you're coming."

"That'd be great. And I need some advice in the romance department. After only one year of marriage, I've managed to alienate my husband. He thinks I'm having an affair with Rick."

Jolene gasped.

"Oh, I'm not, absolutely not!"

After a pause, Jolene replied, "Sounds like you got a lot on your plate."

In a rush, Jane said, "On top of that, there's so much I'm sorry for, so many things. I've abandoned my family, and I want y'all back."

"Honey, you never lost us. We've always been here and always will be."

"That means a lot to me." Jane's eyes stung. "I'll see you in a few hours. I'm just outside Abilene. Almost forgot, I have my cat Tallulah with me. Will that be a problem?"

"No. Max, our Golden Retriever, loves everybody. I'll set another place for dinner. We're having King Ranch chicken. How's that sound?"

Jane didn't hesitate and said with great enthusiasm, "Wonderful! Oh, can I get directions from Route 84?"

If she didn't count the last two nights, Jane couldn't remember the last time she had eaten King Ranch chicken. The casserole appeared to be a family favorite; Shane and Tom both had seconds. At least Jolene's recipe tasted a little different from Rafe's. Had a little extra kick.

Dinner table talk covered the three Bs: basketball, bible, and basketball. Tom was a fanatic on topic one and three. Jolene, a strong proponent of topic two. Jane decided to wait until the children went to bed before broaching family history with Tom. She picked at her food and studied the exchanges among the four Jennings as if they were an exotic tribe whose culture she was researching—*familias normalias*. After the meal, Summer and Shane cleaned up the table and the kitchen without prompting. Jane found that amazing and recalled the lengths to which she had gone to avoid household chores when she was their age.

Tallulah was safely ensconced in the laundry room, away from the curious, goofy Max. When introduced to the dog, the cat had arched her back, hissing, and spitting like a little demon. Tallulah smacked him in the nose and that set off Max, who ran around the house like a furry tornado. After he knocked over a lamp, Jolene sent him outdoors.

The three adults went to sit on the back patio. Max approached Jane cautiously, a few steps at a time. He sat and offered a paw. "Oh, what a sweetie!" She shook his paw, and Max settled at her feet with a groan. Luckily, Tallulah was declawed, so the only injury to the dog was to his pride.

Tom took the initiative. "Kid, somethin' brought you all this way. Spill."

"Goodness, Tom. Am I on a time limit?" Jane asked. She brushed her hair back, wishing she had put it up because of the heat. "Okay, let's just dive right in. I'm sure Jolene told you Daddy is going to sell the house, and he wants me to help him."

"Good. I hope they raze it to the ground and salt the earth," Tom said dryly.

Jane grinned. "Wow! Great minds. You stole my line."

The siblings broke into laughter.

Jolene stood. "I'm gonna let you two work this out. Jane, we can have that girl talk later, if you'd like."

"Yes, I'd like that."

Tom leaned over and took his wife's hand. "Good defensive move, honey."

When the sliding door closed, Jane regarded Tom, speculating how the coming conversation would go. Tom gazed at her as if he were thinking the same thing. Their six-year age difference seemed negligible now, although their life experiences and perspectives were vastly different.

"Well, I got to wonder why you're so willin' to go runnin' back. You gonna be at his beck and call now?" Tom shook his head. "Remember what I said about your old pattern of being Daddy's girl? I just don't get it."

Jane twisted her lips, considering what to tell him. "Believe me, I thought about your resentm—I mean, perspective, a lot. The time just wasn't right to talk to Daddy about it at the funeral."

He raised his eyebrows. "You're way more sensitive than me. You sayin' you *are* gonna confront him?"

"Confront is such an aggressive word."

Tom snorted. "Bullshit! Confront is what you need to do. Ask him why we didn't live in town." He paused but spoke again before she could answer. "I can tell you why—Mama didn't want to. Daddy's a classic enabler."

They sat in silence for a while. Jane was the first to speak. "I'm still trying to wrap my head around my childhood. The whole mess rushed at me like a tsunami when I went back." She leaned forward and touched his arm. "You were my rock until you left for school. I always looked up to you—literally and figuratively. I never suspected how angry you were at Daddy."

Tom scooted his lawn chair to face his sister. "I thought you had come to the same conclusion since you left."

"No, I had a twinge of guilt about leaving Daddy. When I was little, I admired him, thought he could do no wrong." Jane shook her head. "Remember how mad he was at Mama when she got drunk before Grandma June's funeral?"

"So, he got angry with her at times. Never angry enough to dump out her booze. And how long did his being mad last? Until they hustled down the hall to the bedroom at night, is how long."

She scrunched her nose in distaste. "I recall hearing them. Once, I got out of bed and knocked on their door, asking if they were okay. They were quieter after that." She glanced at him. "You think *sex* is why he stayed with her?"

He smirked. "Can ya think of another reason?"

"For us?"

"And how did that work out? He left us at her mercy. We were miserable."

"There was some good. He'd take me grocery shopping," Jane reminded him.

"Well, ain't that grand! He didn't let us starve to death."

Jane leaned forward in the lawn chair. "Compared to Mama, he was a hero. It was Mama who drove me around the bend. Those years I was alone with her, with you at Tech and Daddy gone working—awful."

"Wasn't always that way. The sad thing is, our family life was fairly normal...until Grace died. Daddy was home more. He's the one who taught me my hoop skills. After dinner, he'd take me outside to play. And Mama didn't drink, not that I knew anyway."

Jane's eyes narrowed. "I just can't picture it."

"Why would you? You came along after we moved into that shack in the middle of nowhere."

Jane leaped to her feet, knocking over her lawn chair, and sending Max for cover. "What?" she yelled. "Another secret. Dropping them one at a time is like Chinese water torture—only you're using nuclear bombs!"

Tom held his hands up, palms outward. "Whoa there. Calm down. And I have to say that right there's the craziest mixed metaphor I ever heard!"

She picked up her chair and sat. Her voice returned to normal volume, but her face felt hot. "What *else* don't I know? At the hotel before the funeral, you dropped a couple of bombshells that still have me reeling. Now this. Why the hell can't you just lay it all out?" She stopped for breath. "Okay, I'll bite. Where did y'all live... before I was born?"

"Oil camp near Notrees."

"Oil camp?" Jane's eyes popped. "At school, the only kids lower on the totem pole than us were the oil camp kids. Damn!"

"I never bought into that crap. And it wasn't as bad as *you* seem to think. I don't remember much. We moved before I was five, after...you know. I do recall we had a single-wide. So did most folks. Tons of kids around."

"Anything else left in the arsenal?"

"Nope. The silo is empty." Tom showed his palms and attempted a smile.

Jane stared at him, but her unfocused eyes saw a lonely house in the prairie outside Odessa. They fell silent.

Max approached and stopped in front of Jane, his head cocked to the side. "Oh, Max. Sorry I spooked you, baby." She stroked his head, and he settled between her and Tom.

"Guess I hadn't realized you didn't know the early history of our wretched family. Now you can understand why I hardly ever brought Jolene and the kids to visit them."

"Sorry I blew up at you. I made this trip to come to grips with the past, but now there's more added to the list. Why these revelations rattle me so much is beyond me. Maybe I'm just one raw throbbing wound." She shot him a glance. "Or maybe that house haunts me, and I can't picture our so-called family anywhere else."

He reached out and patted her hand. "I vote for the raw wound theory. You got a hair trigger."

She nodded. "Guess so." After a moment, she said, "I saw Rafe yesterday."

That got Tom's attention. "Oh, yeah? You're makin' the rounds, ain't you?"

"Since I was headed back to help Daddy—" She glanced at him. "I decided to hit it all head on. Put the puzzle pieces together, see the whole picture. If I don't, I won't make any progress in integrating my personality."

"What?" Tom made a face like he had sucked on a lemon. "Sounds like some lofty psychobabble to me. You oughta write a pop psychology book."

Jane matched his sarcasm. "Oh, I have. It's called *When Bad In-laws Happen to Good People.* I have an autographed copy for your sweet wife in my bag. Poor thing didn't know what she was getting into when she signed on with the Jennings family."

Tom hooted. "Ouch, sis." He craned his neck, glancing at the house. "I'm glad Jolene was smart enough to leave us alone." Turning back to Jane, he asked, "What'd Rafe have to say for himself?"

"He confirmed what you told me, about him and Aunt Penny wanting to take me away from...them."

He frowned. "Did ya think I made it up? What'd he say about our par—their reaction?"

She shrugged. "Nothing. He says I should ask Daddy myself. And I intend to."

"Sounds a little like confrontation." Tom gave her a sly grin.

Jane found Jolene in the family room.

Her sister-in-law rose and said, "I've got the guest room made up. Ready for that talk?"

"After my chat with Tom, I'm not quite sure. He and I will just have to agree to disagree about the dynamics of our dysfunctional childhood. But yes, I do want to run something by you."

"Okay, then. Let's head on upstairs."

"I have to apologize for visiting on such short notice. Guess I was afraid you'd say you couldn't see me."

Jolene's brow furrowed. "Oh, honey, never. You're family. I'm just glad we've reconnected, and I hope it continues."

"What did Tom ever do to deserve you?"

"I wonder what I ever did to deserve him," Jolene countered.

"Wow. Y'all sure seem happy. Maybe you can give me relationship tips. I sorely need some."

They climbed the stairs and looked in on the kids. When they opened the door at the top of the stairs, Summer sat up in bed and asked, "Will you be here tomorrow, Aunt Jane?"

"Yes, honey. I'll see you at breakfast."

Peeking into Shane's room, they saw he was fast asleep.

As they entered the guest room, Jane said, "I haven't had a girl talk session since I was sixteen. At least not with someone my age."

"You're overdue."

Jane kicked off her boots and curled up on the bed.

Jolene sat on the chair. "Tell me what's goin' on."

"Well, you know I stayed in Odessa another day to see Rick."

"What d'ya mean 'see,' like a *date*?"

Jane sat up. "I don't know."

"How can you not know?" Jolene folded her arms and regarded Jane with a frown on her usually serene face.

"It wasn't a date. Not really. It was more like catching up. We hadn't spoken since we were kids when his sister Mavis died. You know about that?"

Jolene nodded. "Yes, Tom told me. What a tragedy for that family."

"The worst." A vision of the blond curly-haired Mavis made Jane grimace. *Will that child haunt me forever?*

"Tell me about your…catching up."

"First off, you have to understand I also lost Rick, my best, and only, friend that day—" Jane faltered, "w-when his sister died. You know where we lived. No one around for miles. After Mavis's death, Rick and I were done." She glanced at her sister-in-law. "So, when I saw him in the coffee shop—"

"Wait! When was this? What coffee shop?"

"Oh, a little place in downtown Odessa. I stopped there on the way to drop off the burial dress."

"Got it. You didn't catch up then?" Jolene's forehead wrinkled.

"A little. He was friendly. I wasn't sure he would be, because of the accident." She crossed her legs Indian-style and put a pillow on her lap, resting her arms on it. "We talked for a bit, but I was pressed for time. He wanted to know my story." Jane shrugged. "We didn't have time to talk at the funeral reception, so I stayed the extra day. He took me on a tour of Monahans Sandhills Park where he works, and we had lunch."

"Okay, so what aren't you tellin' me?"

"I-I sort of didn't tell Joshua why I was staying another day."

"Goodness! Why not?"

Jane glanced at her sister-in-law, then averted her eyes. "Because I felt a little…attraction to Rick, you might say."

"Uh-oh. This is serious stuff." Jolene's lips pressed together.

"I know it. Then the day after I got back, Rick called the house and Joshua picked up. When he handed me the phone, I guess my reaction screamed guilt. But nothing happened at Monahans. Or at lunch. And when Rick took me back to the hotel—"

"Hotel?" Jolene's voice rose. "What the heck!"

"Oh, no. God, no." Jane held up her hands as if to ward off the implication. "He just dropped me off."

"Okay. Your story is like a roller-coaster ride. So, why did Rick call you?"

Jane shrugged. "Don't know. He hung up and didn't call back."

"That's odd. How'd y'all leave things after y'all's lunch?"

"He asked me if I felt anything for him."

Jolene's eyes widened. "And?"

"I didn't answer, just booked."

"Honey, you weren't honest with your husband." Jolene stood and began to pace. "What's worse, you're not bein' honest with yourself. Remember what Jeremiah told us: The heart is deceitful above all things and desperately wicked. Who can understand it?"

Jane's lips pursed. "I sure don't."

Her sister-in-law returned to the chair. "Listenin' to you makes my head spin."

"Mine, too." Jane laughed weakly. "I'm getting sick of myself."

"I don't know what advice I can offer." After a moment, she asked, "Are you gonna see Rick when you're in Odessa?" Jolene's down-turned mouth left no doubt how she felt about that prospect.

Jane hung her head. "Yes." She made eye contact with her sister-in-law. "I have to face my demons head on."

"Demons? Maybe that's a clue right there."

Jane winced. "I didn't mean just Rick. There are things I have to address with my daddy."

"You've got some soul-searchin' ahead of you." Jolene walked to the door, then turned back to Jane. "I seem to remember forsakin' all others being part of the weddin' vows. Have a good night." She closed the door softly.

Jane wondered why she couldn't see things as clearly as Jolene. *Do I have a deceitful heart?*

As she fell asleep, she dreaded the last stop on her trail of tears—Odessa.

Dozens of tiny tornados swirled in the West Texas sky. Janie stood in the yard and screamed, "Daddy! Daddy!" He came out of the house, and the tornados disappeared.

Jane woke breathing hard. Sitting up, she put her face in her hands.

What the hell? Another crazy nightmare. This one is particularly ironic.

She threw the covers back and dressed quickly. Tallulah, stuck in the laundry room, was no doubt feeling neglected. She needed a little attention and food. And Jane would have to tend to Lulah's litter box. Lugging the accoutrements of cat care, the litter, the liners, the scoop, was the one drawback of traveling with her feline companion. After making sure Max was outside, Jane released the cat from detention, fed her, and joined the family for breakfast.

"Just toast and coffee for me."

Jolene turned from the stove. "You sure?"

"Yes, thanks. I'm going to head out in a few."

Summer said, "Sit next to me, Aunt Jane."

Shane looked up from his meal, nodded, and mumbled, "Hey." He returned to his bacon and eggs.

Tom had already left. Basketball was year-round for him in some form or other. The kids asked about Tallulah, and Jane told a carefully edited version of the cat's birth, leaving out the c-section, and how she came to own her.

Summer looked at her mother. "Can we get a cat, Mom?"

Jolene put her hand on her hip. "Did y'all see Max's reaction yesterday? I don't think so, honey." She chuckled and joined them at the table.

The kids' breakfast finished, they cleared the table, again without prompting. They chattered about the first day of Vacation Bible School, teasing each other about who else might be in attendance.

Summer came to Jane's side. "Can I come visit you in Austin?"

Caught by surprise, Jane spilled her coffee. "Um, I'll talk to your mom about that, sweetie."

Jolene rose, put her arm around Summer, and moved the girl away from the table. She handed out backpacks. "I hear the bus. Time to go." The kids left in a flurry of goodbyes and hugs.

While her sister-in-law followed the kids outside, Jane mopped up the table. She poured a half-cup of coffee, added cream, and gulped it down.

Jolene came back, and when she saw Jane standing at the counter, asked, "You leavin' already?"

"Yeah, I better get on the road. You've been so welcoming and kind. Thanks for putting up with me and Tallulah."

"Put up with? Honey, it was our pleasure. Okay, maybe not Max's pleasure, but it was great to see you. I'll help you load the car, but you better catch the cat."

Jane chuckled when she found Tallulah already in her crate in the laundry room. "Keeping a low profile, Lulah?"

As they walked out to Jane's car, Jolene said, "I don't think I was much help to you last night."

"Actually, I had no right to drag you into my psychodrama. You and Tom have a good, strong marriage. Maybe I thought I could absorb some wisdom through osmosis—or proximity." She laughed without humor. "I'm an idiot. I have to figure this out myself."

Jolene put Jane's suitcase in the trunk while Jane loaded the cat carrier in the back seat. Tallulah meowed loudly.

"I don't know if Tallulah hates road trips, or she's protesting because she's got unfinished business with Max."

Jolene laughed, and Jane set her feet in anticipation of her sister-in-law's usual exuberant hug.

Three hours later, Jane checked into the same hotel in Odessa she had vacated only a few days ago. She was looking forward to a swim. Before heading to the pool, she dialed Lauren.

"Lauren here. Talk to me."

"Hey, it's Jane. I'm in Odessa, arrived safe and sound."

"Why'd it take you so long to get there? I don't imagine you drove that Mustang twenty miles an hour."

"I made a couple of stops. Saw Rafe in Dallas and Tom in Lubbock. Made my amends to Rafe and got more dirt on my family of origin from Tom."

"Sounds intense. Still sober?"

"Yes." Jane's tone was sharp.

"How'd your hubby take it when you told him you were leavin' again?"

Jane bit her lip. "Not good."

"Details, darlin.'"

"I let it slip that I'd stayed an extra day to see Rick. Joshua blew up. He slept in the guestroom and was gone when I woke."

"Interesting turn of phrase there, girl. 'Let it slip' versus comin' clean."

Jane gulped. "Ouch! You're right. I guess I've been keeping my past from him for so long, it's a habit."

"A habit you need to break. If you want to save your marriage, that is."

Jane gazed at the ceiling and didn't answer directly. "Anyway, he's gone to a convention in Atlanta. He left me a note asking if I'll be there when he gets back."

"Will ya?"

"I don't know yet."

"I hope you find some answers, darlin'. Take care."

Jane hung up, feeling unsettled. She took it out on the water, carving ferociously through the lap lane. After she showered, Jane fed Tallulah and decided it was too late in the day to drive out to see her daddy. An AA meeting might help get her head straight before she saw him. When she called the local AA phone number to find a location, she was relieved to learn that the Baptist Church had a non-smoking meeting at five. At least she wouldn't have to air her troubles at the First United Methodist Church. She put her hair in an updo, dabbed on light makeup, and threw on jeans and an airy chiffon blouse. Riding the elevator to the lobby, she wondered who she might see at her first AA meeting in Odessa.

In her red high-heeled boots, she tapped down the basement steps, following the AA signs to the meeting room. Entering the dim space, she noticed Rick and stopped, staring. He was chatting to a young woman, standing so close a piece of paper wouldn't fit between them. The girl was maybe twenty, with curly tawny hair held back with a headband tied in a bow. She wore a torn t-shirt, calf-length tights, and a tiered skirt. Did she think she was Madonna?

Rick and the Madonna look-alike appeared to know each other quite well—this wasn't a chance encounter. Jane's heart thudded, and she struggled to keep her face expressionless.

And to think...I actually thought...I considered the possibility...

Rick looked up, and his smile faded when he spotted Jane. He stepped back from the girl.

The girl's head swiveled between Jane and Rick. Wide-eyed, she appeared confused at first. But Madonna apparently wasn't stupid. Jane watched realization dawn. Scowling, the girl's mouth formed a pout.

Jane read Rick's facial expression as guilt. And Jane believed she'd earned her spurs in that arena. Determined to behave with dignity, she lifted the corners of her mouth and greeted him. "Hey, Rick! Is this your usual meeting?"

"It is now," the very young woman interjected.

One side of Rick's mouth turned up, a lame attempt at a smile. He avoided eye contact. "Nope. My home group's in Monahans."

"I'm Trish," the young woman announced. "Who're you?" She pressed into Rick's side and took his hand, glaring at Jane.

"Hello, Trish. I'm Jane." She nodded at her childhood friend. "Rick." Head high, she strode to a seat in the third row of chairs. If she hadn't really needed a meeting before, she did now. Looking straight ahead, she listened to the good people of AA share their experience, strength, and hope. As for her, she had some experience to digest, needed strength to do so, and hoped she'd never have to lay eyes on Rick again.

Back at the hotel, Jane dialed the phone.

"Jennings."

"Hey, Daddy. Finally made it. I'm at the same hotel. I'll be out to the house tomorrow, around nine. That okay?"

"Sure is, Janie. I'll be here. I started packin' up." He paused. "But I'd like you to go through Martha's things, if you would."

"Yes, you mentioned that when we talked." Jane pursed her lips. She had agreed to perform that last duty but was not looking forward to it.

"You all right? You sound a little low."

"I'm fine, Daddy." Jane sighed. "Just road-weary. I need some sleep. See you in the morning."

She picked up Lulah and held her close. The hotel bed was nowhere near as comfortable as her bed at home. She fell asleep wondering what Joshua was doing in Atlanta and if he was thinking of her.

Chapter Thirteen

Gigantic Faded Pink Fuzzy Slippers-Odessa to Austin 1984

Driving so slowly she almost stalled the Mustang, Jane down-shifted again, and the car chugged along Kermit Highway. She wasn't in a hurry to get to Daddy's house, and it showed in her sedate pace, so unlike her. She turned left at the track to the house and barely touched the gas as the car jounced down the lane. Stopping to gaze at the place that haunted her, she promised herself this was the last time she would behold the scene of her childhood misery.

Dressed in an old plaid shirt of Joshua's, jeans, and boots, she was prepared, at least with her attire, to perform this last chore for her daddy. What she lacked was emotional and mental preparation. Tallulah was back at the hotel in her crate, unhappy. But not for long. Jane intended to be in and out in short order.

After parking, she took several deep breaths, then unclenched her fists and got out of the Mustang. Her feet scuffed in the dirt as she approached the house. She clomped up the steps, but before she could knock, her daddy opened the door.

He hugged her. "Thanks for comin'."

Jane's body stiffened in his embrace, and he released her at once. "You okay, Janie?"

She stepped back and crossed her arms. "I'm fine. Better get to work. Can't stay long."

"Will ya sit a minute? I made a pot of coffee."

"No, thanks." She glanced at him, saw his puzzlement, and relented. "Half a cup."

Jane sat at the kitchen table. She noticed a newspaper opened to the rental section, a half dozen ads circled in red pen.

He carried two cups to the table and handed her one. Pointing to the paper, he said, "I'm lookin' at a few places tomorrow." He sat. "One of the roughnecks at work is interested in this place."

"Really?" Jane stirred cream into the coffee, trying to imagine strangers treading the floorboards of this shack. She believed the wretchedness of her family life had seeped into the very walls and would be perceptible to new owners, like a haunting. *Caveat emptor.*

"Yeah. He's comin' by with his wife tonight. That's why I got started packin' right quick."

"Speaking of packing, I better start. Like I said, I can't stay long."

The corners of her daddy's mouth turned down. While he seemed perplexed by her curtness and lack of eye contact, he didn't confront her. He jerked his head toward the hallway. "I put some boxes in there."

Jane stood and left the kitchen with her coffee mug. She entered Mama's lair. The blackout shades were raised, and light poured in the space. She couldn't recall ever seeing the room in daylight. The sun shone on dust motes but did nothing to improve the ambiance or erase her memories.

Placing the mug on the dresser, she turned to her task. She dragged a box to the closet and opened the door, wrinkling her nose at the fragrance of "Woodhue." Pulling the tops, pants, and dresses off hangers, she folded the limp, pastel garments and placed them in the carton.

When finished with the hanging clothes, Jane checked the drawers in the dresser and found a few undergarments and three pairs of pale-blue baby doll pajamas. Beads of sweat appeared on her upper lip and hairline. She closed her eyes as the movie reel of Mama on that blockbuster night played in her head.

Swaying on her feet, wearing wrinkled, stained powder-blue baby dolls and gigantic hot-pink fuzzy slippers, Mama howled, "If I could strike you dead and bring Grace back, so help me God, I would."

Had Mama purchased those ridiculous pajamas by the dozen? Handling them with her fingertips, as if they might be contaminated by their dead owner, Jane added them to the other garments. Done with the clothing, she found a small box for the footwear still in the closet.

Pausing to finish her coffee, she dabbed at the sweat on her face with her sleeve. Her mind flitted to the high points of the discussion she planned to have with her daddy. Would she have the nerve to say what needed to be said?

Just get on with it and get out of here.

She grabbed the box and knelt on the floor to gather the various shoes. Her breath caught when she spied the two gigantic, faded pink fuzzy slippers. Were they the same pair from that night? She didn't want to touch them but could not leave them for her daddy.

A transitory fantasy of setting fire to the house with the baby dolls and pink slippers inside teased her. One side of her mouth turned up as she pictured herself dancing and leaping in joy while celebrating the immolation, with Hendrix wailing, "Let me stand next to your fire."

When she pulled the evocative footwear to her, she heard the clang of metal hitting the floor. What looked like coins were strewn across the worn floorboards, along with a folded paper. Puzzled, Jane picked up one coin, thinking Mama had stashed a few silver dollars, although the sound was too tinny. Shocked, she gazed at an AA promise medallion, a silver chip representing the desire to stop drinking.

Mama in AA?

She snatched the paper, unfolded it, and read:

Jane, I know it will be you cleanin out my things. I made yore daddy promise me. This is for yore eyes only, sweet Jane. If you tell anyone, I'll deny it. Ha ha ha! That's a joke. Yore old mean mama made a funnie. I'm prolly in the ground by now, worm food.

My messige is simple—forgive me. I got lots of regrets. Sorry I didn't get to make my amends face ta face.

Heal yore heart. Don't make the same mistake I did, livin in the past, grievin Grace. I didn't see the good rite in front of me. I hope you don't take to drinkin. And I'm real glad you got married. I hope yore happy. I won't live to see it, but you shud have kids. Do a better job than me rasin them up. Move on and be happy.

Eyes widening in disbelief, mind-blowing revisions to her history tore through Jane's brain. *Did Mama love me, after all?* Dropping the coins and the note, she covered her face with her hands. At last, Jane wept for Mama. Shoulders shaking, she cried quietly, not wanting Daddy to hear. Softly moaning, "Mama called *me* sweet."

After several minutes, Jane wiped her eyes with the sleeve of the plaid shirt and gazed heavenward. *The good right in front of me. Joshua.*

She gathered the AA coins and the note and stalked out to the parlor to confront her daddy.

He was taping boxes closed and glanced up when she entered. His face fell when he saw her angry expression.

Jane pushed the words past her dry throat and stiff lips. "Did you know? AA?"

Daddy stepped toward her and stared at the AA medallions and paper in Jane's outstretched hands. A silver desire chip, one red thirty-day, and a green ninety-day chip. Evidence of effort.

He wouldn't meet her eyes. "She started goin' to AA off and on, after Tom told us you was gettin' hitched. Mrs. Foster tried to help her, would come by the house and drive her to the meetin's."

From a place deep in her heart, Jane cried, "I know you didn't have my number, but why didn't you tell Tom? He would've let me know. It might have made a difference."

He stared at the floor. "She wouldn't let me."

"And you always did *exactly* what she wanted, didn't you?" Jane's voice shook.

Daddy took a step forward. His shoulders drooped. "That's harsh."

Jane's lips twisted in anger. "My *childhood* was harsh."

"Your mama wanted to see you again, sober. She made it to ninety days at the end, but her liver gave out. She faded away and told me I couldn't tell anyone she was dyin'."

"And ever obedient, you complied with Mama's orders," Jane snarled.

He hung his head, silent.

"Did you see the note she wrote to me?"

"No." He held out his hand for the paper.

Jane folded the note and shoved it and the AA medallions in her pocket. "And you never will."

Daddy staggered to the couch and slumped onto the plastic-covered cushions, appearing to deflate.

Jane crossed her arms. "That's not all I have to say." She took several deep breaths. "The reason I took so long to get here is that I stopped to see Rafe."

Her daddy didn't reply. He reached for his back pocket and pulled out a handkerchief, gripping it tightly.

"I know." Her words tasted as bitter as bile.

"Know what?"

Cutting off a humorless chuckle, she leaned forward and enunciated with exquisite care. "That Penny and Rafe wanted to take me to live with them."

His mouth opened and closed. Rubbing the back of his neck, he gazed out the window. "Oh, Lord."

"He knows, too." Her brows knit. "I had a chance at a normal childhood. You and Mama stood in the way. Why?" Glaring at him, her lips formed a tight line.

He lifted his chin and with a burst of self-righteousness, said, "The Jennings take care of their own. You're my daughter, not Rafe's and Penny's."

"Take care of your own?" she sneered. "You left me alone with a drunk, for days at a time. How is that taking care of your own?" Jane flung out her arms, beseeching him for an answer.

"I kep' thinkin' she'd get better. Sometimes she stopped for weeks. Whenever I came home, she looked okay."

"Are you kidding?" Jane's nose wrinkled in disgust. "That's not how I remember it."

His forehead furrowed, and he gazed at her. "You were a kid and only remember the bad things."

"Really? There were *good* things?" Jane huffed, incredulous.

Her daddy didn't answer that query. "Honey, your mama never got over losing Grace. She blamed herself, and it drove her to the bottle."

"I know that! Doesn't change a thing." Jane's eyes filled, and she blinked the tears away, not wanting him to see her cry. After a moment, she asked, "How did Grace die? Tom never said."

"Crib death is what they called it. Your mama found Grace dead, with the blanket over her face."

Jane raised her hand to her mouth. "Oh." She gazed at her daddy, feeling manipulated, angry that he refused to address her pain and misery as a child. Why had she idealized this man? She recalled how she adored him when she was little. "Even now, it's all about Grace. My life was lived in her shadow, and I never even knew it." With her hands on her hips, stony faced, she leaned toward him. "Until Tom told me. I was eleven, Daddy."

"Grace's death destroyed your mama. We didn't want to keep thinkin' about it or talkin' about it."

"Her death destroyed the whole damn family! Can't you see that? There's no excuse for treating me like she did, or you leaving us alone with her. Tom is plenty angry, too."

His eyes left her face, and he stared at his feet. "I know."

Jane paced in the narrow space between the kitchen counter and the parlor. Confounding and diametrically opposite emotions from just a few days ago swarmed her. Gone, the pity and regret she had felt for Daddy, the anger at her mama now directed his way. Unsure of what she felt for Mama. *Can I forgive her? Have I already?* Clutching her head, Jane reeled from the psychic explosions and implosions in her brain, neurotransmitters colliding, cosmic conflict. *I can't stay in this loathsome house for another second.*

Whirling to face him, she snapped, "Well, Daddy, I've done my duty. There's nothing for me here. I'll be on my way—"

He lunged from the couch and came to her, imploring, "Please, don't go like this. Sit down and let's talk it out."

She stepped back. "What is there to say? The past can't be repaired."

He held out his hands in supplication. "You and Tom are all I got left."

"You made your bed, now lie in it." A thrill of satisfaction ran through her as she said those words. With that, Jane marched out the door, got in the car and sped away, accelerating hard, tires spitting up gravel.

In the rearview mirror, she glimpsed her daddy on the porch, twisting his handkerchief.

When Jane neared the county road, she yanked the wheel and stopped on the shoulder, shaking as the adrenalin rush of confrontation left her. Not wise to drive with her clammy hands and churning emotions. Besides, on this final time in Odessa, there was one more way station on her pilgrimage. She could not leave without completing the last arc in the circle of her history.

Opening the Mustang's door, Jane waited for the quivering to subside before standing. She drifted over to Rick's family home. A wave of sadness engulfed her as she caught sight of the caved-in roof. Rick had told her his parents abandoned the house a couple of years after he left Odessa. Passing a long-dead campfire, she kicked the ashes and detected a whiff of smoke and burnt hot dogs. The front door lay on the concrete porch. She peered through a broken window and saw a mesquite seedling growing in the shredded couch. Strips of wallpaper hung from the walls and ragged holes peppered the plaster. There were signs of animal habitation, small bones, and nesting material. Shattered beer bottles, cigarette butts, and fast food wrappers littered the filthy wreckage of the carpet. Walking around the corner of the ruin, Jane felt ill at the sight of the wooden siding defaced with spray-painted graffiti—rude, anatomically challenging sexual taunts, pentagrams, and names—'Mavis' in huge red dripping letters.

A memory of Mrs. Mills, dressed to go into town, smelling sweet, kneeling to hug Mavis, struck Jane's heart. She shuddered and bent at the waist, gripping her knees.

She wondered why Rick hadn't addressed the forlorn condition of the property. Was it because of grief, or did he not care? The Mills family had no legacy. Just a son who had never married and was cutting a swath through the female AA population. They deserved better. Well, maybe he would fix up the house and move in with Trish. Jane had expended enough energy on Rick. Lesson learned.

As she turned away toward Rangerland, she pondered the legacy of her own family. Her daddy would die a lonely old man if he didn't make amends to her—or if she couldn't find it in her heart to forgive him. At this point, she wasn't ready.

If Grace had lived, if Mama had not turned to alcohol, what might her childhood have been like? For the first time, Jane felt pity for the infant Grace, a wisp of innocent life, whose brief existence and death indelibly damaged her family.

Tom had done well, far better than he might have. He was settled into a good life, with a family, work he loved. Once he left Odessa, he had thrived.

Her own future stretched in front of her, as long as a lonely Texas highway, nothing as far as the eye could see. Featureless, except for a single landmark—her marriage. If she had learned one thing on this trail of tears, it was that she could not continue her current trajectory. She needed help. And she knew where to find it. Could her relationship with Joshua be salvaged? Summoning the words of the note he left, *will you be here when I get back,* she blew on the embers of hope.

Jane climbed a rise, what her younger self would have called a "hill," and spun in circles, searching for the boundary tree. Eden's Acres, ridiculously named, had never been built except for the doomed Mills home. Several mature mesquite and dozens of saplings dotted the landscape, but she couldn't discern which tree was the marker of her childhood kingdom. Shrugging, she decided that looking further was pointless. Offering a prayer for Mavis and Mr. and Mrs. Mills, she returned to the car. Rangerland was long past, and she needed to focus on the future.

The question was *not* what kind of life she would have had if she weren't raised in that house—but what kind of life she could have despite it. She could spend hours inventing an alternative history for herself—a normal life in Dallas with Aunt Penny and Uncle Rafe, graduating high school, college, marriage, children, career—she was good at that. Foolish waste of time. *I'm heading home.*

Driving back to the hotel, Jane minded her speed despite her eagerness to jumpstart her marriage. The last thing she needed was a ticket, an entanglement with Odessa. This would be a clean break.

Tallulah kicked up a fuss when Jane got back to the room, yowling and smacking the bars of the crate with her paws. Jane soothed her while keeping the huffy feline in the enclosure, not wanting to delay her departure with cat-wrangling. She had packed this morning, and not bothering to change from her work-clothes, wasted no time checking out.

The three hundred and fifty miles to Austin should take seven hours. But like Sammy Hagar, Jane couldn't drive fifty-five. Not on the interstate. She stopped at an auto parts store and bought a fuzz buster. Her trip to Odessa had not held the same urgency she felt for her return to Austin.

When she turned on the Mustang's radio, Greg Kihn's "The Breakup Song" blared from the speakers. She lunged for the dial and snapped it off, hoping the song wasn't an omen.

Cruising down Route 385, a shade over the speed limit, Jane hit the gas once she reached I-10. She kept pace with the long-haul truckers and an eye on her radar detector. As she drove, she considered the roadblocks she had erected between herself and Joshua. After the turmoil of the last week, she had to admit her problems were rooted in her lack of honesty. One of the most important tenets of AA was *rigorous honesty*. Amazing that she had remained sober for eight years—especially during the past few days—with the secrets she kept. You're as sick as your secrets—another AA truism; she had heard that a thousand times, but apparently hadn't thought it applied to her. Had the time come to open up to her husband? She imagined Lauren and the other members of her AA group rolling their eyes and shouting, "Duh!"

Jane slapped the steering wheel. "Miss Tallulah. I do believe I've made a breakthrough. Time to get honest. My secrets aren't protecting me, they're *hurting* me."

Another barrier—she had set up a false dichotomy, pompous and absurd: psychiatry versus psychology. Because she abhorred the use of lobotomy, electroconvulsive therapy, and Thorazine did not mean she couldn't be married to a psychiatrist. Joshua didn't even employ those loathsome techniques. No wonder he walked on eggshells around the topic of mental health, no longer discussing his practice with her and rarely asking her about school.

Realizing that she had been driving without music, she clicked on the radio and perked up at a new Stevie Ray Vaughan song, "Couldn't Stand the Weather." One line grabbed her attention: "sweet as sugar, love won't wash away." Her foot goosed the gas thinking of Joshua, then she eased off, remembering he wouldn't be home until the next morning.

Her growling stomach forced her to pull off the highway in Junction. Parked in a Sonic stall, Jane ordered a burger and jalapeño poppers. Tallulah meowed, but her request wasn't on the menu.

"Sorry, girl. You'll have to wait until we get home for Fancy Feast." Jane scrounged through the cat supplies and found a plastic bag with dry food. "This will have to hold you."

While Jane ate, her mind wandered to her failed attempts at love. As a vulnerable teenager, she had fallen for Jeremy. Homeless, lonely, frightened, and lacking self-esteem, she succumbed to the ocean of hormones in which she floated. Diving in head-first, she thought she found what she craved—true love. But she had her nose rubbed in free love. Through three years of his philandering, spats, and make-up sex, she had clung to him like a stubborn vine. It took time and countless humiliations until Crystal uprooted her.

She had bounced like a ping-pong ball through life, caroming off events, pursuing a new direction without analysis. After Jeremy, she lived like a meek daughter with the Harrises for years, attending First Methodist, but never rekindling the connection with Jesus she had as a child.

Taking on the protective coloration of those around her—never becoming her own person. She laughed at a mental image of herself as Silly Putty—*I am but an egg.* Press her up against a man and his imprint transferred to her, like the elastic clay on the Sunday comics.

While in her early twenties, she put her nose to the proverbial grindstone of school and work, eschewing all fun and joy, trudging through the days like a dried-up spinster. To borrow a term from the Papists, was that some sort of penance for Jeremy? It was inevitable that she would break loose from those chains, and she had done so, spectacularly, with Andy.

The sexy horns from Peggy Lee's hypnotic "Easy Evil" played on her mental jukebox. Indeed, Andy was a purveyor of sensuous sin, a promise of fun; and, oh, she had been taken in—willingly. He had been desperate in his pursuit of her, a function of his addiction, and she had capitulated. She almost lost everything, her standing at school, and her life. During their years together, she had fallen into addiction—something for which she despised Mama and Grandma June. Despite her lack of honesty, she got sober, and it stuck. Why had she been granted that gift? If the thought of Champagne crossed her mind, she felt nothing but nausea. At will, she could access the memory of crawling on the floor, glugging down the dregs of a Champagne bottle and getting a mouthful of cigarette butts. Humbling. And an invaluable reminder.

Those past relationships were based on weakness, and she wondered why it took until now to realize it. With both romantic disasters, she eventually came to her senses—after two or three years of veering off the road.

She finished her calorie-laden lunch, vowing to return to her regimen of yogurt and veggies when she returned to Austin. With a word of reassurance to Tallulah, she pulled back on I-10.

Her thoughts turned to Rick. Her indiscretion, a hideous mistake, was a flirtation with the *idea* of Rick—a romanticized version of reality. She knew him for a few years as a child and had been crazy to imagine that fragile link could be the basis for a life together. If she hadn't been reeling from the geyser of emotion from the onslaught of her past, she wanted to believe she wouldn't have taken that detour. No, she *needed* to believe that. Recalling the scene with Trish, Jane's face flushed with embarrassment.

"Thank you, Trish!" Talking to herself was another side-effect of her recent upheaval.

Lack of judgment about men—her curse. Hiding behind them for cover. Until Joshua. He offered her a partnership and unconditional acceptance. Falling in love with him was the truest thing she had ever done. He always encouraged her, supported her and yet, she almost threw him away.

"I'm an idiot!"

Ever since she answered Daddy's phone call last week, she had not been herself. Her lips tightened at the thought of her daddy—her father. No longer would she be locked in the child's sweet jail of hero worship. With that, she vowed to refer to him as "father," if she ever found it necessary to refer to him again.

As soon as her cruelty registered, Jane regretted it. That line of thinking wasn't good for her soul.

Driving through the "Y," the infamous traffic bottleneck in Oak Hill, she switched off the radar detector. No point in late afternoon congestion. *So near, yet so far.*

Before heading home, she decided to close the loop on her journey by making good on her promise to connect with the Harrises. Constance, a source of wisdom, could give her answers about keeping a marriage fresh and viable.

By the time she got to Tarrytown, the vet hospital was closed for the day. Jane parked in the deeply shaded drive, casting a look at the apartment over the garage, wondering for a moment who resided there. Was there a new waif in town? Tallulah yowled and Jane shushed her. "I'll only be a minute." Leaving the windows half-open, she locked the car and dashed around the house to the back porch. She knocked, smiling at her former mentor when Constance turned from the sink and opened the door.

"I can only stay a minute. Just got back to town, and I've got Lulah in the car."

"Go get her. We'll have a cup of tea."

"Oh. Okay. I guess it's silly to drive over to tell you I can't stay."

Constance chuckled as she filled the kettle.

Jane retrieved the carrier and released her pet. "I hope I can convince her to get back in when I leave."

Constance brought two cups of tea to the table and joined Jane. Sammy, ancient and slow, hobbled into the kitchen and meowed loudly when he spotted his old friend, Tallulah. Jane's cat played it cool at first, but soon settled in, lying next to her buddy at Jane's feet.

Jane grabbed a cheesecake brownie from the plate on the table. "Do you keep Sweetish Hill in business?"

Constance laughed. "I do my best." Stirring sugar into her tea, she said, "Last time you called, we never did find a time to get together. Sometimes spontaneity works better. Anything in particular you wanted to see me about?"

Jane twisted her hands in her lap, not touching her favorite treat. "I've been back to Odessa—twice in the last two weeks in fact."

"It's been years, hasn't it?"

Jane glanced at her. "Half my life." She reached for the teacup but didn't pick it up. "My mother died—"

"So sorry, dear."

Jane waved a hand, swatting away the condolence. "To my surprise, I went to the funeral." She hesitated. "I wouldn't let Joshua come with me."

"Goodness! Why?" Constance's brow furrowed.

"I was ashamed to let him see where I come from. Anyway, after the funeral I returned home, then went back a day later because my father wanted me to help him pack up the house. Joshua had to go to a conference—he'll be back tomorrow—so he couldn't come, not that I'd have wanted him to."

Constance leaned forward and patted Jane's hand. "What on earth?"

"That's what I've been exploring for the last few days. What on earth am I doing? My past smacked me upside the head at the funeral—so many wounds reopened. In addition to that, I had a flirtation of sorts with my childhood friend." Jane's cheeks and eyes burned.

"Oh, honey."

Jane grimaced. "Nothing happened. Well, an ill-considered kiss that I regret to my core. I'm *so* embarrassed at my lack of judgment."

"At least you came to your senses before—"

"Don't even say it. I'd never be able to forgive myself—or face Joshua." Jane picked at her brownie, reducing it to crumbs. "Actually, things have been a little tense between us lately. I've been wondering if I'm suited to marriage. But, after all the turmoil on my journey, I had an epiphany. The best decision I made in my *life* was to marry Joshua. I want it to work."

Constance sighed and sat back in her chair. "Then work at it! I've known you for fourteen years now. I remember all your beaus, the romantic upheavals, the drama. From what I observed of your courtship with Joshua, that relationship is on a whole other level. I'll never forget the way you looked at him at your wedding. And the way he looked at you." She held out her arm. "Still get goose bumps."

Jane's mouth turned up, a frail attempt at a smile.

"What a vision you were that day! That glorious ivory column of a gown." Her brow wrinkled in puzzlement. "For some reason you chose to pair it with red cowboy boots."

Jane grinned. "I had my reasons for the boots. Tell me, what is your secret for a happy marriage? Do you and Doc walk in lock-step, complete each other's sentences, have the same beliefs and opinions?"

Constance threw back her head and laughed. "No, no, and no. The secret is there is no secret. Just love one another."

"Sounds simple."

"It is, if you let it be."

With an indignant Tallulah voicing her displeasure, Jane headed cross-town to the co-op, knowing Lauren would be there at this hour. She needed to see her sponsor in person.

She parked next to the rear entrance, pulled out the cat carrier, and rang the bell.

Lauren held the door open, waved Jane in, and smirked. "I'd say look what the cat dragged in, but I ain't ever said that to someone who was draggin' in a cat." She looked pleased with herself at this pronouncement.

Jane placed the crate on the floor and told the protesting feline, "Last stop, I promise."

"You look a little frazzled and a little country to boot. Nice plaid shirt. Have I ever seen you in plaid?" Lauren touched one fuchsia fingertip to her chin, then shook her head. "Don't think so."

Jane breathed out, raising her long bangs from her forehead. "I'm not here about fashion. Look at this." She dug in her pocket, dropping the AA coins on the floor, and handed Lauren the note. Falling to her knees, Jane retrieved the scattered chips, red, green, and silver.

Lauren picked up reading glasses from her desk and scanned the note, eyebrows lifting and mouth forming an "O" as she did so. She folded the paper, handed it to Jane, and dropped into her desk chair. "Wow."

"Right? I'd never have dreamed. Never."

"I'm speechless. Well, not really, I'm never speechless. Honey, I can only imagine what you're going through."

"Turned my world on its ear, for sure." Jane pulled up a chair and sat.

Lauren's turquoise eye's narrowed. "And yet, you're remarkably calm after the last few days of upheaval. Why's that?"

"I think, for the first time, I've addressed all the ghosts of my past, up front and personal, with all the players."

"Sounds a tad poetic there, sweetie. Maybe with a mixed metaphor thrown in. Care to explain?"

"Tom revealed a few family secrets that stunned me." Jane held up her index finger. "But, instead of scurrying around like a squirrel hiding those nuggets, I faced them head on."

"Secrets? Do tell." Lauren leaned back in her chair and gazed expectantly at Jane.

"When I was little, Aunt Penny and Uncle Rafe wanted to take me out of hell house to live with them," Jane said, studying Lauren for her reaction.

Lauren exploded from her chair, raising her arms, causing her silver bracelets to dance and jingle. "Good God! Tell me you're sober. A whole alternative life—that would rock anyone's world and might could send a person to the closest bar!"

Jane motioned for Lauren to relax. "You're more worked up than I am. But then, I've had time to process. When I saw Rafe, he confirmed it, but refused to talk about my mother and father's reaction."

"No triangulation for him. Wise man." Lauren's eyes widened. "Wait, did you just call your parents 'mother and father' instead of 'mama and daddy?' That, right there, is mighty interesting. Did you talk to your *father* about this?"

"Yes, I did," Jane said with pride. "After that note, and my father telling me 'the Jennings take care of their own,' I realized my anger was misplaced. For the first time, I felt compassion for my mother, understood her depression and inability to function, and redirected my anger toward him, the man I looked to as my protector." She searched Lauren's face. "He didn't protect me."

Lauren returned to her chair. "Tough stuff. How did ya leave things with him?"

"I told him there was nothing for me in Odessa, then I left."

"Kinda harsh. How d'ya feel about that?"

"Liberated," Jane said. Then she frowned. "And maybe a little guilty now that I've had time to cool off. I'm going to rethink how I treated my father, talk to Joshua about it." Jane glanced at Lauren. "You know, sitting here, I feel as if I'm talking to a shrink. You're pretty good at the probing questions about feelings."

"And?"

"And I'm finally answering with 'rigorous honesty.'"

"Good on you! Speakin' of shrinks, when is your hubby due home?"

"Tomorrow morning."

"You haven't mentioned Rick. Did ya see him?" Lauren asked.

Silence.

Lauren got up from her desk and scooted a chair next to Jane, patting her arm. "Oh, honey. What happened?"

Jane, red to the roots of her hair, blinked away tears. "I don't know what possessed me…" She shook her head. "I went to an AA meeting, and he was there with his *girlfriend*. Didn't take him for a thirteenth-stepper, but there you go."

"Good grief! Dodged that bullet," Lauren exclaimed.

Jane shrugged and bit her lip. "But on the drive back, I even managed to find some compassion for him. He must be damaged from the loss of his sister and his parents, unable to form relationships. After all, he never married. Also, he's let the family home fall into ruin."

"Sad. My advice? Forget it ever happened and forgive yourself. Move forward with Joshua. You do mean to?"

Jane glanced at her. "If he'll have me."

Lauren stood and adjusted her curls. "Darlin,' that man is crazy about you. Didn't he ask if you'd be home when he got back?"

Looking at the floor, Jane said, "Yes. But—"

"But what?" Exasperation crept into Lauren's voice.

"I wonder how he can even relate to me. I'm so messed up, and an alcoholic. He's never had issues with drugs or alcohol."

Lauren raised one of her perfectly groomed eyebrows. "Don't you think he, a flippin' mental health professional, thought of that before he asked you to marry him?"

"Oh, I suppose so."

"There you go, ratcheting up the self-doubt."

"What does he see in me?"

"Stop with the poor, pitiful me bullshit. You're tryin' my patience!"

Jane clutched her elbows and bent forward. "I'm a quivering mass of insecurities, a big blob of jello—tap me and I will vacillate all day."

"What an image." Lauren rolled her eyes and grasped Jane's arm, urging her out of the chair. "You know, I think you're tired. Go home, take a bubble bath, and get ready for your man."

Standing, Jane made eye contact with Lauren. "I told Jolene I was sick of myself and I am."

"Then *do* somethin' about it! Can't you see what's right in front of you?"

"*Et tu*, Lauren? First my mother, and now you." She sighed. "You're right. I'm heading home."

Lauren ushered Jane to the exit and handed her the cat carrier. She gently pushed Jane through the door.

Tallulah was silent, perhaps resigned to a fate of spending her life in locations other than her home.

Parking her road-dusted Mustang in the driveway, Jane left the luggage in the car. She carried only Tallulah's crate and her purse inside.

Crossing the threshold, she viewed the interior with fresh eyes. At last, Jane knew she was home. The excitement she and Joshua had felt when they purchased it, the fun they had furnishing it rushed back to her, and she smiled. The air was stuffy, so she adjusted the thermostat to cool the house.

"Come on, pretty girl. Time to eat." Tallulah, released from confinement, padded after her into the kitchen where Jane opened the cat's favorite food and provided fresh water. After eating, Tallulah wandered from room to room, inspecting her domain. The cat purred as she settled on her fleece bed in the corner of the kitchen.

Jane bent to stroke Tallulah's sweet head and said, "You're glad to be home, too, aren't you?"

She lugged in her bags from the car, stashing them in the closet to deal with later. While the water ran in the deep tub, she lit scented candles and set out her various lotions and creams. As she soaked, she sipped ice water and contemplated the emotional journey of the past ten days.

Avoidance of her history had ruled her life and that, not to use a technical term, was crazy. Had she thought she could ignore the events that shaped her? Ridiculous.

Facing the facts about her lack of an identity freed her. Jane knew one couldn't make forward progress until one admitted there was a problem. Had she finally achieved personality integration? If she planned on counseling addicts, she would have to do so. A therapist hampered by unresolved issues couldn't help anyone. Joshua had told her as much, but now she truly understood.

According to the standards in that paper she had struggled to complete while avoiding her own issues—was it just last week—Jane believed she had in fact effectively organized her past and present experience into a harmonious whole. Sloshing water, she sat up. "Yes! I am acceptable to myself!"

She smiled at the realization she had vanquished her crippling self-doubt. At last, Jane knew what she wanted to be when she grew up. Raising her glass of ice water, she toasted, "I'm going to do it! I *can* do it."

Settling back into the warm, fragrant bath, she turned her mind to her husband and fantasized about Joshua's homecoming. He was the perfect combination of love and lust. Kind, intelligent, he loved her despite everything she threw at him, every obstacle she put in their path.

He's my future. I'm going to pour it all out to him—let him see the scars, the damage. Maybe at last that massive psychic wound will heal.

The water cooled, and her fingers and toes puckered. She washed her hair quickly and rinsed with the nozzle on the side of the tub. Once dry, perfumed, and oiled, she slipped into a short silk nightgown, pulled back the covers and climbed in bed.

She and Joshua stood holding hands. They were in the large field at Zilker Park, standing on the flat boulders of Rock Island. She wore a pink and white, hi-low, tiered skirt, and a brown menswear vest with a lace camisole underneath. Red cowboy boots. Yellow daisies crowned her head, and baby's breath was braided in her long hair. Joshua wore a white shirt and jeans.

A small crowd gathered below them. Grandma June, Daddy and Mama, Rafe and Penny, Tom and Jolene, Doc and Constance, Lauren with a hunky date, and Mrs. Foster watched as Preacher Henry pronounced them man and wife. Jane noted the absence of Jeremy, Andy, and Rick.

As she and Joshua kissed, Jane woke, the dream dissolving into the room's darkness. The vision dissipated, but the joy remained. Tugging the bedcovers over her legs, she lay back, floating on a cloud of happiness, counting the hours until Joshua came home.

Chapter Fourteen

True Love-Austin 1984

I woke with a smile. Remembering my dream, I felt like bursting into song. Marvin and Tammy's "You're All I Need to Get By" came to mind. Tallulah hunkered next to my pillow, staring at me. The bedside clock said 10:20. Impossible! Joshua's flight was due at 10:45 and he'd be home soon after.

Running down the stairs with Lulah at my heels, my mind ticked off a list of tasks. I scooped food into the cat's dish, gave her fresh water. In the kitchen, I poured a glass of orange juice and gulped it. I wasn't hungry and had no time to make coffee.

I hurried upstairs and searched my closet for the perfect outfit. Jeans—too casual. A negligee—too obvious. After trying on and discarding a dozen ensembles, I settled on skintight white leggings and a sleeveless tunic with lush layers of fringe and dashed into the bathroom for a quick shower.

My hair took only a few minutes. I decided to wear it long and loose. Minimal makeup—I hoped he would kiss it off anyway. Spritz of Coco. The diamond earrings he'd given me for our anniversary. My reflection glowed with anticipation. Good to go.

Standing there, I watched my smile fade bit by bit in the mirror. My eagerness to see him turned to dread about revealing myself. The blob of jello reared its ugly head, and my twin nemeses—vacillation and ambivalence—descended on me like a shroud. Why couldn't I turn off my mind? At last, I was committed to a future with him and needed to come clean. Since I had a few minutes before he was due, I propped myself up in bed with pillows and opened my book of daily reflections. I read for a few minutes, finding the words about trust and faith soothing. After several deep cleansing breaths, I gathered my resolve. Feeling calmer, I headed back to the kitchen with my mother's note in hand.

The *chunk* of the front door opening sent a thrill through my chest. "Jane? Babe, where are you?" Joshua called.

"In the kitchen, honey." My voice quavered.

I heard his suitcase hit the floor. Out of the corner of my eye, I saw Tallulah lead him into the kitchen. Keeping my gaze on the counter, I opened the canister of his favorite Blue Mountain coffee, a reminder of our Jamaican honeymoon. "I'm making coffee. You're not going into the office today, are you?"

Joshua came up behind me. My breath caught as he lifted my hair and kissed the back of my neck. I swung around to face him.

He placed his palm on my cheek. "You're here."

I pressed my hand into his and smiled. "I am."

He wrapped me in his arms and held me close. I relaxed into his embrace, inhaling deeply: leather and cedar.

"No, I'm not going in today. We have all day."

"I want to tell you everything." Mumbling into his white shirt, "I've been so wrong to shut you out."

Joshua released me, kept an arm around my shoulders, and led me to the kitchen table. "Let me get that coffee going. Then we'll talk."

"Hand me the box of tissue, will you, honey? I might need the whole thing." Taking a deep breath, I dove right in. "I told you my mother drank. My childhood was spent surviving her. When I was eleven, I learned she lost a baby, Grace, as an infant, a few years before I came along." I grabbed a fistful of tissue from the box. "It explained a lot but didn't make it any easier for me. Mama would slurp vodka and sing 'Amazing Grace, so sweet, so sweet…' It was years before I figured out why she got the words wrong. Sometimes, the way she looked at me, so hateful, so angry, so *disappointed*…"

He finished at the counter and came to the table. He sat beside me. "Oh, babe. So sorry."

I picked up the note and offered it to him. "But look what I found. This changes everything."

With the aroma of coffee filling the air, he plucked the paper from my hand. I watched his face while he perused the message. Brow furrowed, tears glistening, he met my eyes, and I knew that he understood.

As the burden of the past lifted, my body lightened, and my shoulders straightened. "She never got over losing Grace. Yes, she took it out on me. But, when she heard I was getting married, she tried to get better, really tried. She wanted to change. That is so important, and something I can relate to." My eyes misted, but I didn't cry.

"Sounds like healing, although I'm sure you'll be assimilating your discovery for some time."

"No doubt about it. In the last few days, I've made such progress. So glad I made the journey. My trail of tears, I call it." I tried a smile that didn't materialize.

He stood, went to the counter, and poured two mugs of the full-bodied coffee. "Cream and sugar coming right up." Returning to the table, he said, "I'm listening."

"I drove to Dallas first. To see my Uncle Rafe."

"How's he related to you?"

"Oh! That's right. I've kept so many secrets. Rafe is my mother's older brother. He went to college and has had a successful career with an oil company. He married Penny, a wonderful, kind woman. As a kid, I adored her and fantasized she was my mother. I wanted to grow up to be an aunt, just like her. Thought I could only pick one: mama, aunt, or grandma." A tear rolled down my cheek.

Joshua reached out and brushed it away. "I can see you in my mind's eye as a little girl, and it breaks my heart."

I met his eyes and saw compassion in his intent gaze. "I learned from Tom that Rafe and Penny wanted to remove me from my parents, because of the drinking. That caused a rift. I never knew, until now, why I wasn't allowed to see them much." I dabbed at my eyes. "The tragedy is that Penny couldn't have children. Although she finally got pregnant in 1969, she died from a hemorrhage late in the pregnancy. Rafe never remarried." Touching Joshua's hand, I said, "I want you to meet him some day."

"How sad about your aunt. And I'd love to meet Rafe."

I stirred cream into the inky brew. "Next, I stopped in Lubbock to see Tom." Warming my hands on the thick mug, I continued, "I've told you he and Jolene have two beautiful children." I glanced at him. "Shane and Summer."

"Great names. How old are they?"

"Shane's thirteen. So handsome. Tall like Tom and just as crazy about basketball. Summer's eleven, all arms and legs, coltish. A sweet girl." Looking at Joshua's face, I believed I saw his desire to have a child, filed that thought away for later.

Gazing out the window, I noticed the crepe myrtles were covered with blooms, scarlet and fuchsia. Beautiful.

"Tom filled me in on a little family history. I learned they lived in an oil camp before Grace died. My brother has faint memories of a normal family life. I don't. After the baby passed away, my mother started drinking, and my father moved them to that isolated house where I grew up. Tom blames him for allowing our mother to drink herself to death with no one around to see." The words came in a rush.

Joshua held his coffee mug, watching me. Silent, giving me the space I needed.

My coffee had cooled enough to drink. After a few sips that reminded me of a certain morning in Ocho Rios, I revealed another piece of my story. "The last time I saw my mother, I was sixteen." I moaned. Couldn't stop the tears. "Sixteen. She was drunk as usual and so cruel. I left home and never went back. For half my life, she was the demon that haunted me."

Joshua's eyes widened. "Jesus God. On your own so young."

I patted his arm. "I survived, honey. After talking to Tom, I realized my father's part. Tom called him a classic enabler, and he's right. But as a teen I had no perspective—or compassion. And no one to turn to for help. At least that's what I believed."

Joshua leaned forward. "Sounds like you're angry with your father. Very different from how you spoke about him after the funeral. And you seem to have had a change of heart about your mother, reached a place of forgiveness. After what you've learned, are you sure you want to estrange yourself from your father?"

I sighed. "I know I didn't handle things very well, storming out and leaving him standing on the porch. He wanted to talk, but I wouldn't listen." Shaking my head in regret, I continued, "I need to rise above my resentment. Forgive him and make amends. He's bereft and alone."

"Give yourself some time. You'll do the right thing." He finished his coffee and held up his mug. "Reminds me of our honeymoon." He raised an eyebrow and smiled.

"I was thinking the same thing, honey." My cheeks felt warm.

We fell silent.

Joshua scooted his chair closer. "Look, you've been caught in a whirlwind of emotions the last several days. Be gentle with yourself. Call your father when you're ready. I'd like to meet him, as well as Tom and his family. Maybe we can host Thanksgiving this year."

I attempted a smile, but it fell short. "I'm surprising myself by not dismissing that idea out of hand. You're a good man, Joshua Anyway, and a good shrink. Speaking of shrinks, I mean psychiatrists, how was the conference?"

"Joshua Anyway? Haven't heard that in a long time." He leaned back in his chair. "The conference was worthwhile. A lot of new research into antidepressants. Lilly may be on to something in serotonin reuptake..."

I knew why he'd trailed off. "Don't worry. I get it. I can have my mental health theories, and you can have yours. How foolish I was to use those differences to set up a wall between us. It's like I was searching for things to distance myself from real intimacy."

"That's great insight, babe. I've been saying all along you're free to pursue your own practice with your own methodology. As for the other wall, after what you just told me, I see why you had such difficulty in opening up about your past."

"You understand me. Sometimes better than I understand myself." At last, I could smile. "Hey! I know what I want to be when I grow up! I'm going to pursue a doctorate, hang out my shingle, and offer counseling to addicts. My self-doubt is gone. I *know* I can do this and have something to offer."

"Never once did I question your potential. I've always believed in you."

"Thanks. But that didn't matter when I didn't believe in myself. My mother's effort inspired me. And the people I've met in AA who've stayed sober despite upheavals in their lives."

"Add yourself to that list, babe. I'll do everything I can to help you achieve your dream."

"You've always been so supportive. There's so much more to tell you, but that's enough for now. You've got a lot to absorb. Let me know when you're ready for the next installment."

"I'll be ready for the next episode of 'life, the universe, and everything' Jane whenever you are." His face grew serious. "You're right. I do have a lot to ponder, but there's one thing you left off your trail of tears. A rather glaring omission."

I winced. Fingers of dread poked my belly. "Rick?" My mouth twisted in distaste.

"Bingo. Did you see him?"

I gulped. "Sure did."

"And?" Joshua ran his hands through his hair.

I laughed without humor. "And nothing. A great big fat nothing. He's not who I thought he was. His own family story is fraught with tragedy. One of those funerals I'll tell you about someday. Because of our history, I imagined a connection that wasn't there. If I hadn't been in such emotional turmoil, I wouldn't have spent that day with him." Gazing into Joshua's eyes, I implored, "Please, forgive me for hiding my past and this...error of judgment."

He stood and pulled me up by my hands. "Come on upstairs, and I'll show you I have."

We lay in the tangled sheets, our breathing returned to normal in the afterglow of our lovemaking. To say we'd reconnected was an understatement. Shattering, orgasmic "thunder and lightning," as Chi Coltrane sang. This man could curl my toes with his kisses. I wanted to melt into him. I knew I was home.

Propping myself up on my elbow, I studied him. His flushed face wore a relaxed smile. It was a good look for him, and I resolved to make him look like that as often as possible for all the years of our union. I ran a finger down his bare arm.

He turned on his side to regard me. "Babe?"

"Why are you the way you are? You were dedicated and focused from the get-go. Never veered from the path of becoming a doctor. Was it because of your upbringing?"

"If you think I can answer that, you endow me with superpowers I don't have."

"Oh, I can testify to at least one superpower. In fact, you just demonstrated it." I gazed into his chocolate eyes and saw his love for me. Accepted it. At last, I understood the A.A. saying about being true to one's self.

He laughed and grabbed me, kissing my neck, nibbling lower.

I giggled. But I persisted in my self-torture. "Then there's me. What's wrong with me? Genetics? Environment? A toxic combination of the two?"

"If you could see yourself the way I do, you'd know there isn't a damn thing wrong with you. You're perfect. Once in a lifetime."

For once, I shut up. His mouth covered mine. The turbine of my overactive, over-analytic mind wound down. I chose to live in the moment.

Joshua is my truth.

The End

Acknowledgments

Sweet Jane began with a writing prompt in a cafe one Saturday morning in Austin, Texas. From there, the character I created came alive, grew, and developed not only in my mind, but also in public, in my critique groups.

I want to give thanks to all my fellow writers who gave solid insight, criticism, and suggestions. The San Antonio Writers' Guild and the Kerrville Writers Association are two of those groups. My beta readers, Daryl Herring, Tom McEachin, Billy Couvillion, Charles Tate, and Shelly Hafernik, all contributed valuable comments.

My stellar source about Odessa, Texas in the Fifties and Sixties was Michael Moore. His personal stories fired my imagination. Any errors are mine alone.

Lastly, I want to acknowledge my husband, Charles, who knows how hard it is to live with a writer.

Joanne Kukanza Easley

A retired registered nurse with experience in both the cold, clinical operating room and the emotionally fraught world of psychiatric hospitals, Joanne lives on a small ranch in the Texas Hill Country, where she writes fiction about complicated, twentieth-century women. Her multi-award winning debut, *Sweet Jane,* released in March, 2020, was named the adult fiction winner at the Texas Author Project and shortlisted for the Sarton Award and Eric Hoffer Award, among others. *Just One Look*, Joanne's second novel, was a May 2022 Pulpwood Queen Book Club Pick. *I'll Be Seeing You,* her third novel, features characters from *Sweet Jane.* Her prize-winning short stories and poetry have appeared in several anthologies.

Just One Look

In 1965 Chicago, thirteen-year-old Dani Marek declares she's in love, and you best believe it. This is no crush, and for six blissful years she fills her hope chest with linens, dinnerware, and dreams of an idyllic future with John. When he is killed in action in Viet Nam, Dani's world shatters. She launches a one-woman vendetta against the men she seeks out in Rush Street's singles bars. Her goal: break as many hearts as she can. Dani's ill-conceived vengeance leads her to a loveless marriage that ends in tragedy. At twenty-four, she's left a widow with a baby, a small fortune, and a ghost—make that two. Set in the turbulent Sixties and Seventies, *Just One Look* explores one woman's tumultuous journey through grief, denial, and letting go.

I'll Be Seeing You

A saga spanning five decades, *I'll Be Seeing You*, explores one woman's life, with and without alcohol to numb the pain. Young Lauren knows she doesn't want to be a ranch wife in Palo Pinto County, Texas. After she's discovered by a modeling scout at the 1940 Fort Worth Stock Show Parade, she moves to Manhattan to begin her glamourous career. A setback ends her dream, and she drifts into alcohol dependence and promiscuity. By twenty-four, she's been widowed and divorced, and has developed a pattern of fleeing her problems with geographical cures. Lauren's last escape lands her in Austin, where, after ten chaotic years, she achieves lasting sobriety and starts a successful business, but happiness eludes her. Fast forward to 1985. With a history of burning bridges and never looking back, Lauren is stunned when Brett, her third husband, resurfaces, wanting to reconcile after thirty-three years. The losses and regrets of the past engulf her, and she seeks the counsel of Jane, a long-time friend from AA. In the end, the choice is Lauren's.